RUBIES *and* REBELS

RUBIES *and* REBELS

a novel

Lynn Gardner

Covenant Communications, Inc.

TO THE READER

This book offers a glimpse into life in a very different world than the one I have inhabited all my life. We lived for eighteen months in Yerevan, Armenia, working with the wonderful young people there, watching month by month as conditions in the country improved slightly, sometimes almost imperceptibly, but always making some small improvement. Flowers were planted and tiny plots of grass nurtured. Remodeling began on houses and businesses. Trees were planted to replace the thousands that were burned as the only fuel available during the war with Ajerbaijan when the gas was turned off, leaving the city with no means of heating in their buildings. Fountains in the parks began being repaired, one at a time, and were turned on again.

We fell in love with the people, with their passion and their music and art. We were entranced with the beauty of the countryside, with the antiquity of the monasteries and churches, and with amazing workmanship that has lasted through the centuries—some even through millennia. We were impressed by the resilience of the Armenian people through their times of terrible adversity when there was literally no heat, no electricity, no money to buy food—if there had been food available. And we were touched by the hope of the younger generation, that theirs would be a much better life than that of their parents.

We were amazed at the generosity of a people struggling to put food on their tables for their families, and yet insisting on sharing whatever they had. We were in awe of their tremendous capacity for learning languages and their emphasis on education.

We went to teach, and instead we were taught by humble, sincere people who continually reminded us that the simple things in life are always the most important. Their reverence for family, living and dead, was inspiring. And their zest for living, best expressed through their music and dance, was exhilarating to experience. We formed friendships that will be everlasting.

Was it a sacrifice to "give up" eighteen months of our lives, miss the wedding of our youngest daughter and the experiences with our grandchildren during that time? Never! It was the grandest, most incredible adventure we could have experienced!

Special thanks to Shauna Nelson for her patience through all of the editing process and to Nikki for her great eye for detail.

For ease in pronouncing the names and places:

i has an "ee" sound—Narine would be pronounced Nah-ree-nay; Lucine would be Loo-see-nay
a has an "ah" sound—Ararat would be Ahrahraht
Echmiadzin: Etch-mee-ah-dzeen
Garik Grigoryan: Gahreek Greegoreeahn
Milena: Mee-lain-ah   Vaghinak: Vah-hee-nahk
Vanik: Vah-neek   Haghartsin: Hah-gahr-seen
Davit: Dah-veet   Lilit: Lee-Leet
Norik: Nor-eek

CHAPTER 1

As I signaled to exit Highway 101 north of Santa Barbara, the flashing lights of an emergency vehicle appeared in my rearview mirror. I pulled to the side of the highway, expecting the ambulance to speed by, heading for one of the state beaches just up the road. With beaches crowded and waves running high and dangerous, accidents happened frequently this time of year.

But the ambulance whipped off the pavement in front of me, kicking up a cloud of dust as it skidded onto the gravel road—the road leading to my parents' estate and the little cottage under the pines that Bart and I called home.

Fear knotted my stomach as I hit the accelerator and followed the speeding ambulance, its siren echoing across the golden hills. It must be a mistake. The ambulance had simply exited too soon. The driver should discover any minute he was on the wrong road, but except for a couple of hairpin curves, the vehicle in front of me showed no sign of slowing as it raced up the hill toward my home.

Why was an ambulance headed for the estate? No one was there. Bart, as usual, was on assignment on the other side of the world, as was Dad. Bart's parents, Jim and Alma Allan, were vacationing in Texas. That left only Mom, but she was in Los Angeles at the Armenian Embassy picking up her visa and wasn't due home until evening.

An unsettling premonition of trouble increased as I approached the top of the hill. That premonition was confirmed when we entered the long circular driveway and I glimpsed Mom's blue convertible in front of the mansion. I caught my breath at the sight of a splash of color at the foot of the white marble stairs and my heart felt like someone was squeezing the life out of it.

Slamming on my brakes behind the ambulance, I raced toward Mom who lay tangled in the garden hose with one leg bent at an alarming angle. My old Momma Cat arched in fight mode at the top of the steps, hissing a warning at something in the rose bushes. As the emergency medical technicians knelt at my mother's side to assess the damage to the obviously broken leg, I knelt and brushed her hair back from her face.

"Mom, what happened?"

"I came out to water the roses while I talked to your father on the cell phone and apparently disturbed a rattlesnake warming himself in the sun. I must have been distracted. I didn't see the tangle of hose." Mom frowned. "I had the distinct impression . . ." She bit her lip and gripped my hand as the EMTs extricated her from the garden hose and eased her onto the gurney.

Momma Cat's hissing and growling turned my attention to the top of the steps. Curled to strike, with tongue flicking and tail furiously rattling a warning, the huge snake still faced the cat. But that old cat had won innumerable battles with rattlers in her fourteen years on the estate. I wasn't worried about her, but I was surprised the viper hadn't disappeared when all the noise appeared on the scene.

"Alli, come with me," Mom pled as the two broad-shouldered technicians lifted the gurney into the ambulance.

I grabbed the cell phone from the steps, left it in the foyer, locked the door and slid in beside the no-nonsense EMT caring for Mom who glared his displeasure at my presence and the sixty-second delay I'd caused him.

Mom closed her eyes and gripped my hand, her pain obvious in her expression.

"Where's Dad?" I asked, trying to get her mind on something besides the uncomfortable here and now.

Mom took a deep breath. "Still in Karabagh. He said the situation is stabilizing and he hopes to be home in the next couple of weeks. He started to tell me about some new development when I fell." She paused and squeezed her eyes shut, but a tear escaped and trickled onto her temple, disappearing into her black hair. I brushed away the next one. I would rather it had been me lying there instead of my mother.

"Thank heaven for your old Momma Cat. I think that rattler would have come right down the steps after me. It started to, but she drove it back and kept it away." Mom managed a faint smile. "Guess that was my payback for feeding her all those years you were away."

"I'm sure it was, but I always suspected she liked you better than me anyway."

Her smile widened. "I probably fed her more than you did, even when you were home. You were a little forgetful of that important item." The humor disappeared from her face and she fell silent for a few minutes. "Alli, I'm scheduled to leave for Armenia tomorrow. I saw my leg. I won't be out of the hospital by then, much less able to get on an airplane. You're going to have to cover for me."

"In Armenia? Mom . . ."

"It'll just be for the first couple of weeks, until I can travel. The schedule at the American University is tight. They've spent six months arranging these classes. I don't want them to have to shuffle everything at the last minute because of me. All my materials are filed in my briefcase according to presentation date. You can do this. You've heard me give these lectures all your life."

"Hearing them and giving them are entirely two different things," I reminded her. "And what about a visa? My passport is good, but I'll never get a visa in two days."

"Mine was complicated because it was a three-month business visa." Mom paused, her face filled with pain. "You can pick up a tourist visa at the airport when you land in Yerevan. Call Barbara at the travel agency and get your name on my ticket. Then make another reservation for me for about two weeks from now. We can spend some time together exploring Yerevan before you fly home."

I nodded, not wanting to answer lest my intuitive mother hear the doubt in my voice. I'd seen her leg, and even the invincible Margaret Alexander wouldn't be making an international flight in two weeks. Not even in the comfort of Anastasia's private Lear jet.

I changed the subject. "What were you doing home so early? I didn't expect you until this evening."

Mom sighed. "Nedra canceled our luncheon date."

"Again? This is the third or fourth time that's happened. Did she have a good excuse this time?"

"I suspect she's had another face lift and the discoloration hasn't disappeared. She complained of a multitude of new wrinkles the last time I saw her." Mom was quiet for a minute, before adding in disgust, "Aging movie stars are so vain."

The stern-faced technician was all ears now.

I laughed. "All but you. You've never had so much as an eyebrow tuck. But then, you've hardly changed in the twenty-five years since you retired from the dizzying heights of stardom, so you haven't needed all that cosmetic surgery in which your peers constantly indulge. Of course, maybe you are getting old," I teased. "I can't imagine the agile 'Margo' tripping on those steps where you've danced for the cameras so often."

Mom looked puzzled. "I was sure I'd coiled the hose yesterday when I watered. Alma would have a fit if she'd seen the tangled mess. Guess I was having a 'senior moment' and forgot to put it back. That's why I tripped over it. It's never like that." She closed her eyes and shuddered. "When that hose tightened around my ankle, I thought it was another snake."

To change the unpleasant subject, I reminded her, "You forgot to ask about my appointment with Dr. Sperry." I leaned close to her ear and whispered, "I have good news. You'll become a grandmother in May."

If Mom had been able to get on her feet, she would have danced with delight. "Your dream in Idaho was right, after all. I must say, I didn't really believe it could be true."

"I told you, in that dream I saw our baby just as clearly as I see you now. She was a beautiful little girl with my black hair and Bart's azure blue eyes. The dream was so real I could almost have touched her."

Mom squeezed my hand. "Are you still planning on naming her Alexandria?"

"I wouldn't dare not to. If I believed in that sort of thing, I'd think it was a bad omen to change anything about a dream that vivid."

Arrival at the hospital in Santa Barbara interrupted our conversation. Over her weak protests, I was relegated to the nearest waiting room as soon as I'd signed the papers authorizing her treatment. She may have thought her instructions and our conversation could continue, but having suffered a compound fracture myself, I understood when the doctor banished me from the room. In another few minutes, she wouldn't know whether I was with her or not.

I curled up on a love seat in the empty room and made myself comfortable for the long wait. Today had been physically and emotionally exhausting thus far. I hated hospitals and doctors' offices with a passion and I'd already filled my quota of hours in waiting rooms. But the good news I'd received earlier from Dr. Sperry offset the discomfort and inconvenience of the interminable wait.

As I'd suspected, I was finally pregnant. Dr. Sperry had announced the diagnosis with an admonition: "Everything looks good. Now if you'll give up that dangerous lifestyle you lead, stay home, eat right, and exercise, you should deliver a healthy baby next May."

That dangerous lifestyle he alluded to was already behind me. My fieldwork as an agent ended in an icy cave in Idaho last month with the escape of the infamous terrorist Osama bin Laden. I'd promised my anxious husband I would fulfill my responsibilities to Interpol's Anastasia from the safety of the Control Room at the estate.

Anastasia, the antiterrorist arm of Interpol which was created by my father over twenty-five years ago in Viet Nam, had been his life's work. On the organizational totem pole, Mom came second, with my husband, Bart, next in seniority. The elite unit numbered only ten agents, but due to its well-trained, highly skilled force, it was feared and hated by terrorists throughout the world.

The ringing of my cell phone startled me and I snatched it from my purse. I hadn't heard from my husband for nearly two weeks, though Bart made his coded check-in to the Control Center computer frequently. That brief message informing Anastasia he was alive and well wasn't the same as a personal call where we could talk, though it did alleviate the fear that built anew each day with Bart in some dangerous foreign environment.

"Bunny! How's your mother?" Dad's anxiety-filled voice boomed through the room.

"Hi, Dad. I can't tell you anything except it looked like a very bad break and she'll definitely not be leaving for Armenia tomorrow. Mom said you're in Karabagh. Any chance you'll be home sooner than two weeks?"

"You can bet I'm doing everything I can to tie this up," Dad said, "but unless I get a lot of cooperation from the other side of the table, two weeks is still just a wild guess. Are you covering her in Armenia?"

"I'd rather not. If I can find someone to take Mom's place in Yerevan for a month, I'd rather stay here with her."

"Do you have someone in mind?" The hope in Dad's voice was almost palpable. "Knowing you were with her would sure relieve my mind."

"Since the major requirements for the trip will be leaving job and family on twenty-four hour notice for at least thirty days, having a valid passport and up-to-date immunizations, and some knowledge of the subject matter, the possibilities are extremely limited. Thought I'd speak to the doctor before I started making phone calls."

There was silence on the other end of the line.

"Dad, are you still there?"

"Still here, Bunny. Just racking my brain to think of someone who could take her place." He fell silent again. "I'll give the doctor an hour, then call you back. Maybe by then you'll have thought of something."

"I'll work on it, Dad. Stay safe. Love you." Dad hung up without saying good-bye. He was worried. I was too. The last thing I wanted to do right now was live out of a suitcase in a foreign country giving lectures to people who knew more than I did about the subject matter.

Dr. Margaret Alexander was an international authority on cultures and customs of native peoples of the earth. When I was young, I'd traveled the world with her collecting and recording stories, songs, folk tales, dances, and oral histories from every country. Mom headed a highly respected department at the local university where she'd compiled her life's work into a tremendous collection that was the basis of many renowned anthropology studies.

She'd been invited to the American University of Armenia to be the keynote speaker and moderator at a three-month symposium, receive a lifetime achievement award in her field, and share her most recent study: a documentation of the far-reaching effects of modern society's intrusion on family and village life as people migrated to cities and multi-generational families disappeared. There was far more to her study than that, but she hadn't had time to share her discoveries and conclusions with me.

I could read her keynote speech, accept her award, and probably do a fairly creditable presentation on the history part, but it had been years since I'd shared her research so her latest studies were totally new and unknown territory to me. I couldn't possibly do justice to the subject when it came to the question and answer sessions. That required an expert in the field so I began listing possible replacements from the professors and teachers in Mom's department.

When the doctor still hadn't returned from surgery, I listed people I might call to stay with Mom in case I couldn't get someone else to go to Armenia, though that would definitely be a last resort. I didn't want to go to Armenia. I didn't want to go anywhere right now. I had a nursery to prepare and I was anxious to complete a list of things I'd been postponing for the last year. I'd call Alma and Jim in Texas only as a final recourse. They needed this break from the highly stressful demands of running the estate and keeping track of all our agents' needs in the field. We'd just completed a tense confrontation with the world's most wanted terrorist and we all needed some downtime, though Bart and my father had plunged immediately back into the danger-filled occupation they both loved.

I glanced at my watch. It had been well over an hour since we'd arrived at the hospital. If the doctor wouldn't come to me, I'd better find her before Dad called back. Being distracted by problems not directly related to his current situation could get him killed.

Tracking down a doctor or nurse who knew anything about Mom's condition—or would tell me anything—proved to be a study in tact, diplomacy, and patience, not to mention the detective skills of Sherlock Holmes. I finally found a friendly nurse who pointed out the room where they were working on Mom's leg. Positioning myself in the hall opposite the door, I remained there until a nurse emerged, leaving the door ajar.

Inside, Dr. Roskelly peeled off her scrub hat and mask and dropped them in a receptacle by the door. She ran her fingers through her short graying hair, then motioned for me to follow her down the hall to a small waiting room and sank into an overstuffed chair, pointing at the one opposite for me.

Her smile was weary. "I thought I'd find you hovering close to your mother."

"How is she? I need the gory details as well as a quick prognosis, Dr. Roskelly. Dad will call any minute from the other side of the world and I've got to have answers for his questions."

She rubbed her temples as if to massage away pain, then sighed deeply. "How many years have I been repairing your family's injuries?"

"At least since I was five years old." I sat up on the edge of my chair. I didn't like the way this interview began. "Why?"

CHAPTER 2

Before she could answer, my cell phone rang. Dad interrupted my greeting, bellowing loud enough for anyone within twenty feet to hear, "And the word is?"

Dr. Roskelley motioned for the phone which I reluctantly relinquished. "Hello, Jack. This is Leah Roskelley. How are you?"

How he was right now, he was too much of a gentleman to reveal. I knew he'd be in no state to chatter with an old acquaintance, even if she were the doctor with the answers he sought.

"I'm fine, Leah, but how's my wife? We were on the phone when she fell so I know enough to be worried sick."

Dr. Roskelley nodded absently, that professional mask falling into place on her attractive face. "Margaret has a compound fracture—worrisome at any age. At her age, it can require a long healing process. She told me she's lecturing in Eastern Europe next week. She's not. She'll still be in the hospital. Then I'm afraid it will be weeks before she gets her walking cast."

My heart sank. It would require a minor miracle to find someone to begin the lecture series and stay for a few weeks. It would take a major miracle to find someone who could stay the whole three months, especially since most of Mom's colleagues were already covering her duties at the University and school was only a couple of weeks into the new semester. Even Professor McGuire, Mom's retired mentor, had been pressed back into service to help while she was away.

Dr. Roskelley handed me the phone and pulled herself from the depths of the chair to get back to work.

"Now what are you going to do, Bunny?" Dad said as I put the phone to my ear.

"Make some very fast phone calls to everyone in Mom's department . . ."

"And then pack your suitcase," Dad finished.

"I'll do my best to find someone to go. I'd much rather stay with Mom, and anyone in the department could do a far better job than I could with the subject matter. If I *have* to go, I'll call Nedra. I'll play on her guilt feelings for standing up Mom at lunch three months in a row and have her come until Jim and Alma get home. I really don't want to interrupt their vacation."

"Bunny," Dad hesitated, then began slowly. "Would you do one thing for me . . ." He fell silent.

"Of course, Dad. You know I'll do anything I can."

"I, uh, I'd like you to call that bishop of yours and have him give your mother a . . . what do you call that?"

My heart nearly stopped beating. "A blessing. A priesthood blessing. I'd planned on it, as soon as we got off the phone. But what made you ask? I thought you didn't believe in that 'hocus pocus,' as you called it."

"I don't," he growled. "But on the off chance that it can help her, I'd like it done. I'll do anything, including calling in witch doctors to chant over her if it will improve her condition." Dad's voice cracked. I knew he was too emotional for this conversation to continue longer.

"That will be the first phone call I make, Dad. Thanks for asking. Don't worry about things here. I'll handle everything. You just be safe and hurry home. I love you."

"Love you, too, Bunny." He was so quiet for a minute I thought he'd hung up. As I was about to disconnect, he added quietly, "I think it will be more effective than witch doctors." Then the line went dead.

I was both stunned and delighted at Dad's request. My parents loved each other passionately. Their greatest fear was being separated from one another by death, especially the premature death of one of them. Since Bart and I had joined The Church of Jesus Christ of Latter-day Saints just over a year ago, I'd hoped my parents would want to know what we believed so fervently, but they'd declined to listen to even the one principle I felt would appeal most to them—that of eternal families.

The fact that my father thought about a blessing for Mom was a major step in the right direction. I quickly punched in Bishop O'Hare's number on my little cell phone, blessing the convenience of these miniature gems.

"O'Hare." A terse one-word reply seemed the normal mode of answering the phone for every FBI agent I knew.

"Bishop, this is Allison. Do you have a minute?"

"For you, always." The Bishop's familiar voice softened immediately and warmed my soul. "What can I help you with?"

"I'm at the hospital . . ."

"Oh, Alli. What now?" I could almost see him reaching for his suit jacket and heading for the door. "I'll be right there."

"Hold it. It's not me this time. Mom broke her leg, a compound fracture, and I'd like you to give her a blessing when you have time." I took a deep breath. "And you won't believe this—I can hardly believe it myself. Dad asked if I'd call you to do it." The emotional impact of that request suddenly hit me. Hot tears stung my eyes.

"Well, well, well. The iron man does have a heart after all." He paused. "Or was this a case of covering all the bases, on the off chance it might help?"

"I'll think about it and let you know. I'll be with Mom until they kick me out tonight. Sorry to have to bother you. I know you just got back in town, but since we're supposed to call our home teachers for help, and you're it, you get all the problems that come with the territory."

"My pleasure, Allison. Besides, your problems are always interesting. If I wasn't in the spook business myself, I'd probably find them unbelievable. I'll call someone to come with me and we'll be there within the hour. How are you holding up?"

"I'm fine. And thanks for not making me feel like a burden, which I have been so often." I hung up before he could answer. The emotions I'd carefully controlled since I'd seen Mom on the stairs finally overwhelmed me. If I'd said one more word, or he had, I'd have cried like a baby.

This good man had performed our marriage; had saved my life, literally, at our explosive wedding by throwing himself on top of me when terrorist bombs started going off; and had been our confidant, teacher, and good friend through all the vicissitudes of our marriage during the last year. He and his wife, Kitty, had even flown to Idaho to be with us when we were sealed in that beautiful little temple by the river a few weeks ago. Knowing he was available was a great comfort as the enormity of my task suddenly registered. With no husband at hand to give support, aid, or advice, no father near to rely on, and Jim and Alma, always so dear and helpful, now absent, I suddenly felt very much alone.

I pulled the phone book from the small desk in the waiting room and began calling Mom's colleagues. As I'd feared, none were able to make the trip on such short notice. That meant I was elected. One call remained to be made, but I didn't have Nedra's number in Beverly Hills. That would have to wait until I got home, unless Mom remembered it.

Now it was time to face my mother. The only thing worse than being in pain in the hospital was having a loved one in pain in the hospital. Reluctantly, I backtracked the sterile corridor to find Mom's room. She was sleeping. No surprise. I suspected she would probably spend the rest of the afternoon sleeping off the effects of the anesthetic. I pulled two chairs together next to her bed, settled into one, propped my tired legs on the other, and began the necessary planning. Checklists were essential in my life and unless I could convince her to just cancel the whole thing, I didn't have time to make lengthy mental plans, then check them multiple times to make sure I hadn't forgotten something.

Mom stirred, opened her eyes, and reached for my hand. I jumped to my feet and began my pitch for canceling the entire trip. She gave one very firm no and closed her eyes.

"Just listen for a minute, please. Mom, stay awake. Someone else can read your keynote address and moderate the symposium. This isn't an earth-shattering presentation you're making. Important, yes. But . . ." No use. She was gone and I couldn't rouse her from the drug-induced sleep. Back to my checklists.

Acquiring a visa would be the first problem, tickets the second, then wardrobe. Even if I could convince Mom later when she was awake enough to think clearly that I didn't need to make this trip, there were things that must be done right now—if I ended up having to go. I called Barbara, our much-used travel agent, to expedite the name change on the ticket, and inquired about the itinerary while I had her on the phone. Unfortunately, I had less than twenty-four hours before I had to check in at Tom Bradley International Airport in Los Angeles to catch my flight. I hung up and stared at the small phone in my hand, paralyzed by the multitude and magnitude of tasks confronting me, and the short time in which to accomplish them.

I leaned my head back on the chair, closed my eyes, and mentally packed my suitcase. My reluctant mind kept taking things out as fast as I thought of something to put in. I did *not* want to make this trip. I forced myself to concentrate. Business dress for three months, casual clothes for Saturdays, and Sunday best for church. I sat up. Assuming there was a church in Yerevan. We were a worldwide church, established in nearly every corner of the world, but Armenia was a small country that had, until recently, been under Communist domination. I'd ask Bishop O'Hare to check for me.

Questions tumbled over one another in my mind. Who would meet me? Where would I stay? What was the climate? The political situation? And possibly the most important of all to a member of Anastasia, what was the terrorist activity level in and around the country now? Still fermenting from the recent assassination of government leaders?

Dad was next door in Karabagh attempting to quell a terrorist group disrupting the peace-making efforts of governments trying to stabilize the war-torn area where thousands had already died. I knew my parents had planned to be together when he finished. It wasn't unreasonable to believe he would come to see me, when and if the situation allowed. That was a comforting thought.

Bishop Matthew O'Hare arrived with Tom Robbins in tow. Tom, a retired FBI agent, frequently accompanied the bishop on these errands of mercy. The two had much in common besides their line of work. I particularly enjoyed Tom's stories of the early days with the Bureau. Today there were no stories. They both understood the special nature of the occasion and their mood reflected that.

I stood and greeted the two old friends, then squeezed Mom's hand to see if I could wake her. This blessing depended as much on her faith as it did on mine and those performing the ordinance. She finally roused enough to understand she had company.

When I explained Bishop O'Hare was there to give her a blessing, she nodded. "I'd like that. I remember how much of a difference it's made in your recovery after you had a blessing. Thank you for thinking to do it for me."

"Would you believe Dad requested it?" I asked, watching her reaction closely.

She closed her eyes and didn't answer right away. For a minute, I thought she'd drifted back to sleep. Then she opened her eyes. "Of course, I'd believe it. Your father knows much more about your faith than you think." She smiled. "And so do I."

With the ordinance performed, Bishop O'Hare and Tom waited for me in the hall while I kept Mom awake long enough to get as much information as possible from her on the seminars. Then I let her sink into oblivion with the help of the pain medication.

"How'd she break her leg?" Bishop O'Hare asked as we walked to his car.

"While she was talking to Dad on the phone, she went out to water the roses. She was startled by a rattler in the rose bushes, and when she stepped back, she got tangled in the hose and fell down the marble stairs, twisting her leg in the process." I still couldn't envision my agile mother clumsily tripping over the hose. Nor could I envision the hose in a tangled mess. "Both Mom and Alma unreel the hose as they go down the rose bushes watering them, then always coil it back up out of sight around the corner where it belongs. Neither of them has ever left it out. She said she must have been having a senior moment and forgotten to put it away."

"Unfortunately, we know about senior moments," Tom laughed. "Mine are happening so often now my wife calls them senior hours."

As they drove me back to the estate, we chatted about their families and then my new assignment and the challenges it would present. I was glad not only for the ride home, but even more for the solace of their companionable presence. With reluctance I climbed out of the car in front of our little cottage under the pine trees. I didn't look forward to my busy night, nor did I feel confident about replacing my knowledgeable mother at the podium.

"Bishop, would you and Tom mind . . ."

"I was hoping you'd ask. If you hadn't, I'd have offered." The Bishop slammed his door with a smile and followed me to the doorstep. Tom hurried out of the car and was at the door by the time I'd opened it.

They gave me a simple blessing, offering comfort and the ability to accomplish what needed to be done. But as the Bishop pronounced the end of the blessing, he paused for what seemed an eternity. When he resumed, he promised I would ultimately return home safely. That phrase caused a little tingle of alarm to run through me, which I quickly dismissed.

As I thanked him and Tom, I teased, "What did you mean by ultimately? Three months isn't that long, although it might seem like forever to whoever replaces me in the nursery every Sunday at church. You will remember to find someone to substitute for me, won't you? I haven't had time to call anyone."

Bishop O'Hare nodded and laughed. "I'll definitely get someone to cover for you. If I forget, it will be me in there with your room full of tiny tots." Then his smile vanished and he reached for my hand. "Alli, be careful. You have such a propensity for finding trouble I worry, especially when you'll be over there on your own."

They said good-bye in the deepening twilight and headed for the car. As I stood in the doorway watching them, Bishop O'Hare hesitated as he opened the car door. He looked back at me, then waved, got in and started the car. But before he drove away, he rolled down the window and called, "Remember your training, Alli, and stay on your toes. That's a very different part of the world."

I laughed and waved them away, "Yes, Father." That was the very thing my father would say to me if he were here. I turned into the house and locked the door behind me. I probably wouldn't have thought to do it without the Bishop's admonition, since I felt so safe and secure on the huge estate, even if I was the only soul out here right now. But training manuals specified locking doors, day and night, so I threw the bolt and headed upstairs, feeling only slightly guilty for not locking it when I left this morning.

My list of "to-do's" had grown long enough to keep me busy right up to flight time, but I could always sleep on that all-night flight to London.

Nedra headed my list, and when I called, she agreed to pack her bag and come immediately. I assured her Mom would be in the hospital for several days, but she said she'd stay nights at the estate and spend all day with Mom. I sent a grateful prayer heavenward for that blessing.

Then I turned to the task of finding the right combination of clothes, while packing as lightly as I could, without wearing the same few outfits over and over. That accomplished, I hurried up the big lawn to the mansion where Mom and Dad lived. A brilliant half-moon lit my way though I knew it so well I could have made the trip blindfolded.

Bart and I had taken over the little caretaker's cottage when we got married, just until we found another place to live. It had now been over a year, and we'd stayed so busy with Anastasia's antiterrorist demands, we'd never had time to look for anything else. Gradually we'd settled in and it became our home, though it was truly the only home I'd ever known. Mom and I had lived there from the time I was five years old while she masqueraded as the caretaker of the estate, living the deception for twenty years to escape a mafia don's contract on her life. My absentee father, finally able to emerge from his under-cover job, had moved with Mom into their mansion.

The phone rang in the foyer as I unlocked the door. By the time I turned on the crystal chandelier and reached the phone, there was no one on the line. I glanced at my watch. Midnight. Who'd be calling at this hour? As I crossed the white marble foyer, I remembered the bishop's admonition and returned to lock the door.

I slipped behind the potted palms under the circular staircase, and sliding my fingers up the wall, pressed the concealed button activating the miniature elevator that would take me to Anastasia's underground West Coast Control Center. In seconds it silently dropped three hundred feet down the shaft carved through solid rock to a tunnel that led to the Control Center, and a few feet farther, to the Pacific Ocean.

As the elevator door slid silently open, tiny lights appeared at the base of the rock wall, affording just enough light to guide one through the tunnel. The sound of waves crashing on rocks echoed through the cave from the far end, and the salty smell of the sea hung heavy in the air.

When Mom was at the height of her successful career as a movie star and Dad was with the military Office of Special Investigations, he'd helped her design the mansion, convincing her this would be a perfect location for a control center for Interpol. She'd accepted his design, and later, his proposal of marriage.

I felt for the indentation in the rock wall that opened the door to the control room, stepped inside the darkened room and closed the door before turning on the lights. When I touched the switch, fluorescent lighting flooded the room filled with computers and communication equipment. I hurried first to the check-in computer where encoded messages were received, and typed in the combination of numbers and letters that automatically decoded waiting messages.

Several had arrived since Mom last checked and filed them. I searched for Bart's code name, Apollo, and found it. He'd sent his "agent okay; all is well" message several hours earlier. Dad's was there, and by habit I thumbed through the rest, finding check-ins for Else, Dominic, Sky, Lionel, David, Oz, and Mai Li. All agents accounted for.

Then I had a disconcerting thought. With me gone, Alma and Jim on vacation, and Mom unable to easily navigate in a cast, who would keep track of our agent's field movements?

I sent a quick note to Oz and Mai Li's message retrieval number, requesting Mai Li return as quickly as possible to man the Control Center, explaining the sudden change in our situation. If she could come, she could masquerade as a nurse's aide hired to help Mom. Having Mai Li here would also alleviate my fear that Nedra might not keep her word and stay until Jim and Alma arrived. Nedra was not high on my list of dependable people, loveable as she might be.

Nedra knew nothing of my parent's involvement with Interpol. I hadn't even known until just before my wedding. For twenty-five years they'd kept their secret life hidden from everyone except Bart's parents, Jim and Alma Allan. During all those years, Jim and Alma had manned the computers, managed the estate, constantly upgraded all the electronic gadgets, and kept operations running smoothly behind the scenes, including coordinating complicated operations when all the agents were in the field. How I missed them tonight.

I called up the State Department website on the computer and asked for information on Armenia. While that printed, I stepped to the next computer and downloaded Interpol's information on that country, including maps. I'd need to know something about the political situation as well as the general layout of the city before I arrived.

From the "M" file in the filing cabinet, I removed what I estimated to be enough money for three months in Armenia, and a couple of credit cards we used for agent's expenses.

As I headed for the door with my printed sheets and expense money, the phone rang. I jumped at the unexpected sound. No one had this special number but Anastasia's tight circle and I couldn't imagine any of them calling at this hour. Then I remembered it was noon on the other side of the world. Excited at the thought it might be Bart, I snatched the phone.

"Hello."

"Alli, I called your cell phone but you didn't answer, so I figured you must be in the Control Center. I needed to give you a few more instructions."

"Mom, what are you doing awake? I thought that medication would put you out for hours."

"I hoped it would, but I've had to ask for some with a little more power. I guess my pain tolerance isn't what it used to be. Allison, my briefcase is on my bed, but I hadn't packed the special tools I planned to take." Mom paused. "These are just in case." Her laughter seemed a little forced. "No well-dressed agent leaves home without them."

"I get the message. What do I need?"

"Take the journal with the ceramic gun hidden in the padding. It can make it through customs and x-ray machines without being detected. Also, take your pretty gold compact with the radio receiver and scrambler. I've arranged to have a cell phone over there, but everything is heavily monitored by both the Mafia and the KGB, so any messages we don't want them to hear must be sent and received on the compact."

I'd been retrieving the suggested items as she listed them. "Anything else?"

"If I think of anything, I'll call. Keep your cell phone handy. Whew, whatever they gave me has started taking effect. I'll talk to you in the morning. Please glance over the materials in the briefcase so I can answer any questions you have before you go. Communication is much easier when we are on the same side of the world. Oh, will you bring my lavender robe and slippers and my hairbrush and makeup when you come tomorrow? Good night, dear."

My family had a disconcerting habit of hanging up when they finished their side of the conversation. I did have some questions, but now they'd have to wait until morning. I jotted them down so I wouldn't forget to ask, then looked over the little case full of special equipment. I always felt "Q" should be here dispensing them as he did to James Bond at the beginning of each of Bond's new assignments.

The small polemoscope had been very useful in Sri Lanka, so I set that aside. It looked like a monocular, but instead of seeing through the lens in front, the arrangement of tiny mirrors inside allowed you to see to the side. One never knew just when a gadget like that would be handy, especially if all my movements were being monitored. I knew the Mafia and KGB were active in Yerevan, so they'd know the minute I landed at the airport and I'd probably be followed everywhere I went. With this device, I could watch them watch me.

I was about to close the case when the "Dick Tracy" watches caught my eye. They had been designed especially for Bart and me to use to keep track of each other. I reached for mine, but decided it wouldn't be much help if I were there alone and closed the case. Then, feeling an urge to take them along, I put the watches with the rest of the equipment, left the Control Center, and returned to the white marble foyer through the tiny elevator.

As the little door concealed behind the circular staircase slid silently open, goose bumps rippled down my arms and up the back of my neck.

CHAPTER 3

I stood silently, listening, waiting for some confirmation that my danger antennae weren't just playing tricks on me at this late hour. Had Bishop O'Hare's admonition to remember my training simply triggered my imagination?

No. Someone *was* in the house. Soft footsteps descended the stairs above me. I waited, finger poised on the elevator button. If they started around the stairs when they reached the bottom, I'd have time to close the panel before they could see it. The door operated so silently one would have to see it to know it was there.

I'd locked the door. How would anyone have gotten in? Of course, they could have broken a window and I wouldn't have heard a thing from the soundproof Control Center. Unfortunately, I hadn't turned on the monitors to view what was going on in the empty house above me. As the footsteps reached the bottom of the stairs, I heard a quiet murmur of voices. Exit time.

I pressed the elevator button and the secret door slid silently closed, sealing me into a comforting cocoon of safety. Hurrying back to the Control Center, I switched on all the closed circuit cameras in the mansion to check each room, beginning with the grand entry. It was empty. So were the music room, the ballroom, and the library. On the other side of the foyer, the living room, dining room, and kitchen were also quite deserted.

I scanned each of the guest rooms, then the grounds: the garden, pool area, and cabanas. There was nothing moving but Momma Cat on her nightly prowl. Puzzled, I plopped into the chair in front of the monitors and went back through each room. Not a soul visible anywhere. That thought sent shivers through me.

Silly goose. You're definitely dealing with humans here, not invisible spirits. Spirits don't make sounds on the steps. Do they?

I could sleep down here in the little room just off the Control Center and feel perfectly safe all night. But I didn't have time to stay tucked away from . . . from what? Had my imagination just been overactive? Maybe my ears had played tricks on me and no one had been there—in which case, I had lost a valuable few minutes coming back down to the Control Center for this fruitless search. I shook off the feeling of disquiet settling over me. Time to get back on track or I'd never accomplish everything that needed to be done in the next few hours.

I glanced at my watch. Twelve-thirty. In less than twelve hours, I needed to be on my way to the airport. No more dilly-dallying. I hurried back to the elevator, but instead of taking the one into the foyer, I opted for the elevator to the ballroom. It would deposit me in the immense fireplace at the end of the ballroom where I'd be hidden by the gold fireplace screen. I laughed at myself. Apparently I wasn't totally convinced I'd been imagining intruders in the mansion after all.

Emerging from the elevator in the side of the fireplace, I stood quietly behind the screen listening intently for any sound that might suggest another presence in the house. I heard nothing but the wind off the ocean singing through the pines. Taking a deep breath, I slipped from behind the five-foot, gold peacock, crossed the ballroom and peeked through the French doors into the moonlit night. Mom's car and mine were the only ones in the circular driveway. The only lights visible were the oil rigs on the dark horizon that looked like huge brightly lit ships on the ocean.

I tiptoed through the music room and stopped before approaching the French doors into the foyer, waited a few seconds, then sidled up to the doors, remaining in the shadow and out of the light streaming from the crystal chandelier in the foyer. I could see or hear no one else in the house.

Quietly opening the French doors, I crossed the white marble tile and, slipping my shoes off, carried them up the spiral staircase. Mom's door stood wide open, as she would have left it. But there was no briefcase on the bed. The dim glow from the foyer chandelier wasn't sufficient to search for the missing briefcase. I quietly closed the door, switched on the light, and waited, almost expecting someone to jump out of the closet. No one did. I chided myself for being ridiculous.

I searched everywhere for the briefcase. It simply wasn't there. The only sign it might have been was a slight indentation the size of the item in question on the foot of her bed. She must have had another senior moment and hadn't remembered moving the case.

That bothered me. It wasn't like Mom to be so forgetful. She was the most "together" lady I knew, extremely intelligent, and certainly not at all the absentminded professor type. Dr. Margaret Alexander was a detail person who never let anything escape her or go undone that was in her scope of responsibility. The events of today didn't make sense: first the tangled hose that caused her accident and now the missing briefcase. Then I remembered Mom's comments about the hose tightening around her ankle.

Had someone purposely placed the hose on the steps, deposited the rattler in the rosebushes to distract Mom, then jerked on the hose when her foot was in the right place? Pretty far-fetched, even for my vivid imagination. However, given the diabolical minds of terrorists, nothing was out of the realm of possibility. Every member of Anastasia was in constant danger from those set on destroying the free world's way of life.

Quickly gathering the robe and toiletries Mom requested, I packed them in her overnight case, turned off the light and opened the door. There, reaching for the doorknob, stood the biggest, ugliest man I'd ever encountered in my life.

He must have been as surprised to see me as I was to see him as neither of us reacted for several seconds. Then I slammed the door in his face, twisted the lock, and raced to the closet on the other side of the room, thanking Dad with every step for his farsighted vision and all the secret passageways in the house.

I quietly closed the closet door behind me, slipped between Mom's clothes and slid open the panel in the back wall. As I entered the narrow corridor of the passage, I heard the bedroom door splinter and men's excited voices. That was definitely not a figment of my imagination. It almost made me feel better, knowing there was nothing wrong with Mom's mind.

Now the questions loomed large: was this another attack on a member of Anastasia, a deliberate attempt to stop Mom from going to Armenia, or just a random robbery?

As I hurried through the winding passageways leading to the elevator and the Control Center, I catalogued the features of the man I'd faced in the doorway. Large misshapen nose, left cheekbone higher and more prominent than the right cheekbone, as if someone had smashed in his face on that side. And a scar that arched in a curve over the right eyebrow. He reminded me of a boxer who'd been hit in the face countless times, like Rocky in the old Sylvester Stallone movie.

I didn't remember ever seeing that face before. Nor did it appear in Interpol's extensive collection of mug shots we kept updated on the computer. I scanned through them a second time, just to be sure. Was he a new recruit to a known terrorist group or were these men part of a newly formed terrorist cell? Then again, it could be a simple breaking and entering and those men had nothing to do with Anastasia's never-ending battle against terrorism.

Why hadn't they appeared on the monitors? I shuddered to think of meeting them all together in another part of the house where I couldn't have escaped as easily. They must have been in the hallway of the guest rooms. That was the only blind spot in the elaborate security system Jim had devised for the mansion—one he'd planned to correct but hadn't yet.

I returned to the bank of monitors and watched the men search for me. There were three in the house. The big man with the boxer's face, a young, slender, agile man with an aquiline nose and black hair, and a man with silver gray, close-cropped hair who carried Mom's briefcase from room to room with him. When they discovered I wasn't in the bedroom or any of Mom's closets, they began searching the mansion room by room.

The older man was obviously the leader. His dark eyes scanned each room as they entered it, then he watched the other two men search, pointing out places they'd overlooked in their haste, or hadn't searched carefully enough. I heard one of the men refer to him as "Fox," and thought it appropriate—he reminded me of a fox with his beady little eyes and devious expression.

When they'd searched the house thoroughly, they held a confab at the foot of the circular staircase in the foyer discussing where I could have gone. Except for the legal technicality that they *had* broken into my parents' home, these three didn't appear to be your common everyday second-story men involved in petty breaking and entering. They were well dressed. Two wore slacks and sport coats. The third, the one carrying the briefcase whom I dubbed The Fox, wore an expensive gray suit, square-toed Italian shoes, and had big time written all over him. They were quiet, efficient, and thorough.

I reached for the phone. The FBI was the authority where terrorists were involved. I just hated to get Bishop O'Hare out of bed in the middle of the night.

"O'Hare," the sleepy voice grumbled.

"Bishop, it's Allison. I'm safe," I assured him, "but there are three men in the mansion."

The voice changed instantly to fully awake. "Where are you? Where are they? Are you sure there are only three?"

"I'm in the Control Center watching them on the monitors. They're in the foyer. Three is all I've seen." I checked the monitors that covered the grounds and gardens just to be sure.

"Allison, stay put. Do not leave the Control Center. I need you there for two reasons: first, to track their movements while we get into place; second, you'll be safely out of my hair and I won't have to worry about you. Anything else I need to know?"

"Mom's briefcase seems to be the only thing they're interested in, except finding me now that they know I'm here. I haven't been able to identify any of them from Interpol's files."

"I'm sending a man to the hospital to watch your Mom. You stay near the phone," he ordered. Then the line went dead. We lived ten to fifteen minutes from Santa Barbara, depending on how fast you drove, and he had to gather his men. It would be thirty minutes at least before anyone arrived. What if the men left with the briefcase before the FBI arrived to apprehend them?

I turned back to the monitors. Evidently a plan had been agreed upon. The big man with the boxer's face took possession of the briefcase and remained in the foyer. The Fox returned to Mom's bedroom. The younger, dark-haired man began a second search of the house.

As I watched Rocky settle on the stairs and lean his head sleepily against the balustrade, an idea formed. Mom's briefcase sat on the floor near his feet between a potted palm and the stairs, out of the way of traffic. I was confident he could not hear the panel open behind the stairs, even in a high state of awareness. Right now, he was one sleepy man.

Checking the whereabouts of the other two men one last time on the monitors, I disobeyed Bishop O'Hare and left the safety of the Control Center, raced to the elevator, shedding my shoes while it whisked me up through the granite cliff. The door slid soundlessly open into the shadows behind the stairs. I waited, breath held, listening. There wasn't a sound from anywhere in the house—or out. Even the wind had stopped.

Creeping softly into the foyer in stocking feet, I slipped from behind the huge green palm fronds. Staying close to the stairs, I reached for the briefcase. At that instant, a door slammed somewhere in the house, disturbing Rocky. He raised his head and appeared ready to stand. I froze. I could clearly see the back and side of his head. If he turned even slightly in my direction, he would see me.

The wait seemed interminable. I felt like a statue atop a bowling trophy, legs and body bent and arm stretched out at the moment the ball was released. Finally, just as Rocky settled back and leaned his head against the balustrade, the door at the top of the stairs closed quietly—Mom's bedroom door, where the man in the suit had been. My fingers tightened around the handle as I heard his footsteps on the stairs above me.

Rocky heard him too. He stood and stretched. I tiptoed back around the potted palm, briefcase in hand, and escaped into the elevator shaft. I wanted to watch the discovery of the missing brief-case on the monitors in the Control Center. I didn't know what Mom had in her case, but at this point I suspected it wasn't just papers on the effects of families moving to the city from villages in Armenia. I dropped the purloined case next to Mom's overnighter and concentrated on the monitors.

It took them a couple of minutes to discover the briefcase was gone. They waited silently for the third man to join them, and when he appeared, the leader asked for the case. Rocky bent and reached around the stairs. As he realized it wasn't there, the stunned expression on his face was priceless. I was more interested to see the reaction of the man in the suit, but movement on another monitor caught my eye and I shifted my focus to the grounds and gardens monitors.

The good guys had arrived in their blue windbreakers with big yellow FBI lettered on the back. My cell phone rang. It could only be one person. "Hi, Agent O'Hare. What a welcome sight you are."

"Do you ever just say hello?" Without waiting for an answer, he asked, "Where are they? Have you seen anyone outside?"

I turned back to the indoor monitors. "All three are in the foyer and we have one furious bossman to deal with. No, I haven't seen anyone outside, but if they were out of camera range, there could be an army out there and I wouldn't know it."

"We haven't come across an army. Are you still in the Control Center?"

"Safe and sound. Your targets are spreading out again with guns. They're looking for me and they don't appear to have party games in mind. I stole Mom's briefcase right out from under their noses, and I think they are a little upset at the loss. They look ready for a fight."

When O'Hare didn't answer, I checked the outside monitors and watched him deploying his people to different entrances of the house. Night vision and infrared cameras enabled the monitors to pick up in shadowed areas outside the range of the lights.

"I'm sending someone in through the garden," he reported. "Can we come in the front door?"

"You can right now, or you could just wait and get them when they come out."

He ignored my suggestion. "Where are they? Specifics, Alli."

"The agile-looking one is in the library, climbing the little wrought iron stairs to the second level. That will keep him there for a minute or two. Rocky's in the kitchen. He doesn't look too fast, but could be very strong. The boss man, The Fox, is back in Mom's bedroom at the top of the stairs. He knows I disappeared from there and seems determined to find out where I went."

"Coming in now."

CHAPTER 4

On the monitor, I watched the kitchen door open slowly. A tall, blond agent named Fred slipped in quietly and caught Rocky with his head in the refrigerator investigating its contents. The big man seemed in shock at being apprehended and gave no resistance at all. Fred quickly disarmed and cuffed him, and they disappeared into the night.

I immediately turned to the other monitors to watch Bishop O'Hare and a small, red-haired female agent enter the house through the front door. He motioned her in the direction of the library while he headed up the stairs to Mom's room.

I held my breath. The Fox didn't look like the type to give up quietly. I wanted to warn Matt O'Hare to be careful, but my words would have been wasted. Of course he'd be careful. This had been his occupation for twenty-five years. He'd expect the unexpected.

Matt crouched in the doorway, gun pointed inside, and yelled, "FBI. Drop your weapon."

The Fox fired as he turned from the closet door, missing the FBI agent by a hair.

"Drop it," Matt demanded once more. The Fox fired again as he swept his hand down the wall, turning off all the lights. I heard another shot as the room plunged into darkness. The monitor momentarily darkened while the camera adjusted to the different light.

The shots alerted the man in the library and he flew down those narrow circular steps as easily as Mom danced down the white marble staircase in her movies. The redheaded FBI agent heard the footsteps on the wrought iron and ducked into the ballroom doorway so when Dancer emerged from the library, there was an empty hall in front of him.

As he raced back toward the foyer, the redhead tripped him. He skidded down the marble tile, arms spread out in front of him. But before he'd stopped sliding, he tucked into a forward roll. He'd almost regained his feet when she tackled him. Dancer was back on the floor in a flash, the redheaded agent on top of him with one knee in his back and her gun pressed into his neck. As she cuffed him, I checked the monitor in Mom's bedroom.

Still no lights, but the infrared camera revealed one man on the floor by the bedroom door. Matt was down!

Where was The Fox? I searched every monitor. The only movement in the house was the redhead inching up the stairs toward the darkened bedroom, followed closely by Fred, the tall, blond agent who'd captured Rocky. No sign of The Fox anywhere. He'd slyly slipped away. But to where? Had he found the hidden passage behind Mom's closet?

My attention returned to Bishop Matthew O'Hare. This man meant as much to me as my family. He was big brother, favorite uncle, and dear friend, all wrapped into one neat package of a man, and he lay motionless on the ground.

Sending fervent prayers heavenward, I helplessly watched the agents creep up the stairs, and struggled to control the impulse to race to Matt's side instead of following his instructions to watch the monitors.

Every room in the house was empty. No movement appeared on any monitor in the bank except the two agents on the stairs. Nothing moved outside. I couldn't even tell where Rocky and Dancer were. But worst of all, there was no movement on the floor in Mom's bedroom. Tears stung my eyes. *Please, please, let Matt be all right.*

Why had I taken my eyes off that bedroom when the lights went out? If I hadn't allowed my attention to be diverted to the library, I'd know to where The Fox disappeared. He couldn't possibly have found the hidden passageway in Mom's closet in those few seconds. The man had conducted an extensive search when he was there before. If he'd found it, he'd have continued his search for me in the passage at that time. So he had to have left Mom's bedroom by the only other means—through the door into the hall—right over the top of Matthew O'Hare. Tears trickled down my cheeks. If he could escape while Matt lay in the doorway . . . The thought was too horrible to finish.

The redhead reached Matt first and knelt at his side while the other agent covered her. I turned up the sound on that monitor to hear what they were saying. Matt was bleeding from a head wound. The redhead radioed for an ambulance. The other agent, apparently determining no one was in the room, turned on the light and knelt beside Matt to help.

The bishop still hadn't moved. It had been at least two minutes, if my muddled mind computed right, and he remained unconscious. Unconscious with a head wound. That didn't bode well. I couldn't let that monster escape who had done this to Matt. When I thought of what might have happened to Mom if she'd been here, I brushed hot tears away angrily.

I had to find The Fox. If he'd stepped over the body on the floor, he'd have gone down the hall in the opposite direction of the stairs. That would take him to the guest bedrooms.

Scanning the monitors covering that wing of the house, I punched in one guest room after another to reveal the interior of the room. There simply wasn't a soul in sight. He could be hiding in any one of the closets, but The Fox didn't seem the type to cower in a corner and be caught. He'd get out of Dodge as fast as possible with the FBI on the scene. So he could be in the hallway where the monitors didn't cover. He could also have taken the stairs down to the garden and pool area. That was the most likely.

How could I alert the two agents with Matt? I dialed the bishop's cell phone and hoped he hadn't turned the ringer completely off when he'd come in. He hadn't. The redhead dug the phone out of Matt's pocket and answered it.

"This is Allison Allan. I think the man who shot Matt is outside or on his way there, probably heading for the garden and pool. If you have someone out there, give them a head's up. If the man hasn't cleared the house yet, he probably will any second." I paused long enough to give her time to radio the agents outside. Fred left immediately, heading down the hall toward the guest rooms where I figured The Fox must have gone.

The redhead hovering over the bishop still had the phone in her hand. I asked, almost afraid of the answer, "How's Matt?"

"Head wound. Lot of blood," she said, telling me nothing I

hadn't already seen from the monitor.

"How serious?" I hoped and prayed it was superficial, but knew it had to be more if he hadn't moved.

"Since I'm not a doctor, I'd rather not make a diagnosis."

Her brusque reply infuriated me. I wanted to shake the woman. Instead, I spoke quietly into the phone I held with a quivering hand. "I'm trying to be eyes and ears for you and find the man who shot Agent O'Hare before he gets a shot at another agent. I'd appreciate it if you could give me some information on Matt's condition. He's very special to me. Please tell me something besides the obvious."

Before she could answer, The Fox emerged from the stairway leading from the guest rooms. He paused for an instant before heading across the pool area.

"I see him!" I yelled into the phone. "Just coming out of the house by the pool."

The redhead radioed that information to the agents outside, and to Fred, following The Fox through the house. I was relieved to know Matt had brought more than two agents with him. I had a feeling it would take everyone available to stop the man with the devious, disdainful expression stamped on his face.

Two agents emerged from the darkness fringing the camera range and moved slowly toward the pool on a collision course with The Fox. Fred emerged from the staircase at that moment and spotted his target. Three good guys to one bad guy. I liked those odds. Definitely increased the chances of capturing the fiend who shot Matt, then casually walked over the top of him to escape.

I didn't think The Fox had seen the two agents, but apparently he had. He suddenly turned and darted toward the cabanas, disappearing into the darkness and from view of the monitors.

If no one waited in that direction to stop him, he could slip out by the carriage house where Jim kept the golf carts. He'd have a thousand yards of open lawn in front of him, lawn studded with huge boulders and large oak trees and a dozen places to hide. Beyond the manicured lawn, golden hills dotted with rocks and caves stretched above the mansion for miles. If he crossed the lawn without being caught, it would take a battalion to find him.

All three agents raced toward the cabanas. My heart sank. The

Fox's half-minute head start would be sufficient to get him across the open lawn to the first cluster of trees. If he were as clever as he appeared, he'd have spent time studying the layout of the grounds and would have planned multiple escape routes. The agents pursuing him were at a disadvantage. They'd never been here before. They didn't know what lay beyond the carriage house.

The wailing siren of an ambulance filled the Control Center and I cut the sound on the monitors. Another agent materialized out of the darkness, and following the radio directions from the redheaded agent, guided the EMTs through the front door and up the stairs to the bishop.

I'd lost track of The Fox and the agents following him. They were out of range of any of the cameras. No point in remaining here. I shut down the monitors and hurried out of the Control Center, leaving Mom's briefcase safely behind. There were too many people about to use the foyer elevator. I took the elevator that opened into the fireplace, remaining behind the peacock screen until I was sure no one could see me, then slipped into the hall from the library. I entered the foyer as they carried the gurney down from Mom's bedroom.

Matt was conscious. Finally. He reached for my hand as the technicians wheeled him toward the front door. I gripped it gratefully.

"Matt O'Hare, you scared me to death. I thought you were dead." He didn't look too far from death right now with his pale face covered in blood. I kept pace with the gurney as they wheeled him across the foyer and carried him down the marble steps outside.

"Call Kitty and tell her I'm okay. Tell her not to come to the hospital. I'll be home in an hour or two." He motioned to the female agent beside him and she handed me Matt's cell phone. I stuck it in my pocket and clung to the bishop's cold hand.

"I can't lie to your wife," I objected. "How can I tell her you're okay when you were shot in the head?"

"I'm okay," he assured me. "My head must have bounced off the door casing as I fell. The lump on my forehead hurts worse than the bullet wound. The bullet just grazed this thick skull of mine, didn't penetrate, but you know how head wounds are. They bleed a lot and look bad." He tried to reassure me with a smile. It didn't work.

"I'll call Kitty. But you know it won't matter what I say. She'll probably beat you to the hospital and be waiting for you when they wheel you into the emergency room."

Matt let go of my hand as they hoisted the gurney into the ambulance, then motioned for me to get in. "I'll leave Kelly here with you while you pack your bag. Then I want you, and that brief-case, at my house by the time I get there."

I started to object but he stopped me. "Don't argue. You can't stay out here alone now. Kelly says the third man got away. Until they apprehend him, you're in protective custody, and I've already sent a man to guard your Mom. Now go get packed. Take what you need, because you won't be back before we put you on that flight to Armenia—if we do."

CHAPTER 5

I knew it would be futile to argue with the bishop. Complying with his instructions, I called Kitty, told her Matt had bumped his head and would be home as soon as he'd had it checked at the hospital. He'd told her not to worry and not to bother to come to the hospital.

Passing the phone back to the bishop, I squeezed his hand. "You were afraid she'd know how bad off you really are if she heard your voice, weren't you? Now you've made me an accomplice in deception and she'll never trust me again."

He pointed his finger at me. "I'll see you in an hour at my house. Be there."

I'd be there, but I wasn't convinced he would. I jumped from the ambulance and joined Kelly on the steps. We silently watched the red taillights of the emergency vehicle disappear around the corner of the circular drive and down the hill. I shivered as the lights vanished, whether from the cold night air blowing in from the ocean or something else, I wasn't sure.

"If you'll wait here, Kelly, I'll grab Mom's briefcase, then we can go down to my house and get my suitcase. I'm actually packed already, so you won't have to baby-sit me for long."

She turned to follow me up the steps. "I'll go with you. I'm supposed to deliver you safely to O'Hare's."

That presented a problem. I wasn't about to show her the Control Center. I wasn't sure even Matthew O'Hare, FBI agent in charge of this area and close personal friend of the family since before I was born, had seen it. Though he knew about it, knew its capabilities, I didn't think anyone but Anastasia's elite group had ever been allowed into the inner sanctum.

"Oh, you don't have to come. I'll only be a minute," I assured her. Racing up the stairs, I reached the open front door several steps ahead of her. Quickly closing the door behind me, I twisted the lock and ran across the foyer to slip behind the huge palms under the circular staircase. I'd opened the hidden panel into the elevator and was safely inside before I heard her rattle the doorknob.

It was a dirty trick, I knew, and she'd be furious at me, but a necessary step in preserving the integrity of the Control Center. She simply didn't have a "need to know," the criteria on which such security issues were judged. I added the ceramic gun, the polemoscope, and the Dick Tracy watches to the contents of Mom's briefcase without taking time to examine what was already there, though I was intensely curious about its contents. What could it possibly contain that someone wanted so badly?

With Mom's briefcase and her overnight case in hand, I took the fireplace elevator back up to the house. A hidden door would be obvious if I materialized in the foyer before Kelly's eyes. She'd have unlocked the front door by now. There weren't many locks that could keep out a clever agent; slow them down, which had been my plan, but certainly not keep them out.

There was no sound in the house when I stepped into the fireplace from the elevator. I paused behind the five-foot, golden peacock screening the immense interior of the fireplace, then slipped out and ran across the parquet floor into the library. I hurried through the library, emerging in the hallway where less than an hour ago Kelly had captured the agile young man I'd called Dancer.

The redheaded agent stood in the foyer fuming. "Where have you been?" she demanded. "How can I protect you if you're going to lock me out and disappear?"

"I'm sorry the door locked behind me," I apologized, sincerely meaning it. I hadn't wanted to lock her out. It was just one of those necessary steps one must sometimes take that makes others acutely unhappy. "I have Mom's briefcase and overnight case, so if we grab my bags, we can go to town and you'll be rid of me."

That didn't mollify her. After turning off the lights in the mansion and locking the doors, we walked through silent darkness down the lawn to the little cottage. Kelly was a new agent in the area, one I'd never met before and I wasn't sure how much Matt had told her about our family. Apparently not much because the surprise on her face was apparent when I opened the door and turned on the light to reveal the interior of our humble abode.

I laughed. "No, I don't live in the mansion. I never have. This is where my husband and I live." Then it was my turn to be surprised. Unpleasantly so. As I stepped into the room, I realized the door had been unlocked—the door I'd so carefully locked when I left for the Control Center.

Kelly sensed the change and without a word, drew her gun. We stood silently, listening, assessing. Someone had been here. The cozy, secure atmosphere had been disturbed. Someone had violated the sanctity of my home.

Were they still here? Had The Fox brought his men to the cottage before they came to the big house, or had he sent someone else—who remained here—to wait for me?

I reached for my purse I always left on the roll top desk by the front door. My leather bag lay open on the desk, its contents dumped and scattered on this morning's mail. The little Beretta Bart designed especially for me was missing. Opening the bottom drawer, I touched a spring revealing a false bottom and retrieved the gun we kept hidden there.

As Kelly silently raised her eyebrows, I pointed toward the little kitchen, motioning for her to check there and the lower level. I crept toward the stairs leading to our bedroom loft. Avoiding the creaking stair, I tiptoed across the balcony to check the little spare room, then our bedroom. No one was upstairs. Kelly arrived quietly beside me to report the results of her search. We were the only ones in the house.

My clothes were strewn all over the bedroom. The suitcase I'd so carefully packed a couple of hours ago had been thoroughly searched and emptied. Only my slippers remained inside.

"Any idea what they were looking for?" Kelly asked as she tossed clothes from the floor to the bed.

"I suspect it's something in Mom's briefcase. The Fox carried it through the house, and was furious when it disappeared."

"The Fox?" Kelly's expressive eyebrows went up again.

"That's what his men called him. I don't know whether it's his given name or a nickname, but he does sort of resemble a silver fox with his gray hair, beady little dark eyes, and devious look on his face." I was about to add that I hadn't found him in Interpol's gallery of bad guys, but changed my mind. I'd let Matt tell her whatever he wanted her to know about us.

"You have a license for that gun, and know how to use it properly?" she asked, nodding at the weapon I'd placed on the bed by my suitcase.

"Of course," I smiled. "Matt would see to that, wouldn't he?"

Kelly stepped out of the bedroom and got busy on her little radio to whomever Matt had left on the estate. She leaned over the balcony, surveying our living room below, speaking so softly into the radio I couldn't hear what she said.

I quickly replaced my clothes in my bag, then headed downstairs with it and Mom's mysterious briefcase. To say I was anxious to examine its contents was a gross understatement. My curiosity had nearly overcome my better judgment and I'd almost opened it while Kelly had her back turned, but I'd mustered enough self-control to wait until we got to O'Hare's.

Kelly tripped lightly down the stairs after me and reached for the briefcase. "Here, let me help you."

I reluctantly relinquished it while I gathered the scattered contents of my purse. I didn't want to let the briefcase out of my possession, but had no valid reason for not accepting her offer of help. I locked the door, not sure why I bothered, except that locked doors keep honest people honest. Dishonest people always find a way if they want in badly enough.

Kelly rode with me in my car since she had come to the estate with Matt. Another agent had driven Matt's car back to town. We made the trip to Santa Barbara in silence, not even attempting small talk. I mentally checked my list of things to do before leaving the country and determined I had more list than time. Then I had a thought that was both comforting and disconcerting. What if Matt decided I shouldn't make the trip?

I wasn't anxious to go, especially to stay alone for three months in a country with which I was totally unfamiliar, delivering talks on a subject with which I was just as unfamiliar. Definitely not my idea of fun. On the other hand, I hated to disappoint Mom who was counting on me to fill her now-empty slot. I had to admit, it would leave a lot of holes in the symposium without her: keynote speaker, moderator of the panels, and presentation of her own paper.

The sun was still nowhere near rising when we arrived at the O'Hare home, but lights in every window blazed brightly, as if the inhabitants had already plunged into a busy day. I glanced at the car clock as I parked in the driveway. Though Kitty was an habitual early riser, this was early, even for her. Maybe she'd gone to the hospital and left all the lights on in her haste to see her injured husband.

But she greeted us at the door with her usual enthusiastic welcome, shepherding us into her big comfortable kitchen where she had a pan of hot chocolate waiting on the stove and muffins just coming out of the oven.

"Matt called from the hospital. He should be here momentarily. He didn't sound too chipper," she added, a frown creasing her forehead. "How did he get hurt? And just how bad was it?"

As the oven timer went off, I took the pot holder from Kitty's hand and turned to busy myself removing muffins from the oven, leaving Kelly to face the barrage of questions fired by Matt's worried, curious wife.

"What was going on out at the estate?" she asked, pouring the hot chocolate into mugs. "How is your Mom, Alli? I was so sorry to hear about her accident. Kelly, you didn't tell me what happened to Matt."

As I put the muffins on the breakfast bar in front of Kelly, our eyes met, and for the first time, I really looked at her. Her eyes were as green as my own and she had the faintest dusting of freckles scattered across her nose, as I did. Her hair was as red as mine was black and we were about the same size.

Kitty placed the hot chocolate and the muffins on the kitchen table and waved her hand toward it. "Sit. I want to hear everything. I want your version before Matt arrives and glosses over the gritty details."

Kelly and I looked at each other and laughed. The animosity I'd sensed earlier dissipated in Kitty's friendly kitchen. I decided I could like this redhead, given a chance to get to know her. She gave a quick two-sentence report on Matt, saying that was all any of us knew. We'd have to wait for anything further until he'd seen a doctor.

"Your turn, Alli," Kitty instructed, waving her knife still dripping with honey. "And don't give me the edited version. I want the full, detailed report."

"Where do I start?" I asked, hoping to consume at least one delicious smelling muffin while it was still hot.

"Let's have the medical report first. You had a doctor's appointment today and you didn't call with the results like you promised. Then tell me about your Mom." Kitty settled back in her chair as if prepared for a long story, warming her hands on the mug of hot chocolate.

I glanced at Kelly who had leaned forward, ignoring the steaming hot muffin she'd just cut open. Pushing the honey jar toward her, I took a quick sip of chocolate, not sure how much I wanted to tell in front of this comparative stranger.

Turning to Kitty, I tried to keep my voice steady and unemotional. "The tests were positive. Our little Alexandria should make her appearance in early May."

Kitty reached for my hand and squeezed it, tears filling her big dark eyes. "Oh, Alli. I'm so happy for you and Bart. I know it's the best thing that could happen to you. You'll be much happier, and much more fulfilled being a mother than chasing bad guys all over the world. I don't care what anyone says. Cradling a gun in your hands can't compare to cradling your newborn baby. Even capturing the FBI's most wanted can't compare to the capturing embrace of your toddler."

I glanced uncomfortably at Kelly, sipping her chocolate with amusement in her eyes. "I take it you do know how to use that gun," she said with a smile. "Matt should have told me a little more about you."

I returned the smile. "Not much to tell."

Fortunately, Matt arrived at that moment, leaning heavily on the arm of a colleague. He wore a gauze bandage like an Indian headband, and still looked like he didn't have an ounce of blood in his veins.

Kitty jumped and rushed to his side. "Matthew O'Hare, you lied to me. You said you weren't hurt!" She brushed away the sturdy agent, looped Matt's arm around her shoulder and helped him to a chair at the table. Then she turned to the man still standing by the door. "Is he supposed to be here, Craig, or did he bully his way out of the hospital?"

Craig's shrug and broad smile told the story. Kitty invited him to the table to join us, but he declined, saying he needed to get home.

The bishop turned to Kelly. "I'm sure you're ready to hit the sack, too." He glanced at his watch. "Allison can crash on the sofa in the den for a couple of hours before the pandemonium of kids getting ready for school begins. I'll grab a little shut-eye, then see you two in the office about ten o'clock. Thanks, guys. Craig, will you drop Kelly off?"

Having been dismissed, Kelly reluctantly retrieved her purse and followed Craig into what remained of the night, her disappointment evident at not learning what the mysterious case contained.

Matt took a long gulp of the hot chocolate Kitty placed in his hands, then leaned back and asked for the briefcase. "Let's see what Margaret has in this baby that's so valuable."

CHAPTER 6

If the Bishop and Kelly were curious and intrigued, I was even more so. I'd tried to imagine what Mom could possibly have in that briefcase that anyone, or three anyones, as it happened, would break into the mansion to acquire. If it did contain her presentation to the American University in Yerevan, certainly nothing in that series of papers would interest thieves—or terrorists.

Had she neglected to mention something else? Something related to Anastasia? Was she delivering sensitive information difficult to send via traditional methods? Matt had probably entertained these same thoughts.

As he flicked open the locks on the front of the briefcase, he turned to his wife. "Kitty, love, you don't have to stay up. We'll hit the pillow after a quick peek at the contents."

"I'm wide awake, Matthew O'Hare, and you can't dismiss me as easily as your agents. Get on with it so we can go back to bed before the alarm goes off."

I pulled my chair around so I could see inside the briefcase. Kitty rinsed Kelly's cup and spread honey on a muffin for Matt, placing it next to his mug of chocolate, but it remained untouched as we searched through the sheaf of papers filed neatly inside the case.

Mom was efficient. She'd clearly labeled each day's presentation in a separate folder. Another folder contained the same information I'd downloaded in the Control Center—State Department data on Armenia, and the country info I'd planned to read on the airplane. Her tickets were tucked in the pocket in the top, along with the symposium schedule and her contact person in Armenia. That, an Armenian-English dictionary, and the four items I'd added from "Q's case" appeared to be the sum total of the contents.

Matt frowned. "Margaret didn't give you any hints about the contents?"

I picked up the folder with the State Department data to place it on the top of the other folders. "We found exactly what she said was there. In fact, this is a duplication of the information I just downloaded from the computer tonight." I flipped through the pages again. "Wait. There are six pages here. I only printed five from that site."

I peeled that sixth page from the stack and placed it on the table. It wasn't from the State Department at all, but a photocopy of a Los Angeles Times newspaper article on precious artifacts that had recently been stolen from Echmiadzin Cathedral in Armenia. Some of the items had been recovered, but two valuable rubies, which had been removed from ninth century gold crosses, were still missing.

"Interesting." But even with this intriguing new discovery, I yawned, having a hard time keeping my eyes open. "I wonder where she got this, and why she was taking it with her."

Matt shook his head without comment. Kitty stood and cleared the rest of the table. No one spoke. There simply were no answers. And we were all probably too tired to even think of the right questions.

"Since we obviously have no ideas, why don't we catch a couple of hours sleep and just ask Mom in the morning?"

Matt nodded absently, his mind apparently occupied with our search of the briefcase. Was he thinking of what we had found, or what we hadn't?

Kitty jumped on the suggestion. "Good idea. I've got a busy day and I'm going to need all the energy I can muster. And you need to get that head on a pillow, Matthew." Before he could object, Kitty shut the briefcase, clicked the locks, and reached for his arm to help him out of the chair.

Suddenly fatigue hit me. My body might have been filled with lead, my limbs felt so heavy. I reached for the briefcase, but Matt beat me to it. "I'll keep this with me, Alli. Then you won't have to sleep with one eye open."

"You know where the den is," Kitty said, steering her husband toward their bedroom. "Just shut the door and pull the afghan over you. I'll try to keep the kids quiet as long as possible."

I didn't object. I entertained the idea of loading the dishes into the dishwasher, but only for a second. My tired body wouldn't cooperate with my noble thoughts, heading instead for the over-stuffed sofa in the study. Once off my feet, I could ponder the problem of strange men, mysterious briefcase, and missing rubies, and how they were connected, I rationalized. But as soon as I stretched out and pulled the crocheted afghan snugly around me, I fell into a deep, untroubled sleep, dreaming about neither the men in the mansion nor the bothersome briefcase.

I awoke to the sun in my eyes and five-year-old Sara patting my face. "Alli, your phone is ringing." She plopped my purse on top of me and hurried out to answer her mother's call to breakfast.

Mom's worried voice banished all traces of sleep. "Allison, what took you so long to answer the phone? I've called three times and let it ring forever. Are you okay?"

"I'm fine, Mom." I struggled to free myself from my afghan cocoon and sit up. "How did you sleep last night? How's your leg?"

"Answering both your questions in a single word—beastly. Did you have a chance to look over the material for the lectures?"

"As luck would have it, yes." I squinted at my watch "What time is it?"

"7:30." She paused then asked, "What does luck have to do with it?"

I ignored her question. We'd go into that at the hospital. "I'm bringing the briefcase to go over your data with you. I'll be right there."

Kitty shook her head from the doorway.

"Right after breakfast," I amended.

Kitty nodded as I hung up. "You don't skip breakfast when you're pregnant, unless, of course, you're one of the unlucky ones who can't keep anything down. Doug brought your suitcase in from your car so you can change out of your wrinkled clothes."

"Thanks, Kitty. You think of everything. How's Matt this morning?"

For a moment she sagged against the oak doorframe with her head bowed and eyes closed. She took a deep breath, then turned and forced a smile. "He's still sleeping. He was restless until the alarm went off, then he slept through our scripture study and the kids getting ready for school. I thought I'd just let him sleep as long as he can." She bit her lip to control its quivering.

I crossed the room in three long strides and put my arms around her. "I guess my question should have been, how are *you* this morning?"

Kitty leaned her head on my shoulder, put her arms around me for a moment and accepted a hug, then stepped back with a rueful smile. "Just fine until someone offers sympathy," she said, brushing tears from her cheeks. "When I think how close that bullet came . . ." A shudder shook her slender body.

"Momma, I spilled my milk," Sara wailed from the kitchen.

Kitty sighed and hurried to help her child. I quickly changed into travel clothes and carried my suitcase to the hall. From the brief glimpse I'd had earlier at Mom's papers, I knew this presentation would be a problem. I'd need to spend every minute I could with Mom to bring me up to date on her studies. I used to be familiar with the terms and jargon of her work. Not anymore. Four years of college away from home, a couple of years in New York working as a translator at the United Nations, and then traipsing all over the globe for Anastasia with and without my husband had left me clueless about her current project.

"Kitty, could you bring me Mom's briefcase? I'm on my way to the hospital to learn about the presentations I'm supposed to be giving the next three months. I haven't a clue what Mom's been doing lately."

Kitty hesitated. "Are you sure you should take it?"

"You saw for yourself there was nothing in that case except her papers. If Matt's awake, you can ask him, but if he's not, don't bother him about it. I'll be at the hospital all morning if he wants to come over. He did send someone to be with Mom, so the briefcase, and the two of us, will be under guard."

Kitty acquiesced and hurried to their bedroom to comply with my request while I washed down a warmed-over muffin with a glass of milk. She stood in the doorway and waved good-bye while thirteen-year-old Doug carried my suitcase to my car and ran to catch his school bus.

As I drove to the hospital, I pondered the events of the night before. Had I overreacted in supposing the intruders were terrorists instead of merely well-dressed burglars? Being so heavily involved with the twisted terrorist mind, I had probably become paranoid, seeing their greater evil everywhere. But then, it was everywhere today, which is what kept my husband—my whole family—so busy.

As my thoughts turned to my tall, blond husband, I realized I hadn't heard from him in over forty-eight hours. He'd been eagerly anticipating the results of my hospital tests yesterday and promised to call last night. The fact that he didn't gave rise to worrisome questions, but as I thought of all the things that could prevent him from making that call, I decided the most constructive thing I could do was simply pray for him. All the worrying in the world couldn't help. Prayer could.

When I reached Mom's room, the guard Matt said he ordered was nowhere in sight. The usually busy corridor was unusually empty. Maybe the bishop had decided there was no threat after all and canceled the protective custody order.

Mom wasn't her normal, beautiful, put-together self this morning, and from the looks of the dark circles under her eyes, even the make-up I'd brought wouldn't help much. My astute mother read my thoughts at a glance. "I'm sure I look like death warmed over. Well, that's exactly how I feel. Or worse. My apologies, Alli, for not being more sympathetic when you broke your arm. I never imagined anything as simple as a broken bone could be so painful."

I placed the robe and slippers and her makeup on the bed beside her, dropped the briefcase on the chair next to the bed and leaned over to kiss her cheek. "First of all, a compound fracture isn't simple by any definition, and second . . ."

She shook her head and waved her hand, interrupting before I could finish. "I don't want to hear the second. I'm sure it's only more bad news." She pointed to the clock. "You have under three hours before you leave for the airport. What questions do you have on the presentations you'll make before I get there?"

I'd reached for the briefcase, but her comment stopped me midway. "Haven't you talked to the doctor this morning?" Did she still really believe she'd be able to travel to Armenia before the completion of the symposium?

"Not yet. They keep promising she'll be in at any time." Mom motioned impatiently for the case. "Let me show you . . ."

She paused to listen to the conversation just outside the door. I recognized Dr. Roskelley's distinctive voice. "Can I help you?"

"Uh, yes," a deep male voice answered. "I'm, uh, looking for Margaret Alexander's room." He paused as if uncertain what to say next. "I'm assigned to—"

Another female voice interrupted the stammering man. "It's about time. That other agent disappeared thirty minutes ago. We were told Mrs. Alexander was supposed to be in protective custody. Anybody could have walked in here in the last half hour." She poked her head around the corner to look in on Mom, saw me, and gasped. "How did you get in here without me seeing you?"

Mom and I looked at each other. Her forehead creased in a deep frown. My danger antennae sent a shiver through me. I tossed my cell phone to Mom. "Call Matt O'Hare. Number eight on automatic dial." I slid the briefcase behind the chair and slipped my hand into my open bag, locating my gun as I stepped to the door. I stood in the doorway so neither the nurse, Dr. Roskelley, nor the man could enter.

As I looked up into the uneasy brown eyes of a tall, round-shouldered man, my fingers tightened immediately around the gun. "May I see your identification, please?" If this was one of Matt's men, he was the most different breed of FBI agent I'd ever met.

His eyes narrowed as his right hand started under his coat jacket. I pulled my gun from my purse, and pointing it at his heart said quietly, "Open your jacket—slowly—so I can see what you're getting. And do it with your left hand, please."

The nurse gasped and backed away. Dr. Roskelley shifted slightly toward me until the door to Mom's room was completely blocked. An expressionless mask instantly replaced the look of surprise that passed over the man's face.

"Be careful with that, lady. Guns aren't toys, you know." He began a quiet monologue on the danger of civilians carrying guns while his left hand awkwardly probed his inner jacket pocket. As he spoke he glanced up and down the hall. I did not imagine for a minute he watched for innocent civilians who might be injured if my gun went off accidentally.

With a flourish, he finally produced his ID and thrust it toward me. My eyes never left his. "Dr. Roskelley, will you look at it, please?" I asked, ignoring the extended identification.

"Dave Hernandez is the agent on duty," Mom called from her bed.

"That's not the name on this ID," Dr. Roskelley said quietly.

The man's eyes narrowed slightly. He shrugged his shoulders and tried a smile. "Dave called me an hour ago and said he wasn't feeling well. Asked me to cover for him. I told him I'd be right there, but an accident on the 101 held me up. He knew I was coming, so he must have left about the time I said I'd arrive."

I raised my voice so Mom could clearly hear me. "Did you clear the change in assignment with your boss, Jonathon Hendricks?"

"Of course. Dave said Hendricks approved the switch. Will you put the instrument away now, lady? You're making me nervous. And I'll want to see your permit. You could be in big trouble for holding an agent at gun point and interfering with official FBI business."

If Mom did what I expected, and if I could keep him talking long enough without making him suspicious about the delay, I hoped to prove this man wasn't FBI and have him in custody within the next couple of minutes. His story was plausible. But not probable.

"What's your name?" I said, attempting to prolong the interview.

"It's right there. See for yourself," he said, then changed his tone to a softer, friendlier one. "Charles Courier." He shot Dr. Roskelley a condescending smirk.

"Dr. Roskelley, what's the name on the ID?" I asked, stalling for time.

She read the name from the identification. "Charles Collin Courier."

"Same as on the ID. Imagine that." This time he didn't attempt to hide the sarcasm in his voice, nor his impatience. "Now give me that weapon. I'd hate to press charges against a pretty lady like you."

I held out my hand for the ID, which Dr. Roskelley placed in it. "Please step against that wall. I definitely don't want you to press charges, but I do have to be careful, you know." *Think fast, Alli. Do something to befuddle him, throw him off guard until Matt gets here.* "When you have an injured murderer in the hospital, and no one there to guard her, any family member could come in to take their revenge and she'd never make it to court."

The nurse, who had moved to the edge of the next doorway and had been motioning away anyone who approached, gasped at the statement. Charles Collin Courier looked confused, then instantly masked his expression. "So what are you doing here with a gun?" he asked, attempting to put me on the defensive. "Revenge?"

My mind raced. The longer this interchange lasted, the uneasier this man would become if he were not a legitimate replacement for the agent Matt assigned. When he'd agreed with the fictitious name I'd tossed at him, I'd discounted his legitimacy. That meant he was not one of the good guys. I'd called his bluff. His normal reaction should have been to escape as quickly as possible after being challenged. Or act immediately.

I saw only three possible outcomes to this confrontation if help didn't arrive at once. I could arrest him, but if he was connected to the men at the mansion last night who I suspected were affiliated with terrorists, he wouldn't give up without a fight. The terrorist mentality would forfeit his own life to complete his assignment. I didn't want to chance innocent people getting hurt.

The second possibility was to allow him to leave, follow him, and try to apprehend him in a less public place than a hospital corridor. The outcome of that scenario would probably be a shootout. Terrorists I'd dealt with previously would not allow themselves to be taken by a woman; they'd rather die than suffer the disgrace.

The third possibility was to press my luck, stand my ground, and pray for reinforcements before this man took the offensive, forcing me to react to his actions. That was my least favorite option, the one no agent should ever allow to happen.

"Revenge? Yes, as a matter of fact," I said, answering his question. "Dr. Roskelley, please get on with the 'euthanasia' we planned." I motioned to the nurse. "Come and help her." Hoping Dr. Roskelley understood what I wanted and would aid me, I stepped toward the man standing near the wall on the other side of the narrow corridor, leaving room for the nurse to slip into Mom's room behind me. She didn't move.

Dr. Roskelley's authoritative voice was quiet but firm. "Come quickly, Sharon. I need your help."

The nurse moved cautiously toward the door. Now was the critical moment. If Dr. Roskelley got the nurse inside Mom's room and they shut the door, I had three less people to worry about. If Mom had reported our situation to Matt, help could be on the way. If some of those medical personnel the nurse had motioned away were on the ball, even hospital security could arrive in time to help. But I couldn't depend on any of those "ifs."

And the man facing me suddenly took the offensive.

CHAPTER 7

"What's going on here? Lady, put down that gun and turn and face the wall." Hospital security arrived, running down the corridor waving their guns. The distraction was all the man facing me needed.

"Be careful. She's dangerous," he called. "I'll go after her accomplice. You hold her here until I get back."

The security guards dropped to one knee, steadied their guns with both hands, and demanded I drop my gun. I watched helplessly as Charles Collin Courier ran down the hall in the opposite direction.

"Dr. Roskelley," I called. "Come quick." The door swung open behind me and Dr. Roskelley poked her head out.

"Tell these idiots I'm not the bad guy. They just let him get away."

The good doctor lashed the apparently untrained guards with an Irish blessing that left my ears burning. As soon as they lowered their guns, I raced after the imposter, but he'd disappeared. Kelly and Craig arrived at the entrance to the hospital the same time I did. Two minutes too late. I explained what happened, described the man, and left them to organize a thorough search of the hospital and grounds while I hurried back inside.

"Alli, what on earth was that all about?" Mom demanded as I entered her room.

I thanked the hovering nurse and excused her to go about her duties, then turned to my mother. "That's exactly what I want to know. What's in that briefcase? What are you doing besides presiding over a symposium in Yerevan?"

Mom struggled to sit up. "What do you mean? What are you talking about?"

"Someone broke into the estate last night and attempted to steal the briefcase. Thanks to Dad and Jim's handy-dandy secret passages, I got it back. Matt and his crew caught two, but the leader got away. Matt was hit, grazed by a bullet, and knocked unconscious as he fell. I stayed with him and Kitty last night and we searched your briefcase, but found nothing I thought anyone would want. Unless, of course, educational espionage is in and they were after your presentation."

Mother's face paled further and she sank back into her pillows. "Someone broke into the house? What did they do? Oh, Alli, you were out there alone."

I sat on the edge of the bed and patted Mom's hand. "No, I had plenty of company," I smiled. "First three intruders, then a passel of FBI agents. Apparently, the briefcase was all they wanted. Matt and I searched it and found nothing, so you must have it well hidden. What's there that's so important?"

"Nothing." She rubbed her temples as if to erase an oncoming headache. "There's nothing but my presentation and tickets."

"Are you sure you don't have sensitive documents stashed in a hidden pocket? It must contain something unusual. Three men wouldn't break into the house to take nothing but the briefcase unless they sought something special. Or is your presentation going to rock the educational world?" That off-the-wall comment gave me another idea. "Do you have a rival, or someone jealous of your success in your field, someone who doesn't want you to receive this award, present your paper, or receive the recognition that goes with all of that?"

Mom shook her head. "Doesn't make sense. I could just print another copy of the presentation from the computer and get replacements tickets. Stealing the briefcase wouldn't be anything more than a temporary setback."

"They've accomplished more than that already. They've prevented you from going to Yerevan."

"Another temporary setback," Mom insisted. "I'll be there before the month is up."

"Apparently you haven't talked to Dr. Roskelley yet. Mom, I don't believe your 'accident' was an accident. I think someone doesn't want you in Yerevan." A frightening thought since I was now in the hot seat. Certainly a challenge. But I'd never walked away from a challenge or a mystery. I looked out the window and watched plain-clothes men and police swarm through the parking lot. I turned back to Mom. "We're not going to have much time alone. There'll be too many interruptions with FBI questions. You'd better tell me, as concisely as possible, what you want stressed, what areas I should concentrate on."

"Hand me my papers and we'll go over the first month's classes." She looked at her watch. "If we're lucky and have no interruptions. Then I'll arrive in the country in time for the second set." She held up her hand when I began protesting. "Listen, don't talk. This old bird is tougher than you think." She smiled. "Besides, I have a date with your father I don't want to miss in that historic city."

I wouldn't burst her bubble, but I was afraid the indomitable Dr. Margaret Alexander was sidelined for the duration of the symposium, and if the goal of the mysterious men was to keep her from attending, they'd accomplished their mission.

We were interrupted countless times, but Matt, head still wrapped in the bandage, did his best to keep those interruptions to a minimum so I could have as much time with Mom as possible. Then he returned to report they'd found their missing agent. Dave Hernandez had been shot and stuffed in a utility closet in the same corridor of the hospital where he'd been standing watch outside Mom's room. He was dead.

"I think you should cancel this trip, Allison," Bishop O'Hare advised. "We don't know who these people are, or what they want. The two we have in custody haven't told us anything and we have no record of them in our files. Until we know what's in the wind, it's simply too dangerous for you to go over there on your own."

Mom and I simultaneously voiced our objections.

"At least until we know who we're dealing with," Matt countered. "Give me that."

"I'd like to cancel completely, Matt. I don't want Allison going at all now. But I can't leave those people without a keynote speaker and moderator. If you knew how hard we'd worked to set this up and how many postponements we've had, you wouldn't even think about it. I hate to sound egotistical, but the world desperately needs to hear the message I have to deliver at that symposium, and there are far too few forums available in which to present it."

"Margaret . . ."

"Matt," Mom interrupted. "It's not like Allison can't take care of herself. She's a trained agent."

"So was Dave Hernandez," Matt said quietly, "and he'd had twenty years of field experience. Think about that before you send your daughter into danger." Bishop O'Hare turned on his heel and walked out of the room.

Mom patted the bed for me to sit beside her. "Let's finish. You don't have much time." When I sat down, she took my hands. "How do you feel about going?"

"I absolutely did not want to go and would have done just about anything to get out of it when you first proposed it. But now, nothing will keep me from making the trip. I refuse to be intimidated by terrorists."

"Good girl. You are your father's daughter."

"And my mother's," I laughed. "You still think you're going to Armenia with a compound fracture that actually will keep you incapacitated for the next three months."

"I'm a quick healer," Mom said. "Let's get back to the presentation."

We managed to cover most of the first month's material before it was time to leave to catch my flight. As I replaced the folders, I saw the one with the State Department information—and the article on the stolen artifacts from Armenia. "What were you doing with the newspaper article on a robbery in a cathedral in Armenia?"

Mom's forehead creased in a puzzled look. "I found that article on my desk one morning last week in my office. I assumed one of my colleagues had put it there because of the Armenian connection and would talk to me about it later, but no one ever mentioned it. I guess I tucked it in the file to read later, and forgot about it. Maybe you'll have time to visit the cathedral. They call it the Armenian Vatican, I think." Mom looked at the clock. "But you've got to scoot or you'll miss your flight."

I stuffed the folders back in the briefcase. "I'll leave my car in long-term parking at the airport. Have Jim or someone pick it up as soon as they can. The extra keys are in the roll-top desk." That triggered a thought. "Mom, have the locks changed on both houses. And don't you go back home without Nedra or someone there with you. I left a message for Mai Li to come home as soon as she can to help, but I don't know when that will be." I kissed her cheek.

"Stay safe, Alli. Please be careful," Mom said, squeezing my hand.

I scooped the briefcase from the bed, swung my purse over my shoulder, and headed for the door. I hated long good-byes, and this was a particularly hard one. I needed to be with my mother, especially upon her release from the hospital. I wanted to be the one to care for her, but I'd caught the vision of her presentation and her determination to have it made public as well as her enthusiasm for the entire symposium. I wasn't about to be deterred by would-be thieves or terrorists who may or may not follow through on the first attempt at the briefcase. And right now we had no proof there was a connection between the break-in at the mansion and the death of Dave Hernandez.

I hoped to talk to Matt before I left, but I didn't see him on the way to my car and there wasn't time to search for him and still make my flight. Despite the warm October Santa Barbara sun, I felt cold—and alone. A word of encouragement from Bishop O'Hare would have dispelled that, I thought. Then again, maybe he would have continued to try to dissuade me from going. I understood his concern. If Bart knew what I planned, he'd try to stop me, too. I guess it was fortunate we hadn't communicated during the last couple of days. I'd be on the plane and committed before he could voice his displeasure at the change of events.

The sun sparkled on the silver surface of the Pacific Ocean as I headed down the 101 Freeway to Los Angeles. I loved this peaceful corner of the world, this beautiful Spanish-flavored haven from the hurried pace of the rest of the planet. Well, it used to be peaceful. My mind replayed and pondered the events of last night and this morning and I suddenly found myself at Los Angeles International Airport without any memory of the past two hours on the freeway.

The next two hours were a blur of security checks, luggage hassles, ticket verifications, and long lines. My breakfast muffin seemed a distant memory, one my empty stomach had long since forgotten, so I grabbed an ice cream cone at Haagen-Daz to tide me over until the flight meal. I sat in a quiet corner on the second floor watching entertainers from Switzerland perform folk music on the floor below accompanied by a ten-foot long wooden alpenhorn, apparently trying to entice tourist dollars to the Swiss Alps. I wondered what Armenia did to entice tourist dollars to their country.

I scanned the faces of people walking by, wondering if I'd eluded those who'd shown such interest in Mom's briefcase, wishing I knew who they were and what they wanted, how badly they wanted it— and if they still did.

As I finally settled into my seat on the plane, I glanced at my itinerary. We were scheduled to leave at 4:30 p.m. Thursday, arriving at Heathrow Airport in London at 2:30 p.m. Friday their time; an eleven hour flight with a five hour layover before the final segment of the flight to Armenia at 7:30 p.m. Then an overnight flight, arriving in Yerevan at 7:30 Saturday morning. Not long enough to get properly acquainted with Mom's notes and I'd have jet lag to contend with on the other end of the journey. I plunged into the materials I'd have to begin presenting less than four days from now.

I read until my eyes would no longer focus, napped briefly, and read again, ignoring the man at my side who kept trying to strike up a conversation. When my mind wouldn't absorb any more information, I reread the newspaper article and tried to make a connection between it, the rubies, Mom's presentation and the symposium, her "accident," which I was convinced was no accident, the three men at the estate trying to steal the briefcase, the break-in of my little cottage, and finally the death of Agent Dave Hernandez at the hospital. Perplexing. I found no connection, but felt an unsettling certainty that something very unpleasant was in the wind. And the wind was blowing my way.

I vaguely remember an in-flight meal, but the trip mostly was a blur of typed pages and cramped, aching legs. At Heathrow, I showered in one of the traveler's convenience rooms and felt alive again. I walked for three hours, wandering the airport shops, getting the kinks out of my body before the next imprisonment in a too-small airline seat. I sent a postcard to Mom, mailing it in a bright red "post" box used everywhere in England, and nibbled on various taste treats from around the world.

At boarding time, I found my gate for the Yerevan flight, but instead of an airplane, a bus waited at the gate. We boarded the bus and were driven around the perimeter of the airport to a small plane waiting on the far side of the huge airport complex. I felt like I'd been relegated to Outer Mongolia. None of the other passengers seemed bothered by the distance from the terminals, or the fact that there was nothing out here besides the lone aircraft. If there hadn't been fifty other people climbing the stairs which the crew rolled to the plane as we arrived, my paranoia would have kicked in and I'd have suspected we'd been kidnaped and were being spirited away in a stolen, broken-down airplane.

Beautiful dark-eyed, dark-haired children chattered happily as they climbed aboard the plane and settled into their seats. Armenian wasn't one of the dozen languages I spoke, and since I didn't understand what they were saying, I only assumed they were Armenians. Catching snatches of a whispered conversation in Russian between three men behind me, I understood they'd be disembarking at our stop in Tbilisi, Georgia.

I settled into my seat, hoping the space next to me would remain empty so I could curl up and sleep for a couple of hours in flight. In the meantime, I pulled the article on the stolen artifacts and reread it. Somehow someone had snatched several valuable artifacts, priceless historic chalices and crosses precious to the Armenian Apostolic Church, from right under the noses of the priests who were giving tours of the cathedral's museum. Two of the items, crosses too large to carry out inconspicuously, had their center rubies pried out. Most of the chalices and crosses had been recovered. The rubies had not. The article raised more questions than it answered.

When we were finally airborne, I stopped reading long enough to peer out the small window and watch the intriguing pattern of London's twinkling lights below. They glittered like topaz and diamonds set in gold and swirled in intricate designs on black velvet.

Unfortunately, the flight was filled to capacity and a large woman overfilled the seat next to me. She kept shifting in her too-small seat, constantly poking me with her elbow. I tucked against the window, giving her as much room as possible, and turned to the State Department information on the country that would be my home for the next three months, along with the Armenian-English dictionary. A few phrases of the language would be handy to know, as well as something of the country, its people, and their history. What I learned was astounding. The missing rubies were immediately forgotten as I plunged into Armenia's past.

When I was younger, I'd accompanied my mother as she recorded the oral histories of various cultures throughout the world. I must have been too small to remember anything about Armenia, because what I read horrified me. Situated at the crossroads between Europe and Asia, Armenia had been overrun and conquered numerous times by different civilizations. But it was one thing to conquer a people. It was quite another to attempt to annihilate an entire race. From the late 1800s until 1915, Turkey, their Muslim neighbor to the West, had carried out a series of attacks designed to destroy the Christian nation—to totally wipe out their population.

That was the first tragedy. The second was that the other nations of the world had turned their heads and ignored the systematic slaughter of one and a half million Armenians. The third part of that unbelievable tragedy occurred when Hitler noted the world's apathy, and proposed to do the same thing to the Jewish race. When told it wouldn't be tolerated, he replied, "Who remembers the Armenians?" And thus the second genocide of this century came about—and was called the holocaust.

At one time the borders of Armenia had stretched approximately from the Mediterranean to the Caspian Sea. Now its territory comprised an area smaller than the tiny state of Maryland. One incredible fact surfaced through all my reading—these people had retained their Christian beliefs throughout the last seventeen centuries, forgiving their conquerors, and refraining from becoming the aggressor after they were converted to Christianity.

The last two nights of limited sleep caught up to me. I put the pages away, turned my back on my obnoxious seatmate, put the airline's tiny pretend-pillow against the window and succumbed to sleep's inviting embrace. I woke as the airplane descended into Tbilisi, Georgia, and the woman next to me jabbed her elbow into my ribs trying to get her seat upright for landing.

The lights of the former Soviet city sparkled in early morning darkness, sprawling for miles across undulating hills. Thankfully, the fat lady and her skinny husband exited the plane along with three-quarters of the passengers, leaving their two seats empty next to mine.

Ignoring the refueling process going on outside my window, I stretched out in all three seats under the thin airline blanket to finish reading the historical sketch of Armenia. The brisk breeze entering the open doorway may have been refreshing to some. To me, it was one more addition to a long list of uncomfortable circumstances. I was more than ready for this interminable flight to end.

The last leg of the journey was a short hop over the Caucasus Mountains to Yerevan. We'd barely reached cruising altitude, it seemed, when we began descending. I slipped the State Department pages back into the briefcase in time to watch the breathtaking sunrise on Mount Ararat. The first rays of the sun hit the jagged snow-covered peak, turning the snow shades of violet, blue, pink, and then gold. Noah's ark should still be enclosed in a glacier near the top of this historic mountain after all these centuries. Little Ararat's perfectly formed peak sat beside her famous sister, Big Ararat, or Sees and Masees, as Armenians called them.

Two men across the aisle shared their knowledge of the famous mountains in tones loud enough for everyone on the plane to hear. According to one, Armenian money, and nearly everything else in Armenia, contained the profile of the two mountains. Since for centuries the Ararats were within their country's boundaries, the distinctive profile of the mountains and their sacred relics became their national symbol. When the Turks overran Armenia and borders were realigned, the famous peaks ended up within Turkish boundaries. That didn't change the Armenians symbolic view of "their" mountains.

When the Turks asked why Armenia continued to use the symbol of the Ararats on their money, the Armenians countered with a question, asking why the Turks used "their" moon on Turkey's flag and money. Interesting bit of local humor I hadn't read in the rather staid information from the State Department.

I noted the four distinctive towers of the controversial nuclear reactor as we descended into the airport at Yerevan. It provided much-needed electricity to the area, but had also contributed contamination to an area already over-polluted by careless disposal of factory wastes during Soviet domination of the little country.

Vineyards stretched for miles in every direction from the airport, alternating with golden fields of harvested grain. Gray stone farm houses with gray stone barns dotted the rural landscape, while the capital city of Yerevan spread over its seven hills a few miles distant.

Zvartnots Airport's circular terminal looked modern and inviting from the air, but stark and forbidding as we disembarked into the cold marble interior. Definitely Soviet designed: massive blocks of sand-colored marble which were functional but not aesthetically pleasing to the eye.

As the escalator descended into the entry control area, I scanned the faces of those waiting on the other side of the glass partition. One tall, striking-looking young man, standing apart from the crowd pressing close to the window, watched me as I moved toward the booth where credentials were checked. Mom said someone would meet me, but hadn't had time to tell me about my contact person and I'd forgotten the name listed in her notes. I assumed they'd find me, since I was one of the very few non-Armenians on the flight, although I did fit in better with all the black-haired locals than the middle-aged blonde just in front of me.

Temporary visa obtained, I retrieved my luggage and was directed toward two doors, a green one and a red one. Customs officials motioned me toward the red one. Tapping on the window caught my attention as I began to comply with the guard's directions. The tall, good-looking young man motioned me to the green door. Wheeling my suitcase after me, I gripped the briefcase tighter and headed toward the green door, not knowing what might happen if I ignored the official at my elbow. The blonde in front of me was also trying to go to the green door, much to the consternation of the official insisting she enter the red one which apparently was a customs baggage check station. That distracted the man at my elbow enough for me to slip through the green door.

I suddenly found myself free of officials and inspections, and surrounded by taxi drivers eager to grab my luggage and load me into their cabs. The tall young man rescued me, sending the disappointed horde of drivers off to find another fare to fight over.

"Welcome to Armenia, Mrs. Allan. I'm Dr. Garik Grigoryan from American University." He took the briefcase from me with his left hand and thrust out his right hand to shake mine. "I am sorry about your mother's accident. I hope she join us before end of symposium."

I grasped the outstretched hand and looked up into sober dark eyes. "Thank you. Please call me Allison. Mrs. Allan is too formal."

Without releasing my hand, he tipped his head in a slight bow acknowledging my request as his eyes met mine again in a steady, appraising gaze that made me suddenly uncomfortable. I pulled my hand from his and reached for the briefcase. "Thank you for meeting me, Dr. Grigoryan. I prefer carrying the briefcase, but I will let you wrestle with my luggage if you don't mind."

"I am Garik, please, and I take care of both. This way." He pointed toward the double glass doors and waved to a waiting taxi driver who scurried in to take charge of my luggage.

I didn't want the briefcase out of my possession for even a minute, but didn't want to commit a cultural faux pas by insisting that he return the case. He opened the door on a small ancient car whose model I was unfamiliar with and whose worn seats were covered with pieces of brightly colored tapestry. I sat down, expecting Garik to go to the other side of the taxi and enter. Instead, he squeezed in beside me. As I slid across the seat, I retrieved the briefcase he placed at his feet. After all the trouble I'd had getting it, I wanted it no further away from me than arm's length.

"You are authority in Professor Alexander's field?" Garik asked as the taxi driver turned up the music and sped out of the airport like a driver on the first lap of the Indianapolis 500.

When we whipped around a curve, I clung to the seat to keep from sliding into the lap of my handsome Armenian escort. "Sorry to disappoint you, Garik. That's not my area of expertise. I'll be a poor substitute for my mother's knowledge and insight into traditional cultures and customs and their transitions into the modern urban world. I truly hope she'll be able to join us before the completion of the conference, for your sake and mine, but I honestly don't think she'll make it. She has a compound fracture of the leg and her doctor led me to believe she wouldn't be able to travel for at least three months, so you're probably stuck with me."

"No problem. We are happy you come to our University. You have been to my country before?"

I shook my head, gripping the seat for stability as the taxi continued at breakneck speed dodging potholes in the road, cows nonchalantly wandering in the street, and vans that seemed to stop indiscriminately half on and half off the street. A small flock of sheep crossed in front of us, herded by an old man in his suit jacket, carrying a tall walking stick in one hand and a bandana wrapped around something in the other.

In the city and out, the same stone seemed to be the building material of choice, and elaborate rusting iron grillwork covered nearly every window. There had been money here at one time, but apparently none was available for upkeep now. The information I'd read stated the economy was depressed and unemployment high since the Soviet Empire crumbled in 1989 and they subsequently pulled all money and support out of their satellite countries.

I could see evidence of that everywhere. Men who would have been working by this hour back home sat watching traffic along the road, or two or three hunched over a game board on a tiny table in front of an open door. These scenes occurred repeatedly along the road.

"Our country suffer greatly when Soviets leave," Garik offered as an explanation for what I saw on every side. "They leave projects unfinished when they walk away with financing. Armenians not prepared for independence. We only want more say in how we governed." His voice contained no bitterness, just a quiet resignation that these were the facts and he would live with them.

"Will these be finished?" I asked, pointing to a massive concrete building with four floors partially completed and unfinished concrete corner beams pointing starkly at the blue sky. Two cranes with beams hanging halfway to their destination rusted next to the project.

"No. There is no money." Garik casually slid his long arm across the back of the seat, glanced out the rear window and frowned slightly. I turned to see what displeased him. A shiny black Mercedes with tinted windows sped up behind us.

"Someone you know?" I asked, clutching the briefcase tighter.

He nodded, sighed almost imperceptibly, then turned to me as if to change an unpleasant subject. "You have less jet lag and become accustomed to our time more quickly if you remain active today. We'll take luggage to apartment, you can refresh, then I acquaint you with city so you find your way around and be independent. Do you have questions I can answer for you?"

"What do you do at the American University?"

The serious expression that had seemed to be a permanent fixture on Garik's handsome face relaxed the slightest bit as he explained his major in business administration and how, with the help of his professor and mentor, he'd created the position he now occupied of arranging special conferences and symposiums for the university, and attracting famous lecturers for those events.

"And instead of the renowned expert you expected for this one, you ended up with me. I'll try to not be a disappointment. At least Mom's research and conclusions will be the real thing, even if the presentation won't be quite as the illustrious Professor Alexander would have done it. Garik, your English is very good. Do you speak other languages, too?"

He nodded. "My parents Armenian, but compelled to speak Russian during Soviet occupation. I learn both as child. We speak Armenian at home, and study Russian at school. I also studied Italian and some German at university when I earn first degree in engineering. No work for engineers, so I continue my studies with second degree in business administration and public affairs."

Garik's speech patterns intrigued me. He seemed well educated, pronounced most English words quite clearly, yet omitted almost all articles as he spoke.

"We begin tour here," he said, pointing out the window. "Left on hill is American University of Armenia, and right in trees is metro station you use every day to University. This street is Marshall Baghramian. Foreigners say, Embassy Row. There United States Embassy." He pointed to a building blocked by a high wall of pink stone with Marine guards standing outside. The houses and buildings on this street were huge, grand mansions, most showing signs of neglect and decay, but it was apparent they once had been splendid behind their high wrought-iron fences.

Garik pointed to an immense official-looking building set back from the street with armed guards patrolling the sidewalk outside the fence and the grounds inside. "This is House of Parliament. You hear about assassinations here some years ago?"

I nodded. The State Department information reported the political assassinations as occurring in a country that still had a young, unstable government. Not too much different, I remembered thinking, from much older stable governments. Someone always seemed to oppose the ruling party. Sometimes the opposition even resorted to violence, as in this case.

The grounds of the imposing structure were beautifully landscaped. Most buildings had some green growing in what would have been well-manicured lawn space at home, but what appeared here at first glance to be casual English-style gardens. Upon closer examination, they seemed to be two to three-foot tall weeds with an occasional flower colorfully poking up here and there and a bent old man was taming the overgrowth with an old-fashioned scythe. Not a lawnmower in sight.

The boulevard was supposed to be four lanes, but at any given time six vehicles occupied those four lanes. Brightly colored electric trolleys guided by overhead wires vied for space with regular auto-buses, as Garik called them. Vans of assorted size, age and design performed a remarkable choreography darting in and out of traffic to pick up and discharge passengers who stood at the side of the street and with a downward flick of the hand signaled the van to a stop.

"Those *marshutkas,* main transportation in Armenia. Each has route, identified by number in window," Garik explained. "If you miss one, another comes in maybe ten minutes. You travel anywhere in city for one hundred drams."

A quick mental calculation figured that at about twenty cents. Pretty reasonable transport, if you didn't mind being packed in like sardines.

A gray-haired woman in apron and dark dress bent over a short-handled reed broom sweeping the street. "She fortunate to have job," Garik explained as I turned to watch her out the back window. "She paid three thousand drams a month to sweep little section of street each morning."

Another quick calculation. Less than six American dollars. "You mean, three thousand drams a week?" I asked, hoping he had his terms wrong.

Garik shook his head. "Each month she receive three thousand drams."

The big, black car still followed close behind us and I watched in horror as it made no attempt to veer around the woman who had reached out to sweep an area away from the sidewalk.

"They nearly hit her," I gasped. "Who's in that car? They could have killed that old woman."

Garik's dark eyes narrowed. "Mrs. Allan, in Armenia only cars have rights on street. Must be very careful crossing street. Better to cross in middle with only two lanes to watch, than intersection where many cars turn. Pay no attention to traffic lights. No one else does. If driver knows you see him, if your eyes meet his, it is your responsibility to get out of his way. He not slow or stop for you."

I looked back at the car with heavily tinted windows that remained less than a half block behind us. If they were tailing us, they were being very obvious.

"Garik, you said you knew who was in the black car. Is it friends of yours, or . . . ?" As a guarded expression closed over Garik's face, I suddenly remembered the Armenian KGB and Mafia.

CHAPTER 8

Garik ignored my question and leaned forward, speaking to the taxi driver and pointing to a street paralleling a park. The driver turned up the street, narrowly missing a car passing another on the approach to the intersection. I closed my eyes and gripped my seat. Driving in Armenia was certainly an experience. A frightening one. So much for renting a car. I'd be terrified to share the streets with these wild drivers.

I glanced behind us. The black Mercedes stuck right with us, even when we went the wrong way on a one-way street. We drove half a block, weaving in and out of pedestrians and *marshutkas* maneuvering to park, and turned into a narrow alley, barely missing a man pushing a small cart loaded with bright red tomatoes and purple onions.

Garik pointed to a garish green wrought iron gate. "That is good *shuka*. Market," he explained as I began to ask for a translation. "They sell many fruits and vegetables. It is right around corner from your apartment."

The taxi driver dodged another vendor headed for the *shuka* carrying bulging bags of potatoes while a bald man dressed in a faded tweed jacket stepped aside with his bucket of copper-colored dried fish. We slowed at a high, vine-covered wire fence and stopped under two trees whose golden leaves reminded me winter would arrive before I left here.

Garik stepped out of the cab and extended his hand to me, expecting me to slide across the back seat. The driver ignored the door I sat beside, walked right by it to the trunk and retrieved my luggage. Maybe the door didn't work. That would not be a surprise, considering the apparent condition of the ancient car. The surprise came when the black car with tinted windows pulled into the alley behind us, paused, then proceeded slowly out into the street. The hair on the back of my neck stood up. I could feel eyes watching me from behind those tinted windows. I feared I knew to whom they belonged, even if Garik remained silent on the subject.

As I exited the taxi, I faced three dented, rusting square garbage cans overflowing with trash. I shuddered, imagining the number of rats that would attract to the area. The entrance to the building didn't offer any more encouragement regarding my accommodations. Cigarette butts littered the dirty marble stairs. Paint peeled from the stained walls in huge chunks. My spirits plummeted.

Garik led the way; I followed, clutching the briefcase and my purse, being careful not to brush against the wall, and the cab driver trailed behind carrying my suitcase. We labored up five flights of chipped, gray, dirt-covered marble stairs without conditions improving in the least as we ascended. Not only was I out of breath, I was devastated at being accommodated in such a filthy place. It seemed an insult to invite someone to your country to live for three months, and then house him or her in a slum. There had to be some-thing better than this somewhere in the city, even if the people were poor and the economy was depressed.

Then Garik produced a gold key and opened the door. The sight rendered me speechless. Behind that nondescript door at the top of those grimy stairs was hidden a jewel of an apartment. The wide hall with twelve-foot high ceiling led to four large, light, airy rooms, all beautifully furnished with elaborately carved and lacquered antique furniture. Persian or Armenian carpets partially covered shiny parquet hardwood floors in every room.

Garik pointed out the "toilette" room, a tiny three-by-four-foot tiled cubbyhole also with a twelve-foot ceiling, and the tiny bathroom containing a sink, tub, and little washing machine. Overhead two tanks held water: one for the shower, and one for the washer and to flush the toilet.

"Water come about five-thirty each morning for maybe two hours, and most evenings." He pointed to four gallon-sized turquoise jars and various buckets and pans. "Fill these bottles to use when no water comes. There be no running water except those times, and," he paused, then continued with an apologetic tone, "not always then."

He led me to the kitchen, a long narrow room with a huge window at the end, and stopped at the sink. "This your filtering system." Three twelve-inch high white plastic canisters perched on the back of the sink. "Americans and foreign visitors drink only filtered water. They prepare all food and wash dishes with it."

"But you don't?" I asked, intrigued by this apparent special consideration for visitors to his country.

He shrugged. "We accustomed to water," he said simply, and continued pointing out items he thought I should know about, including a cupboard filled with dishes, drawers containing kitchen linens and utensils, and a refrigerator and pantry stocked with essentials.

The cab driver had deposited my suitcase in the bedroom and disappeared back down the stairs. Garik suggested I unpack later, refresh myself now if I desired, and we'd continue our tour to familiarize me with the city. "Yerevan is easy city for visitors to get around. I'm sure you find your way after today without help."

I assumed that was Garik's subtle way of saying I'd better pay attention to where we were and where we went, as I'd be on my own from now on. That would certainly be nothing new. With my husband gone so much, I frequently found myself alone in strange cities.

What an interesting contrast to a trip to Spain on which I'd accompanied Mom a few years ago. A car, furnished by the University, met her every day at the entrance to her villa, also furnished by the University, to deliver her to the lecture location or excavation site, or wherever she wanted to go. Definitely different economics involved.

I deliberated briefly about the wisdom of leaving the briefcase unattended, but finally decided it might be safer here behind these three locks on the door than on the street with me. While Garik waited for me outside in the hall, I took the precaution of stuffing it under the rusty cookie sheet in the pantry, which would only slow down an experienced burglar, but I didn't have to make it easy for anyone trying to steal it. I knew it was a useless gesture if the men in the Mercedes were interested in the case or its contents. They'd leave nothing intact if they searched for it. And they would not leave until they found it.

Before we'd traversed the short distance from the front door of the building through a small alley to the busy street in front of us, I'd learned that this country was Hyestan to its people, and they called themselves Hyestanis, or Hys. I was an Amerigatsi who spoke Anglaren or English.

Our first stop was at the entrance to Abovian Street, Yerevan's equivalent of New York's Fifth Avenue, Garik informed me. I followed him down half a dozen steps to a tiny shop where a bespeckled money exchanger named Van changed my US dollars to Armenian drams. Five hundred fifty drams for one American dollar. Van's serious expression melted into a smile at my attempt to say thank you in Armenian.

The counter across from the money exchanger was filled with cheeses, Russian butter, sour cream and yogurt. Garik pointed to a corner in the little market where a man in a once-white jacket wielded an axe to a huge side of beef.

"This good place to buy meat," Garik explained. "Sassoon bring it fresh from the villages every morning. Show him what you want and he cut for you."

Garik proved to be an entertaining and knowledgeable guide as he acquainted me with places he thought I might need in my neighborhood, adding a running commentary on Armenian customs and people. I met the old man selling fresh, wonderful smelling bread from a tiny trailer on the corner of Abovian and the park. The windows were filled with dozens of different sizes, shapes, and varieties of unwrapped fresh bread. I peeked in the pass-through window to say *barev-dzez,* which meant hello if I remembered right from my brief study of the language on the plane. The old man beamed and passed me what looked like a skinny bagel. No sack. No bag to put it in. Just handed it to me with his fingers.

"We go first to American University so you see where to go each day." Garik pointed down the little one-way street filled mostly with pedestrians crossing to and from what looked like a gigantic concrete pipe sticking out of the ground. "This entrance to Yeritasardakan Metro Station." We stopped in front while he motioned at the alley directly across the street. "That other entrance to your apartment."

I recognized the narrow little alley that led to the *shuka.* Within a few steps from my shabby front door, I could buy meat, cheese, bread, and fresh fruit and vegetables. And music. As we stood at the entrance to the Metro, music blasted from three different directions: American music from across the street at a CD and audio shop; an Italian tenor warbled behind us at the outdoor café with bright red umbrellas; and in front as we entered the metro, or subway, a young man turned up the volume on Armenian music he sold from a kiosk.

Garik showed me how to buy subway tokens, gave me the handful he'd purchased, then explained that I must never put my token in the slot and hurry on through the stile without making sure the red circle of lights disappeared and a green arrow of lights appeared. If I tried to pass through without the green arrow, a barrier would slam into my legs. Effective way to make sure no one rode the metro without paying.

The steep escalator plunged us quickly two hundred and fifty feet down to the train platform below. A huge marble hall with squared arches on both sides and chandeliers hanging from the high ceiling stretched at least three hundred fifty feet to a massive white marble mural at the end.

"To travel south in city, board train to right as you enter metro. To travel north, take one on left," Garik suggested. "You soon recognize metro station names and travel with confidence." We passed through the arches on the left as a cold wind whistled through the dark tunnel. The stone floor vibrated under my feet, and then I heard the roar of the approaching train. Seconds later two Metro cars appeared painted the blue, orange, and red colors of the Armenian flag.

A stream of people poured from the open door as Garik stepped right into the midst of them, not waiting for them to disembark before he entered the car. As I stood, waiting for the last to exit, Garik reached out and grabbed my arm, pulling me into the car.

Someone pushed in behind me, and not a moment too soon. Suddenly the doors slammed shut and the train lurched along the track. If Garik hadn't been standing in front of me, I'd have gone flying down the aisle or landed in someone's lap. As it was, I fell full force against him. His arms closed around me, pulling me tightly against him in an intimate embrace.

As I stammered an embarrassed apology for nearly knocking him over and struggled to regain my footing, Garik's serious dark eyes looked deeply into mine, searching, I felt, for acceptance of his attention. His actions and attitude caught me so totally by surprise, it took a minute to react. Regaining my balance, I extracted myself from his arms, murmured a second apology for my clumsiness and grabbed the pole for stability as the train sped along the track.

I sneaked a quick look at the person who'd crowded into the metro behind me. Designer sunglasses hid his eyes so I couldn't tell if he, too, watched us, but we seemed to be the focus of nearly every other passenger seated along both sides of the car. I felt my face flush with embarrassment.

"You must enter and exit metro quick," Garik explained. I glanced up. The serious expression he'd worn all morning had been replaced by one of amusement. "They only pause at stops. If you hesitate, doors slam in your face and you'll be left."

I nodded. Unless you were standing close, communication was difficult because of the noise of the cars on the rails. I avoided standing that close to Garik. If his intentions were romantic and he was testing my reactions, he needed to know I wasn't the least bit interested in becoming involved with anyone—anyone but my absent husband. I suddenly remembered Bart wouldn't have the slightest idea I was now on his side of the world, and in fact, there should be only two small countries between us at the moment.

Not that he always remained long in his last reported region. Trailing terrorists usually involved travel rather than sitting surveillance in a given location. Terrorist leaders were mobile, never remaining in one place for any length of time. They slipped into a city, delivered their motivating message of hate and holy war to susceptible disciples, then moved quietly on to contaminate another group of ill-advised devotees.

The network of security surrounding them rivaled, or excelled, that of the President of the United States or any other head of state of a major power. That Bart and my father were able to apprehend many of these terrorist czars spoke volumes of their dedication to duty, adaptability to customs and cultures, and their tenacity at trailing these masterminds of hatred and destruction. Both Bart and Dad had become skilled at disguising themselves, enabling them to slip in and out of identities as easily as changing clothes.

It was understandable that my father could do this. Jack Alexander's appearance was that of any man anywhere—middle-aged, medium complexion and build, graying hair, and gray eyes. He could instantly become one of any number of nationalities with little more than a change of attitude, accent, and expression. But Bartholomew James Allan was another story completely. Tall, blond, and blue-eyed, Bart was the epitome of the California beach boy. How my husband managed to assimilate different nationalities, especially those of the Middle East with their dark hair, dark eyes, and olive skin never ceased to amaze me.

Twenty years ago, Osama bin Laden began preaching the holy war, or jihad, against all infidels with the express and advertised purpose of Muslim domination of the world. The acceleration of their holy war, especially against Americans, finally alerted the world about the very real menace Anastasia had been covertly fighting all that time. My father and mother had been fighting terrorist regimes even before that, and now Bart and I were the second generation involved in the on-going war that seemed to escalate with the passage of time.

The metro screeched to a stop only two or three minutes after we boarded. This time I clung tightly to the overhead rail as I watched other passengers brace for the stop and the final lurch of the car. Garik grabbed my hand and pulled me behind him through the stream of people pushing to board the train before it left them.

The press of bodies around me was disconcerting. In America, we prefer our space, keeping almost at arm's length from others when possible unless they're intimate acquaintances. Here I noticed everyone walked arm in arm, or hand in hand—mothers and sons, friends, old women, especially grandparents and small grandchildren, and even men. Two young women linked little fingers as they disentangled themselves from the exodus of passengers and walked down the long sand-colored marble hall toward the exit. Two men in their forties walked with arms touching.

"This is Marshall Baghramian station, one metro stop after Yeritasardakan. You will arrive at University in only minutes each day," Garik explained as I tactfully extricated my hand from his.

"That will be handy. Then I won't have to rent a car."

"In Armenia," Garik said, pointing to another escalator, "You rent driver. He bring car."

Novel idea. The escalator carried us quickly up to the station entrance and as we exited into the warm autumn sun, we faced a long flight of wide stairs, stationary this time, leading to street level.

"Yerevan built on seven hills," Garik said as we trudged up the sidewalk reminiscent of some of San Francisco's famous hills. "Yerevan, originally called Erebuni, pre-dated Rome on its seven hills by twenty-nine years. Erebuni compete in time with Babylon and is world's first gate to threshold of Christianity." Garik recited those interesting tidbits of information like a memorized phrase he repeated to all his visitors.

Older than Rome. Contemporary with Babylon. I was impressed. As we approached an intersection, my host pointed out the Sherlock Holmes Restaurant on one corner, recommending the food and convenient location as a good place for lunch, and almost directly across the street, a tall attractive building perched on the hill.

"That is American University of Armenia," Garik said, his voice filled with pride. "You will spend many pleasant hours here, I hope." He stood for a minute, looking at the building the color of golden sand with an expression of obvious devotion to the place. My alma mater held a special spot in my heart, but it certainly did not invoke what I saw in Garik's face.

I felt grateful for the opportunity to stop a minute and catch my breath after our climb up the steep sidewalk, especially when I noted the two long sets of wide stairs curving from the street to another set of even wider stairs, which led to the multistoried university. It appeared it would be easy to follow my doctor's instructions to walk at least a couple of miles each day, but I wasn't particularly excited about climbing those long flights of stairs today to see the university. Lack of rest during the last day and a half of travel had caught up to me and my energy lowlight came on. Bed definitely sounded like the most inviting thing on my itinerary.

Garik may have noted the fatigue that suddenly overcame me, or maybe the university wasn't on his agenda for today; whatever his motivation, he turned back toward the metro station. "Now you can find your way to University, we do something you enjoy to keep you awake."

"Do you promise that's the best antidote for jet lag?" I asked as we retraced our steps down the hill. I secretly hoped he'd admit it wasn't and would take me to my apartment and leave me for at least a couple of hours so I could crash.

His expression remained stoically serious, without a hint of a smile even in his eyes. "It is hard only today. Tomorrow your body remember the hour you go to bed tonight and adjust. Then your body clock—is that how you call it?—is set for Armenian time."

I nodded. It did make perfect sense to my tired mind, but my tired body wasn't buying into the idea. As we reached the metro, a young man sat on the marble bench near the entrance, eating sunflower seeds. His face seemed familiar, but I couldn't remember where I'd seen him before, especially since I'd only been in the country a few hours. I reminded myself of the old adage that somewhere in the world, everyone has a double. I must know this man's double from my side of the world. I did like the fashionable navy blazer he wore.

"I give you now some things to remember," Garik said as we entered the spacious marble station and walked toward the escalator. "When you want taxi, agree on price before you make trip, even before you get in. Best to use marked taxis. Many private taxis here. Americans safe in Armenia, but their wallets not so safe from crafty cab men who take you for ride the long way and charge you much."

Garik stepped onto the escalator, then turned to face me. "Armenians basically honest people, but it is good to be sly, to be clever. If you can be clever enough to get away with something, it is not wrong."

I hoped I'd misunderstood him. "You mean, if you don't get caught doing something dishonest, then it's okay?"

He shrugged. "There is much to overcome from time of Soviet domination and other times of oppression by conquerors. My people have had to be very clever to survive as national entity. Now we must be clever to eat."

Someone clattered down the escalator behind me. I stepped to the side so they could pass, and recognized the young man in the navy sport coat who'd been eating sunflower seeds at the station above us. Was this another Armenian idiosyncrasy? Leisurely lounge in the sun, then race down the already fast-moving stairs to catch a train that came every five minutes?

I watched over Garik's shoulder as the man hopped off the escalator and hurried toward the platform under the square stone arch on the right. He would be traveling south. But not on this train. I heard the doors slam and the train leave just before he reached it. All that rushing had been in vain.

We too were taking the south train. Garik led me toward those arches and we emerged on the other side in time to watch that young man embrace another man and kiss his cheeks. I glanced up at Garik who also saw the gesture.

"Is that an Armenian custom?" I asked. In my experience, only a few cultures still retained that old form of greeting, but it had been contemporarily adopted in most countries as a salutation between members of the Mafia, even in the United States. And the information I'd read indicated the Mafia was not only active in Armenia, but thriving.

"*Ha,*" Garik nodded. "When friends meet, also relatives, it is greeting of affection."

"*Ha?* Does that mean yes?" I was puzzled. "In the Armenian dictionary, it listed 'io' as the word for yes."

"'*Io*' is formal yes. '*Ha*' is casual. '*Voch*' is formal no. '*Che*' is casual. Armenians have many words for one meaning. Is very complicated language."

That I believed. In my short study of the language dictionary on the plane, I'd discovered most root words were verbs, and Armenians simply added a different suffix to the verb to indicate tense and action. But learning the language required, first of all, learning the thirty-nine-character alphabet, and then memorizing the verbs and the suffix meanings. Something that probably wouldn't happen in my three-month stay, especially with the amount of homework I'd have each night before the next day's presentation.

This language wasn't related to any of the dozen languages I already spoke, but I thought it might be interesting to see if I could find any similarities to other Eastern European languages, given time to do that, of course. Again, probably not in my short stay.

The train swooshed into the station immediately behind the blast of cold air that preceded it, and we boarded. This time I was able to take in the passengers without the distraction or embarrassment of being off balance and embraced. And of course, every eye in the car seemed to be watching me as I studied them. I'd thought with my long black curly hair, I'd not be out of place in this country of women with long black hair, or at least, not so visible. Maybe it was my green eyes that had everyone staring. Few people I'd seen thus far had light-colored eyes.

Garik leaned over. "Next station where you live. Do you remember name of station?"

"Yeritasardakan," I said, hoping I'd put in all the syllables. "It means youth station. Is that because all the universities are located near it?"

A look of surprise replaced Garik's serious expression.

"I read about it in the guide book on the plane." I braced myself for the lurch that came with each stop and watched the man in the navy jacket do a fancy step toward the door enabling him to stay on his feet while the train car screeched to a halt. As the doors slid open, he exited quickly, stopped directly outside, then just before the train started, he reentered the car. Puzzling behavior. Guess he changed his mind about which station he wanted.

He was an interesting study, slightly taller than medium height with the build of an athlete: thick neck, muscular shoulders, trim torso. Like all other Armenians I'd observed, his haircut was neat and short. Totally refreshing after all the "artistic types" in Hollywood who could be identified by their long, straggly hair and almost unkempt appearance that supposedly marked them as freethinkers.

Most Armenian men wore suit coats or sport coats as jackets, usually black or dark shades of gray, with either an open-collared shirt or turtleneck shirt or sweater. He was the only one on the train dressed in navy blue, and where most other jackets were of a plain, basic design, this young man wore a double-breasted style with shiny brass buttons and a matching navy turtleneck sweater. One little old man wore a brown jacket on which he had pinned his war medals. I wondered for which war he'd received them. Armenia had been involved in many wars as various nations attempted to conquer them, some succeeding.

At the next stop, Garik linked arms with me and hustled me off the train. "I think now you will be able to stay awake. You like to shop, no?"

"I like to shop, yes, depending on who it's for, where, and how many hours I've already been awake." I hoped he'd take the hint and let me go home to bed. Home to bed. Already I was thinking of this as home.

After the usual steep escalator ride to the top of the metro station, we emerged in an area still one level below ground. A huge circular fountain in the center of the plaza, attractive even without water, looked like it hadn't operated for some time. Massive scalloped concrete overhangs opened above the fountain revealing brilliant blue sky. Each scallop ended with what I thought was an elaborately carved dragon, but on closer examination, I discovered it was a stylized bird and scrolls copied from what looked like the Babylonian era. What a lovely place this would have been if the fountain worked and the outdoor café still operated under the arches surrounding the plaza.

As we approached the stairs to ground level, an old woman in a worn cardigan and long faded dress with a tattered scarf covering her silver hair sat near the top with her hand held out. She didn't speak, just sat silently, patiently, waiting for people to help her. And they did. In the time it took us to climb the twelve or fifteen steps, nearly every person ahead of us had dropped a bill in her hand, even young people. Garik pulled a ten-dram note from his pocket and added it to the tiny stack of small bills she'd accumulated from this batch of passengers disembarking from the metro.

"In my country, families most important," Garik said. "We take care of each other. Several generations live together in small apartment and help one another. She probably have no family to care for her, so to eat, she beg. Ten drams buy nothing, but 40 drams take her home on the metro, 60 drams buy bread for tonight, and 100 drams buy kilo of tomatoes and cucumbers. She have no rent if she owns apartment given to everyone by Soviets, but probably has no electricity unless people generous enough each day for her to pay for it."

We stepped into the warm October sunshine and I felt ashamed for not helping the old woman sitting on the cold stone steps. I turned to give her a thousand dram note, not quite two dollars, and saw a well-dressed woman bend over her with a paper cup of steaming coffee and a sandwich she'd apparently just purchased from the vendor at the foot of the stairs. What a compassionate gesture.

Garik was right. These people did take care of each other. I hurried down, dropped my meager contribution into her worn apron, and rejoined Garik at the top of the stairs, my heart much lighter.

"First, I show you Republic Square," Garik said, pointing to a huge open space in front of the sand-colored marble building across the street. "Then we shop."

As we stepped into the street, a big, black Mercedes with three yellow lights on the front screeched around the corner, accelerating as it came. It headed directly for us.

CHAPTER 9

The unexpectedness of the threat immobilized me. I froze, mind and body unable to respond to the danger. I felt Garik shift at my side, watched as the car sped closer and closer without veering from its course, but still couldn't make my feet move from where they seemed firmly rooted in the street, couldn't take my eyes from the mesmerizing golden circle of light in the center of the shiny chrome grill.

Then as if my responses finally awoke and realized the peril, adrenalin shot through me. I spun and threw myself toward the sidewalk, colliding with Garik who had stepped out of harm's way. As it zoomed by me, the speeding car came so close it hit the purse I held in my outstretched hand.

Garik staggered but maintained his footing, holding me up at the same time. As he embraced me again, he looked down with just the slightest smile in his eyes and said, "Twice today you throw yourself into my arms. I think maybe you like it there, yes?"

"I think maybe, no. But thank you for saving me from skinned knees. I think maybe I'm too tired to stand on my own feet." I extricated myself once again from the strong arms of this handsome Armenian and stepped back onto the sidewalk, making sure I was still intact.

"Remember, I tell you people have no right. Only cars," Garik said, reaching for my hand to lead me back into the street. "You must be cautious all time."

I nodded numbly, but looked carefully this time before I left the safety of the sidewalk. If he hadn't already warned me about drivers not watching for pedestrians, and if I hadn't already seen one near miss this morning, I'd have sworn that car deliberately tried to run us down. Us? In replaying the past minutes in my mind, I had the distinct impression that Garik had moved out of the way without warning me, had left me standing in the street in front of that speeding car. I shook off the feeling. Not likely.

We crossed the busy street uneventfully and emerged on what Garik called Republic Square, but which was, in fact, an immense circle. Three pink multistoried buildings and a sandy-colored one, each built in an arc, formed the ring with the sand-colored National Gallery and Museum and dancing fountains at the top of the circle and at the foot of the loop, a large, rather tacky-looking, modern-art, steel cross.

Garik pointed to it. "Cross only there to celebrate seventeen hundred years of Christianity this year. Then it go." He shook his head. "Good thing. Not show Armenian artistry." Then his narrative voice continued. "With exception of Hotel Armenia there with flags, these are government buildings."

"I can't believe all the marble. Everything in Yerevan seems to be built of either concrete or marble."

"This native Armenian stone called *tuff.* Have many colors. Black, white, orange, pink, gold, even green. We build like Soviets. Everything concrete, then face concrete with beautiful Hyestani stone. Yerevan called 'pink city' because of all pink tuff." Garik grabbed my hand and pulled me back toward the street from which we'd entered the Square. "But you explore later. Now I show you Hyestani art."

This time all my senses were on alert but we had an almost uneventful street crossing, scurrying out of the way of a big red trolley bus as we reached the other side. A little old man in a beige beret had his paintings spread on the wall of a fifty-foot long fountain that apparently no longer worked. Other vendors displayed their wares the length of the fountain and on the sidewalk.

Garik stretched his arms wide, gesturing proudly toward the plaza that extended as far as I could see. "This is Vernisage. You find anything you need here, from fine art to custom jewelry, needlework to used telephone, dishes to plumbing needs." The serious side Garik had presented all morning disappeared in his enthusiasm for his countrymen's art.

He wasn't kidding about finding anything here. A young woman exhibited handmade cloth dolls in Armenian costumes. Another had woven beautiful handbags that looked like the carpets for sale next to her. Then we walked down an aisle that resembled a garage sale at home: shiny chrome bathroom and kitchen fixtures, old telephone parts, well-worn tools of every kind, various nuts, bolts, nails, screws, new and used, and right next to them, old sterling silver, crystal bowls, and Russian war medals.

When we reached the end of the "garage sale" section and passed the used books spread on the sidewalk, the art section began. Beautifully embroidered linen, tatted doilies, and needlework, then paintings of every size and medium. Favorite subjects seemed to be Noah descending from Mt. Ararat with his family and animals streaming two by two behind, or the uniquely styled domed monasteries that dotted the Armenian countryside and adorned cities.

But the art I immediately fell in love with was the wood carving. The craftsmanship was incredible, and many of the artists sat behind their clocks or vases or carvings of churches or crosses, working with the simplest of tools on another creation.

"You like this?" Garik asked, his face expressing the same pride and love I'd seen when he showed me the American University of Armenia.

"I love it. But there's so much to see." I truly couldn't see the end of it. "This is wonderful."

"You are no longer tired?" Garik's smile reminded me of the pure delight of a small child delivering a dandelion or daisy to someone dear.

"Oh, no. Not now. This is stimulating, revitalizing. Is it here every day?"

Garik shook his head and steered me to yet another art form. Polished onyx and obsidian. "Only Saturday and Sunday. But just as well. You too busy at University. You couldn't come anyway."

People packed the place, jostling one another to get through the crowd. I clutched my purse a little tighter, knowing this was the perfect place for pickpockets, which I assumed were as active in Armenia as in every other large city in the world.

Live music emanated from some quarter down the plaza, an accordion, violin, and flute, probably like the wooden ones we'd just passed, playing a gypsy rondo that made me want to dance. If Bart had been here, I might have. Fatigue fled at the sight of all these beautiful things. I felt like a little girl again, going to the fair. But Bart had always been with me, watching out for me, pointing out things he knew I'd like, buying me an ice cream, or hot dog, or cotton candy. How I missed him.

We finally reached the end of the first aisle, and started back up the second when Garik pointed to some bright red umbrellas under the trees. "Would you like cup of coffee or tea?"

"Thanks, I don't drink either, but I would like a drink. Water or soda would be great." And a chance to sit for a minute. Energizing though this was, my lack of sufficient rest was telling. Getting off my feet would be a welcome treat. I couldn't believe we'd been wandering these ancient uneven stone sidewalks looking at artwork for over two hours already. No wonder my feet hurt.

Garik led me to a little round white table sheltered by a big red umbrella with Coca-Cola written all around the fringe. Coke certainly had a monopoly in Armenia. I could see no other soft drinks advertised anywhere besides Coke products: Coke, Sprite, and Fanta. I ordered a Fanta Limon instead of a Fanta Narange when Garik explained one was lemon-flavored, one was orange. While we waited for the waitress to bring our drinks, I observed people's drinking choices: tiny cups of steaming black espresso, larger cups probably containing tea, many bottles of Coke, Sprite, Fanta, and several brands of what was probably beer.

I turned to survey the tables behind me, and looked directly into the piercing black eyes of the man in the navy jacket with the brass buttons. He stared at me without blinking, as though he were looking right through me and reached for the red and white box of cigarettes lying on the table. He slowly withdrew one and lit it with a slender black obsidian lighter, blowing the smoke directly at me, yet never once acknowledging he was aware I watched him or that he was even conscious I was there. Casually he pulled a pair of designer sunglasses from his pocket and slipped them on, hiding his eyes.

Now I realized why the man eating sunflower seeds at the metro station by the American University of Armenia had looked familiar. He was the one who had crowded into the metro immediately behind me at the first stop. This man was following us!

I turned back to Garik to report my discovery, but found Garik's attention on a striking, slender young woman in a tight, black leather miniskirt split almost to the waist on one side, with a leather halter top that had nothing in the back but crisscrossed laces holding the shaped front piece in place. Her skin was flawless, make-up masterfully applied, and her long raven hair gleamed in the sun with indigo highlights. But the focus of Garik's attention was the amazing length of leg revealed by the minuscule skirt. I had to admit, it was quite a view. Even the shoes were attention getting: an eight-inch wedge sole in leather to match her brief outfit.

In my astonishment at the brevity of the costume and the beauty of the woman displaying it, I totally forgot the man in the navy jacket. When the woman and her entourage of ogling, admiring young men moved on and our drinks were served, I turned to point him out to Garik, but the table was empty. It actually could be coincidence, I thought, his being at the American University metro stop, then on the metro, and now here. In order to get here, he would have had to follow, precede, or travel with us. Yes, probably coincidence.

There was a fine line between being cautious and aware of people and surroundings and becoming paranoid that everyone was following you, watching you, or out to kill you.

And speaking of killing, that seemed a viable option at the table directly behind Garik. The conversation between four older men had gone from what sounded like friendly banter, to a heated discussion, to voices raised in anger. Garik didn't seem concerned, in fact, never even turned to see what all the shouting was about. But their voices were no long friendly; their expressions now were down-right angry, and their animated arms were raised in accusatory gestures.

Garik chose that moment to excuse himself. He walked casually toward the refreshment booth and disappeared behind it. The couple at the table next to ours picked up their drinks and moved to a table at the far end of the pavilion. Others simply left their empty or near-empty glasses and bottles and quietly exited the area.

The phrase "When in Rome . . ." came to mind, and I followed the example of the Armenians, picking up my drink to leave. Not a moment too soon. One man stood abruptly, sending his chair flying backwards. As it crashed against our table, I sidestepped it and scurried out of the way, hurrying in the direction Garik had taken.

But Garik was nowhere in sight. The restroom I assumed he'd headed for was non-existent. He'd simply disappeared around the corner of the refreshment booth. I didn't want to go too far from where he'd left me, so he could easily find me when he returned, but I didn't want to stay too close to the argument that had gotten out of hand. I'd read that Armenians were volatile, passionate people. I believed it and didn't want to be on the receiving end of their passion.

I left the pavilion and sat by a fountain near the end of the Vernisage where I could still see the action but was far enough away not to be physically affected by it. The sound of cascading water drowned out the angry voices and restored the peaceful feeling of the afternoon.

I finished my drink and waited. Still no sign of Garik. Where had the man gone? Had he deserted me? Or had he gone to find a restroom? It occurred to me that I hadn't seen a public restroom since I'd arrived in Armenia.

The warmth of the glorious October sun and the pleasant sound of water splashing in the fountain had a relaxing effect that was dangerous. I could easily fall asleep right here on the edge of the fountain. I glanced at my watch. Garik had been gone over twenty minutes. I'd give him ten more, and then see if I could find my way home. I had too much preparation remaining on Monday's presentation to bask in the sun all afternoon, pleasant though it might be.

Since tomorrow was Sunday, and I had nothing on my agenda from the University, I'd hoped Garik could find out if there was a church I could attend if only to partake of the sacrament since I probably wouldn't be able to understand a word of the meeting.

Ten minutes passed, then fifteen. I decided Garik wasn't coming back. At least there was no sign of the man in the navy jacket and fancy sunglasses. Guess he hadn't been following us after all. I'd spotted the entrance to the metro station from which we'd emerged hours before, and with one more look around to make sure Garik wasn't coming, I descended the steps to the station, passing the little old woman still leaning against the wall on the stairs.

I had no trouble finding my way through the glass doors, down the escalator, and even remembered on which side the train going north would come. Feeling like a seasoned metro rider, I checked the time clock to see how long since the last train had left, and how much time before the next one came. One minute and fifty seconds. So the next one was due in another two or three minutes. I watched people hurry through the arches, check the clock, and visibly relax when they noted they had minutes to wait. Some just stood without moving and waited. Some walked back and forth along the embarkation area, but some wove in and out through the arches into the main great hall and back.

As I watched a couple of children running back and forth, I caught a glimpse of a tall, slender man enter the embarkation area at the far end, then quickly step back out of sight under the arches. Curious, I walked into the great hall, but he wasn't there. That entire end of the hall was empty. Of course, the arches were six feet thick, so he could be standing under an arch having a conversation with a whole group of people and remain hidden from either side of the arch.

My train blew into the station, literally. The whoosh of cold air that preceded it would feel wonderful during the hot summer. Right now, it sent a chill through me. Or was the chill caused by the knowledge I'd been deserted by my escort in a strange city, was being watched by a sinister-looking man with piercing dark eyes, and had been the target of a speeding automobile? One thing for sure, this trip would be anything but boring. The bishop's caution came to mind: "Remember your training and stay on your toes." Good advice anytime. Looked like it would be essential here.

I stepped quickly through the open door of the first metro car, but remained near the entrance holding tightly to the chrome rail. My apartment should be at the next stop on the line, so I didn't bother to sit. I did peer out of the door just before it closed to see if the dark-eyed man in the navy jacket was anywhere in sight. He wasn't, but he could have boarded the last car and I missed seeing him. Or it could have been someone else entirely, since Armenia seemed to be full of tall, dark, handsome men.

The female voice announced Yeritasardakan Station next, and I exited quickly, climbed the steps and hurried through the long curved tunnel to ride the escalator to the top. I wondered exactly how deep the metro tunnels were, but my fact-finding tour would wait for another time.

The smell of freshly baked bread as I emerged from the station reminded me I hadn't really eaten today, at least, not anything substantial. The alley leading to my apartment was right in front of me, but I remembered the bread kiosk on the corner and went there first, buying a flat oval of bread like the two customers in front of me had purchased. One hundred drams for a hunk of fresh bread that measured over nine by thirteen inches. That equaled about fifty-five cents per loaf. Unheard of!

The little old man handed me the bread without wrapping or bagging it. I stood for a second wondering what to do with it, then turned and headed for my apartment, carrying it in one hand and my purse in the other, the way I'd seen the Armenians do. Everyone seemed to have a plastic bag they used for their purchases. Guess I'd better get one too, so I wouldn't have to carry my bread in my hands.

The shabby front doors still stood wide open at the entrance to my apparently once-fashionable apartment building. Evidently they were never shut. Certainly not like the apartment I'd had in New York when I worked at the United Nations where no one could enter without being buzzed in by the tenant.

By the time I'd reached the top of that fifth flight of dirty stairs, my heart was pounding like I'd just run five miles. As I juggled the bread, dug out my key, and opened the door, goose bumps tingled down my arms. I paused in the doorway, hesitant to enter, and yet afraid not to. I stood motionless on the threshold, listening for movement in the apartment. There wasn't a sound coming from that direction.

I stepped back into the hall and listened for movement across the hall behind the scarred wooden door that sagged on its hinges. Someone could be watching me through the peephole, but they were being very quiet if they were.

That left the filthy cluttered stairs leading up another flight. Interesting. Garik said I was on the top floor which was the fourth floor, but I'd climbed five flights of stairs to my apartment, and here was still another flight leading even higher. I quietly closed the door to my apartment and moved slowly, carefully up through the higgledy-piggledy collection of discarded radiators, cinder blocks, white bags half-filled with what looked like sand, and rusty cans containing debris. At the top of this flight of stairs, not only the window was missing, but the wooden casing as well. There remained just a gaping three-foot square hole in the concrete wall.

I peered up the next level of darkened stairs, fearful of stumbling over something—or someone—if I continued without a light. As my eyes adjusted to the gloom, I could see a chain and padlock on a door to the right at the top of the stairs, and on the landing, a huge armoire lay on its side blocking the entrance to the door on the left.

Still clutching the loaf of bread in one hand and my purse in the other, I wished I'd left the bread in the apartment and retrieved my gun from its journal case in my luggage. I'd have to be very creative to use the bread for self-defense, in case I met someone or something at the top of those dark stairs with other than friendly greetings in mind.

To be as quiet as possible, I carefully placed my feet on the grit-covered, marble steps; but my shoes crunched with each step. And each stair seemed dirtier than the last, so I made more noise the higher I climbed. As I reached the halfway point up the dark passage, something moved behind the armoire.

CHAPTER 10

I froze on the staircase, unable to move. I heard the noise again. A very small movement, but someone—or something—was definitely there. A body shifting behind the armoire? Children playing hide and seek? A rat? I shuddered, remembering the overflowing garbage cans across the alley.

Think about this, Alli. Before you go poking your head into something that doesn't concern you, think about what you're doing. Do you care if someone or something is hiding up there? Is it any of your business? Can you do anything about rats in your building? And remember it's not just you you're putting in danger now.

Ignoring the little voice that always urged caution when curiosity overcame good sense, I took one more step. *Just one*, I told myself. *Then if I can't see what's here, I'll go lock myself in my room and unpack.*

But my eyes were riveted on that huge, old wooden armoire lying on its side at the top of the stairs and I didn't watch where I put my foot. As I stepped up, a piece of broken glass under my shoe splintered, making a loud crunching sound that echoed up and down the stairwell.

A blur of black and white fur hurtled past me, yowling as it flew down the stairs. Startled out of my wits, I fell back against the dirty wall, crushing the loaf of bread against me. I stayed there, weak-kneed, trying to catch the breath the cat had scared right out of me. Then I laughed. I wasn't sure who was more frightened—the cat or me.

When my heart rate had returned to normal, I climbed up the rest of the stairs to check out the apparently empty apartments above me. The door on the right had a chain and padlock across the front, but a wide crack in the bottom panel enabled me to peek into the room beyond. It wasn't an apartment, but an attic, with dormer windows open to the sky. A wonderful nesting place for birds of all kinds, probably even the huge gray and black rooks I'd seen in the neighborhood. Or rats from across the alley, unless the cat population did, indeed, keep the rat population contained. At least the hole wasn't big enough for children to crawl through. A fall through those open windows to the ground five stories below would probably be fatal.

At first glance, the armoire didn't seem to be damaged. The glass was still intact in the door. But it blocked the entrance to the door on the other side of the hall so I couldn't tell, without climbing over it, if that door was locked.

The wonderful aroma of fresh bread I still clutched in one hand overcame my curiosity. Further explorations would wait for another day. It was time to eat and unpack, and then—time for bed. My body was still on California time, which was—I glanced at my watch as I made my way back down the cluttered stairs—three o'clock in the morning. No wonder numbing fatigue had set in.

I opened the door to my apartment again, stopped and listened once more, but all was quiet, upstairs and down. Carefully bolting all three locks on the door behind me, I kicked off my shoes, put the bread on the kitchen counter, noting the crushed corner where I'd clasped it so tightly, and prepared to wash my hands. Though I hadn't touched a thing on the filthy stairs, my hands felt like I'd been playing in the dirt.

I turned on the faucet. Nothing came out. Then I noted the bottle of water on the sink and remembered there was no running water except from the holding tank in the bathroom. This would take some getting used to—washing from a bottle instead of running water from the tap.

Hands clean, I headed for the briefcase, still hidden right where I'd left it, apparently untouched. Breathing a sigh of relief, I tore a piece of bread from the flat oval and popped it into my mouth as I explored the fridge and pantry to see what might accompany my meager meal of Armenian bread.

The telephone rang in the study, shattering the pleasant silence in the apartment. I hurried to answer it, chewing furiously on the crusty bread. Probably Garik calling to see if I'd found my way home and apologizing for deserting me on my first day in a strange city.

I picked up the phone, held it while I swallowed my mouthful, then answered. "Hello. This is Allison Allan."

"Princess! What in heaven's name are you doing in Armenia?"

"Bart!" I sank into the office chair at the desk, suddenly weak-kneed. "Oh, Bart, it's so good to hear your voice. How did you find me? Where did you get this number? Where are you?"

"You answer my question first. What are you doing in Armenia? Don't you know that's one of the hottest spots in this part of the world right now? What was your mother thinking, sending you there in your condition?"

"You've just answered your own question. I'm covering for Mom. Apparently you've already talked to her or you couldn't have found me. And what do you mean, in my condition? I'm pregnant, not sick or incapacitated." Then disappointment flooded through me. "Oh. You know already."

"Margaret told me. I'd been frantically trying to reach you for two days and finally got Mai Li in the Control Center. She told me about your Mom's accident. When I connected with Margaret at the hospital, she was so happy she couldn't keep the news to herself. She should have. I was ready to strangle her right over the phone for sending you and our baby into harm's way."

"I could strangle her too. I wanted to tell you myself. Of course, it doesn't matter since it would have to have been over the phone. I don't know why I envisioned a nice, intimate little setting where I would coyly reveal my wonderful condition, and you would sweep me into your arms with joy. Must have been from watching too many old movies. In real life, Anastasia always interferes with my romantic plans."

"I had some plans of my own when we finally determined this was for real, Princess. You would have been surprised by the scheme this unromantic clod devised to celebrate this great news. But the plan now is your immediate exit from Armenia." Determination filled Bart's voice.

"There's nothing I'd like to do better, love of my life, as long as you'd be with me. But I can't leave until someone else comes to fill Mom's responsibilities during this symposium. Now if you'd like to do it, I'll be more than happy to get on the next airplane home, which, by the way, is not until next week. Air service in and out of Yerevan is limited."

"Then call and make reservations on the next plane out, because I want you on it. Alli, please listen to me and do as I ask." Bart's insistence unsettled me.

"What's going on? Why the urgent need to get me out of Armenia? I checked both the State Department and Interpol's travel advisories. Neither had any troubling new developments."

"Princess, call and make reservations right now. See if there is anything—anything at all—even on Armenian Airlines—and get on it, though the thought of you flying with them is almost as scary as having you stay in Yerevan."

"Bart, you're making strange sounds. I need to know why." A funny feeling began in the pit of my stomach and I knew I wasn't going to like what I heard.

There was a long pause on the other end of the phone. Finally Bart asked, "Did you bring any of Q's gadgets with you?"

"Yes." I knew immediately what Bart wanted. "Is there anything else you want to tell me before I hang up. I need to put on some make-up and get ready for an important appointment."

"Just that I love you more than life itself. Please take care of our little Alexandria, and get her home quickly." My husband abruptly hung up, leaving me holding a dead phone.

I raced into the bedroom, unpacked the gold compact and turned on the miniature communication set it contained. Via satellite, I could connect with anyone almost anywhere in the world. I took it into the bathroom, turned on the shower connected to the filled holding tank, and pressed a small curved indentation on top that looked like a decoration, activating the "send" mode.

I spoke into it. "Hi, handsome. Are you there?"

"I'm here." Bart's welcome voice came through clear and strong, even over the noise of the shower. "And I wish you were anywhere else in the whole world but there, where you shouldn't be."

"What do you mean? I'm in the bathroom with the shower running so if my rooms are bugged they can't hear our conversation."

"You know what I mean, and you can bet your rooms are bugged," he assured me. "By now, every KGB agent in town knows which flight you came in on, what time you landed, where you're staying, for how long, and why you're there. As does every member of the Mafia who might have an interest, as well as the police. By the end of the day, every beggar in your neighborhood will know an American has moved into that building and which apartment is yours, so don't open your door to anyone you don't recognize. It does have a peephole, I assume."

"It does." I sat down on the blue tile floor and leaned against the deep old-fashioned tub. "Now what's the big deal about me being here?"

"Princess, you've got to vamoose immediately. The Jihad is escalating smack dab toward that little spot of real estate you're currently inhabiting."

"Why are they bringing their holy war to Armenia now? It's been going on for months, and there haven't been more than a couple of tiny incidents here, both of which were probably not even related to the current phase of the Jihad." I had done my homework, so I wasn't totally ignorant of what had been happening.

"The remaining leaders of the defeated Taliban are on the run, accompanied by al Qaeda. Most Americans vacated that part of the world already, since Americans have been Osama bin Laden's main targets. Christians are the next most obvious target of his disciples of hate. Armenia's made a lot of noise lately about being Christian for over seventeen hundred years. In case you didn't check the map, that little pocket of Christianity is surrounded on three sides by huge Muslim countries. Armenia shares only one-hundred forty kilometers of border with mostly Christian Georgia."

"How do you know this is where they're coming?"

"Because I'm hot on the tail of three of them and it appears that's where they're leading me." Bart was quiet for a minute and when he continued, his voice contained an entirely different tone. "When I remembered your doctor's appointment and couldn't get through to you or Margaret, I was afraid something had gone wrong with the baby. Princess, I can't tell you what that did to me." He paused for a minute. "Alli, I am *so* happy. No, more than that. Thrilled. Ecstatic. I don't know what. I'm so over the top that we're going to have a baby—then suddenly I find you've brought the two most precious things to me in the whole world right into the path of bin Laden's holy war. Tomorrow's headlines will probably have a Yerevan dateline. Princess, if anything happened to you, I wouldn't even want to live. Get out now. Please."

"I'd love to, if you'll tell me how when there isn't a flight sched-uled out of Yerevan for at least two days." I pulled a towel off the rack and sat on it. The cold in the tile floor soaked into my tired bones, making them ache even more.

"We have an operative there that I'll have contact you as soon as I can get in touch . . ." Bart's voice abruptly disappeared.

I shook the little electronic marvel I held in my hands. Now wasn't the time for it to go on the fritz! Then I had a horrible thought. Maybe the problem wasn't on my end. Had something happened to Bart? I sat for a minute waiting for his message to continue, waiting for his welcome voice to tell me about this operative that would get me out of Armenia, but the compact remained silent. Apprehension wrapped me in its anxious arms. If one satellite rotated out of position, the next one picked up the transmission and continued the beam without missing a beat, so unless someone had been shooting down satellites right and left, that shouldn't be a problem. What had happened?

Suddenly remembering the holding tank above the bathtub, I turned off the shower. This wasn't like being at home or in a hotel with an unlimited supply of water. In fact, it looked like I barely had enough left in the plastic tank for a hot shower. If my stomach hadn't growled just then reminding me how long it had been since I'd eaten, and how hungry I was, I'd have used the rest of the water right then to wash off the grit and grime of two days travel.

Instead, I grabbed the portable phone from the study and the suddenly silent compact, as well as the cell phone Mom had arranged to have, and headed for the kitchen to find something to appease my starving body. If any one of the three worked, I wanted to be sure I didn't miss the call.

In the pantry, I spotted a jar of Snicker's Peanut Butter—one of the few items on the shelves with a label written in English. My Russian was good so I could read the food labels in that language, as well as those in Arabic, German, and Italian. I had an international pantry.

I smeared the peanut butter, swirled generously with chocolate, caramel and nuts, over the flat bread, poured a glass of milk from a little square container with a German label, and sat at the tiny table in the kitchen where I bowed my head and blessed my meal, sending a fervent plea heavenward for Bart's safety.

My first bite was pure bliss. Just like eating a Snicker's candy bar, only better because the bread was so good. But I don't remember the rest of my dinner. My thoughts were consumed with Bart. What happened during his transmission? Had my receiver quit? Improbable, since all the equipment was kept in top working order and not returned to the case in the Control Center without being cleaned and checked. And satellites didn't usually fall from the sky, and certainly not in multiples. That left the one thing I hated to acknowledge. Something had not only interrupted Bart, but had prevented him from continuing our conversation.

With a heavy heart, I cleared the remains of my meal and headed for the bedroom to unpack essentials. I decided, in view of Bart's concerns, not to unpack everything, especially if I'd need to leave quickly. In the morning, I'd call the travel agency whose number was listed on my ticket jacket and make arrangements for the next flight out of town—probably to Vienna, Austria leaving Tuesday morning—if I remembered right. I took both phones and the compact, still in receive mode, into the bathroom and used the last of the water in the holding tank to shower. Just as I finished, the water came on and began filling the tank with cold water. My shower turned icy cold.

But I was so tired, even a cold shower couldn't revive me sufficiently to stay awake any longer. I donned pajamas and robe and headed for the sun-drenched balcony to towel-dry my hair. Tall, straggly flowers filled the fenced courtyard four stories below. A white-haired old woman and raven-haired boy hand watered each one with little red plastic buckets they filled from a short length of hose.

The alley running next to the fence teemed with people hurrying somewhere: kids with backpacks; mamas and grandmas with heavy bags of produce from the vegetable *shuka* at the end of the alley; an old man selling bundles of fresh herbs and one selling lemons shared a sunny spot conversing while a big German shepherd barked his disapproval from the other side of the tall, vine-covered fence behind them. A noisy hand-trolley filled with bright red tomatoes and deep green cucumbers rattled up the alley from the *shuka*, pushed by a man laboring to keep the heavy cart moving up the bumpy little incline.

On the third floor balcony below and to the side where the building angled toward the alley, a plump, dark-haired woman with streaks of gray at her temples hung dainty, lacy lingerie on a line. Obviously not hers.

Piano music floated from the window of the apartment next to mine, a piano student at music lessons. I shared a balcony with this apartment, but someone had stood a huge piece of plywood on end, then wired it, sort of, into place to separate the balconies. Unfortunately, it looked like a strong wind would topple it. And it certainly wouldn't keep anyone from coming onto my balcony if they wanted to. All they had to do was walk along the stone balustrade from one balcony to the other. I guess its main purpose must have been to provide a little privacy, though I could see the entire length of that balcony and the laundry hanging from the lines stretched across it.

A flattened cardboard box leaning against the back of a cement stairwell in the alley started flapping with no apparent wind or human in sight to cause the motion. I moved a few steps down the balcony to get a better view. There was not one, but several pieces of cardboard stacked against the wall, and as I watched, a small, dark head poked out, looked up and down the alley, then jumped out of what actually was a hole underneath the stairwell, covered by the cardboard. A little, dark man, who reminded me of the gypsies Mom and I met in Romania, scurried up the alley toward the garbage cans and began searching through the refuse placed there. Then he spotted a plastic bag hanging on the fence and a huge smile spread across his face as he withdrew a chunk of bread and piece of white cheese. Someone had left him some dinner.

I leaned over the balcony, watching the peaceful scene below, listening to the laughter of children playing around the corner, hearing the sounds of traffic from busy Abovian Street filter up the alley, and feeling the warmth of the late afternoon sun as it dried my hair. Was something terrible on its way to disrupt the tranquility I could feel here? How would I know if I couldn't communicate with Bart?

I replayed our conversation over and over in my mind. He'd said it *appeared* they were headed toward Armenia. Not that they were definitely coming here. The only thing you could predict with terrorists was their unpredictability. So I wouldn't plan on them arriving until they did. However, I would get those plane tickets for the next flight out of the country, just so I could relieve Bart's mind when he called back. I stopped the negative little voice in my mind that started to say, "If he does."

It would have been nice if I could have stayed awake long enough to read through Monday's presentation, or even tried again to call Mom and report my conversation with my husband and his insistence that I leave, but I was so groggy I barely remembered to lock the French doors to the balcony and check locks on the front door before I crashed with both phones and the gold compact next to my pillow.

It would also have been nice if my mind had ceased activity the same time as my body. Assorted KGB agents in trench coats, Mafia in black turtlenecks and jackets, and the man with gold buttons on his navy sport coat inhabited my dreams, popping out from behind trees, peeking in my windows, and trying to run me down with their big, fast, black cars.

When I awoke from a troubled sleep, it was dark outside. My watch said 7:30, but was that A.M. or P.M.? Had I slept through the night or only for a few hours? As I lay trying to clear the cobwebs from my mind, I heard a small shuffle overhead, then footsteps on the stairs, quiet footsteps that I probably couldn't have heard at all if my bed had not been next to that wall. Someone had been up on that dirty landing leading to the attic and was sneaking softly down the stairs on little cat-feet. But it wasn't a cat.

I willed my tired body to leap out of bed and see who it was through the peephole in my front door, but my body simply would not move, except to turn over and snuggle deeper into the covers. It must be evening, I reasoned, or I'd have had over fifteen hours of sleep and be more than ready to get out of this bed. So I closed my eyes and went back to sleep.

The German shepherd barking furiously in the alley below roused me from a deep sleep to find the bedroom filled with the soft gray light of morning. As I pulled the covers closer around me, trying to decide if I was really ready to get up, I heard water running somewhere in the apartment. I leapt out of bed, fearful that in my tired state I'd left it running last night. I hadn't. The holding tanks had refilled and the overflow from the toilette and washer tank trickled into the bathtub.

Now thoroughly awake, I grabbed an apple from the bowl on the kitchen table, the jar of Snickers peanut butter and a portion of the oval bread, the telephones and gold compact, and curled up on the sofa in the study, the only room with a heater. Every room contained built-in radiators, but Garik had explained there was no gas in Armenia to heat them. During the war with Azerbaijan, the gas supply had been cut off. Cement buildings got cold-soaked during the night and unless you had an electric heater to warm the rooms, or a wood burning stove, you stayed in bed to keep warm, suffered with the cold, or piled on layers of clothing.

The beautifully carved wooden clock on the wall chimed eight o'clock. That would make it eight P.M. in California. Mom should have called by now to check on me. She had this number. I licked the peanut butter from my fingers and started to dial the Control Center, the only number I had memorized. There was no dial tone on the phone. Great.

I tried the gold compact, which didn't rely on phone service, but on satellite relay waves. But there was no communication of any kind. I tried the phone again. Still no dial tone. Had all the communication in the world been disrupted? I tried to contact Bart, but if he were in any kind of situation where he couldn't answer, he'd ignore it until it was safe to return the calling number that would be stored in his device. No answer there either.

I suddenly felt isolated, totally alone in a little country where I knew only one person—and he had deserted me yesterday in the marketplace. I picked up Mom's presentation—my presentation now—that had to be made tomorrow morning and tried to bury myself in it, to get the facts and figures and stories into my mind that she told so well so I could present at least some of it without reading from her notes. But I simply couldn't concentrate.

Maybe I needed a trip to the American University of Armenia to get the feeling of the place and become acquainted with the great hall where the symposium schedule said most of the presentations would be made. Maybe even meet some of the other people involved in the conference—anything to rid myself of this terrible feeling of isolation.

I stuffed tomorrow's presentation in my purse and disbursed other portions of Mom's studies in various hiding places in the apartment, then returned the almost-empty briefcase to its place in the pantry. If someone did try to find the briefcase, at least they couldn't easily walk off with all of her hard work.

The "Dick Tracy" watches I'd tossed in at the last moment lay nestled in a corner in the bottom of the briefcase. No sense leaving them here for someone to find. They wouldn't do me any good without a partner to wear the other one, but at least they wouldn't fall into the hands of the enemy. I dropped them into my purse, along with the polemoscope and the gold compact, which currently was useless but hopefully would be valuable when communication was restored. I prayed that would happen very soon.

I even remembered my gun. I debated briefly whether or not to leave it hidden in the little padded journal and take the whole thing along, but the journal, small and compact though it was, made my purse heavier than I liked. I opted to simply drop the weapon into the pocket of my bag where it could easily be reached, and hoped I wasn't supposed to have a special permit to carry it in Armenia.

The dilemma of what to wear was quickly solved when I swung open the huge kitchen window to test the weather. Cold, gray mist curled down the hillside behind the apartment, so thick I couldn't even see the monument atop the hill. Definitely weather for my warmest pantsuit. I dressed quickly, not bothering to wheel the portable heater into the bedroom, but considering purchasing one for each room if my stay was going to last the entire three months. I was not into freezing and Anastasia had enough money to foot the bill for a little comfort.

I remembered the little man in the alley and took him an apple and the remainder of my bread smeared with Snickers, leaving it hanging in a plastic bag on the fence where he had retrieved his supper last night. It wasn't much but would suffice for breakfast if he didn't find anything better.

When I walked through the alley onto Abovian Street at nine o'clock, it seemed the city came to life at that moment. *Marshutkas* disgorged dozens of passengers all along the street. Streams of people poured from the metro station. I'd never seen so much black leather in my life. Everyone wore it—in every style and length—from short, fitted jackets with matching skirts or pants to long, flowing coats.

Even many of the men wore long leather coats. I thought Garik said many were unemployed and these people had no money. Unless some benevolent soul had passed out a truckload of leather coats *gratis,* there was money somewhere.

I dutifully looked both ways before leaving the safety of the sidewalk to step into the little one-way street I had to cross to reach the metro. But careful as I was, I wasn't prepared for, nor could I have seen, the big black car with gold lights on the front that screeched around the corner the minute I reached the center of the lane.

CHAPTER 11

This time I didn't freeze. When I saw that big gold light in the middle of the silver grill speeding toward me, equal amounts of anger and adrenalin energized my inert system. The madman hidden behind those dark tinted windows so intent on killing me would be disappointed this morning. But as I began to sprint toward the safety of the sidewalk, someone bumped me from behind, knocking me off balance.

I saw myself in one of those excruciatingly slow motion videos, falling, falling, falling slowly toward the ground. I'd land face down in the wet street approximately the same moment the car reached the spot where I'd be spread eagled.

Suddenly a full body tackle hit me from behind. The momentum carried us the remaining ten feet right into the middle of a group of young men standing at the edge of the street. Three went down with us. As we all hit the ground, the arms around my waist loosened and my benefactor rolled to one side, clear of the pile of arms and legs and bodies sprawled in a heap. I tried to see his face, to see who had risked his life to save mine, but he jumped quickly to his feet and disappeared into the fog.

Concerned, polite young men helped me to my feet, returned my purse which had landed several feet away, and tried to tell me something I didn't understand. I finally held up my hands in a futile gesture. "I'm sorry. I don't speak your language."

"Ah. Anglaren," one said with a huge smile. "You are not Hy?"

"High?" No, I wasn't high. If anything, I was rather low, literally. Being only five feet four inches tall, these good-looking, well-dressed young men all towered over me. Nor was my mood high. It was at an all time low at the moment. Then I remembered—Armenians call themselves Hyestanis, or Hys. "No," I laughed, "I'm American."

"You must take much care crossing streets," he cautioned with a most serious expression on his face. "Cars don't look out for people."

I thanked him for the advice and withdrew from the group, walking slowly toward the metro while replaying the scene in my mind. That good-looking young man was wrong. That particular car did look out for this particular person—and with deadly intent. But why? Yesterday could have been an accident. I probably wasn't watching as closely as I should have been. But the same car, screeching from a standstill right toward me this morning, was no accident.

Yesterday I'd avoided being hit by that car because my guardian angels woke me from a daze in time to get out of the way. Who was my guardian angel today? And why had he disappeared without a word?

Now what? Should I flee to the safety of my cold, lonely flat and study the presentation I wasn't prepared to make tomorrow? I shuddered thinking about it. Right now I needed to be surrounded by people and activity in a place where I could ponder the incidents of the past few days and try to make some sense of them, or if not, at least try to find some pattern in senseless events.

I paused at the entrance of the metro, turned slowly in a circle to observe the people in the area to see who might be watching me. Apparently no one. Even the group of young men I'd just left had re-formed their circle and resumed their conversation. I'd descended only a few steps down toward the entrance, when I stopped and looked again. Probably my messed up psyche this morning, but I still felt I was being watched.

When no one seemed to be paying the slightest bit of attention to me, I boarded the metro heading north to the American University of Armenia. The school should be filled with people and activity, even on a Sunday morning. How I wished I knew where to find the Church. I could have used some friendly company this morning, but with no phone book in my flat, which I couldn't have read anyway, I had no way of knowing if there was even one in Yerevan.

The doors on the train slammed shut and I slid into my seat, feeling every eye in the car on me. But none of the passengers appeared to have more than a slight curiosity and quickly looked away when my eyes met theirs. I didn't see any obvious Mafia or KGB types, or even any of the cold-eyed terrorist types I frequently faced. Just grandmas and grandpas with small children, young people who appeared to be students, older women carting heavy bags of produce, probably to sell at market, and an old man selling newspapers through the car.

As I disembarked from the train, someone bumped me from behind and I suddenly remembered the sensation of being pushed off balance when I started to run for safety in the middle of the street. Had someone unintentionally knocked me off balance and the man who saved me saw the danger? Or did he shove me into the path of the car, then have a change of heart at the last minute and push me out of the way? If so, he'd endangered his own life in the process. We'd barely avoided being hit as the car sped by. No. That didn't make sense. But nothing did any more. Only one thing seemed certain—that it had been a deliberate attempt on my life. A second attempt.

Why?

It all began with the briefcase. Who wanted it? And why? To get something out of it? Or to put something into it?

As I climbed the long flight of stairs up out of the Marshall Baghramian Metro station, I began the process of "what if." What if Mom was supposed to bring something into the country, either knowingly or unknowingly? Her trip had been widely advertised in university circles in California. With as many Armenians in Glendale and Fresno as there were in the capitol city of Yerevan, they could have planned to send something into the country with her.

What if I'd thwarted that course by slipping the briefcase away from the man who reminded me of a fox before he could add something to the case? What if people on this end didn't know it wasn't in the briefcase and were trying to retrieve it? No. That scenario didn't hold water either. Any second-story-man worth his salt could have been into my apartment in two minutes, found the briefcase and absconded with the whole thing, or any one thing he wanted from it. I'd been gone for hours yesterday, and the only thing that happened was a near miss by that murderous black Mercedes with the gold headlight in the center of its massive silver grill.

That's what didn't make sense. Since arriving in Armenia, *I* seemed to be the target, rather than the briefcase.

Then again, what if the briefcase had a secret compartment that we hadn't found, with something valuable hidden there? My what-ifs were getting more far out all the time. We'd examined it carefully and hadn't found any secret compartment.

Did the article on the robbery have anything to do with the mystery, or had one of Mom's colleagues simply placed it on her desk because of its connection to Armenia and her trip there?

When we reached street level, I tagged along with a gaggle of girls headed up the hill toward the university, staying close enough that I appeared to belong with them. No more solo street crossing. If there truly was safety in numbers, from now on I'd cross only with others.

I continued the "what if" process as I walked through the misty morning. What if all this was to simply scare me off and prevent Mom's participation in the symposium and her presentation from being made? Was there something earthshaking in there I'd missed? Admittedly, I hadn't read through the entire paper yet. I'd have to do that as soon as I found a suitable spot at the school.

As we reached the foot of the stairs in front of the university, the hair on the back of my neck prickled. I spun around and looked up into the serious dark eyes of Dr. Garik Grigorian.

"You out early. You not sleep well?" He extended his hand to shake mine, and when he had clasped it, he turned me around, linked his arm through mine and, without waiting for an answer, almost pulled me up the long set of stairs to the university atop the hill. He indicated no surprise at my being there, and offered no apology or even made mention of his disappearance yesterday as he chatted about his job and the marvelous conference he'd organized.

I was speechless at being drawn through the mist by this man who acted as if we were the oldest and dearest of friends, had met as planned at the foot of the stairs, and were simply continuing our agenda for the day.

He proudly pointed out the marble grand foyer, then led me up a wide set of winding stairs to the second floor and the great hall where the daily presentations would take place, continuing his monologue of praise and adoration for his beloved AUA.

"Tomorrow at ten o'clock is first session here. Today at twelve o'clock is tour. I see you downstairs soon." Garik turned and left me standing alone between the dimly lit stage and the rows of theater seats stretching up into the darkness where the muted light didn't reach.

I stood dumfounded. I had not spoken one word in the last ten minutes—had not even been expected to, apparently. Was the man so self-engrossed that he did not notice, or was his monologue designed to keep me off balance so I didn't press for an explanation of his strange behavior of yesterday?

At the sound of a door softly closing somewhere in the darkness above, the music from *Phantom of the Opera* played through my mind, its pulsing beat matching that of my heart. Cold chills shot through me. I quickly exited the poorly lit lecture hall to search for an area containing bright lights and friendly people. The term "safety in numbers" again came to mind.

As I chided myself for allowing the atmosphere to get to me, I began exploring the multistoried building, looking for a teachers' lounge or student gathering place where I could lose myself in Mom's first lecture and prepare for tomorrow's opening session. I needed to be totally familiar with the material so I could present it with the passion that she would have for it, and see if I could find anything contained in those innocent-looking pages that would cause someone to want me dead.

At the end of a long hallway of classrooms, I heard excited voices emanating from behind a double door with frosted glass panes. I opened the door slightly and peeked around. Yes. Exactly what I'd been seeking: a lounge with small tables and chairs in one end and comfortable-looking overstuffed furniture in the other, and in the center, a group of students in the midst of an animated discussion.

At first I thought it was a heated argument, but as I watched, I decided the passion of their feelings would probably be the same if they were discussing the weather. After all, this was Armenia, and I'd been told these people were passionate about everything. What I'd seen thus far bore that out.

I slipped into the room, took a seat in the corner where I hoped to be inconspicuous, and pulled Mom's notes from my purse. With the atmosphere as I'd hoped, I could relax, study, then possibly ponder the problem of the deadly Mercedes.

As I opened the notes, I heard the word satellite, then sun spots. A girl with a mass of frizzy black hair waved her cell phone. If that

phenomenon were occurring, that would explain the sudden inter-
ruption of Bart's call.

A young man, looking decidedly out of place with his sandy
blond hair, interrupted in English with a marked British accent. "My
roomie just informed me someone is shooting down satellites. Those
aren't sunspots, those are explosions."

"Where is CNN when you need it?" someone lamented. With the
Brit joining them, the conversation turned to English. It was then I
noticed the silent TV with blank screen on the other side of the room.

"Two hundred thousand Muslims gather on border to invade
Armenia. I finish my exam next hour, then go to my grandmother's
village in mountains. They won't come there." The wide-eyed girl
who spoke didn't appear old enough to attend university, much less
be working on a master's degree. Since the AUA offered only masters
programs, her appearance must be very deceiving.

"Where did you hear that?" the Brit demanded.

"My uncle come from Azerbaijan this morning. Muslims from
Iraq, Serbia, Afghanistan, Pakistan, Libya—from all over—come to
finish what Turks didn't do in 1915." Her terror-filled eyes glanced
from one student to another in the group. Was she looking for
someone to refute the rumor? No one did.

"I hear that, too. Taliban remnants and radical Muslims incited
by bin Laden. I think it just a story someone tell to scare everyone."
The tall young man with the prominent Armenian nose towered over
the petite little girl with the huge dark eyes. No one agreed with his
theory the story was just that, a story.

Someone else offered his opinion, but I tuned out the rest of the
conversation. The rumored two hundred thousand probably equated
to two thousand or even two hundred, but two would be too many
if they were actually coming to Armenia with mass destruction in
mind. Was it coincidence that satellite communication had been
disrupted just now?

What had Bart said? Osama bin Laden's holy war was escalating
into Armenia via the remnant of the Taliban and al Qaeda. If that
group's recent performance indicated their current agenda, Armenia
was definitely not the place to be right now. But if this was where
they were headed, and Bart knew that, he'd be right behind them, or

possibly even with them. His mode of operation was to infiltrate the group and destroy it from within.

If I couldn't get out of the country immediately, maybe I could sit tight and he'd find me. He had my phone number, so maybe he had the address of my apartment, too.

I didn't like it when my life involved so many *maybes* and *what ifs*, and it seemed right now that's all I had going. It wasn't enough that someone was trying to kill me every time I set foot into the street—there had to be terrorists, too? As terrible and unimaginable as it had been at the time, today's terrorist tactics would make the genocide of 1915 look like a Los Angeles street fight. Too horrible to think about. How did I land right in the middle of this mess?

I tuned back into the conversation as most of the students left the room, some of them in an apparent rush to get somewhere. Only one couple remained, sitting at a table near the center of the lounge. They were speaking quietly in Russian, a language I spoke and understood. I listened to their conversation for several minutes as a beautiful young woman with fear-filled, brown eyes poured out her anxiety to the young man, explaining her reasons for the terror she feared because of the reports they'd just heard.

The young man named Armen kept reassuring the distraught young woman that the stories were simply rumors, nothing more; they were perfectly safe in today's world and this would definitely not be a replay of that horror.

I shook my head at Armen's naivete. If anything, men had become more wicked and perverse than they were at the beginning of the century. One man, or even one dozen, could not possibly have killed the million and a half Armenians that were murdered then. It had taken the Turkish Army. With today's weapons, a single terrorist could destroy the capitol city of Yerevan and its million and a third inhabitants in a matter of minutes. No wonder Bart wanted me out of here. The more I thought about it, the more I wanted out of here, too.

The report I held in my hands suddenly didn't seem nearly as important as it had in the safety of my secluded little world above Santa Barbara. In fact, at that moment, I couldn't remember how Mom convinced me it was imperative she be represented at this symposium—and that I be the one to do it.

Nothing seemed as important as getting out of town. I gathered the papers without having spent a single minute studying tomorrow's presentation. If I could arrange it, I wouldn't be here tomorrow. No one said you had to fly out. There were, after all, roads. And with Interpol's clout, and my own inheritance, I should be able to finance about any mode of travel that was available, no matter how exorbitant the fee.

As I passed the table where the young couple engaged in quiet conversation, tears streamed down the girl's face. Armen wiped them away, promising to find a way to get out of Armenia as soon as possible. Their next words stopped me in my tracks.

"But it will be very costly, Maria, and very dangerous. Possibly more dangerous than staying here."

"Armen, it's better that we die trying to escape. If we make it, we'll have a real life together. Maybe we can even find our way to the temple."

I dropped the sheaf of papers I hadn't yet stuffed back into my bag and watched them flutter to every quarter of the area. As I'd hoped, Armen and Maria quickly jumped to their feet to help me gather the scattered sheets. It was the opening I needed. I introduced myself as we worked, and by the time the presentation had been gathered and reassembled, they invited me to share their table and talk with them.

"Where did you learn to speak Russian?" Maria asked. "Do Americans study Russian in school?"

"Not generally. I traveled extensively with my mother when I was a child and picked up several languages. I seem to have an aptitude for learning them, so I studied a few more in college and worked at the United Nations as a translator. I can't tell you how delighted I was to hear you speaking Russian. Armenian was not one of the languages I learned and it is frustrating to not be able to speak to or understand anyone around you."

Armen smiled. "Almost everyone speaks and understands Russian, and some families still speak that language in their homes. In other families, only the very young may not have learned it. While the Soviets were here, Russian was the official language of our country. If you did not speak and read Russian fluently, you couldn't work. It was a mandatory class in all schools. Even today, we use it interchangeably with Armenian. Sometimes it's easier to express your thoughts in Russian than to find the right word in Armenian."

"Did I hear you mention a temple?" I asked, attempting to steer the conversation down the avenue I wanted it to go.

Armen and Maria glanced at each other, then back at me.

"I'm a member of The Church of Jesus Christ of Latter-day Saints. We have many temples all over the world. I wondered if you were speaking of one of those."

"You're a Mormon?" Maria gasped. "We are, too."

I leaned forward. "Then there is a church here?"

"We have nine branches in Armenia, six in Yerevan proper," Armen said. "We're struggling to become a stake so we can have our own temple in Armenia. Not a large one," he quickly explained. "Just a small one. Our members can't get out of the country easily to attend a temple, so we're praying the prophet will give us one here."

"And you are ready to go to the temple now?" I asked, noting Maria wore no rings on her fingers.

Maria looked at Armen, then down at her delicate white hands folded on the table in front of her. She spoke quietly without looking up. "We have no money for that. We are both studying at university only because we've received student loans from the Church, but there are no jobs available when we graduate, so it may be many years before we can go. But none of that will matter if we don't leave now."

I waited, but neither of them spoke. "To go where?" I asked quietly. "What's the urgency that you must leave now?"

Maria twisted her fingers nervously, bit her lip, then looked up at Armen, her eyes pleading for him to say something, but he sat silently, waiting for her to speak.

Placing her hands palm down on the table, she took a deep breath and began to speak. "In 1915 the Turks issued an order to annihilate every Armenian in the country. Everyone from my people's village was driven into the desert by the soldiers and forced to walk for days without food or water. The women and girls were raped repeatedly. Those who survived the march were massacred. Every member of my family was killed except one fourteen old boy who escaped to Aleppo, and from there to the United States. That boy was my grandfather. He was the sole survivor not only of his family, but also of his entire village." Maria clenched her fists and lamented bitterly, "Why did my father ever feel the need to move to his father's birthplace?"

As emotion overcame her, she stopped her narrative, wiped the tears streaming down her cheeks, and when she'd regained control said fiercely, "I will not stay here and let history repeat itself."

"Where will you go?" I asked. When no answer was forthcoming from either of them, I asked, "Do you have family or friends outside of Armenia?"

Maria stared at Armen. She didn't speak. She didn't have to. Hopelessness and frustration filled her beautiful brown eyes.

Armen reached across the small table for Maria's hand. Without taking his eyes from hers, he spoke quietly, deliberately, as if tutoring both of us at the same time. "In order to leave Armenia, you must have a visa from the country you wish to enter. But countries that allow us to enter are few because Armenians leave here and don't return. They become refugees, seeking work and a better life, but many end up depending on the welfare of that country to eat."

He paused, stroking her small hand, then continued, his eyes still on Maria. "We cannot cross into Turkey or Azerbaijan. Those borders are still closed to Armenians. Iran does not welcome us right now. Georgia leads to Russia, Eastern Europe, Turkey, and then to Europe. People going that route pay high prices for false papers or to be smuggled across borders. But they are caught and brought back to Armenia. Or they freeze to death crossing the mountains. I will not take you that way, Maria."

"Then we die here," she said simply.

CHAPTER 12

The door burst open. "They are coming! It's true. What Tatevik said is true," a young man shouted in Russian. "We are at war! The president asked for volunteers to help the regular Army. Armen, you've already served. They need you again."

"No." Maria stood so suddenly her chair fell backwards with a loud clatter. "No, Armen." She rushed around the table, threw her arms around Armen's neck and clung to him as though that could prevent him from leaving.

"Who's coming?" I asked the breathless young man I recognized as one who had been in the lounge earlier.

"Osama bin Laden's radical Muslim army. They've knocked out all communication. We have no radio, TV, or telephones."

"How did you find out if there's no communication?" I asked.

"Mher's father is head of KGB and his uncle is head of Mafia," Armen said. "He knows everything."

"Where are they coming from?" I still did not believe this story.

"Mostly Azerbaijan, but a few up from Iran, and some into Gyumri from Turkey." Mher sounded so certain, so knowledgeable, but then, most rumor mongers did. They had to be convincing for the rumors to start.

"How many have gathered?" I pressed, hoping Mher's information was scant enough to cast major doubts on his story. "The last few months the world coalition against terrorism has about decimated his followers. They can't have much of an army left."

"The report my father received said they were estimating at least two thousand well-trained guerilla fighters, but my father believes that estimate is too low. He personally knows of four training camps in the Pankisi Gorge in Georgia the coalition never found. They have about one thousand soldiers in each camp and are continually getting new recruits from the radical Muslims, plus sympathizers to their Jihad cause."

This can't be happening, my head kept saying over and over, but his story was beginning to gel with what my own father and husband had told me. Two more students joined our little circle around the table.

"Why are they coming to Armenia?" I asked. "This tiny country is certainly not a strategic target."

For the first time the young man hesitated. "That is not totally clear yet," he said. "My father has several ideas, but even he asked that same question."

Several more students quietly congregated, all listening intently to our exchange.

"Supposing that al Qaeda actually is sending soldiers here, when are they supposed to arrive?" I couched my question in very doubtful tones.

"They have already crossed the borders, infiltrating individually, in pairs and in small groups."

"If you know they've crossed the borders, why weren't they stopped?" I welcomed the doubts Mher's last statement aroused.

"Kasark," Armen said quietly. "It's a common practice on all borders."

"Kasark?" I repeated.

"Bribery. Money under the table," Armen explained. "For enough kasark, you could move an entire army across any border in this part of the world." He turned to the young man with all the information. "Mher, your father must have some idea what they plan to do when they get here. There is too little money or wealth among the people to help their cause. Ransacking the entire country wouldn't get them enough to feed their army for a month."

Mher ran his finger thoughtfully across the back of a chair. "My father . . ." He paused, seeking the right word. "My father wonders if one of the dissident groups in Parliament hasn't joined forces with al Qaeda in order to gain control over the government and have power to bring about the changes they want for their minority." He paused again, then added slowly, "Personally, I think it may have more to do with world opinion. If Osama bin Laden's men can gain a victory, even a small victory, they can show the world they still have the ability to fight against the super powers of the coalition. That will bring them more followers, more soldiers to fight their cause."

Armen agreed with Mher. "The Armenian Air Force is small, but even the few airplanes in our inventory would be immeasurable help in the war these men have been fighting with mostly small arms and explosives."

"Could a group like bin Laden's ragtag remnant actually take over your air force?" This theory was hard for me to believe.

Armen nodded. "Our military has not been trained in the Jihad terrorist camps. It's possible they could take our air force. Training is radically different for holy war terrorists who blow themselves up for Jihad than for regular army and air force who need to stay alive to fight for their cause."

No one spoke after that pronouncement. I hated to think this could actually be happening, but with my father in Karabagh trying to control the terrorist-led rebels there and bring peace to that war-torn area, and my husband trailing terrorist leaders headed in this direction, Mher's story now didn't seem so unbelievable.

Bart said tomorrow's headlines would probably have a Yerevan dateline. I hoped he was wrong, but I was beginning to be convinced.

One of the students who had listened to the whole exchange quietly spoke. "So if they have already come into the country, how long before . . . before . . ." She left that alarming question dangling in midair.

Yes. Before what? I thought. *What will happen?* I looked at Armen. He shook his head and turned to the KGB leader's son. "Mher?"

"My father thinks it may take days for everyone to filter into the country and get into place. So he believes we are not going to see action . . ."

"Define action," someone broke in.

"He believes we will not see shooting in the streets or physical evidence of the invasion for several days. I think he is wrong. I believe those already in Armenia are the forward wave sent to disrupt communication, which they've already accomplished. The next phase will be a surprise attack on the Air Force and Army bases to gain control of the weapons and men."

"Has anyone informed the military about this?" a familiar voice with a disdainful ring asked from the doorway.

Dr. Garik Grigoryan leaned against the door casing, an amused smile on his usually serious face.

Mher flushed. "Yes. My father immediately informed the military as soon as he received word of the invasion."

"Good. Then we don't have anything to worry about for the next few hours, so I suggest you all get to your appointments." Garik made a small motion in my direction and reverted to English. "Mrs. Allan, please come. Group waits for you."

I couldn't help noticing the difference speaking a native language made to Garik. He exuded self-confidence, a cool poise in his own language, but when he spoke English, there appeared a hint of apology in his manner all the time, an uncertainty or hesitation that was clearly absent when he was on the sure ground of a mother tongue.

I turned back to Armen and Maria, not ready to end our conversation. Maria grabbed a pencil from the table and scribbled a phone number and address on the folder with Mom's presentation, then thrust it at me. "Where are you staying?" she asked quietly.

"Twenty-nine Abovian, number seven," I whispered, scooping up the rest of my belongings. I turned toward Garik and quickly followed him out of the room and down the hall, wondering why Maria had spoken so quietly, and why I had whispered my reply.

I caught up with Garik. "You heard what the students were talking about. Is it true? Is your country being invaded by Osama bin Laden's al Qaeda?"

He continued striding down the hall and answered with a simple, "*Che.*"

"*Che?* No?" I struggled to keep up. "Mher said his father . . ."

"Mher is dramatic young man. Likes attention."

"Then there is no army coming? No threat of war?"

Dr. Garik Grigoryan dismissed the whole thing with a wave of his hand. "You are safe in Armenia, Mrs. Allan."

"What about the communications disruption?"

"You are in Armenia now. We suffer these small trials frequently. No money for new equipment. Must repair old equipment. Everything stop while that happen. Hurry, please. We must not keep group waiting longer."

"Group? What group is waiting?"

"We take tour. Everyone on bus waiting." As we hurried down the stairs Garik linked his arm familiarly through mine, a gesture I neither welcomed nor appreciated.

"What tour? I think you mentioned it this morning, but that was the first I'd heard about it." I slipped my arm from his under the pretense of adjusting my bag on my shoulder. I didn't want to hurt his feelings, but I certainly didn't want Garik to feel comfortable with this touching thing. It may be the custom in Armenia, but in America, it would indicate a relationship that I definitely didn't have with this man, and would not have in the future.

"I assumed you read schedule I sent Dr. Alexander. Presenters tour Echmiadzin and sister cathedrals of St. Gayana and St. Hripsime today before conference begin tomorrow." He flashed a charming smile. "Play today, work tomorrow."

"I'm sorry. I guess I haven't paid much attention to the other papers Mom had in her case. I was just worried about the presentation." *Which you haven't spent nearly enough time on*, I chided myself. I stopped as we reached the front doors. "Maybe I should skip the tour today and spend the time studying."

Garik grabbed my hand and pulled me through the door. "You study later. I show you our history now. I think maybe you like Echmiadzin."

Echmiadzin. That was the cathedral mentioned in the article persons unknown left on Mom's desk. Curiosity about the stolen rubies suddenly overcame every reluctance I'd felt about the tour. I would keep Garik at arm's length and I could study the presentation later. I couldn't pass up an opportunity to learn about the missing gems, and if I got really lucky, maybe I'd figure out why Mom was given the article.

A small modern tour bus filled with people waited at the foot of the stairs. I felt embarrassed to have them all waiting for me. I glanced at my watch as I hurried down the stairs. It was only 11:45. I vaguely recalled Garik mentioning something at noon.

"This morning did you tell me the tour began at noon?" I asked as Garik helped me into the bus.

"*Io*. But presenters not Armenian," he smiled as he pointed to two empty seats right behind the driver, the only two empty seats on the bus. "If people Hyestani, bus leave at 12:15, maybe 12:30. But presenters gather early so we leave early. I think maybe everyone anxious to see Hyestan's treasures."

I settled into the seat by the window and Garik took the remaining seat on the aisle. He hooked a small microphone to his lapel, tapped the driver on the shoulder to signal we were ready, and began an historical narrative to set the stage for what we'd see at the cathedrals. Since history was my favorite subject, I found the whole thing riveting.

In A.D. 300 a group of virgins traveled to Armenia from Rome preaching Christianity to King Trdats III. He rejected the message, but fell in love with Hripsime, one of the virgins, and asked her to denounce her religion and marry him. When she refused to do either, he tortured and murdered the virgins, all thirty-two of them.

The king began taking on the countenance of a pig, or went mad thinking he was doing so. His sister dreamed Trdats' only cure was to release the Christian, Grigor, from his well-prison in Khor Virap where he'd been cast for preaching Christianity nearly fifteen years before. Convinced no one could survive that long in the well, Trdats refused to make the trip, but as his condition worsened, he went to the well and found Grigor miraculously alive. According to legend, Grigor had made friends with the rats, scorpions, snakes, and other creatures that inhabited his horrible surroundings and survived by drinking his own tears, or had been fed by some unknown woman. King Trdats released Grigor, recovered from the disease, embraced Christianity, and declared it the national religion in A.D. 301.

As we arrived at St. Hripsime monastery, Garik hurried me off the bus, pointing out the unique architectural features of the ancient stone church with a huge round dome on top and a smaller one above the columned bell tower entry. Inside, an immense iron chandelier hung from the dome high over head, but its meager light did nothing more than cast shadows into the corners of the main chapel area.

I stood in the center of the circular sanctuary under the chandelier and gazed at the cold, stark stone walls adorned only by patterns of soot from centuries of burning candles. There were no chairs, no benches, no place for worshipers to sit. A totally different world from our comfortable, carpeted chapels radiant with light and warmth and padded pews.

As my eyes adjusted to the dark interior, sunlight suddenly streamed through the high arched windows of the dome, illuminating the worn stones on the floor.

"Your first Armenian miracle," Garik whispered in my ear pointing to the sunbeams that highlighted the smoke from candles curling toward the blackened dome. Linking his arm through mine, he drew me toward the altar. In the shadowy gloom, two-foot-high pictures of the apostles painted in bright colors and adorned in gold would have remained unseen across the base of the altar without the sun shining on them. The altar itself was carved of marble with four candled tiers leading to an ancient image on the marble of Mary holding the Christ child.

On the wall to the right, an immense picture caught my eye. A crown released from heaven by a dove and guided by a cherub descended toward the head of a woman dressed in royal blue with a tall wooden cross in the crook of her arm. She stood on the fallen body of a king still brandishing his sword, and in the background of the picture, one woman was being stoned to death while another's tongue was being cut out.

"Explain this picture, please, Garik." I extracted my arm from his and walked to the foot of the picture, trying to put a comfortable distance between us.

"Woman in blue is St. Mariam, mother of Christ. You call her Mary. Hripsime being stoned to death. Gayana's tongue being cut out before she beaten to death."

"That's monstrous." I shuddered at the graphic sight and the thought of those women suffering so for their beliefs.

He shrugged. "But they become martyrs, then saints, to bless lives of believers. All work out for best."

For whose best, I thought. A couple of older women approached Garik, asking questions about the Armenian Apostolic Church and I took the opportunity to slip away to explore the rest of the church. I followed a couple that had bought a pamphlet and were reading the Russian text aloud. Apparently St. Hripsime was buried under the main altar. We descended five deep stone steps into a small room with bare stone walls and high windows, which afforded the only light in the room. Ancient stone crosses, or *khachkars*, leaned against the walls beside a pair of huge carved wooden doors no longer in use. The workmanship of the carvings on both wood and stone was incredible and the patterns so intricate, it made the stone crosses look like lace.

I followed the couple down through a small tunnel that led to a tiny low-ceilinged room lit only by one small light bulb. An exquisite white marble tomb with a life-sized painting of the sainted Hripsime on the top filled the center of the small space. I listened as they read how Grigor and the repentant King Trdats III recovered the remains of the martyred women and buried each of them with their belongings.

The couple quietly left the small space and I took their place to examine the extraordinary gold detailing on the sarcophagus and the serene look on the sainted woman's face. As I bent over the coffin, the hair on the back of my neck prickled. Suddenly the tiny stone vault plunged into darkness.

CHAPTER 13

I froze where I stood, still bent over the marble casket. Possibilities for the power failure flashed through my mind. The one I clung to was the memory of the single thin wire leading along the tunnel wall to the tiny bulb lighting the burial place of Hripsime. Someone brushing against it accidentally could have disconnected it from the power source.

But my danger antennae didn't buy into that theory. The lights had been turned off purposely, and now someone in the tunnel crept quietly toward me, blocking the airflow. I straightened, touched my purse silently to retrieve my flashlight and my gun, and remembered I'd left the gun pocket carefully zipped closed. I didn't dare make a sound to open it.

The movement in the tunnel stopped. I held my breath, hoping the next sound would reveal the intent of the person in the tunnel. I waited. Neither of us moved. But someone was there, someone breathing so heavily I could hear them.

Just in case the creature blocking the tunnel had some doubt in their mind of my presence in this utter blackness, I wasn't about to make it known for certain. We played our waiting game for what seemed an eternity, each waiting for the other to move, to reveal our position. I stood silently on that cold stone floor, praying Garik was simply playing a joke, perhaps testing my mettle, or maybe hoping I'd fly into his arms again.

But it wasn't Garik. A strange, coarse voice whispered something in a foreign tongue. I didn't respond. Didn't move. Again, faintly whispered words wafted across the tomb. The image of dead leaves rattling across dry bones filled the tiny cubicle. I swallowed the claustrophobia rising in me.

I'd never been able to stand small, cramped places. To be trapped in the cold, dark tomb with the only entrance blocked by someone who may have malicious mischief in mind was not just terrifying. I felt suffocated. Unable to breathe. My throat tightened, closing off the air to my lungs. I clenched my fists and prayed—for air, for control, for safety.

Then he moved slowly, quietly, two steps into the tiny tomb. I stood frozen near the head of the coffin with nowhere to go for escape. He stopped at the foot of the coffin on the other side, only an arm's length from me.

"Amerigatsi die," the throaty voice whispered, nearer than I'd imagined the man would be. Too near. Involuntarily I stepped backward. I bumped into the cold stone wall behind me just as something hit my purse with force enough to tear it from my shoulder. At that instant I heard Garik's very welcome voice—from somewhere too far away—clearly calling my name.

The man with the raspy voice muttered something I didn't understand and quickly left the tomb, no longer being quiet, but running up through the tunnel and up the steep steps. I heard voices, a heavy door slam shut, and then nothing at all.

I breathed again, for what seemed the first time in minutes. Cold shivers quivered through me. That was close. Way too close. I bent to retrieve my purse, feeling in the dark for the bag that had been torn from my shoulder. I found it, dug out the penlight I always carried, and discovered the bag's thick leather strap had been cleanly sliced all the way through.

Suddenly weak-kneed, I sagged against the cold marble coffin. That was far closer than I'd imagined. If I hadn't moved back that one step, that knife would have sliced through me, not my purse. Whoever they were, these guys weren't just trying to scare me, They were seriously intent on killing me. But why? And who were they?

I shuddered at the thought of my blood seeping across the white marble casket and hurried out of my frightening surroundings. There could easily have been one more body in that tiny tomb and I wasn't about to give anyone another opportunity to accomplish that.

But when I reached the stairs leading to the main sanctuary, a huge heavy door blocked my escape. I put my ear against the door but couldn't hear a sound through the thick carved wood. Had Garik and the tour left without me? He'd walked away and left me before. But whoever had just tried to kill me wouldn't walk away. They'd wait for the next opportunity, which would be when everyone had left the monastery.

I pounded on the door and yelled as loud as I could. If only I could get the attention of the man stationed near the front door selling brochures and candles before Garik deserted me again, maybe I could leave this fearful, frigid place unscathed. But there was no quick rescue. I pounded again and screamed, a sound born of panic and claustrophobia and absolute terror at being imprisoned in this dark, cold, stone place that had already been the site of too much wanton bloodshed.

Finally I heard someone on the other side of the door. The rusting ancient knob rattled, but the door didn't open. Then all was silent again. I pounded once more and yelled for help. They couldn't go away and leave me here. I pounded on the heavy door till my fist hurt. Then I heard a key in the lock and the door swung slowly open.

Garik stood at the shoulder of the stooped old man with the huge key in his hand. "Allison. Mrs. Allan. How you be locked in?"

I stifled the urge to throw myself into the arms of the tall, handsome Armenian who seemed my only friend at the moment. I desperately needed physical warmth and comfort after that terrifying ordeal. Where was my husband when I needed him?

"How indeed?" I stepped quickly to Garik's side and away from the entrance to Hripsime's tomb—which had almost become my own. "Apparently someone locked the door while I was down there." I looked around. The sanctuary was empty except for the three of us. "Where is everyone?"

"We ready to leave. I not find you. Dr. and Mrs. Famas say they see you downstairs so I come back but door locked. I think you not there. Then I hear scream. I think someone being killed."

"Someone would have been if you hadn't come back." I turned to the old man still holding the key. "Thank you." Then I headed for the front door. "Come on, Dr. Grigoryan. Let's get out of this place."

I hurried from the damp, dark, smoke-filled sanctuary into the damp, dark, mist-filled afternoon. "What happened to the sunshine?"

Garik smiled. "I tell you. Your first Armenian miracle. God send ray of sun to show he pleased with holy place. Did you like?"

I literally ran down the stairs to the waiting busload of people. "Garik, I can truthfully say I will never forget that place. It will remain forever etched in my memory."

As I entered the bus, I took the opportunity to scan the faces of those who would be my colleagues for the next three months at the symposium—if there would actually be one. And if I lived long enough to participate, both of which seemed doubtful at the moment. None of the faces seemed a match for the voice in the tomb. Garik pointed out Dr. and Mrs. Famas seated in the seats immediately behind ours. I leaned over and thanked them for sending Garik down to Hripsime's tomb, then settled into my seat as the bus lurched onto the road.

Garik turned to me. "I not understand how you get locked in."

Mrs. Famas leaned forward. "You were locked in? Down in that tiny dark tomb?" English was not her mother tongue, nor was the Russian they'd been reading from the brochure.

I turned around and looked more closely at the couple that apparently had been my salvation. They were a pleasant looking couple with laugh lines etched into their sun-tanned faces. "Famas is Greek, isn't it?"

They smiled and nodded.

"My grandparents are Greek. They live on Skiathos Island." I reached over the seat and shook hands with both of them. "I'm Allison Allan. Where are you from?"

"Mykonos," they answered simultaneously, then looked at each other and laughed.

"I've been there many times." I felt like I'd found family in the friendly couple.

But Garik had begun his narrative over the microphone, so I reluctantly settled into my seat to hear about our next stop, Echmiadzin, Armenia's main monastery, cathedral, and residence of the Catholicos, head of the Armenian Apostolic Church. My conversation with the Famases would have to wait. While I listened, I worked on a temporary repair of the slit strap on my purse.

Settled in the third century B.C., Echmiadzin was the capitol of Armenia from A.D.180 to A.D. 340, but it wasn't until A.D. 303 when

Grigor received a vision that the site became holy. According to legend, Christ himself came down from heaven, pointed to the spot for Grigor to build a place to worship the Lord, and named him The Illuminator.

"*Echmiadzin* means descent of the only begotten," Garik intoned. So the man held in the well-prison for fifteen years became St. Grigor, or Gregory, the Illuminator, the first Catholicos, and head of the Apostolic Church. Interestingly enough, the site revealed in Gregory's vision happened to be in the exact location of the Temple of Fire, a popular place of worship of local pagans since the fifth century B.C.

We arrived at Echmiadzin a few short minutes after leaving Hripsime, but there was no comparison in the two churches. Where Hripsime had been a solitary church with walled grounds, Echmiadzin was a huge complex of buildings. The new bell tower built for the celebration of seventeen-hundred years of Christianity seemed decidedly out of place with its modern lines of gray marble, whereas everything else in the complex constructed of beige or tan stone looked appropriately ancient to match the cathedral.

Several Armenians, both young and old, descended on us as we left the bus, selling their handmade souvenirs: elaborately carved wood crosses, wooden pomegranates on a jute string, and pictures, in case you didn't bring a camera. Garik hurried us past them, pointing out the long building next to the parking lot where they made candles by running a rope on a pulley through a vat of wax. I wanted to see, but a peek in the window was all I got. Garik was not a lingering, wordy guide.

We passed a brigade of broom ladies with kerchiefs on their heads and multiple sweaters over old print dresses sweeping the sidewalks with their little half-brooms. Garik pointed out the monastic cell building on the right where twenty-five priests lived while training, and a bookstore on the left where we could stop on the way back, but he didn't dawdle as he did so.

Garik's destination was the acclaimed seventeen-hundred-year-old cathedral with an elaborately carved center dome, double bell tower over the entrance, and smaller delicate towers over each of the three wings of the building. Ornate designs carved in the stone gave each tower a lacy look, and around the center dome, the faces of the Apostles stared down from their lofty perch several stories above.

After the stark stone walls of Hripsime, Echmiadzin was a delightful surprise. Ancient Armenian designs in rich colors and gold leaf adorned the elaborate entrance to the cathedral. Inside, the high ceilings and Gothic arches were covered with intricate patterns in beautiful colors highlighted with gold. Elegant crystal chandeliers illuminated the interior.

I stopped just inside the door to take in the marvelous artistry before me and heard a lovely melody sung so quietly I thought at first it was a figment of my imagination. I looked around for a priest performing the liturgy, but saw no one, and couldn't locate the source of the beautiful music. Then I saw a young woman standing near me, with head covered by a heavy scarf, sign the cross on her forehead, shoulders, and heart, and resume the quiet song she sang in her personal worship. It was a precious moment, listening to the clear beautiful tones of the young woman singing her praises to her Lord.

Then Garik intruded on that magical moment, introducing me to Archdeacon Gasparyan who had agreed to take our group on a tour of the antiquities room filled with the treasures of the Armenian Apostolic Church. The tall, black-robed priest led us past the elaborate main altar into rooms beside and behind the altar.

Light from the huge crystal chandelier reflected from a roomful of precious gold and silver artifacts displayed behind glass. Archdeacon Gasparyan stroked his graying beard a couple of times while the group gathered around him, then plunged into his narrative, describing the priceless items. He stopped by one case containing a beautiful piece of framed wood about twelve inches square with an ornamental cross in the center—a remnant from Noah's Ark, one corner of which had been broken off and sent as a gift to Catherine the Great, Queen of Russia in the 1700s.

There were several gold or silver forearms, resembling the gloved armor of a medieval knight, each differently decorated, and each containing a relic of a saint: one held the right hand relic of Gregory the Illuminator; others contained relics of Stephen who had been stoned to death, the first martyr of the original church; the Apostle Andrew, John the Baptist, and even St. George of dragon fame who figures prominently in both Armenian and Georgian history.

Archdeacon Gasparyan indicated a huge tapestry depicting St. George spearing the dragon, which represented evil, and trampling it under his horse's feet, explaining St. George was a Christian who fought to preserve the church and defend the area against Muslim invaders.

The archdeacon pointed out beautiful ancient illuminated manuscripts, heavy silver chalices, gold crosses, one for which he showed particular reverence. At first glance, I saw simply a uniquely shaped case with open doors containing an ornate, gem-encrusted cross with a large, gold-colored jewel in the center. Looking closer I saw imbedded in what looked like poly-resin a small sliver of wood—a relic of the Cross upon which Christ had been crucified.

Preserved the same way in a glorious sunburst of gold eighteen inches high was a thorn from the crown of thorns that had been pressed cruelly onto the head of the Savior by the mocking Roman soldiers.

But the artifact the Archdeacon reverenced most was a simple diamond-shaped piece of iron, almost rusty looking, probably sixteen inches high, displayed in an elaborate gold case: the sacred lance, he called it—the head of the Roman spear that pierced the side of Christ as he hung on the cross.

Gasparyan waited for the gasps and murmurs to cease before he continued his narrative, quietly answering a question from a member of the tour group.

"Could these be real?" Mrs. Famas whispered.

"Supposedly Thaddeus and Bartholomew, two of the apostles, came to the area and converted Gregory. Thaddeus was supposed to have brought the spearhead with him," Dr. Famas answered quietly. "The leaders of the early church could have preserved these things and sent them to the outer reaches of the kingdom hoping they would strengthen the faith or belief of the members and converts."

I nodded. "It is possible, I guess. You would certainly protect these relics with your very life if you were a priest in charge of them, so they could have survived the wars and conquerors that swept through here century after century."

I considered that as I looked at engraved and bejeweled silver book covers, jewel-encrusted altar crosses, a huge crystal cross made in A.D. 966, ancient chalices too numerous to mention, and a collection of miters worn through the centuries by the Catholicos, the head of the Armenian Apostolic Church, an office comparable to the Pope of the Catholic Church.

When we finished marveling at the wondrous collection of artifacts, Archdeacon Gasparyan asked if we would like to go down under the main altar and see the ancient altar stones from the fifth century B.C. Temple of Fire. Everyone pressed toward the steep narrow stairs, but when I saw the heavy door and the huge key the archdeacon pulled from his robe, I immediately stepped aside to let the Famases take my place in line. No way was I voluntarily going into another dark, confined space.

Garik, however, had other ideas. He looped his arm through mine and firmly steered me toward the steps leading to the underground room.

I tried to disentangle myself from his grip. "Thanks, Garik, but I'm going to pass on this portion of the tour."

"You cannot miss this. It is the birthplace of our religion."

"Oh, but I can miss it. Do you know what claustrophobia is?"

He stopped at the top of the stairs, arm still looped through mine, but his forehead suddenly creased with worry and his eyes filled with concern. "I do not know this word. Is it disease?"

"Claustrophobia is a fear of tight, enclosed places. I can't go down there with all those people."

Garik released my arm and actually laughed out loud. "I think you have bad disease. Maybe I catch sickness from you. We go."

The reprieve I thought I'd received when he released my arm was short-lived. Garik's arm slipped around my waist and he nearly lifted me to the top step.

"Garik, no. I don't want to go down there. Truly, I don't."

Archdeacon Gasparyan, who had been inside the underground room cautioning people to watch their head and their step as they went through the low door now came out and held out his hand to help me down the steps.

With one man pushing me from above, and one pulling me from below, I seemed to have no choice in the matter and descended the four steep steps to the low door that even I had to stoop to enter. I shuddered as my eyes became accustomed to the dim light.

Hripsime's tomb seemed spacious compared to this. I had to turn slightly sideways and sidle around the curved chest-high concrete passage that surrounded something in the center of the low-ceilinged room. The one bare bulb didn't offer a great deal of illumination, which only magnified my discomfort. Garik stood right behind me, blocking my exit. There wasn't room to even squeeze by him in the narrow space.

Archdeacon Gasparyan began his description of this sacred spot by pointing to the circle of stones in the center of the area: the original altar stones from the fifth century B.C. pagan Temple of Fire.

He explained when Christ came down and pointed to the spot where Gregory was to build a place to worship him, the site the Savior chose just happened to be the exact location of the Temple of Fire. Gregory didn't destroy the old altar, he simply built a new altar over the top of it and reconsecrated it as a Christian place of worship to show Christianity was victorious over paganism. The people continued to come and worship, willingly embracing the new form of religion so there was no violent transition from paganism to Christianity, as happened so many times in history.

The archdeacon concluded his brief recitation saying Echmiadzin was called the Armenian Bethlehem, a place of pilgrimage for not just Armenians of the Apostolic faith, but for Christians of all faiths from all over the world.

Very interesting, but as people shifted to see the fifth century eternity symbol carved into the stone wall, I'd had all I could take of tight, dark places. I needed sunlight and air and plenty of space—and I needed it fast.

"Garik, I've got to get out of here. Please turn around and go out so I can leave."

"*Che.* Another minute or two, please." Garik strained to hear the quiet voice of the archdeacon as he answered questions from the group.

Nothing Archdeacon Gasparyan or anyone else had to say could interest me enough at this point to keep me in this confined space even one minute longer. "Now, please. If you don't let me out right now, I'm going to scream."

I'll never know if he would have actually let me out or refused my request. At that moment, the one small bulb, the only source of light in the creepy underground cavern, suddenly went out, plunging the place into total, absolute blackness.

CHAPTER 14

Screams of fright and gasps of surprise filled the tiny, crowded space. I didn't scream. I couldn't. My throat began closing up and no sound could escape. Panic surged through me for the second time in less than an hour.

Archdeacon Gasparyan raised his voice to be heard above the anxious voices of those crowded around the ancient altar but I didn't hear what he said. I wanted out, and I wanted out right now, even if it meant climbing the frame of the stubborn man standing between the door and me.

"Mrs. Allan—Allison—be patient," Garik said as I pushed him toward the door. "You in Armenia now. These things happen often. We lose power, but it return soon."

"Not soon enough, Garik. Get out of my way. My claustrophobia just kicked into high gear and I can't breathe. Move, please. Now."

Suddenly Dr. Famas jostled me on the other side.

"Ouch. Be careful," Mrs. Famas exclaimed. "You're walking on my feet."

"Hold on there," Dr. Famas said. "I'll let you by if you'll give me a minute."

That did it. I put my shoulder in Garik's ribs and pushed, propelled by pure panic. It was entirely possible someone else suffered from claustrophobia and needed to exit this place immediately, but from the history of recent events, it was also possible someone was trying to get to me. I wasn't about to analyze whether or not I was being paranoid. Garik staggered as I hit him with my full weight but recovered to stand his ground.

"Oh, I'm bleeding." Mrs. Famas's voice raised in fright. "Ray, I'm hurt."

With one final shove, I moved the stubborn Armenian the necessary two or three steps to reach the heavy wooden door. Noise from the frightened tour group increased as Dr. and Mrs. Famas contended with whomever tried to squeeze past them in the too narrow passage. Frantically I felt for the knob, the latch, whatever handle would release me from this nightmare.

Finally my fumbling fingers found the knob. As I turned it, a body pressed tightly against mine. I threw myself against the door. The heavy wooden door creaked slowly open. I squeezed through the opening and fairly flew up the steep stairs, colliding with a young black-frocked priest on his way down.

Not bothering to stop and apologize for knocking him off his feet, I raced back through the treasury museum, and through the cathedral. Even the spacious, high-domed chapel didn't have enough room and light for me right now. I needed no walls at all. No bodies pressed close to mine, no one close enough to touch me.

As I reached the entrance, I heard footsteps running across the marble floor, echoing through the nearly empty cathedral. This time I'd be prepared. Ducking behind the spiral column, I pulled my gun from my purse and waited. Now I'd find out who was after me and why they were trying to kill me.

But it was Garik Grigoryan who burst from the cathedral. "Mrs. Allan. You are okay?" Then he saw the gun in my hand. He stopped, backed away a couple of steps and stood silently staring, first at the gun, then at me.

I slipped my gun back into my purse, out of sight, but kept my hand on it. Whoever had been down there had to come up and I could wait right here until he came out.

"Why you have gun?" Garik asked.

"To protect myself. Who came out behind you?" No one exited the cathedral. I couldn't even hear anyone in the chapel.

Garik shook his head. "I see no one. I come to find you."

"Please go see if there is anyone with our group that you don't recognize. And check on Mrs. Famas. She said she was bleeding. What happened?"

He nodded. "I go." Garik spun on his shiny Italian shoes and disappeared back into the chapel, making no pretense of being reluctant to leave. That was certainly okay with me. His presence was smothering most of the time. He hovered too close. He touched too often. But as I stood alone at the entrance to the ancient cathedral, I wondered if I had been too quick to send him off. Was I smart to be alone?

I looked around the empty courtyard. The gray mist hung low, covering not just the tops of the trees, but hiding most of the golden leaves still clinging to the branches. Even the top portion of King Trdates ancient arch was hidden from view. Directly behind the arch I could make out a high wrought iron gate, but the fog obscured whatever lay beyond the gates. Bells from an unseen belfry tolled mournfully across the courtyard. A perfectly creepy day.

A perfect day for murder.

I shuddered and banished the thought. What kept the tour group? Why weren't they coming? Had they been locked in that awful dark place? Should I go see? I wasn't anxious to go anywhere near the Temple of Fire again, but as the minutes ticked away and Garik hadn't returned and no one else from the tour emerged from the cathedral, my imagination created all sorts of scenarios, none of them pleasant.

Curiosity overcame fear and as I turned to reenter the cathedral, a voice at my elbow scared me out of my wits.

"May I help you? You seem distressed," said the voice in perfect English.

I whirled around and gazed up into the clear gray eyes of a tall, white-bearded priest dressed in a white frock trimmed in deep violet.

My mouth opened but no sound came out.

"Is something wrong? How can I help you?" His voice was deep and pleasant, reminding me of my own grandfather's soothing, comforting tones. Then my eye caught the elaborate cross hanging from his neck on heavy gold chain. It contained a ruby the size of a quarter. The rubies! I'd forgotten about the rubies.

"Thank you," I stammered. "I'm just waiting for the rest of my tour group."

"Have you seen the cathedral?"

"I've been in there, yes." But had I seen it? Now that he asked, I couldn't remember anything about the cathedral except the beautiful colors on the ceiling. And the dark, smothering confinement of the Temple of Fire under the altar, which I wanted very much to forget.

"I hate to admit that I hurried too quickly to appreciate what I was seeing." And I missed learning anything about the stolen rubies.

"Would you like me to show you the birthplace of Christianity in Armenia?"

I didn't even hesitate. "Yes. I'd like that very much. Where are you from? You speak English with a Midwestern accent—I'd guess the Chicago or Detroit area."

He smiled and nodded. "Very astute. Chicago." The white-haired priest motioned inside the cathedral. "Come. I'll tell you about Echmiadzin." As we entered the nearly empty cathedral, none of the tour group was in sight. One kerchiefed old woman dusted the altar railing and a couple of others lit candles beneath a huge painting of Mary holding the Christ child.

"First tell me about your robes. I've never seen a priest in a white frock before. What is the significance of that, and the purple trim? And what are you doing here?

"Briefly, studying the history of the Armenian Apostolic Church. These are the robes of office at my church in America. You're obviously American. What are you doing in Armenia? It isn't exactly a 'destination' spot."

I nodded in agreement and explained my purpose at the American University of Armenia. Then I had a crazy idea. I pulled the newspaper article about the stolen rubies from my purse. "Can you tell me anything about this? Have the rubies been recovered yet?"

The priest smiled and shook his head as he glanced at the headline. "You are surrounded by priceless antiquities and history and yet you ask only about some stolen jewels. Is it the generation or is it an American trait to not be impressed by antiquity?" he asked as he guided me toward the elaborate main altar.

"Probably neither. I'm just intrigued by a mystery. Have they been found?"

"No."

"Were they in the glass cases in the treasury?"

He nodded.

"How were they stolen?" It looked like I'd have to drag the information out of him one bit at a time. "During a break-in at night?"

"No. During the middle of the day, when a tour was in progress." He stopped under the main dome and pointed up. "Can you appreciate the beauty of the workmanship here?"

I leaned my head back to view the artistry above me. "Yes, it's incredible." I did take time to examine and appreciate the designs on the arches and around the lacy ironwork balcony railing and on up into the dome. "Did they have to break the glass or were the cases unlocked?"

The priest pressed his fingers together almost in an attitude of prayer. His way of expressing patience? "Why are you so curious about the rubies?" he asked quietly.

"If it was important enough to fill this much space in a newspaper halfway around the world, there must be some significance to the robbery."

He turned and looked at me for a long moment. "I think there is something more than your 'curiosity about a mystery,' as you said." The smile had disappeared from his eyes and he looked like a priest about to receive a confession.

As I looked up into those warm gray eyes, I decided now *was* the time for confession. I needed to talk to someone and he might just be that one. Adding to that was the impression that if I didn't level with him, I'd never get the story of the rubies I so desperately wanted.

I pointed to an apse with padded benches that had just emptied of its lone worshiper. "Can we sit there for a minute?"

He bowed slightly and waved his hand toward the apse in a gesture I interpreted as "after you." I hurried up the four shallow steps and took a corner where we could talk quietly without disturbing anyone who might wish to worship here. He sat on the other bench so our knees were almost touching. I didn't waste time, as I wasn't sure when Dr. Garik Grigoryan might appear to drag me off on the next phase of the tour.

"Someone left this copy of the article on my mother's desk at the University of California at Santa Barbara a week ago. She was supposed to come to Armenia to moderate a symposium at the American University of Armenia, but ended up with a broken leg—which I'm convinced was not an accident but caused deliberately to keep her from coming. There was an attempt on her life in the hospital, and I've had several very close calls since I arrived in Armenia. I can't give you a logical reason why, but I feel strongly all of that is tied directly to this article about the stolen rubies. That's why I'm so curious." I stopped and looked at the priest. "And that is why I need you to tell me everything you can about the rubies. I must figure out what they have to do with us, and why someone thinks it's necessary to . . ." I paused, not sure quite how to say it.

"Do away with you?" The priest finished the sentence. The smile had returned to his eyes.

"Yes. So I'd appreciate it if you'd tell me everything you know about the robbery. What was the significance of those particular rubies? Were they the only ones taken? The article says other artifacts were stolen but were recovered. Where were they found?"

The priest held up his hands. "One question at a time, please. As far as I know, the rubies were removed from their crosses because the crosses were too big and cumbersome to easily carry out."

"Did the thieves break the glass case or was it open?"

"The cleaning lady had been dusting in the case when the large tour group came, so she stepped aside while they examined the artifacts. She said she never left the room and was watching the group the entire time."

"But if it was a large group, she wouldn't be able to see the cases." I paused, remembering the young priest and the cleaning lady who sat at a desk in the corner while Archdeacon Gasparyan told us about the treasures we were seeing. "If she was sitting where the cleaning lady sat today, she couldn't see anything but people. They could have emptied all the cases and she wouldn't have been able to see it being done."

He nodded. "I was appalled at the security—or lack of it—when I came. Much of what is displayed is priceless, not only because of the historical value for Christians and the incredible antiquity of many of the pieces, but also because of the monetary value of some of them. The rubies, for example, were dated from the 800s and were perfect. Many of the gems in the treasury are flawed—pretty pieces of gemstone placed in ornate settings that outshone the jewels so it didn't matter that they weren't of the highest quality. These two particular rubies were famous because of their perfection. The crosses that held them were of impeccable workmanship. It was interesting that only the rubies were taken. One cross contained four large emeralds that were high quality gems."

"Were the crosses in the same case?" I asked. "Maybe it had something to do with accessibility."

"No, that was the strange thing. One ruby was in the first case—next to the door. It was understandable that they would pry the ruby from the center of that sunburst. It would have been extremely difficult, if not impossible to have carried the huge piece from the room without being seen."

"Sunburst? But I thought you said they were both taken from crosses."

"The first case contains a tall golden sunburst with about four-inch golden points radiating from a cross in the center and a miniature version of Echmiadzin as a base."

I nodded. I did remember that particular piece. And it was far too big for someone to simply walk away with it. "But none of the jewels was missing in that piece."

He shrugged. "A paste copy to replace the ruby until it is found. But the second ruby was taken from a cross in the third room—the room with the crystal cross. Did you get in there?"

"In the case by the miters?" I did remember one cross, even in the midst of so many beautiful pieces because of the large emeralds it contained. I am partial to emeralds so they had caught my eye. My engagement ring was a five-carat emerald, "to match my emerald eyes," Bart had said when he gave it to me.

"Why didn't they take the whole cross? Or even take all four emeralds when they took the ruby?" That intrigued me. Why just rubies and not the emeralds which would have been just as valuable? I looked up from my musing and caught the priest smiling at me. "I'm sorry. I didn't even ask your name."

"Father Ohanyan."

"Ohanyan? Is that Irish or Armenian?"

He laughed. "I haven't discovered the origin of the name, but my Russian mother told me my father was from a long line of rebellious Armenians, so there may have been some Irish mixed in somewhere in the generations. But that's another story. I don't have an answer to your question. If it had been me, I would have taken the four emeralds, too."

"What else was stolen and how and when was it recovered?"

"Several other crosses were taken, all containing rubies, but the rest of the jewels were still imbedded in the crosses. A cleaning woman came across the thieves in the bell tower prying out the rubies. Apparently they hadn't had time to remove all the stones before she discovered them."

"They were still on the grounds with the stolen crosses? How stupid is that? Were they caught?"

Father Ohanyan shook his head. "Unfortunately, no. And the woman was so rattled, she didn't remember what they looked like, except they all had dark beards."

"Dark beards? Does that exclude Armenians from the suspects? I haven't seen an Armenian that wasn't clean shaven since I arrived here."

"It doesn't necessarily exclude them. Beards make good disguises. I think the average Armenian is too loyal to his country and his church to do something like this. Their ecclesiastical history and their national history are closely entwined. The Catholicos was not only the head of the church for centuries, he was also the political, and often the military leader. In fact, Armenians have survived as a national entity in spite of all their conquerors because of the continuity of the Catholicos' leadership. But that doesn't mean Armenians weren't involved. There are several political factions, many remaining from the Soviet era, that have no allegiance to or consideration for the Apostolic Church. They would be happy to see the power the church wields in Armenia vanish altogether. The Communist Party is one of those."

"Then you see this more as a political crime than something simply for monetary gain?" I looked closely at the man sitting knee to knee with me in the dimly lit corner of the ancient cathedral. Priest he may well be, and historian, but I suspected he was also something of a detective. Was that a personal interest or an official assignment? His replies to my questions reminded me too much of all the FBI and Interpol agents I knew to discount some kind of law enforcement training.

"I think the rubies were taken to raise funds for some political group. When that has successfully been achieved, I think the rubies will reappear. I believe it was simply a means to an end for some misguided Armenians needing funds, but they will ultimately repent and return the gemstones to their rightful place."

"Sort of like holding them for ransom?"

Father Ohanyan nodded, then threw a series of questions at me. "How do you see the attempts on your life? What kind of threat are you—and to whom? What other purpose do you have for being here besides the seminar at the American University?"

Before I had time to answer even the first question, Garik appeared at the head of the group and came directly to our little corner as soon as he saw me. "You miss very good history lesson."

"Father Ohanyan, this is Dr. Garik Grigoryan from the American University. He's serving as a tour guide today for those participating in the symposium." As the two men acknowledged the introduction, the Famases appeared at the end of the group.

"Mrs. Famas seems to have recovered. Was she hurt badly? What happened? Did you find anyone down there that didn't belong with the group?"

Garik reached for my hand as he answered my questions. "We must go now. She scratch on rock. Just small cut. No, only our group surround Temple of Fire."

A cold shiver ran through me. Mrs. Famas had not scratched herself on a rock. If it was only our group down there, I'd better be very careful in this company. Someone here had murder in mind.

Father Ohanyan caught my reaction. "Excuse me, Dr. Grigoryan. I have one more question for Mrs. Allan before you take her away. I promise I will bring her right along."

Garik reluctantly released my hand. "We go to bus now to see St. Gayane church."

"You shepherd the rest of your flock to the bus. Father Ohanyan can walk me there. I promise I won't hold you up."

The handsome Armenian hurried down the steps into the main cathedral with a worried backward glance to see if we were coming.

"What happened to Mrs. Famas?" Father Ohanyan asked as we followed the tour from the cathedral.

"This is only my perception, of course. I'll have to talk to her to find out her opinion, but when the lights went out unexpectedly while we were surrounding the Temple of Fire, someone tried to get past the Famases who were standing next to me. Of course, there was no room, but suddenly in the pushing and jostling, Mrs. Famas screamed she had been hurt and was bleeding. I was standing next to the door and fled the scene. I'd already had one knifing incident at Hripsime. I wasn't about to stick around for another."

"That's when I found you standing wide-eyed under the bell tower."

I nodded as we left the cathedral and followed the group out into the misty afternoon.

"Tell me about the incident at Hripsime."

I recounted the story and showed him the severed, thick leather strap on my purse. He stopped and took the purse from me to examine it. "I can see why you'd think someone was after you again in the dark after an episode like that. What are you planning to do now?" He returned the purse, but I noticed he'd taken the opportunity to feel the contents through the soft leather as he handled it. "I assume you are able to protect yourself?"

I smiled up into the clear gray eyes. "So far I've been able to. Of course, I think my guardian angels are on duty full time, so that has been helpful. I just pray they don't take a Twinkie break when I need them." Would he mention the gun I knew he'd felt in my bag?

He ignored it. "You didn't answer my first question. What are you planning to do? Will you go home now that you feel your life is in danger?"

I tried not to laugh. Going home wouldn't lessen the danger for a member of Anastasia as long as there were still terrorists in the world. In fact, as soon as I could communicate with my family, I must remember to have Jim beef up the security on the estate. Perhaps now was the time to build the fence Jim and Dad had talked about so many times. I stopped. Communicate.

"Father Ohanyan, are you aware communication in Armenia has been interrupted? None of the phones work and radio and television transmission has stopped. I haven't been able to call out or even get a dial tone since last night. At the university today some of the students were talking about an invasion by the remnants of al Qaeda." I watched his face closely for his reaction. I wanted desperately to think that strange conversation in the university lounge was a nightmare.

Garik called from the bus and I looked up as the Famases boarded. The last ones on besides me.

Father Ohanyan put his hands on my shoulders and bent down slightly so he looked directly into my eyes. "I suggest that you go home immediately. Forget about the rubies and your seminar. Go home, young lady. And be careful getting there." Then he turned me to face the bus and sent me off with a little push in that direction.

I'd only gone two steps when he called after me, "Oh, just in case you do have some trouble getting out of the country, here is my number." When I turned back to him, he folded my fingers around his card, patted my hand as if to make sure I'd keep it safely with me, then thrust his hands into the pockets of his frock and wheeled away, his long skirts whirling as he turned.

I didn't have time to deliberate on his advice. Garik called impatiently and I hurried to board the bus. I seemed always to be keeping these people waiting. As I crossed the parking lot, I glanced at the card Father Ohanyan had given me. Behind his name strung an alphabet of degrees, including doctor of theology, doctor of history, doctor of juris prudence, and criminal investigation. The only mystery now about the good priest was which agency he was affiliated with and the real reason for his stay in Armenia. Studying the history of the Armenian Apostolic Church was merely a smoke screen for the agent. But his certainty about the rubies being returned puzzled me. Did he have inside information that's what had happened? At any rate, it was nice to know I had an ally in the country.

I knelt in my seat and leaned over the back to talk to Mrs. Famas. "What happened down there? Are you okay?"

She held up her handkerchief-wrapped arm. "I must have scratched it on a sharp piece of rock when that man tried to squeeze by me. It's fine, but I had a hard time stopping the bleeding. No one else seemed to have come in contact with that particular spot and I couldn't find it when the lights finally came back on, so I'm not sure exactly how I did it."

I leaned further over the seat and asked quietly, "Would you mind if I looked at it?"

Mrs. Famas looked up in surprise.

"If you cut it on a rock, there is a good chance of infection," I explained. "I brought some antibiotic salve with me if you need it."

Satisfied that I had a legitimate reason instead of just idle curiosity for examining her wound, she unwrapped the large blood-stained handkerchief. I turned on the overhead light and focused it on her arm. The cut was about two inches long, with perfectly clean edges. No jagged flesh wound. No dirt.

"Looks like you bled enough to clean the wound, but I'll bring some salve in the morning, unless you'd like me to get you some tonight."

Mrs. Famas shook her head. "No, tomorrow is soon enough. Besides I'm not sure I'd be able to tell you how to find our apartment yet." She smiled. "We've been here three days and I still get turned around when I go out the front door. If that big black Mercedes ever left before we did, I'd be in real trouble."

"Mercedes?" Her comment puzzled me.

"When I come out my front door, my natural tendency is to turn left and go up the hill because the university is on the hill. But then I see the Mercedes and remember that I must go down the hill to the intersection where we begin the climb up the next hill to the university. Invariably, just as we've passed the car, I hear the doors slam and the engine starts and it drives slowly on past us. Wish I could see in those tinted windows." Mrs. Famas laughed and leaned forward so no one else could hear her next comment. "Ray said it's just my imagination when I told him it was probably the KBG following us. He said they aren't functioning anymore." She paused and looked around, a worried expression replacing her smile. "Do you ever feel like you're being followed here?" she whispered.

CHAPTER 15

I glanced at Dr. Famas. He looked quickly away and began an intense examination of his fingernails. At that moment Garik began his monologue about St. Gayane cathedral and our conversation ended.

"I'll talk to you later," I whispered, watching Dr. Famas's closed expression for a few seconds before I turned and settled into my seat. Why would he tell her the KGB wasn't functioning anymore when it was common knowledge they were very much in evidence in Armenia? And for that matter, in all the former Soviet satellite countries. Though it was now the Armenian KGB, it contained many of the same people in the same basic organization as when it was the Soviet KGB. Was he simply trying to keep her from worrying?

I tuned out the questions and tuned in to Garik's narrative on the other famous martyr, St. Gayane, missionary companion of the sainted, murdered Hripsime. Her story closely paralleled that of Hripsime, except she hadn't been proposed to by King Tidates. Just foully murdered like her companions.

The church, barely five minutes from Echmiadzin, seemed far more beautiful to me, even at first glance, than the more famous memorial to Hripsime. Garik informed us this church had been built in A.D. 630 and he made sure I appreciated the lacy-looking edges carved in the arch as we passed beneath it onto the grounds. I marveled again that stone could be carved into such intricate, delicate designs.

Unlike her famous sister's memorial, and even the Father Church at Echmiadzin with their single arched entries, Gayane's memorial had triple arches spread across the wide front and matching alcoves with delicate bell towers on both sides of the covered entry. But inside those arched entries, instead of the normal blocks of stone, long, thin, red bricks formed the arched ceiling. The only other place in the world I'd seen such beautiful and unusual brickwork was in the Boone Hall Plantation outside of Charleston, South Carolina.

Above the door into the church a fading fresco portrayed the presentation of the Christ child in the temple. Fortunately, Mrs. Famas had many questions for Garik, so I wandered along behind, half listening to his answers, until he informed the group we could go down a set of stairs to a little room where Gayane's remains were interred.

I abruptly fled the church for the safety of the courtyard. Absolutely no more dark, confined spaces for me, no matter how famous the person or elaborate their coffin. I preferred the open air, even if it was heavy with mist. Making sure I was truly alone, I wandered in the courtyard and found three ancient khachkars mounted on a marble base. Two of the elaborate stone crosses carved into the massive stones were over fifteen hundred years old; the third dated a mere eight hundred years ago.

Not taking any chances on someone slipping up behind me, I found a sheltered spot against the wall where I could see the entire courtyard, the church, and the long brick buildings behind it that reminded me of Ivy League colleges in the east. Under normal circumstances, I would have been the one next to the tour guide asking all the questions. I loved learning the history of ancient places, hearing the stories that made historical figures come to life. But these were not normal circumstances.

Leaning against the cold stone, I visualized the knife that had cut my purse strap instead of me in Hripsime's tomb below her church. Then I pictured the scene in the Temple of Fire below Echmiadzin's main altar. If the same person wielded that knife—if he had it in his hand as he pressed past Mrs. Famas trying to get to me—I could easily see how her arm had been cut.

As I relaxed, fatigue seeped deep into my bones. Exhaustion over-whelmed me. This was not a physical exhaustion caused by jet lag, but the heavy burden of fear and uncertainty, of not knowing whom I could trust or what waited in the shadow or around the corner. I was weary of people trying to kill me when I didn't know why.

It was one thing to be the target of terrorists because of Anastasia. I could understand their reasons for wanting me dead—me and every other member of our antiterrorist group. But for some reason, it was very different when I had no idea who wanted to terminate my existence. Or why. It was like watching for suicide bombers in the middle of a crowd—any man, woman or child could be the one delivering death.

Life used to be much simpler for the good guys. Criminal profiling helped law enforcement people everywhere catch the bad guys. But everything changed so quickly after September 11, 2001, and even more when people like Saddam Hussein offered huge amounts of money to the families of those who would offer themselves to Allah by becoming suicide bombers and blowing up the unbelieving infidels. Life became a nightmare for everyone.

As a shiver ran through me, I moved away from the cold stone wall. I'd been on my own many times and in many different places in the world, but I didn't remember when I'd felt quite this alone. Was it the dreary weather, the mist that seemed denser, closer, more smothering with each passing hour? I suddenly felt a great need to be surrounded by people. At this moment, even Garik and his group harboring someone with murder in his heart would be welcome company.

I hurried through the swirling mist toward the church, then broke into a run as I reached the huge tree halfway across the courtyard, propelled by an urgency I didn't understand, but one I didn't question.

As I reached the tree, pieces of bark flew everywhere, exploding off the trunk like buckshot. Someone was shooting at me with a silencer on their gun. I didn't stop, didn't even hesitate, just raced faster toward the church, plunging headlong through the mist which I no longer cursed. As I flew past the *khachkars*, pieces of stone pelted me from the first and the third. Finally I reached the safety of the entry arches and slid behind the wide pillar.

I whispered a prayer of thanks for my guardian angels, adding an additional one for continued help, then leaped across the few steps to the heavy wooden doors. They were curved to fit into the arched doorway, split down the middle to open from the center, but I couldn't remember which side had opened, the left or the right. I hit them both, right in the middle, and hoped one side or the other would open quickly and easily. Another too heavy, too slow door could prevent my little Alexandria from entering this mortal existence.

With that thought, adrenalin—or was it pure panic?—surged through me and as I shoved, the door on the right swung open. I plunged through it, right into the astonished arms of Dr. Garik Grigoryan.

"Mrs. Allan." The surprised man could say nothing more as he staggered to maintain his balance and hold me up at the same time.

"My dear, you look like you've just seen a ghost," Mrs. Famas said, reaching out to take my arm and help get me back on my own feet. "Even in this poor light, it looks like you don't have an ounce of blood in your system."

"Maybe she encountered a vampire out there in the fog," Dr. Famas quipped. "Does that mean we all have to find a silver cross and wear garlic around our necks?"

"If it does, you're in luck. I've never seen so many crosses as they have in Armenia so you shouldn't have any problem protecting yourself against vampires." *Protecting yourself against men wielding knives and guns is another story*, I thought, extracting myself from the clinging arms of Garik. "And there were bags and bags of garlic in my *shuka* so it's readily available, too," I added with a smile, pleased to talk about anything that forestalled questions regarding my wild entry to the church.

"Thank you, Dr. Grigoryan, for saving me from scraped knees once again. You always seem to be in just the right place at the right time."

"And you seem to have difficult time staying on feet. Your feet," he added, then laughed out loud that he had made a joke.

I was glad this turned into a lighthearted moment. I didn't want to have to explain what had just transpired in the courtyard, nor alarm Mrs. Famas unduly since she had already been on the receiving end of one attack. I was sure that knife had been meant for me and not for her and that she was in no danger, at least from my assailant. The danger we were all in from what might be happening all over Armenia was quite another story.

If it really was happening. That was a major question. Was Armenia being invaded? That would be the first thing I did when we returned to Yerevan, and I was most anxious to get back and find out. If I could find out. I shook my head. There were always too many *ifs* in my life.

I turned to Garik. "Are we through here? Is this the end of the tour?"

The rest of the group had gathered around their guide and were ready to leave. The press of bodies close around me was comforting at the moment. An unusual feeling for me, as I usually couldn't stand to be in the middle of crowds.

"We have additional stop at Zvartnots Temple ruins," Garik said as he led the group outside. "On road back to Yerevan."

Good. At least we were heading in the right direction. I stayed in the center of the group as we exited the church noting the faces of those surrounding me, some of which were becoming familiar. None looked threatening in the least, but then, that particular face should be outside, not inside. I wanted to see if someone joined the group from out of the mist, and decided the best place to do that would be as we went under the arch. They'd be out of sight, and as the group exited through the arch toward the waiting bus, someone could simply slip back into the crowd and no one would even notice.

I tried to move to the front of the group so I could be one of the first through the arch and watch anyone trying that very thing, but two hefty people plodding in front of me prevented me from doing so. I endeavored to slip around them, but to no avail. I should have been satisfied with my human shield, slow as it was, and thankful for the safety I felt in the middle of the group, but I was filled with impatience at not being able to at least glimpse, if possible, the person determined to kill me.

I failed. We streamed slowly into the bus and I sank exhausted into my seat, too tired to continue my conversation with Mrs. Famas. Too tired, in fact, to even remember what I was going to talk to her about. Since I couldn't see anything out the window because of the mist, I closed my eyes and listened to Garik's narration of our next and last stop—the ruins of an ancient Christian temple built in A.D. 643 and destroyed by an earthquake in the tenth century. Zvartnots had been one of the most beautiful buildings in all of ancient Armenia, which covered considerably more territory in those days than now, taking in almost all of what was now Turkey all the way to the Mediterranean.

My mind wandered from ancient Armenia to contemporary Armenia. Apparently not much had changed during the ensuing millennia. Someone still wanted possession of this last remaining piece of property claimed by the Armenian people, no matter how small their country had become. It was as if someone was determined this part of the world should be all Muslim and the tiny band of Christians was expendable.

And I had brought my precious child right into the line of fire. No wonder Bart had been so upset with me. I sat up in my seat, anxious to get off this bus, anxious to do something, anything, to dispel the feeling of complete helplessness that suddenly swept over me.

Even if terrorists were not at the moment laying claim to the Republic of Armenia, even if al Qaeda was not preparing to occupy the country, and even if Mom's prized paper was never presented and her award received, I needed to get myself and my baby out of Armenia immediately. One thing that was not an *if* was the fact someone very much wanted me dead. And I'd never wanted to live more than right now.

The bus turned off the highway and stopped at an elaborate gated entry, but the gate was closed. The driver honked his off-key horn loud and long, but no one appeared to open the gate. He shrugged, spoke to Garik, apparently received permission to return to Yerevan, and pulled back onto the highway. Garik apologized through his little microphone for the change of plans and promised to add this historic site to one of the other tours the university had planned for the group during the next three months.

While he had everyone's attention, Dr. Grigoryan took the opportunity to give instruction about tomorrow's scheduled events, urging everyone to please check their printed agenda as there were no changes to the program and things would go as outlined for the rest of the week. We'd see about that. I planned to make one change in his agenda. A drastic change affecting both him and me.

Bless him. Garik had the driver drop people at a convenient spot in their neighborhood, so I didn't have to travel the distance from the university alone. One other person stood to get off at my stop on Abovian, a big man, both in stature and girth. I panicked for a moment as he followed me off the bus.

Darting quickly back on under the pretext of a last-minute question for Garik, I watched the man walk briskly up Abovian without a backward glance. Assured that he was truly on his way away from me,

I jumped off the bus and ran up the little alley to my front door, passing a line of ladies selling vegetables out of the bags in which they'd brought them from their gardens.

An assortment of small older model cars lined the parking space in front of my apartment building—and one shiny new big black one with heavily tinted windows. I didn't give it a second glance. I wanted desperately to lock myself behind that heavy door to my apartment and shut out the world. At least, most of the world. I needed to connect with my family, any one of them would do at the moment, but I longed to talk to Bart.

As I ran up the five flights of stairs, I dug my keys out of the bottom of my purse so I wouldn't have to stop and find them when I reached the top. I had locked two of the locks this morning when I left the apartment, so it would require two keys to get in. Some thoughtful person had strung them on a stretchy cord so both could be inserted in locks about five inches apart and turned at the same time, a process requiring two hands.

Mentally blessing the person who designed shoulder bags that freed your hands for other things, I inserted the keys and shoved the heavy door open, happy and relieved to be back in my safe haven once again. At least I hoped it was a safe haven. I stopped momentarily in the doorway to see if I could hear anyone in the apartment. Hearing nothing, and feeling a sense of safety, I closed and locked the door behind me.

I kicked off my shoes, then ran through the apartment, turning on every light in the place. I'd had enough of dark dismal corners today. I mentally wrote my agenda for the rest of the day. Number one: get comfortable; two: find something to eat. I was starving. And three: get on the phone—if I could—and connect with my family. Bart and my father might be a challenge—they were frequently inaccessible, but Mom should be available to the phone, held captive in her hospital bed by her injury. Then book the next flight out of here on whatever plane left the country first, no matter the destination.

I started to change clothes, but felt the chill in the room when I took my suit jacket off, so I put it back on and dug in my suitcase for my slippers. While I searched, I added one more item to my agenda. A long, hot shower, as soon as I'd completed my mental to-do list.

When I couldn't find them in my suitcase, I thought I'd forgotten to pack my slippers, but finally discovered them at the very bottom of the case. Then I remembered they were the only items left in my suitcase when someone unpacked it for me—all over my bedroom in Santa Barbara.

Slipping my foot into the first one, I encountered something hard in the toe. Puzzled, I turned the slipper upside down. Two huge rubies tumbled into my hand. I just stood and stared at them, unable to believe what I saw. Before my dazed mind could comprehend the implications—the significance, the import—of my find, someone knocked on my door.

CHAPTER 16

The quiet but persistent sound intensified the shock of my discovery. I crept quietly to the door and peeked through the peephole expecting to see a face looking back at me. All I could see was the door across the hall. Then movement down in the corner caught my eye.

A child huddled close to the door, tapping a quiet staccato and whispering something I couldn't hear well enough to understand, even to discern what language was being spoken.

Should I or shouldn't I? One part of me said open it and find out what the child wants. The other part was aghast that I would even consider opening the door.

Then I heard my name whispered, "Meesus Ollon." Maybe this was the contact Bart said would get me out of the country. But a child? Maybe the child was sent so whoever was watching my apartment would not suspect I was being contacted. I couldn't ignore this possibility of help, no matter how loudly my cautious, inner self screamed.

I unlocked the door and it flew open, nearly knocking me backwards off my feet. But it wasn't a child that pushed his way into my apartment and locked the door behind him. It was the little, dark gypsy man I'd seen in the alley.

"Meesus Ollon, KGB come. Put on shoes. We go." He headed into the living room and turned, waiting for me to follow. When I didn't move, he commanded, "Now. They wait for you downstairs. You come home. They come here."

I remembered the big black car parked in front of the building. Then I heard voices in the stairwell and footsteps pounding up the stairs.

"I'm coming!" I grabbed my purse, dropped the rubies into it, and slipped into my shoes, snatching my raincoat from the rack in the hall as I followed the little man into the living room. He had the balcony door open and was waiting for me atop the railing of the balcony. I pulled the doors shut behind me and climbed onto the railing, holding tight to the steel pole supporting the metal awning overhead.

Balancing on the cement railing four stories above the ground, I felt like the tightwire walker in a circus. The gypsy balancing in front of me didn't detract from that image in the least. We traversed the six-inch concrete balustrade for ten feet or so before we jumped down onto the neighbor's balcony.

His plan suddenly became obvious. The building was designed in a U-shape, with a separate entrance for each section of the "U." We could escape through the other entrance.

The gypsy tapped on the door and when there was no answer, he opened it anyway, motioning me to follow him into the apartment. I didn't even hesitate. I could plainly hear the pounding on my door, almost as loud as the pounding of my heart.

Apparently the strange little man had been here before. He went immediately to the front door through a series of rooms, opening each door into the next room and leaving me to shut it behind me as he hurried on. I stayed right on his heels all the way, not stopping to examine the décor and furnishings, but feeling I'd gone back in time about fifty years as we swept through the interesting apartment.

Manipulating the locks on the door, he pulled it open a crack, listened, then flung the door open wide and without a backward glance, hurried out into the hall and down the stairs. I closed the door quietly and followed as close behind him as I could stay. As he reached each landing, he grasped the iron railing and swung himself around the corner to the next set of stairs, reducing the number of steps he had to take on his descent.

He reached the bottom a full flight of stairs before me, stood half-hidden in the doorway looking up and down the alley until I'd caught up with him, then darted down the half dozen steps to the street and headed for the *shuka*, glancing over his shoulder only once to make sure I was still with him. We ran through the vegetable *shuka* and out the back entrance, then through another alley to a street I'd never been on before.

My strange little guide stopped, looked up and down the misty street, then pointed at the intersection to the left. "That is park. Walk in park. Stay out of sight. I meet you in Opera Square in two hours."

"Where in Opera Square?"

"I find you. You disappear while I handle KGB." With that, the man turned and vanished into a crevice between two buildings that looked only big enough for a cat to slip through.

He'd disappeared. I'd better do the same. I hurried down the street toward the park, dodging a *marshutka* that suddenly pulled out in front of me as I stepped into the street. I jumped back up on the sidewalk, frightened as much by his blaring horn as the proximity of his battered van to my knocking knees.

Safely crossing with a couple of brave Armenians who hurried to the center of the street and waited with cars streaming by on both sides until the other lane was empty, I tried to get lost among people enjoying a leisurely stroll in the fog. Most were lovers, arms tightly entwined, gazing into each other's eyes as they meandered along the curved sidewalks, oblivious to the statues and fountains and other people in the park.

When I reached the center of the park, I felt safe enough to stop, sit at a table under a bright red umbrella by a beautiful pond with fountains and study my map of Yerevan. This wasn't a time to wander aimlessly. I needed to know exactly where I was and where I was going, and have a general idea of escape routes.

As I unfolded the tourist map I kept tucked in the pocket of my purse, a waitress approached me. Having no idea of the offerings available since there was no menu, I ordered a Fanta Limon and a bag of popcorn, both of which I could see from my table. The man with the popcorn vending machine scooped delicious-smelling fresh popcorn into a clear plastic bag. Not what I'd had in mind for dinner, but certainly not an unpleasant substitute.

I spread the map on the checkered tablecloth and searched for street names I recognized. Fortunately, Garik had chosen a map that showed buildings and trees and even statues and fountains, the caricatured kind you buy at the airport for a souvenir. Very helpful to someone like me who knew only a few main streets and fewer landmarks.

The city was laid out in a circle, with a block-wide park forming a horseshoe-shaped greenbelt around the inner portion of it. At the top end of the horseshoe, the fifty-meter-high monument to fifty years of Soviet domination of Armenia towered over the Cascades. The Cascades, a series of marble steps and fountains, led from the monument down the hill toward the round opera and ballet house.

With my finger, I traced the park until I found the cement tube sticking out of the ground that was the Yeritasardakan Metro Station across the street from my alley. Following the green belt to the next block with my finger, I located the mast and stylized big blue sail I could see at the restaurant across the pond from where I now sat.

The waitress brought my Fanta Limon, poured it ceremoniously into a small glass and left my popcorn in the bag on the checkered tablecloth, apparently uncertain how popcorn should be served graciously. Nibbling popcorn, I studied the streets, alleys, and landmarks around the famous circular opera building that housed the Armenian Philharmonic Symphony in one half and the Armenian National Ballet Company in the other.

Satisfied that I could find my way around this area of the city without getting lost, and having identified several approaches to my apartment, I decided it was time to put my new knowledge to the test. A bird's eye view from a map with numbers identifying everything was not the same as walking the streets and locating those same buildings without the little round numbers printed on them.

I stayed in the safety of the center of the park until the park ended, then crossed the street, heading for Opera Square a few short blocks away. The mist had turned into a light rain and brightly colored umbrellas popped up everywhere. I didn't have one.

As I crossed a triangular shaped park leading to the Opera House, the hair on the back of my neck stood up, causing shivers down my back. I paused to examine a statue of a man leaning on a tree branch and looked behind me. People strolled on by under their umbrellas or hurried past me without any covering from the rain, but no one seemed interested in me. Still, I felt the unquiet stirring of things not quite right.

I hurried on through the park and waited with a group of people for the traffic light to change so we could cross the busy street. Another crowd of people lined the sidewalk waiting for *marshutkas*, straining to see the number of their route in the window of the van. Maybe I could hop on one of those and ride the route. That should get me out of the area for a couple of hours. But what if I got on the wrong *marshutka* and it headed out into the country instead of staying in the city? And what if the little gypsy man came for me before the two hours expired? Better do as he said and go to Opera Square.

Who was the strange little man? Was he my contact, or just someone my contact had sent? He wasn't someone who could get lost in a crowd, or was he? Most people don't really pay much attention to "street people" if they are going about their business.

I reached Opera Square and explored the grounds, beginning in front at the unique statue of the composer Aram Kachatryan with a robe across his lap, the man for whom this portion of the opera was named. As an excuse to look around, I stopped every few feet to study whatever thing of interest appeared. That nagging little feeling persisted that I was being followed but whoever it might be, he was good, as I couldn't spot him.

Lively music emanated from a sidewalk café along one side of the opera where couples snuggled at tables under red umbrellas sipping from tiny cups of steaming liquid. A delightfully romantic spot before or after a performance at the ballet or symphony. Would Bart and I ever lead lives that would allow us to enjoy leisurely hours like that?

I rounded another portion of the huge circular building and stopped at a statue atop a tall pedestal. I couldn't see the man for rain and mist but remembered from the tourist information in Mom's briefcase there were two statues on this side of the square: an author, Tumanyan, and a composer and conductor, Spendarian, after whom this half of the building was named.

I stopped midway between the statues in the middle of the circle where sidewalks converged from three points into the large paved area. People crisscrossed the open area, hurrying to their destinations, probably a nice warm dry place where someone waited who loved them. How I wished I had someone waiting in my apartment that loved me—instead of the KGB.

An old man and his son loaded tricycles, bicycles with training wheels, and kiddie cars into a battered homemade trailer. Not much business on a rainy evening. Who wanted to play in the rain?

I looked for the little Swan Lake with its famous statue I'd seen on the map, then hurried on around the remaining portion of the building, discovering a bar and restaurant under the opera house. A place to wait for my little gypsy man? A little shiver quivered through me. No, not here. It didn't feel right, so I continued my tour until I discovered the ticket kiosk. A short line of people waited to buy tickets, and a crowd coursed toward the front doors.

That would be a perfect spot to hide. An evening at the opera. If he didn't find me outside, would the gypsy look for me inside? Why not? Not knowing or caring what I saw, only that I would be safely off the streets and lost in the middle of a crowd of people, I watched the man in front of me put 4000 drams through the window and receive a ticket. I did the same, then followed him through the crowd and into the famed opera house.

What a wonderful place this must have been when there was still money in Yerevan to pay for upkeep. Crystal chandeliers hung in the high-ceilinged halls that were in need of a coat of paint, and worn Persian carpets led up the marble stairs to the second floor. I stared out the floor-to-ceiling windows that overlooked the misty park below filled with statues and fountains. This must have been one of the most beautiful, enchanting cities in the world about 1988, while Russian money still flowed freely here.

I examined my ticket, couldn't read anything on it except numbers that I assumed was my seat number, and showed it to a matron who seemed to be directing people to their seats. She pointed to the wide stairway and I melted into the crowd of people streaming up the stairs. Many people were speaking Russian and I gathered from snatches of conversation the philharmonic symphony would perform tonight with a guest pianist. I'd enjoy that.

The disquiet I'd felt outside disappeared now that I was safely surrounded by throngs of people. Maybe my mind had been playing tricks on me. Maybe no one had followed me at all.

A matron with coal black hair piled atop her head guided me to a seat in the middle of a long row, telling me in Russian she hoped I would enjoy the performance. It was not a seat I'd have chosen, though the view was good and I could clearly see every musician and instrument on the stage below. But there was no quick and easy escape. At best, I'd be hemmed in on all sides by patrons, unable to leave if I needed to. At worst—I really didn't want to think about that.

Since there was no safety in my apartment or on the street, I could only hope I'd escaped detection and could relax for a while without further attempts on my life. I desperately needed a breather from bad guys and fervently hoped this would be the safe harbor I sought.

People from about fifty years old and older were all speaking Russian. The younger ones, for the most part, conversed in what I assumed was Armenian since I couldn't understand what they were saying. I saw a few Americans in the audience, heard a smattering of Italian and German, and even heard a couple of students practicing their Spanish on each other.

As the orchestra tuned up, I relaxed, enjoying the cacophony of sounds from below and the bits and pieces of conversations going on around me. The seats on either side of me remained empty as the audience hushed, awaiting the appearance of the conductor. Feeling a satisfying sense of safety for the first time all day, I removed my coat and settled in to enjoy the performance.

Removing the little polemoscope from my purse, I pointed it at the orchestra and studied the patrons on either side while they thought I watched the musicians. I turned slightly in each direction to watch the audience file in. Hiding in the audience at the symphony may have been a good decision. I didn't see a single threatening face in the crowd.

I glanced at my watch. 7:10 P.M. So much for starting on time. Garik had said Armenians weren't noted for being on time, but I noticed most people were in their seats, with only a few stragglers scrambling down the aisles to slip into their seats before the symphony began.

I did observe a number of people who had the wrong seats. They simply shrugged their shoulders and left quietly when a patron with a ticket claimed that seat. After watching two young women ousted from three different sets of seats, I decided they were trying for a better seat than the one assigned them on their ticket. Apparently seat-hopping was a common practice.

The conductor finally appeared to enthusiastic applause, but whether it was because of his popularity or that his appearance signaled

the beginning of the concert, I couldn't tell. He was young, slightly
built, with very black hair. He gave a slight bow to the audience, turned
his back and faced his musicians, shaking hands with the white-haired
concertmaster, then raised both hands and plunged into the first movement of one of Beethoven's symphonies—without a copy of the music.
I'd never seen a conductor who had memorized an entire score.

I watched with fascination as he led the different instruments
through their parts, pointing first to the French horns, then flutes as
their solos approached. This was not a small group of musicians. I
began counting the instruments: twenty-six violins, seven violas, six
cellos, and eight big bass. I never got to the brass and reed instruments
or percussion. As I finished counting the stringed instruments, movement just off the stage to the right of the bass caught my eye. Someone
came in late and found his seat filled. There was something familiar
about him. I looked a second time. The man in the navy jacket.

My heart pounded. I took a deep breath and held it, afraid to
breathe lest the slightest movement up here would cause him to look
up and see me. Or had he already seen me? Was his appearance at the
symphony a coincidence or had he been following me?

I looked both ways on my row of seats, trying to find the
quickest, easiest exit. There wasn't one. What a mistake this turned
out to be. I envisioned tomorrow's headlines, "Murder at the Opera."
Sounded like a Margaret Truman novel.

While I was thinking things couldn't get much worse, being
trapped in a narrow row of seats with no escape except over the toes
of patrons, in plain view of the man I suspected had been following
me ever since my arrival in Armenia, a commotion on the center aisle
of my row caught my attention.

Someone attempted to pass the dozen or so patrons to occupy the
empty seat next to me. I only had time for a quick glimpse of the
person before the bulky man next to the empty seat stood to allow
the latecomer to reach his seat. Silver gray suit, purple shirt, lavender
tie, black hair. I didn't get to see the face, but had the general impression of a tall, neatly dressed Armenian.

Why was he so intent on getting to this seat when there were
others more easily accessible? My first instinct was to flee in the other
direction, but that would call unwanted attention to myself. I leaned

my elbow on the armrest and shielded my face with my hand, pretending to be engrossed in the performance. If I could have shrunken like Alice in Wonderland to the size of a mouse and scurried out of the hall, I'd have gladly done it.

The first two minutes after he settled into his seat were quiet and uneventful. I'd almost lost myself in the marvelous music of Beethoven when the man tried to share the armrest with me. I quickly surrendered it and leaned toward the empty seat on my left. He stretched his long legs sideways, encroaching on my space. I ignored him.

Another few minutes of the symphony passed without incident, until I felt his leg press against mine. Granted, he didn't have enough space to be comfortable in his own seat area, and he certainly couldn't turn the other way as the huge man sitting next to him took more than his share of the limited space available, but he didn't need to touch me. I was huddled on the far side of my seat from him as it was. But I could solve the problem. At the first break in the music, I could move to the empty seat on my left.

I glanced at my watch. We were fifteen minutes into the symphony. This portion should end in five to ten minutes, at which time I might even be able to exit the whole row. If not, at least I could put one seat between those long legs and me.

When several minutes passed uneventfully, I began to relax and be immersed in the music once again. Suddenly I felt a shoulder against mine. The man had not only taken over the armrest, he was leaning so heavily on it his broad shoulders extended beyond his seat.

Thank heaven the first portion of the concert ended. The audience burst into enthusiastic applause and people began popping up in a standing ovation. As the spectators around us stood, I jumped to my feet, clapping my hands in the measured beat the audience used, and slipped in front of the empty seat next to me. The long-legged man rose to his feet and shifted slightly, standing with one foot in front of his seat and one foot in front of the seat I had just abandoned.

When the audience resumed their seats, I took the empty one on my left. The tall man settled into my former seat! As I prepared to jump and run, the conductor raised his arms and the music began. I was furious. First someone had tried to kill me with a car, then a knife, then a gun, and now someone was trying to pester me to death.

I clenched my hands in my lap, trying to decide whether to just ignore him or cause a major disturbance by leaving. When the next few minutes passed without further incident, I decided the man was simply an inconsiderate bore who hadn't realized he encroached on my space. Shrugging the tension out of my shoulders, I allowed the haunting melody to carry me back into the symphony and temporarily forget the man in the navy jacket and even the nuisance sitting next to me.

Suddenly his long arm reached over and his hand covered mine. That was the last straw. Picking up his heavy hand, I dropped it in his lap and turned to glare at the boldly impudent, presumptuous male next to me.

I looked up into two azure blue, laughing eyes above a stubble of dark beard. My heart nearly stopped. I turned quickly away, confused and flustered. It couldn't be. I peeked back, but the man had turned away leaning his head on his hand, apparently intent on the music. I couldn't even see his profile.

Puzzled and intrigued, I watched him out of the corner of my eye. He didn't move, keeping his face hidden by his hand. I was tempted to take over the armrest. That would force him to change positions and remove the hand shielding his face.

I retrieved the polemoscope and, pretending to study the orchestra again, watched him carefully to see if what I suspected— what I hoped—was true.

As the music swelled to a crescendo, my eye was drawn back to the musicians and the percussion instruments doing their thing. The kettle drummer took his cue and rolled his drums into a thunderous swell. The cymbalist anticipated his big moment with instruments raised to strike and I leaned forward to watch him. As the cymbals resounded across the hall, my seat felt like someone kicked it. I turned to see what happened and was stunned to discovered a huge hole next to my shoulder in the padded upholstery.

The man sitting next to me whispered hoarsely, "Get out of here quick. Someone is shooting at you."

CHAPTER 17

As the music reached a deafening climax, the audience jumped to their feet in an enthusiastic ovation. I turned to look at the man with the strange accent. He leaned toward me and pretended to cough in his hand.

"Don't look at me. Go out the other way. Now," he commanded.

That command removed all doubt about the identity of the stranger next to me. I grabbed my raincoat and turned quickly, stumbling past the applauding patrons, squeezing between them and the seats too close in front of them to allow easy exit. When I reached the aisle, I didn't look back to see if Bart followed—I just fled toward the exit.

Only then did I notice the armed guards slipping in during the applause, taking their places at every exit. As I hurried toward the double doors at the top of the balcony, I could see patrons glancing uneasily around, whispering about the unexpected uniformed presence. If they were here because of the shot, they were incredibly fast. If they were here because of me, I was in big trouble.

When the matron at the door looked like she was going to block my way, I put my hand over my mouth, and grabbed my stomach. She immediately threw both doors open and stepped aside. A young guard had moved forward, as if to stop me, but he too, quickly stepped aside to let me pass.

I raced down the empty hallway, keeping my hand to my mouth and my arm wrapped around my stomach. It had worked once to get me past the guards. I wasn't naive enough to believe there wouldn't be more on the ground floor I'd have to bypass before I could reach the safety of the square.

"Safety" of the square? Hardly. Hurrying down the fading carpets on the marble stairs, I almost laughed. As far as I could tell, nowhere in Armenia was safe, at least for me. Wherever I'd been, someone followed with murder in mind. My murder.

As I reached the bottom of the stairs, a fresh contingent of uniformed guards entered the opera house. I felt the blood drain from my face as their leader turned to watch my progression toward him. I renewed my act, hoping the fear that clutched at my stomach translated to a fear of being sick in the opera house, not fear at being stopped.

I threw in a good imitation of a retch for his benefit and pretended to look frantically around for a container. At his brusque command, his men immediately parted, leaving an aisle for me to pass through—straight out the door. I raced down the stairs to a grassy area and performed what they would expect to see if they still watched me. I didn't imagine for a minute that I wasn't under surveillance; just wasn't sure if they'd followed me.

I pulled a tissue from my purse, and turning around to see, wiped my face, as I would have done had I truly been sick. Two uniformed men stood just outside the entrance watching my performance. But what were the uniforms they wore? Army? City police? The security guards I'd seen at the metro wore similar attire. How did you tell who was what?

I slipped into my red raincoat and sat on the park bench under the nearest tree. Keeping up my act, I rocked slowly back and forth holding my stomach. The rain had almost stopped, the mist had dissipated slightly, but the gloom of dusk now settled across the dimly lit square.

The captain of the guard appeared in the doorway with a brute of a man by his side towering over him. He nodded toward me. Uh, oh. I jumped to my feet and turned to the grass again, giving what I hoped was a convincing performance. I grasped the back of the bench as if for support, then slowly turned around and collapsed on it, wiping my face with another tissue. Apparently satisfied with my act, the guards disappeared back inside the opera house.

My next dilemma was what to do now. My husband said to leave, but he hadn't said where to go. Should I wait here and make it easy for him to find me? Or should I leave before the man with the gun came looking for me?

The gypsy told me to wait for him at the Square. I'd trusted him and had arrived safely at the opera. But whom had he sent to find me—my husband or the gunman? Had the gypsy set me up? Or had the gunman found me on his own? If I hid too well, I might escape the person intent on killing me, but I might also elude those I wanted to find me.

Far too many questions and too few answers.

A man in a long black coat suddenly appeared out of the mist, walking briskly on by me. He didn't slow or turn to look at me, but said simply, "Follow me—at a distance," and hurried on around the opera house toward the sidewalk café.

I stood, turned to depart in the opposite direction, then looking around as if I discovered I was going the wrong way, I turned and followed my husband. His long legs allowed him to cover a great deal more distance than my short ones, so as soon as I was out of sight of the guards, I ran to catch up. I couldn't stand the thought of losing Bart now that I'd found him. It would be so easy to do in the mist and gathering darkness.

Keeping a distance between us wasn't hard. Keeping up with him was. I mentally tracked us on the map I'd studied, trying to figure out where we were going. I followed him through another sidewalk café, a bright spot in the dark filled with patrons, glowing lights, and lively music.

Bart exited Opera Square through high, wrought iron gates and hurried across the busy intersection, stopping at a flower kiosk on the corner. How did he know without turning around that I didn't make the traffic light and had to wait for a stream of cars before I could follow him? I kept one eye on him and one eye on the traffic. Apparently he watched traffic too, because as soon as I stepped into the street, he immediately set off down the sidewalk at his usual fast clip.

Halfway down the block Bart crossed the street. I raced between cars and *marshutkas* to the other side, barely keeping him in sight. How could I watch my footing on the uneven brick sidewalk and see where my husband was going at the same time? If he stepped off the sidewalk into a store or alley as I glanced down to make sure I wasn't stepping into one of the frequent holes in the sidewalk, I could easily lose him.

Dodging a group of boys spread arm in arm across the breadth of the sidewalk, I panicked when I looked up again and couldn't see Bart ahead of me. *He won't leave you*, I reassured myself. *He'll know if you aren't there. He'll wait.*

I hurried to the corner, but still couldn't see him. Had he crossed the street or turned the corner, or stopped somewhere along the way? I stopped, waiting just outside the dim light of a street lamp, hoping for some clue as to which way to go.

Out of a darkened doorway on my right, the most welcome voice in the world spoke quietly to me. "Cross to the other side of the street, then turn right. We have a block and a half to go."

Relief flooded through me. I waited for a car to turn the corner, then crossed at the intersection, and turned right. This was not a major street and there were no street lamps to light the way, just lights from a couple of shops. Confident that my husband knew where I was, even if I didn't know exactly where he was, I slowed my pace, being careful of the uneven sidewalk and unexpected missing bricks.

When I reached the corner, I crossed the street and continued straight ahead, hoping Bart would intercept me at the proper time. I panicked again when my sidewalk came to an end in a parking lot of a tall apartment building. I paused, uncertain where to go from there. From the darkness behind a van, an arm reached out and grabbed me, pulling me into a smothering embrace.

I threw my arms around Bart's neck and clung to him, laughing and crying at the same time I was so happy and relieved to be with him. He kissed my tear-wet cheeks and covered my mouth with kisses until a quiet voice from the darkness interrupted. "We go now."

I jumped, startled to hear the unexpected voice so close behind my husband.

"We'll follow you," Bart said, moving aside so the man could get by.

He headed toward what appeared to be a dilapidated high-rise apartment building, skirted a travel agency and a computer store on the bottom floor, then turned a corner and entered an unfinished dimly lit portion of the building. He waited for us in the dirty, malodorous, concrete entry that had an opening for a door and window, but both were missing or had never been installed.

I couldn't quite put my finger on all the unbearable odors, but it seemed a bad combination of too many stray cats, sour milk, and heavy stale cigarette smoke. A frightening-looking elevator opened off to the left and a stairway beside it led to the many-storied apartments above. I was relieved when the man opened the door directly in front of us. Thank heaven I didn't have to get in that elevator. It didn't look like it could make it up one story, much less the dozen or so to the top of the building.

As our guide stepped aside so we could enter the open door, he noticed my wrinkled nose. "Sorry for smell. We move to new building soon. Welcome to Yerevan Branch of Church of Jesus Christ of Latter-day Saints."

We entered a narrow hall about ten feet long with a door at the end. Music emanated from a door on the left, a familiar hymn in an unfamiliar language. Once inside with the door shut, the unpleasant odor disappeared.

Bart introduced me to Norik his Armenian contact, with an unnerving statement that sounded like deathbed instructions. "I trust this man with my life, but more than that, I trust him with your life and Alexandria's. Whatever happens here, do as he says."

An involuntary shudder ran through me at Bart's almost ominous words, but as I shook hands with the stout, round-faced man in front of me, Norik's warm smile put me instantly at ease. His piercing dark eyes radiated intelligence and deep laugh-lines crinkled the corners.

"I'm happy to meet you," I said sincerely.

"I give you five minutes. Then we go." Thrusting a bouquet of peach rosebuds at Bart which he'd held behind his back, Norik turned and parted heavy tapestry curtains, revealing a long room with rows of wooden chairs. He disappeared behind the curtains and I could hear a child's voice above a quiet murmur of other voices.

I rushed into Bart's arms and clung to him, trying to keep from smashing the beautiful flowers between us. "When did you get here? How did you find me? Why didn't you call me?" I looked up into those wonderful azure eyes. "How did you get a black beard?"

Bart put his finger to my lips to stop the flow of questions. "Whoa. Save the questions. Just listen for a minute. I didn't call because all communications are down."

Like a bucket of cold water, fear washed away my high spirits at seeing my husband. "Then it's true? Armenia is being invaded?"

"Infiltrated might be more accurate at the moment, but it is a precursor to an invasion." Bart's eyes narrowed. "Unless we can stop it in the next forty-eight hours."

"We?" Had Bart changed his mind about my leaving the country? "You and me?"

"No. You're on your way out of Armenia as fast as I can get you out, though it probably won't be tonight. Norik is taking his family to safety in the mountains. We're going along so I can get you to Tbilisi. You'll fly home. I'll work with Norik and his people to stop the incursion of terrorists before they can whip the local political rebels into organized action and complete their takeover."

Disappointment and relief vied for top billing on my emotional thermometer: disappointment at not being included and able to work with Bart again, and relief that I might get safely home without endangering my baby.

Bart didn't give me a chance to reply. "Norik's family is here, ready to go. Hope you've got everything important with you because you're not going back to the apartment. The place is swarming with KGB. What did you do to get them all riled up?"

"What did I do? As far as I can tell, I just came to Armenia." Then I remembered the rubies in my purse. "Oh! I think I've got the stolen rubies."

"What rubies?" Bart shook his head in disbelief. "Stolen from where?"

I handed Bart my beautiful bouquet of peach roses. While I dug in my purse to find the rubies and the article, I briefly sketched the story beginning with Mom's "accident" on the front steps, the break-in at the estate, and the assassination of the FBI agent assigned to watch her, concluding with the four attempts on my life.

"Five," Bart corrected. "You didn't mention the near miss at the opera."

I dug to the bottom of my purse and produced the rubies, the "Dick Tracy" watches I'd forgotten were there, and the article. Bart scanned the printed sheet while I examined the rubies, mentally replacing them in their respective crosses. The largest one would go in the center of the cross with the four emeralds at the cross points.

Bart tore the paper into shreds. "I'll get rid of this. If we're stopped, you might explain the rubies if they're found, but not if they see this article. How did you get them?"

I told him about finding the clothes all over the floor I'd packed for the trip, except my slippers, in which I'd discovered the rubies a scant two hours ago.

"Stash them somewhere besides your purse. That's the first place they'll look if we're stopped."

I did have a zippered pocket in my raincoat, but the rubies weren't exactly tiny objects that would escape detection in a shakedown. That done, I handed Bart his portion of the matching pair of watches a friend had fashioned for us to use in our work with Interpol.

"I didn't know if I'd have a need for these, but here you are, in the flesh, and here is your watch. I assume the satellites will be up and running soon and if we actually need these, we'll be able to use them."

Bart strapped the communications watch on his wrist. "I need to have him devise one that uses the sun instead of relying on satellites so I'll be able to keep track of you all the time. You're such an unpredictable creature, I never know where you'll turn up next."

"That's like the pot calling the kettle black. I never know where you'll turn up next, but I'm sure glad you turned up here—and now."

The curtains parted at that moment and Norik led his family into the hall, introducing Narine, his petite dark-eyed, dark-haired wife, their teenage son, LeVon, and Maggie, a bright-eyed shy little girl I guessed to be about eight or nine years old. Each of them carried an overnight case or backpack and a plastic shopping bag

"We go." Norik spoke like Dr. Garik Grigoryan. No articles.

Bart was about to toss the bouquet of roses into a wastebasket near the door when it opened and chattering young adults spilled into the hallway. Seeing that I was going to lose the flowers anyway, I caught them before he could act, and gave them to the first young woman I saw. Narine greeted her as she passed, calling her Milena.

"Here, Milena, these are for you. Enjoy." I thrust the bouquet into the surprised young woman's hand and hurried down the hall behind Norik and his family, urged on by my edgy husband. "Thank you for the roses, Romeo. You even remembered my favorite color. Were you just marking time while I crossed the street and that gave you something to do or . . ."

Bart interrupted my question with a quick kiss and hustled me out the door. I glimpsed a gleam in his eye before we stepped into the foul smelling, dingy entry. "What do you think?" he asked.

"I'll regard it as a thoughtful, considerate act by a loving husband." I linked arms with his as we hurried down the steps into the parking lot.

"Good, because that's what it was." Bart leaned down and kissed my nose. "Princess, I can't tell you how good it is to see you. I just wish . . ."

Norik interrupted him. "We go to meet van. You follow, but not too close." The four of them left the parking lot, walking quickly in the opposite direction from which we had just come. We waited until they were into the alley, then followed.

Light rain fell in a soft, silent mist as we dodged puddles illuminated only by the lights from tiny stone houses lining the ever-narrowing alley. Within a few minutes, the alley opened into a narrow strip of park with one dim lamppost in the center. Norik and his family turned right at a large statue in the park. Bart and I waited in the shadows until they entered a huge, black hole underneath a tall building built on the hill above it. From where we stood, which was probably three stories under the glassed-in lobby, I could see beautiful chandeliers with only a few bulbs lit. This once beautiful building now had a very shabby appearance.

As soon as they disappeared, Bart and I hurried across the end of the park and followed them into the tunnel. Light fixtures zigzagged on the high ceiling the entire length of the tunnel, but so few worked now I could barely see the next few feet in front of me. I did see the outline of a young man who appeared to be waiting for us.

"I will go with you to show where we meet the van," LeVon said, as we approached him. Then he turned and hurried to stay close enough behind his family to see them. We caught up to him.

"Where does this lead?" I whispered. I couldn't see the end of the tunnel, only that it sloped gently downhill.

"To Children's Railway Park on the gorge," LeVon answered quietly. "The van should be waiting for us when we get there."

"What is the building on top?"

"The main post office." LeVon spoke nearly perfect English.

I had a dozen other questions, but decided silence was preferred at the moment. The tunnel stretched on endlessly with every sound echoing and amplified. Just when I thought we were going to walk all night, LeVon slowed, then stopped. I peered into the darkness. The mouth of the tunnel was barely discernible a few feet ahead of us.

Rain pounded the street outside. How long had we been in the passage? It seemed hours but was probably not more than ten or fifteen minutes. In the dark, and in strange new surroundings, time and distance take on different dimensions.

We stood at the mouth of the tunnel against one wall, waiting for a signal. Wherever we were, it was not a main traffic area, either pedestrian or vehicular. Just as I supposed the place to be void of any other people, I heard a sound on the opposite side of the tunnel. My heart drummed as I clutched Bart's hand and peered into the darkness. Someone was there. Someone waiting for us? The contact to get us out of town? Or the KGB to keep us here? Where were Norik and Narine?

No one moved on either side of the tunnel. Were we playing a waiting game, to see which side would reveal themselves first?

Suddenly the crunch of tires signaled an approaching car. With headlights off, the vehicle pulled right to the entrance of the tunnel and stopped. I sidled closer to Bart. The defining moment arrived. We could either be whisked out of town and on our way to safety, or we could be on our way to a very unpleasant and possibly painful interrogation by the KGB. The third possibility entered my mind but I banished it. Bin Laden's men would love to get their hands on a couple of Anastasia's agents. They would make a KGB confrontation seem like a confab of kissing cousins.

I held my breath as the door opened and footsteps crunched on the gravel.

"Norik?"

"We are here," Norik answered softly.

LeVon, Bart, and I hurried across the passage and joined Norik and Narine on the other side.

"Please to get in quickly," Norik instructed his family in rapid-fire Russian, and LeVon and Maggie climbed into the van, each taking a row of seats in the back, LeVon furthest back. Maggie fluffed a pillow she found on her seat, curled up and pulled a blanket over her, ready to go to sleep. Narine took the first seat, closest to the driver, and Norik climbed in beside her, pointing at the front seat beside the driver for us.

He introduced Ruben as the best driver in Armenia, then amended his description with a short laugh. "Maybe fastest driver is better." I squeezed in between the two big men, wondering why I needed to be up front when there was so much room in the back.

Norik answered my unspoken question as Ruben slipped the van into gear and eased away from the tunnel. "We make one stop before we leave city. Narine's sister and mother come with us."

"Where are we going?" I asked as Ruben maneuvered the van up a winding entryway, between parked cars and out onto the street.

No one answered. Bart, Norik, and Ruben concentrated on the street ahead and beside us. I glanced in the rearview mirror. LeVon watched out the back window and Narine nervously leaned forward to stare out the front, then turned frequently to look behind. The silence was oppressive; the suspense even more so.

We wound through darkened side streets, avoiding the lighted main roads where the traffic was heaviest, and, I thought, where the chances of being stopped would be greatest. I was about to ask Bart if it were permissible to talk, when Ruben pulled into an alley across from a plaza containing a brightly lit, many-tiered fountain and stopped at an entrance behind the building.

"Do you need some help?" Bart asked.

"You stay," Norik said as he and Narine jumped out and ran into the building. Ruben stepped out of the van to adjust the windshield wiper.

"Why all the silence?" I whispered, not wanting Maggie and LeVon to hear, just in case they were the reason no one was talking.

Bart slipped his arm around me and pulled me close to him, speaking softly into my ear. "They've lived with fear of authority all their lives. The Soviets were hard taskmasters who rewarded any kind of initiative with prison sentences. Norik worked at two places as an electrician to support his family. That wasn't allowed. Only one job per person, so the communists slammed him in prison for a few years. Everyone had their boundaries and no one stepped outside of them without suffering severe consequences."

"But those days are over," I whispered. "Surely they can come and go as they please now."

"Probably, unless they encounter the Mafia which controls the commerce and the KGB which controls everything else."

"It would be terrible to live with fear all your life. It makes me feel guilty for having such a happy, carefree childhood."

Bart kissed my ear. "You were pretty spoiled all right, and I intend to spoil Alexandria even more." Suddenly his arms surrounded me and pulled me hard against him. "When I think how any one of those attempts on your life could have . . ."

I silenced his lips with mine. I didn't want to think about it either, any more than I wanted to think about what lay ahead in the next few hours. I just wanted to enjoy the here and now, feeling safe and secure in the arms of my husband.

The van door opening startled me. No introductions were made as a woman about Narine's age climbed quickly in with her bundles and settled next to LeVon on the back seat. Narine helped her mother into the seat next to her as Ruben climbed back into the driver's seat and started the van, not waiting for Norik to shut the door. Norik slid it shut as we pulled out of the alley and back onto the street.

"Now we go to Dilijan," Norik said, and I thought I detected a more relaxed tone in his voice. Narine conversed quietly with her mother in Russian, getting her settled with a blanket across her legs and placing the little bag of belongings she'd brought with her where she could reach out and touch it.

Bart leaned behind me and in a low voice so no one else could hear, dropped what turned out to be a bombshell. "You ought to know, Norik, Allison has some rubies she thinks were stolen from Echmiadzin."

Norik leaned forward, his tone incredulous. "You bring rubies back? You have them here?"

"I have them with me, but I'm only assuming they're the rubies stolen from the crosses at Echmiadzin. I don't know for sure." Well, that was really a matter of semantics. I *did* know they were the stones that had been pried from the golden crosses. There wasn't any doubt in my mind, but if I had to present proof how I knew, I couldn't. "Will that be a problem?"

"*Ha,*" he nodded. "*Ha.* That will be problem." He frowned. "I think on it."

I assumed that meant "don't bother me with anything else for a few minutes," so I snuggled against my husband and watched the circuitous route we were taking out of the city. Someone would have to be right on our tail if they were following us or they'd have lost us long ago, and there were no lights at all in the rearview mirror, nor had there been any since we left the church. Apparently Ruben was taking no chances.

As we left the city limits and the road ascended into the hills, the tension in the van diminished somewhat. I could hear LeVon conversing quietly with his aunt, and Narine and her mother speaking softly behind me.

"How you get these rubies?" Norik asked.

His abrupt question startled me. I whispered to Bart, "The whole story or an abbreviated version?"

"Better give him all the details. Maybe he can shed some light on your little mystery."

I began with Mom's scheduled visit to Armenia for the symposium, wound my way through the story of her "accident," the break-in of the estate, the murder at the hospital, finding the newspaper article in the briefcase, the attempts on my life since I'd been in Armenia, and finally the shock of discovering the rubies in my slippers in my suitcase.

Norik interjected "uhuh" and "ha" several times during the story, and when I finished he said, "That is all?"

"That's it. Any idea how the rubies got from Armenia to California and why they were brought back in once they were safely out of the country?"

My question went unanswered. As we rounded a curve in the road, police cars and army vehicles lined both sides of the highway. Traffic was stopped in both directions—an effective roadblock we could not avoid.

What if they were searching vehicles and passengers? Where could I hide the rubies?

CHAPTER 18

Ruben pulled to the side of the road and stopped behind a police car. Two police officers and a man dressed in camouflage fatigues approached the van. None of us spoke as Ruben rolled down the window and began answering questions. His conversation with the authorities was lengthy and heated at times, but I couldn't catch everything they were saying. Norik sat forward, listening to every word but not speaking.

A sick feeling began in the pit of my stomach. I'd heard far too many stories of foreign prisons and Americans being held in horrible conditions, suffering for months for minor offenses—and years for major ones. Stolen national treasures wouldn't be considered minor in anybody's book. Thoughts of going to prison weren't pleasant to begin with, but the thought of having my baby born in a foreign prison was too horrible to contemplate.

Bart must have been having identical thoughts. His arm crept around my waist as if to shield his unborn child from harm. I think it was the only movement in the van. We were all paralyzed with fear.

Ruben produced his driver's license and passport. The men scrutinized his papers and us with flashlights in our faces. While the police kept up the animated dialogue with Ruben in Russian, the man in army fatigues, whose uniform strangely bore no insignia, stood silently observing the interchange. Ruben's answers to their questions were becoming louder and longer, until I was sure we were going to be dragged from the van and carted off to prison, all nine of us, including little Maggie who was sitting up wide-eyed watching everything.

I caught snatches of the conversation, mostly Ruben's answers to the police's questions. Ruben's cover story seemed logical: we were going on a short family holiday before bringing Norik's bees back from their summer production in the wild flowers of Dilijan.

If they asked for our papers and discovered we were foreigners, things would probably go downhill fast. One phone call to Dr. Garik Grigoryan would quickly establish I wasn't supposed to be taking a family holiday anywhere. I was supposed to be at a symposium in just a few hours and had no time for holidays of any kind on the university's tight schedule.

Bart's story would be anybody's guess. I'd like to hear it, along with how my husband's white-blonde hair and beard became Armenian black. I prayed they wouldn't ask for our identification or look closer at the two of us. The slightest suspicion that we were not natives could be disastrous. I shuddered. Or fatal if the man in the fatigues was not regular army but one of the rebels or terrorists.

Just as I thought I couldn't sit still another minute listening to the exchange, the police handed Ruben back his papers and waved us on through the roadblock. We all breathed a deep sigh of relief.

"What was that all about?" I asked.

Norik answered while Ruben concentrated on the road. "They wonder what we do on road this time at night in van not belonging to us."

"The van doesn't belong to you? Or to Ruben?" I glanced at Ruben. I hadn't considered that it was borrowed.

As Ruben sped up the road concentrating on dodging potholes, Norik remained the voice for the two. "I not have this kind of money to buy car." The lights from the dashboard illuminated his fascinating face and he smiled at me. "But man with friends no need money."

Interesting philosophy. "So who owns the van?" I asked.

"Ruben is driver for mission president. Church owns van."

"What does the mission president think about Ruben using his van for this kind of non-Church activity?" I wondered if we were going to be in trouble with the Church authorities as well as the local gendarme.

"President Beckstrand in Tblisi for meeting," Norik explained. "Ruben have van to use as he need. We pay for gas."

"What did Ruben tell them about where we were going?" Bart asked.

"We go on holiday for two days to visit family, then bring bees back from village for winter so they not freeze in mountains."

Bart turned to make sure he'd heard right. "Bees?"

"Norik has several hundred bees he leaves in the country in the wild flowers during the summer, then brings them back to the city where it is warmer during the winter," Narine explained. "They give us plenty of honey for cooking and eating and sharing with the missionaries, and a little money from that which we sell." Narine's English was very good, the best I'd encountered so far in a native Armenian.

"Where are we heading now?" I asked, straining to see through the light rain trickling in tiny streams down the side windows.

"To village near Dilijan."

Narine elaborated on Norik's brief answer. "Norik was born there and his younger brother lives in the family's home in the mountains." She lowered her voice so she couldn't be heard in the back. "We'll stay there until the danger is past."

No one spoke for a few minutes as we watched the mist swirl in the headlights. We were definitely driving up into the mountains. As the road became steeper and the rain harder, I broke the uneasy silence. "How long will it take us to get there?"

"With Ruben driving, one and half hours without rain and fog." Norik shrugged. "Maybe two, three hours with bad weather."

Deciding Ruben could drive just fine without my fierce concentration on the road, I snuggled against my husband and laid my tired head on his shoulder. "Tell me what's been happening in the world the last couple of days while I've been out of touch. How did all the communications systems get down at the same time?"

Bart shifted to make me comfortable. "Al Qaeda sent men to take over every satellite dish in Armenia as well as all phone and radio equipment. They've been in place for weeks, waiting for the signal to cut off the country from all communication with the rest of the world."

"And they just happened to choose the only time I'd spoken to you in days to do it. One of the students at the university said they'd taken over the Armenian Air Force base this morning. Is that true?"

"It would have been," Bart acknowledged, "if we hadn't known about it beforehand and alerted them in time."

"How did you find out?"

"One of the al Qaeda moles became good friends with a girl at the base and when he suggested today might be a good day to take a little trip outside the city, she immediately alerted the commander. Apparently she's active in Armenian politics and their political cell had been reviewing Armenia's geographical position and the routes the remnants of the Taliban and al Qaeda were taking."

I nodded. "Right through Armenia into Georgia, probably into the Pankisi Gorge where there are dozens of terrorist training camps hidden among the refugees who fled there from the Chechnyan war."

"Where did you garner that little tidbit?" Bart asked, his voice filled with surprise.

"Would you believe from the head honcho of the KGB?"

"Princess, nothing you say or do will surprise me."

Apparently it surprised Norik. "How you get information from KGB?"

"At the American University this morning the students were discussing the communication blackout. One of the students is the son of the KGB head here and he repeated what he'd heard his father say. Dr. Grigoryan pooh-poohed the whole story and said it was nothing more than one of the usual Armenian inconveniences."

"I think maybe he didn't want you to be concerned," Narine said, "since it was what? Only your second day in country?"

I nodded, then remembered she might not be able to see my acknowledgment. "Yes, my second day. Mmm. Maybe that was his reasoning. I never could figure him out."

"What do you mean?" Bart asked.

"I never could decide if I really trusted Dr. Grigoryan. When I had that first attempt on my life, I couldn't decide why he had stepped back out of the way of the car, leaving me to save myself or be killed. Isn't it a normal reaction to grab the person next to you and pull them to safety with you? Then he totally deserted me at the Vernisage. Left me to find my own way home. He wasn't present— that I knew of—the second time the car barely missed me, unless he was the one who pushed me into the street." I paused, remembering the incident. "But someone else was. The man in the navy jacket."

"Someone tried to run over you with a car?" Narine asked. She had moved up to the ledge behind the driver's seat to hear the conversation in the front seat. Apparently she had missed the story the first time through.

"Yes. Twice. Then someone tried to stab me at St. Hripsime's tomb." I shivered remembering how very close that had been. "They attempted again at Echmiadzin. Then someone shot at me at St. Gayane, and again at the Opera."

"My goodness, you've had an exciting time the last two days." Narine fell silent for a minute. "Why is someone trying to kill you?"

"I think it has something to do with the rubies." Once again I recited the story, beginning with Mom's planned but aborted trip, up to my discovery of the rubies in my slippers. That reminded me of the gypsy. "Norik, do you know the little gypsy man who lives under the stairs near the *shuka* in my alley?"

"Gypsy?" He thought for a minute, eyebrows furrowed in concentration. "I think no. What this 'gypsy' look like?"

"He's very small, probably about the size of a ten or eleven year old, and has curly black hair and dark eyes. His hair is longer than most Armenians wear theirs and his clothes looked like he slept in them. I thought they might be the only ones he had."

Norik shook his head slowly. "No, I think I not know this gypsy person."

"If you didn't send him to get me out of my apartment when the KGB came, who did? He even knew my name."

"What did he say that convinced you to open the door?" Bart asked.

I thought for a minute, trying to remember the scene at the door. "He knocked quietly, and when I looked out the peephole, all I could see was this little person huddled in the corner that I thought was a child. He said, 'Misses Allan,' so I thought he was the contact you said would come to help me."

"No."

I looked up into my husband's face at his quiet, terse reply. "Then who could he have been?"

"Maybe he not like KGB," Norik said. "He think you not like KGB either."

"But how would he know my name?"

"How did you get from the airport to your apartment?" Narine asked. "Did someone bring you and say your name where he could have heard?"

I thought about that for a minute. "I guess he could have been on the landing above my floor. I heard footsteps a couple of times up there. He could have heard Dr. Grigoryan speak my name. But why did he send me to the park when the KGB came, and tell me to wait in Opera Square? And if he wasn't your contact, how did you know I was at the opera?"

"I can answer that question. My contact had been watching your apartment—and you. When he saw you leave your apartment in that unorthodox way across the balcony railing and enter your neighbor's apartment, he followed you through the park."

"He's good. I only had the feeling a couple of times I was being followed, and I never saw anyone even then." Suddenly I remembered the man in the navy jacket coming into the opera. "What does your contact look like?"

"Tall, dark, and handsome, like all the rest of the Armenians," Bart said.

"Did you notice what he was wearing?"

"Mmm." Bart thought for a minute. "I think he had on a navy blazer with gold buttons."

"Then maybe he's not as good as I thought. I did see him, almost from the minute I landed. He was everywhere we went on Saturday. And I suspect he was the one who pushed me out of the way of the car Sunday morning." I stopped. "That was this morning, wasn't it? It seems like such a long time ago."

"He didn't tell me about that," Bart said. "He did say he stayed close enough so you could contact him if you needed him, but that you'd never asked for his help."

"How was I supposed to know he was on our side? I would have loved to know there were good guys hanging around acting like guardian angels."

Bart chuckled. "I can tell you, he was definitely surprised to see you get off the plane instead of Margaret. That threw him for a minute. And since Margaret had previously been in contact with him, he assumed she'd passed along the information on how to get in touch with him. He also assumed I knew of the change and would have told you about him. I would have, if I'd known you were in Armenia. You were here before I even knew you were coming." Bart paused before adding, "I can assure you, if I'd known the plan, you wouldn't be here now."

I nodded. "If I'd known what was happening here, I wouldn't have been so anxious to help Mom out."

Bart's arm tightened around my shoulder. "I can't understand what Matt O'Hare was thinking, letting you come here. As your bishop, I'd have thought he'd stop you, even if his FBI persona wanted you to come."

"Actually, both of his personae tried to stop me."

Bart sighed in mock exasperation. "But my headstrong wife ignored all advice to the contrary and came anyway, plunging my wife and my baby literally in the line of fire."

I elbowed him in retaliation, happy to lighten the somber mood in the van. "I wouldn't have ignored him if Mom hadn't felt so intensely the need to have her assignments covered here." I knew Bart was teasing me with the first part of his statement, but he was one hundred percent right about the second part. I had brought our baby into a very dangerous situation.

I thought about Mom confined to her hospital bed and the frustration she must be feeling at not being able to be here herself, not to mention the pain she must be in. "But now that paper may never see the light of day and I don't know about the award—or the symposium. She'll be so disappointed."

"Disappointed, maybe. But anything can happen in the next few hours. The whole thing could even be canceled. And I'm sure when she finds out what's going on over here, she'll blame herself for getting you into the middle of this mess. She'll just be happy that you're safe."

"I wish they would cancel it. Then I wouldn't feel bad at all about leaving the country before I finish what I came to do."

"We hope you can leave country," Norik said quietly leaning up where he could hear our conversation.

I glanced back at him. The grim expression on his face matched his tone.

"What do you mean?" I asked, puzzled by the ominous tenor of his voice.

"This not going to be . . . what you say? Cakewalk?" He glanced at Narine for confirmation of his term.

"Piece of cake is what you mean, I think," Narine said.

"Yes." Norik nodded vigorously. "This not going to be piece of cake. Not easy getting out of Armenia. Not easy getting into Georgia. And not easy roads to travel for baby. Good thing Narine here."

"And why is that?" I asked, turning to look at Narine.

"She is doctor. Work many years in emergency room at hospital." Then as if he realized he might be scaring me, he added quickly, "But we hope we not need her. You have no problem with baby."

"No problem," I assured him. Now if I could just assure Bart, and myself, it might dispel some of the tension that had reappeared in the van.

"What kind of problems might we have at the border?" I asked, remembering we were in Eastern Europe and this wasn't like a Sunday drive in the States. Border crossings could be an ordeal, which is why so many people opted to avoid them by going over the mountains.

Narine answered my question with a question. "What kind of visa do you have?"

"A twenty-one-day tourist visa. There wasn't time to get anything else. But I don't have a visa for Georgia." I caught the look that passed between Norik and Narine in the rearview mirror. "That will be a problem, right?"

"*Ha.*" Norik's terse, one word reply was not encouraging.

"So what will we do when we reach the border and they won't let me into Georgia?"

"First problem on Armenian side. You not get out of Armenia without proper visa and residence permit."

"And how do I go about getting those papers this time of night on a Sunday?" I asked, hoping for a quick answer. When none came, icy fingers of fear clutched my heart.

I glanced up at Bart. Dim lights from the dashboard revealed tense muscles working over his tightly clenched jaw. "Does that mean there's no way out of the country?" I almost hated to ask the question, fearing the answer I'd receive.

The van rumbled noisily through the night. No one spoke. I stared out the windshield, waiting for an answer, watching the windshield wipers flip-flop back and forth in a hypnotizing rhythm. I'd watched silently for several minutes before I realized that wasn't just rain being swished away. Very wet, slushy snow was falling.

"How much money you bring, in case other plan doesn't work?" Norik asked quietly. His expression was somber as he looked at Bart.

"Probably enough for both borders, unless we have to pay off a whole platoon of guards." Bart looked down at me. "How much did you bring?"

"Ten thousand dollars. I figured one hundred dollars a day for expenses for three months and threw in an extra thousand for emergencies. Will that do?"

We both looked at Norik.

"It help," he nodded. "But situation might be different at border now if rebels or terrorists beat us there."

Neither Bart nor I had a reply to that terse comment. We rode without speaking for several minutes before Narine broke the silence. "It might be a little different if there has been a change of guard from the regular army, but I think it won't have changed too much. Underpaid soldiers supplement their meager income with bribes, just like the police. *Kasark* is a way of life in Armenia. That won't change overnight, no matter who is in charge. Until the government can pay them a decent wage, these hungry men will continue to feed themselves however they can."

There was a short pause, then Norik and Narine said simultaneously, "Unless Davit is there."

"Davit?"

"*Ha*. Davit." Norik seemed to think that was sufficient explanation and fell silent, shaking his head.

While Norik continued to shake his head in consternation, Narine explained. "Davit is a bright, young member of the Church who served a mission to Samara, Russia. Before he left, he finished his studies to be a forensics lawyer. When he came back and wanted to practice, he found so much corruption in the government, he couldn't work there." She paused. "It's a long story, but he decided to go back into the army, hoping to help our young men who must all serve a mandatory two years. So many fall away from the Church in that environment; he hoped a strong example would help them so they could also serve missions when they return home."

Norik picked up the story. "But Davit, he have principles and integrity. He not like *kasark*. He think someone not be able to break rules because they have money, and someone else who have greater need but no money, not be able to have his dream." He looked at me. "You understand? My English not so good."

"Your English is fine," I assured him. "You're saying Davit doesn't allow bribes to get someone across the border if their papers are not in order." Since that was the only way we'd be able to make the crossing, we could be in a heap of trouble tonight if this principled young man stood between us and safety.

"I can't imagine that makes Davit a popular fellow among the other soldiers if that's how they make enough money to get by," Bart said. "Hunger can be a huge deterrent to honesty."

"You have to know Davit," Narine explained. "He has a very strong personality and a way about him of making people feel good when they do good. He draws the best to him, and the worst avoid him. But I think he was on the Turkish border the last time I spoke with him. That was a better place for him because not so many people try to cross into Turkey."

That relieved me immensely. Surely between the two of us, Bart and I had enough money to get us safely out of Armenia, across both borders into Georgia. Even with two sets of guards, we ought to be able to handle that.

Then I thought of my reaction—relief because an honest person would not be on guard and I'd be able to complete a dishonest transaction to bypass a law that was inconvenient for me. I felt a twinge of shame until I remembered all the attempts on my life and the danger we were in from the terrorists and/or rebels trying to take over the government. Inconvenient wasn't quite the right word for our situation. I'd have to dwell on the moral implications of breaking laws to save lives. Later. When my own baby's life wasn't endangered.

I turned to Narine. "Are you coming with us or are you really staying in Dilijan?"

"No, we'll stay in the mountains with Norik's brother and his family. We have no reason to leave Armenia yet." She paused. "When Norik can leave legally, with papers in order, we will think about it. Our daughter in America has a baby he's never seen. We'd like to visit her and take the whole family. But we are Armenians and this is our country. We want to see it strong once again. We need to be here to do what we can to help build it back up."

"Ha." Norik affirmed, nodding vigorously. "Our people need someone to show them how to do things. Seventy years is long time. Soviets cripple Armenian thinking. They have no . . ." Norik rattled a long phrase in Armenian.

"Initiative," Narine said, giving him the word he sought.

"Ha. When someone always tell you what to do, how to do, when to do, you stop thinking for yourself. You become . . ." He rattled again a phrase and Narine gave him the word.

"Robot."

"You become like robot. Without mind. Take long time to learn to think for yourself. Take long time to get confidence you can do things without supervision every minute." He stopped. "Supervision? Is that right word?"

"Ha," I said.

Norik laughed. "You quick learner."

I shook my head. "That was an easy one. Tell me more about this border crossing. Is Dilijan close to the border?"

Bart joined the conversation. "As the crow flies, it's not far. But we're into the mountains and the roads don't just go straight to the border."

"Of course not. That would be too easy. So is this an all night trip, or is there a bed somewhere in my foreseeable future tonight?"

Bart's arm tightened around my shoulder and he kissed my forehead. "Tired?"

"Only from the top of my head to the tip of my toes. Dodging bullets and bad guys sort of wears me out."

"Surprising." Bart rubbed my arm in a comforting gesture. "I thought you were like the Energizer bunny and just kept on going no matter what."

"Not tonight." I laid my head against Bart's shoulder. "I suddenly feel like someone just removed the battery."

Narine spoke from over my shoulder. "We should be in Dilijan in about thirty minutes, then it's another twenty or thirty minutes to Norik's brother's. We'll all stay there tonight, then you three can leave early in the morning for Georgia."

"Maybe more than thirty minutes to Dilijan tonight," Ruben said, peering intently out the windshield.

I looked out. I could see nothing but thick, heavy snowflakes swirling around the van. The ground was covered with snow, obliterating any sign of the highway. We'd climbed right into a blizzard.

CHAPTER 19

No one spoke in the van. Visibility decreased rapidly and drastically. We all focused our concentration on the beam of light trying to pierce the heavy snow, as if that would help Ruben see where to drive.

Snow built up in the corners of the windshield. Each swish of the wiper blades compacted the accumulation. The viewing area out the front window diminished as I watched. Ruben slowed the van from ten miles an hour to five miles an hour. If a car stopped in the road ahead of us, we'd be on it before we could see it.

I shuddered to think about the edge of the road. Where was it? It would be possible to drive right off the edge of a cliff in this weather and never know we were in any danger until it was too late and we were over the edge.

"If I stop to clean windshield, may not get traction to start again." Ruben looked at me. "You drive while I clear snow?"

I nodded. "Yes, I can drive."

"Put foot on pedal. I take mine off. Keep pedal in same place, so it give no more, no less petrol. Keep steering wheel in same position. Ready?" He gave me a reassuring smile and waited for my assent.

I maneuvered around the gear shift and slid close to him on the seat. I put my foot next to his on the gas pedal and gripped the steering wheel. "Ready."

What I wasn't ready for was the blast of cold air as both Bart and Ruben opened their doors and leaned out into the blizzard to scoop the snow from the corners of the windshield and allow the wipers their full sweep.

I peered intently into the blinding snow that pelted the windshield with wet heavy flakes, praying fervently nothing blocked the road ahead, pleading for guardian angels to keep us on the highway. The snow was so deep I realized I could drive right off the pavement and never be able to tell I'd left the road. There would be no change in the sound of tires on the roadbed, no difference from the smooth surface to the gravel berm.

It seemed an eternity before the windshield was clear and the men sat back in their seats and closed the doors. As Ruben replaced my foot with his on the gas pedal and took control of the steering wheel, I immediately turned up the heater in the van.

Bart had to share his wet, icy fingers with me, wrapping one hand around my neck and pulling me close to his freezing, wet face. The black whiskers were now white.

I shivered and pushed him away. "At least with snow on your face, you look more like my husband than with that black stubble. How did you manage that? You never did tell me. Dying hair, I understand. I didn't know you could dye whiskers, too."

"Your father, the master of disguise, taught me the trick. Don't shave for a week, then dunk your head in a bucket of hair dye."

"Really?" I looked up into two laughing azure eyes. "Bart, you're teasing!"

"That way you get the same color for eyebrows, hair, beard, nose hair, the whole nine yards."

I jabbed him in the ribs with my elbow. "Be serious. I want to know how you did it."

"Actually, they have this little pill. You can choose the color you want from the color chart, and then take the corresponding pill. Voila. Instant red head or blonde or brunette."

I looked at my husband who was having a hard time not laughing out loud at the ridiculousness of his own story.

"This is true?" Norik asked. "This new spy tool?"

"My husband is not telling the truth." I started to explain Bart was just joking, when he interrupted me.

"Instant meaning about two days," Bart amended, trying to keep a straight face. "There is just one bad side effect. You occasionally end up with zebra stripes or leopard spots if you don't take a strong enough dose."

"Enough! Your nose will grow like Pinocchio's if you don't stop!" I elbowed his rib cage again and he wrapped both arms around me in a bear hug to stop me.

I relaxed in his arms and let him hold me. Obviously Bart had been trying to relieve the tension in the van. It had worked. The atmosphere was definitely more relaxed and Norik and Narine conversed quietly in Armenian while I enjoyed the immense comfort of being close to my husband. Everyone in the back must be asleep. We'd heard nothing from them, even when the doors were opened and the blizzard's icy blast blew through the van.

Of course, the atmosphere inside only changed temporarily. Too soon the windshield iced up and Bart and Ruben had to repeat their clearing activity.

There were no tracks in the snow ahead of us. Apparently we were in the only vehicle on the road. At home, we'd be able to follow trucks through the snow. There was never a highway or an hour of the day without some truck traffic. As much as I'd cursed them at other times, I'd have blessed them now if they were breaking through the snow in front of us, leaving tracks to follow.

Time passed excruciatingly slowly, and the miles went even slower. It felt like we would spend the rest of eternity in these conditions, but as we crested the summit of the mountain pass and started down the other side, the snow diminished with each mile and the blizzard abated. It hadn't snowed as much over here, and as we hit a stretch of highway with steep descent and hairpin curves one after another, I uttered over and over a prayer of gratitude the blinding blizzard was on the other side of the mountain.

"I can't believe the difference in the weather as soon as we crested the mountain. Not only did the storm let up, but the road on this side looks like it has a heating element under it to melt the snow."

"That may be," Narine said. "Dilijan is famous for its hot mineral springs. They bubble up all over this valley. During Soviet times, this was a favorite getaway for Soviet leaders from all over Russia and the satellite countries because of the mineral baths and the supposed healing properties of the mineral water, which they bottle here. You can't see it in the dark, but the contrast between this side of the mountain and the other side is amazing. We passed Lake Sevan in the blizzard so you didn't see it, but the hills there have fewer trees. On this side, it is heavily wooded with many different kinds of trees. One of our truly beautiful vacation spots."

"But who have money for vacation now?" Norik asked quietly. It must have been a rhetorical question as no one answered and he didn't press the issue.

Narine patted my shoulder. "It won't be long now. You must be exhausted after your flight yesterday. Are you still feeling jet lag?"

"Actually, I'm not feeling much of anything. I think I'm sort of numb all over. Garik said if I stayed up all day yesterday instead of going to bed immediately after reaching my apartment, I'd be able to overcome the time difference much faster."

"He was right, you know. Those first few hours after that flight are very hard to stay on your feet, but after a good night's sleep, your body seems to adjust quickly."

Norik leaned forward and asked Ruben a question. Ruben pulled the van to the side of the road and stopped. Ruben explained in English, "Police always park around this corner going into town. I go see if they are there alone, or if they have company."

"I'll go with you," Bart said, opening his door. The cold night wind flushed all the warm air from the van. I shivered from head to toe with a sudden chill. I was grateful for my warm pantsuit, but would have been even more grateful for a warm winter-weight coat instead of my lightweight raincoat.

"Is this a place they'd put a roadblock?" I asked, trying to remember the map of Armenia I'd studied on the plane.

"It's on the main road to Azerbaijan. It would be one of the easy points to funnel troops through if there really were to be an inva-sion." Narine was quiet for a minute. "We have had so much war, so much hardship. It would be cruel to have it happen again just as Armenians are beginning to get back on their feet."

As I began to make sympathy sounds, the doors opened and the men jumped back inside. Ruben started the van and whipped it around in a tight U-turn. No one spoke. I didn't get to ask what they'd found. Narine beat me to it. "What did you see?"

"Roadblock with squad of soldiers. I think they expecting many peoples from Yerevan to come here." That was all the explanation Norik gave.

I turned to Bart. "Give me your version, not quite so abbreviated, please."

"He said it all. They're stopping all traffic and they have enough personnel to handle busloads of people. There were a lot of empty cars parked on this side of the block."

"Which means?" I prompted, when my husband fell silent.

"Which probably means they are detaining everyone coming through town, finding out where they are going and why they are in Dilijan."

"Do I have to pry every bit of information out of you a piece at a time? Who are the soldiers? Armenians being careful or . . .? Or what? Rebels? Terrorists? How do you tell the difference? Or is there any difference? Enlighten me here, please."

Ruben silently concentrated on his driving, taking back alleys, twisting and winding through the empty back streets of Dilijan. Norik left the explanation to Bart.

"No one wore insignia. There was nothing to identify them," Bart said quietly.

"And that means?"

"That means they are not the Armenian Army."

"Bart, give me more than one sentence replies. Tell me what you're thinking. Please tell me what's going on."

"Armenia being invaded—again." Dismay and disbelief tinged Norik's brief quiet statement.

"Is it really that bad?" Narine asked, her voice barely above a whisper. "Maybe they are volunteers called back into the army to man checkpoints and help stop the infiltration of terrorists."

Bart turned to her so he could speak quietly, without anyone in the back hearing him. "I suspect they were rebels trying to control the highways, the travel and transportation routes. The terrorists are already in place, at least the first contingent. Osama bin Laden sent key members of his al Qaeda here months ago to work their way into major positions in critical areas to prepare for this. They've also been quietly working the parliament to stir up opposition to President Kocharian . . ."

"That not hard," Norik interrupted, his voice filled with contempt. "Kocharian not keep his promises. Still no water all day.

No jobs. Much corruption in government. He helping his friends get rich while people still suffering with no heat, no water, bad roads."

"A perfect atmosphere to start a quiet rebellion among the different political factions," Bart explained. "They stir up a lot of unrest among members of parliament, creating alliances between the most radical groups to strengthen that bloc. At the same time, they create deep divisions among the more conservative groups so they remain fragmented and fighting each other instead of working together. The al Qaeda infiltrators have had nearly two years to stir the pot and get their people into the key places."

"Are you sure?" Narine said. "We don't have any foreigners in the parliament. They are all Armenians."

"But Armenians from where?" Bart asked. "And what are their politics? Think how many Armenians live in Iran alone, not to mention every other country in the world. How many hundreds of thousands were moved, entire towns and villages at a time, by their conquerors? How many millions fled the genocide? How many more left with the Soviets to find jobs?"

"*Ha.* More live outside Armenia than in," Norik agreed. "Then Satan work his devilish ways with people like Taliban and al Qaeda. Give them evil heart. They become like Gadianton robbers in Book of Mormon with secret combinations to get gain. Evil spread fast through unhappy, dissatisfied people. Promise poor man he can come back to his homeland and have property and position. He forget about right and wrong. He forget about justice and commandment to have charity for neighbor. He think only of himself and big house for his family. Many good men blinded by lies of Satan."

"So it doesn't matter whether you call them terrorists or rebels. They are from the same source," Narine said.

"Exactly. The only difference is in their motivation. Some were blinded by the craftiness of men and may even think what they're doing is for the best good of the country. Others are blinded by the total control of their leaders, like bin Laden's men. They truly believe their mission in life is to rid the world of the infidel Christian so the Muslim can reign supreme. And the rest, like bin Laden, just thrive on the power they wield over others."

We had wound our way out of Dilijan on back streets and were heading into the mountains on a tiny little twisting road that climbed higher and higher into the snow-covered hills where it resumed snowing. The higher we got, the heavier the snowfall became until I feared Ruben would no longer be able to find the road. At least at each hairpin curve, I could see trees illuminated by the van's lights through the falling snow so I knew we weren't on the edge of a chasm.

We rode in silence for what seemed like a very long time. The falling snow and constant movement of the windshield wipers must have hypnotized me, or I fell asleep on Bart's shoulder. Suddenly the van veered around a sharp corner and I sat up as Ruben slowed the vehicle. The snowstorm had subsided somewhat, leaving only a gently falling snow. The headlights revealed the wall of an ancient church, and as the road turned, I could see the pointed roof of another building, and up a pathway through the snow, the outlines of still another.

"Where are we?" I asked.

"This is Haghartsin Monastery complex. It is high in a mountain canyon. Norik's family lives another couple of miles up the road. A cousin lives here, just across a little ravine and keeps the keys to the complex. Haghartsin doesn't have a priest here anymore, nor even a caretaker, so as Henrik herds his goats, he watches for cars to come up the road, then he comes and unlocks the doors so visitors can see the churches."

Norik leaned forward. "We stop here," he said quietly. "I get Henrik's keys. This good place to leave rubies."

Ruben parked under a huge, twisted tree with snow-covered branches. Norik jumped out of the van, softly closing the door so as not to wake whoever might still be sleeping, then disappeared over a little hill at the edge of the parking lot. I tried to see where he went, but lost him immediately in the darkness.

From behind me, Narine pointed over my shoulder out the windshield. "See that light over on the hill? That's where Henrik lives with his family."

I peered through the window to where Narine pointed and could just barely make out a light through the trees and snow. "I hope Norik's cousins aren't asleep. I'd hate for him to have to wake them to get the keys." Since there had been no movement in the back of the van to indicate the children had awakened, I whispered. Narine kept her voice low as well.

"Armenians stay up late. For the most part, they are not early risers. At least, not now that there is electricity. When we had none, we went to bed when it was dark and got up when it was light. Now I think this is a luxury for them to stay up late and have light, so they enjoy it."

"I hate to inconvenience anyone, but I particularly hate the inconvenience these rubies have become already. Unfortunately, I'm sure they will only complicate my life further. Narine, tell me about the rubies. Was it highly publicized here when they were stolen?"

"Yes. The Catholicos pled for their return on TV and in interviews for the newspapers. It was believed at the time that Muslims had stolen them from the Christians. These were not just famous rubies, but the crosses that held them were important relics for the Armenian Apostolic Church. Since probably ninety-seven percent of the people in Armenia are members of the Apostolic Church, people did not want to believe that Armenians would steal their own treasures."

"Would they?" I asked, knowing what the answer would be in America.

"Of course." I didn't have to turn around to know Narine was smiling at my question. I could hear the humor in her voice. "We like to think that Armenians are a very principled people, that we are more Christian since we have been Christian longer than most everyone else in the world." With a small sigh she continued, "But we are just like everyone else. Hunger and deprivation bring out the worst in us. When someone's family is starving, all those beautiful treasures in Echmiadzin can lose their sacred meaning and become nothing more than a lamb and a loaf of bread for their hungry children."

I was curious to know Narine's opinion on the robbery. "Why do you think the rubies were taken to California?"

"There are thousands of Armenians living in California; actually, all over America, and many of them are very wealthy. They constantly send money here to support family and to support many programs that would otherwise go unfunded. About twenty-one million dollars per month come into this country from Armenians for their families who are out of work. The Diaspora—those who dispersed to other countries—was the saving grace for the suffering people here when the Soviets pulled out. It's common knowledge that's where the Armenian money is, except for what lies in the treasury at Echmaidzin, of course. If the thieves were to take the stones to America and show them to the right people among the Diaspora, they would pay the ransom for the rubies and see that they are returned to where they belong."

"So you think the robbery was simply a money-raising enterprise and it was done so the rubies would ultimately be restored to their rightful place?"

"That make sense to me," Narine said.

Bart's quiet voice startled me when he entered the conversation. I'd thought he might be dozing. "Then the theory that it was Muslims who stole them doesn't hold water. Muslims wouldn't want the rubies returned."

"You're right," Narine agreed. "Whoever stole them apparently wanted to get them into the right hands so they could be replaced in their crosses. They could rationalize that there was no harm done if the rubies were returned, and they would have the money they needed for whatever their purpose."

"And because Mom's trip was so highly publicized in the Los Angeles area, everyone knew she was coming to Armenia. They get the jewels to her to bring into the country, then someone here retrieves them after she arrives. She unwittingly becomes a carrier for stolen jewels, but if it is handled right, she would never know what she had done."

"Mmm." Bart thought about it. "That theory seems to have a few holes in it for me, but you may be on the right track. Did Margaret say anything about the rubies?"

"No. When I asked Mom what someone would want with the briefcase, she had no idea. Of course, I couldn't ask her about the rubies, per se, as I didn't know about them at the time. I wasn't aware they were in my suitcase until tonight. My little gypsy friend who got me out of the apartment by telling me the KGB was there could have been clearing me out so whoever wanted to retrieve the jewels could get in to search for them."

"You can bet neither the KGB nor the Mafia would be concerned with getting them back to Echmaidzin, so if your theory is correct about a simple fund-raising scheme, it's someone else who wanted the stones." Bart was silent for a minute. "Try this: a political faction wanting power and influence in the government for their agenda but without funds to promote it comes up with this bizarre way to get their hands on some money. Is it coincidence that bin Laden's al Qaeda is on the run at the same time? Or is this part of that grand plan to take over a little country to make a big impression?"

We didn't have time to answer Bart as Norik returned at that moment with the cousin and the keys.

"Come. I show you place for safekeeping." He reached under the front seat and retrieved a flashlight, then waited for us to exit the van before he proceeded up the path between ancient stone buildings. Ruben stayed in the van with Narine's sister and mother, and Maggie. Bart and I got out, followed closely by Narine and LeVon.

"I've never seen the place the priests used to hide church treasures from invaders." LeVon's quiet tone couldn't hide the excitement in his voice. "Is that where you're going to hide the rubies?"

So much for keeping secrets from children. He must have heard everything we'd said while we thought he was sleeping.

We walked through the snow up a wide, uneven, cobblestone path past what looked like a large church, then between two more buildings. I tried to walk in the tracks made by the men preceding us to keep the snow out of my shoes.

"How many buildings are here?" I asked, surprised at the size of the complex hidden so far up the canyon.

"Nine," Norik answered, "if you count *gavits* of each church."

"What's a *gavit*?" I asked. "And how many churches are there?"

"*Gavit* is entrance or foyer or gathering place. Three churches here: biggest is St. Astvatsatsin which mean Mary, Holy Mother of God." He turned to his cousin and asked in Russian when it had been built.

"Year 1281 they build St. Astvatsatsin," Norik repeated in English. He pointed first to the big church on the left, then to a smaller one on the right. "This one, St. Grigor, or Gregory, is oldest. Built in tenth century. This where hiding place is."

I marveled that they seemed in such good condition after over a thousand years. But we trudged on through the snow past both buildings to a smaller one set apart from the rest.

"This St. Stepanos. This one built in 1244. Henrik want to show us something before he reveal St. Gregory's secret," Norik said, as his cousin stopped at the door to a small stone church set behind and slightly askew from the other buildings. He flashed the light on the huge padlock as the cousin fumbled with a set of keys on a large, round key ring. Henrik finally got the lock undone and swung open a heavy door which creaked on noisy hinges.

A perfect background for a mystery, I thought. Ancient church. Isolated canyon. Creaking doors. All we needed were a few bats flying around and a full moon to complete the setting. Then Henrik dispelled the eerie ambience with the flick of a switch, turning on a lone bare electric bulb that hung from a huge wrought-iron chandelier in the small chapel. It didn't offer a great deal of illumination, leaving corners in shadow, but definitely changed the atmosphere from one of intriguing suspense to one of shabby antiquity.

I was surprised at the temperature when we stepped inside. The other churches I'd been in had been as cool as—or cooler than—the outside temperature. This was almost comfortably warm. Much nicer than the outside temperature right now.

Norik, also apparently surprised at the temperature, asked his cousin if he'd been working here. As they conversed in Russian, I was able to follow the conversation.

"Yes," Henrik nodded. "I let Petros tend the goats while I carve *khachkar*. See my work?" He pointed to a slab of stone laying across a couple of crude saw horses. Norik shined the light on the stone. The top portion contained an intricate pattern that actually looked like openwork lace.

"How do you make stone look like dainty lace?" I asked in Russian, marveling at the beauty of the carving.

Henrik beamed. "With these two hands, the talent that God gave me, and these simple tools." He picked up a small chisel and hammer. "I chip away the stone and leave the lace." He demonstrated, tapping the hammer against the chisel, chipping away a small portion of stone, then blowing the chips away to show his work. "One little piece at a time." He was obviously proud of his beautiful work and had reason to be.

"Henrik, we not come to admire your talent." Norik said. "We come to leave something valuable in ancient hiding place. Please to open St. Grigor for us."

Henrik led us from the comparative warmth of St. Stepanos back into the wintry night, backtracking down the snow-covered walkway to St. Grigor's *gavit*. Another large padlock, another large key chosen from the many on the key ring. The stone column wasn't even in the chapel, which was up steep stone stairs, but in the *gavit*, or entryway, that was over twice the size of the chapel.

Henrik turned to one of the stone columns and placing his fingers in a deep groove, pulled a section of what had appeared to be solid stone away from the rest of the pillar. The sound of stone grating on stone echoed through the high-ceilinged room. Inside was a hollowed out area large enough to hold several books or scrolls, and even a candlestick or two, which is what I'd imagined had been hidden there from invaders throughout the centuries of Armenia's turbulent history.

"Do they still have the silver candlesticks they used to hide in here? How about the silver chalice with the jewels? Is it still around?" LeVon's enthused curiosity created a refreshing excitement in the group.

Norik turned to him in surprise and asked, "How you know about candlesticks and chalice?"

"Petros told me. He said that every night when it was time to close the church, the old priest would wait until everyone was gone, and then hide the valuable silver candlesticks and chalice, as well as the illuminated manuscripts so the poor people who lived here wouldn't be tempted to try to steal them and sell them. One night one of his assistants hid under the altar curtain so he could discover where the hiding place was, but when the old priest sensed some-thing different in the chapel, he didn't put the treasured pieces away. Instead, he spent hours polishing them and working in the chapel, until he heard snoring and found the assistant fast asleep behind the curtain. He then hid the things where he usually put them, here in the column, quietly went out and locked the door, locking the assis-tant in the cold chapel for the night. That was the end of the assis-tant's curiosity." LeVon's face dimpled in a pleased smile as he finished his story.

"Petros knows the stories," Henrik laughed. "He's heard them all his life."

"He also told me there is a secret passageway from one church to the other so the priests could get away when invaders came." LeVon's expression was now serious. "But he couldn't show me so I didn't believe him. Is it true?"

Henrik nodded. "It is true. Tunnels link all of the buildings. Not just handy to avoid raiding Persians or Turks or Mongols, but when the snow gets a couple of feet deep and the blizzards are raging outside, it's easier to go from one building to another. My grandfather, your great-grandfather," he said to LeVon, "was the priest here all of his life. Even the atheist Communists couldn't drive him out, though they tried to close the churches. They were going to tear these down, like they did so many of the wonderful old churches in Armenia. But he bought them off with the only valuables he had— the silver candlesticks and the jewel-encrusted silver chalice. So the church has no treasures anymore to hide in the column."

"Well, for a few days at least, there will be valuable treasures hidden there again," I said, retrieving the rubies from the zippered pocket in my raincoat. I untied the scarf from around my neck and nestled the rubies inside.

LeVon peered curiously into my hands at the jewels. "So those are the famous rubies from Echmiadzin?"

"Well, we think they are. No one—"

Henrik cut me off in mid-sentence with a hand to his mouth signaling silence.

CHAPTER 20

Without a word, Henrik leaped across the room and flipped off the little light bulb, plunging the *gavit* into total darkness.

"Henrik, what games you play with us?" Norik asked.

"Listen," Henrik said.

All we could hear was the sound of a dog barking somewhere in the distance.

"So? I hear dog," Norik said. "Nothing more."

"Listen again and tell me what you hear," Henrik replied patiently.

There wasn't a sound in the stone chapel as everyone held their breath, straining to hear what Henrik had heard. Finally I heard a sound that probably brought fear to the hearts of the people living in this isolated canyon many times before—the sound of an engine, a large engine, chugging up the hill.

Norik and Henrik flew into action. "I have Ruben move van. You hide tracks," Norik instructed, and the two men raced out of the church into the snowy darkness, followed closely behind by Narine.

I pulled my little penlight from my purse, wrapped the rubies carefully in the silk scarf and deposited them in the ancient hiding place. LeVon slid the section of fluted column back into place and I played the light over it to make sure everything looked normal once again.

"Now what?" I asked Bart, standing silently at my shoulder.

"You wait here with LeVon for Norik and Henrik to tell us what's going on," he said quietly. "I'll help Narine."

"I'll come, too," I said, following Bart to the door.

"Please stay here. You aren't dressed for this weather. You can't afford to catch cold right now and be sick. You need to take good care of my baby." Bart kissed my nose and disappeared down the snowy walkway.

"LeVon, where does the road go from here?"

"Only to my grandfather's house where my uncle lives. The road ends there at the top of the hill."

"So a truck coming up here this time of night would not just be traffic passing through?"

"No," LeVon said, his tone serious but not frightened.

"What do you think they are doing out there?" I wasn't used to being shut away from the action. I hated staying here not knowing what was going on.

"I think they bring my grandmother and Maggie and my aunt in here and take the van somewhere else. They will need my help to carry our food. I go, but you stay to open door and help my grandmother." As LeVon pulled the door open, a flurry of snow drifted in. Apparently he couldn't stand being left behind either.

I followed him outside and pulled the door shut, stepping out between the churches just as Bart hurried up the cobblestones carrying Maggie, still bundled in the blanket.

"They said to go to St. Stepanos," Bart said. I wheeled around and ran back up the walk to the tiniest of the three chapels, which was, gratefully, also the warmest. I opened the door, flashing my penlight so he could see the steps into the church, and find the old wooden bench to lay her on. Since this little church was well hidden by the big church, and the truck was still down the road beyond the curve, I didn't worry about my little light being seen just yet.

"Narine is right behind me with her mother. Better shine the light for them," Bart said, settling Maggie onto the bench and tucking the blankets around her, then hurrying out again into the snowy night.

I turned back to the door and focused the little beam on the threshold so Narine and her sister could safely help their mother navigate the ancient stone steps. LeVon, laden with bulging plastic bags, followed the three women into the sanctuary, deposited his bags and hurried out again. I quickly closed the door, shutting out the snow that blew in with them, then shined my light on the bench next to Maggie's.

Narine and her sister helped their mother get comfortable, placing her small bag of possessions next to her on the bench and wrapping her lap robe around her legs.

"Now what?" I whispered to Narine.

"Ruben is moving the van up to the house. Petros will come and help LeVon and Henrik sweep the tracks from the snow so no one will be able to tell how many were here or where they went."

"You really think this is someone following us?" I asked. "Not just someone lost on the wrong road?"

Narine was silent for a minute, then said with a deep sigh, "I would like to think it was coincidence and someone just happened to be coming up here to this dead end minutes after we arrive, but I am not naïve."

"But no one followed us out of town," I protested. "I watched in the rearview mirror. There were no lights behind us."

"The KGB keeps records on everyone," Narine quietly explained. "If someone disappears, they look at the records, locate the relatives' addresses, and that is the first place they look. Also, the relatives become the first ones harassed."

"Or persecuted," Narine's sister added quietly, so no one else but the two of us could hear. Narine introduced her sister, Aida, and the three of us moved to the door, away from Maggie and their mother. It was apparent they wanted to shield the youngest and eldest members of the group from what was going on.

"I think they will send your husband back here to stay with us, but Norik and LeVon will go with Petros and Henrik to the house. When the truck arrives, they will be talking about the bees and getting ready to play Nardi into the wee hours of the morning." Narine opened the door a crack to hear the sounds that echoed through the snowy night.

"The truck is just at the corner by the funerary shrine. In about one minute they will be at the monastery turnoff. Then we will know if they come here or go on to Henrik's house."

Suddenly she stepped back and threw open the door. Henrik burst through with Bart close on his heels.

"Come," he said in Russian. "I think we get you into secret passage so we don't have to worry about you. Narine, you go back to house now with Norik and the boys."

Narine immediately left the chapel to follow Henrik's instructions. As Henrik turned to the altar of the little church, Bart scooped

Maggie and her blanket from the bench. "Give your penlight to Henrik, Princess, so we can see where we're going."

I slapped the tiny light in Henrik's outstretched hand as Narine's sister hurried to help her mother. Collecting the packages left behind, I followed the group through the opening in the altar railing and up three small stairs to the altar platform. Henrik pushed aside the threadbare red velvet curtains that covered the altar and moved a high slender table that stood in front of a life-sized painting of Mary holding the baby Jesus.

He grasped the edges of the frame and with what seemed a mighty tug, pulled the painting from the white marble to which it appeared to be attached. The huge heavy painting swung away from its marble backing, revealing a white marble slab with a horizontal seam in the middle, apparently two pieces stacked together to provide a backdrop for the painting. With another mighty effort, he shoved at the right corner of the bottom block of marble and it swung silently back from under the top piece. Henrik shined my little penlight on the floor, revealing steep stairs descending into a black hole.

"Come quickly," Henrik motioned. "If you back down the steps, it's easier. Count down ten steps, then you'll be on even ground. There are candles and matches, and even some blankets if the rats haven't chewed holes in them."

I shuddered. Not a comforting thought—descending into a rat infested hole. I could not be like Gregory the Illuminator and befriend them.

Aida immediately stepped forward, guiding her mother toward the hole. The older woman, who had given the impression of advanced age and infirmity of step suddenly demonstrated surprising agility.

"Watch your head as you go down," Henrik cautioned.

Aida disappeared into the black void, followed by her mother, and then Bart carrying Maggie. I was the last to go. Henrik tucked my penlight into my hand as I backed down the top step. My head had barely cleared the marble overhang when he swung the marble block back into place, locking us into the dark unknown.

I descended counting the steps and when I reached ten, stepped back onto the rough stone floor. I shined the light around so we could see where we were. The very small room had such a low ceiling

Bart could barely stand upright. Rough-hewn wooden planks that served as benches lined the walls, ending at a narrow door in the corner of the little room. Bart immediately tried the door, opening it a crack to make sure it wasn't locked, then closed it again.

The temperature of the room was surprisingly moderate, considering the blizzard outside. It was like a fruit cellar; cool, but not uncomfortably cold. Aida settled her mother on the bench along one wall and Bart placed Maggie on the bench next to her grandmother. Maggie's bright dark eyes flashed from one of us to the other, but she remained silent. She didn't seem frightened at all, just appeared to be quietly taking it all in. I wondered if this had happened to her before, being bundled up in the night and spirited off to some hiding place for a time.

I lined up Norik and Narine's plastic bags on one of the benches, next to a big black plastic garbage bag.

"Do you want to see what's inside here?" I asked Bart. "It must be the blankets Henrik said were here."

"Go ahead, Princess," Bart grinned. "Check it out."

"Thanks, but no thanks, love of my life. I'll let you do that since you're much better at handling ugly surprises than I am. I'm not interested in disturbing a rat, or a nest of mice. But if there are blankets in the bag, dig them out. We'll definitely need them before the night is over. I don't know about you, but I've had just about as much excitement as I can handle in one day. I'm ready to crash, and even that hard wooden bench looks inviting."

Sad to say, it was true. There had been too many adrenalin surges today and I was ready to settle my exhausted body on the nearest flat surface, snuggle under something warm, and go to sleep. At this point, I didn't even care whether it was a bed with a soft mattress and clean sheets or a wooden plank full of splinters and a musty blanket. Once I laid my head down, it wouldn't make a bit of difference.

Bart fumbled with the string that tied the top of the bag closed, finally got it open, and found a neatly folded stack of old gray wool army blankets. I pulled a couple out and gave them to Narine's mother to put around her shoulders. She pulled Maggie's head down into her lap and tucked Maggie's quilt around her little shoulders, quietly soothing the child back to sleep. Aida took a couple of the blankets and settled next to her mother with one of the blankets around her shoulders and one over her knees.

"If no one minds, I claim this one." As I pointed to an empty bench, Bart plopped down on one end of it.

"Not fair. That one is mine," I objected.

"Guess you'll have to share it with me since I already occupy it," he said, patting the bench next to him.

I tossed him a blanket, pulled a couple more from the bag and folding them lengthwise, placed them on the bench beside him.

"Anyone need anything else?" I asked.

Aida shook her head and motioned toward the bench. "Go ahead. I think we'll be here the rest of the night so you might as well get comfortable."

I was so grateful for my Russian language skills and equally grateful almost everyone I'd met so far spoke both Armenian and Russian fluently. This would have been an unbearable ordeal if we weren't able to communicate. Interesting that some used one more than the other. What factors determined whether they spoke Russian or Armenian in their home everyday?

"Aida, you all speak Russian and Armenian equally well. How do you decide which language to use?"

"It depends on who we are talking to and the setting. We are Armenians, so we take pride in our unique language, but when the Soviets were here, it was required that we all study and speak Russian. It was the official language to be used in school, business—everywhere. All books and reading materials were printed in Russian, the world's great authors translated into Russian. Nothing in Armenian. Even now we sometimes have to use a Russian term or expression because it is better, or more descriptive, or easier than Armenian which is a very difficult language to master, even for Armenians who wish to speak it properly."

"Thanks, Aida. That answers a lot of my questions." But not all of them. I made a mental note to ask Narine the rest. Right now I wanted nothing more than to sleep.

I stretched out on the bench, using Bart's proffered lap as a pillow, and he tucked the musty gray wool blanket around my shoulders. Certainly not the most comfortable bed I'd ever had, but maybe the most appreciated.

To save the batteries, I turned off the penlight and tucked it back in my pocket. As I began to relax and the tension eased, I prepared to sink into a deep sleep of oblivion. But as my body wound down, my mind geared up.

What was happening on the surface? Who was in the truck? Bart trusted Norik, but what about Henrik? Was he totally trustworthy? Were the rubies safely hidden in the ancient hiding place or would they be too much of a temptation? Were we safe down here in this old stone room, or simply being kept on ice until the bad guys got here?

I felt the muscles in Bart's leg tense under my head. Apparently my husband couldn't relax any more than I could. "Had all the relaxation you can handle?" I whispered.

"'Fraid so. Sorry, Princess. I'm going to see where that door leads. I'm not comfortable without some known avenue of escape. I'll get you a blanket to use as a pillow and you can stay here and rest."

"Not on your life, Charlie. I'm with you until the bitter end. Now that I've found you, or you found me, you're not leaving me behind, even for a minute." My curiosity about what was going on above, my fear of being betrayed, and my claustrophobic tendencies at being confined in small spaces were almost enough in themselves to get my exhausted body moving again. But the thought of my husband leaving me behind was the factor that weighted the decision scale. I absolutely could not take a chance that he'd leave me here, thinking I'd be safer locked away in this ancient room than with him and go off chasing terrorists or rebels and forget about me.

I turned the penlight on again, located the candles and matches and put them within reach of Aida. "We're going exploring to see where this passageway leads." I figured the simpler the explanation, the better. I certainly couldn't promise that we'd be back soon, or at all. The only certainty in my life right now was that I would not leave my husband's side.

Bart stepped to the door and glanced back at me. I knew he was going to suggest that I stay, get some rest, and take care of the baby.

"Whither thou goest, I will go," I said, handing him the penlight.

"Lead on, Lochinvar. I'm right behind you."

Bart gave a little sigh of resignation, bent over and kissed my nose, and pushed open the door. A dusty, musty odor assailed my senses as I followed my husband into a cold, dark, narrow stone corridor.

CHAPTER 21

We closed the door behind us and stopped for a minute, listening. The only sound I could hear was the beating of my own heart. Apparently satisfied we were alone in the narrow tunnel, Bart started forward, shining the light on the walls, floor, and low ceiling, making sure we'd encounter no surprises during our exploration.

After passing several feet of roughly chiseled stone walls, we came upon a small door on the right. Bart paused, pressed his ear against it, and cautiously pulled on the rusting iron ring that hung in place of a doorknob. Breath held, I anticipated the loud screech of seldom-used hinges as we'd heard on the door into the chapel upstairs, but the ancient heavy door swung silently open.

Bart and I looked at each other in surprise. He shined the light on the door hinges. Though they were, indeed, rusty and old, they also had been lubricated recently as attested by the oil on Bart's finger when he touched them.

"Someone's keeping these old tunnels in good working condition," I whispered. "We weren't expected. So who was?"

"Good question, Princess."

"I hope Norik's cousin is trustworthy. If he's not . . ." I left the sentence dangling. We both knew the ramifications of the rest of that thought.

Bart shined the light in the little room, a replica of the one we had just left: rough wooden benches lining each of the walls and a steep stairway leading up.

"Would you guess this led to the big church?" I whispered. "What did they call it? St. Astvatsatsin?"

My husband nodded absently. "The tunnel must be under the cobblestone walk between the buildings. Guess we ought to see if we can get out this way." He climbed the steep stairs and stood at the top shining the light over the slab of rock that blocked the way.

I waited until he reached the top, and then followed him up the steps, not anxious to get a foot in my face by following too close. "Try pushing," I suggested, when there didn't appear to be any handles or levers or openers of any kind anywhere around or on the smooth stone blocking the apparent door.

He handed me the light and put his shoulder to the stone. Nothing happened. He tried again. Still nothing.

He turned to me just as I touched his arm. "Maybe we'd . . ." we started to say simultaneously. I stopped and waited for him to finish his sentence. "Maybe we'd what?" he asked.

"I was going to say maybe we'd better leave this one and explore the rest of the tunnel."

"That's exactly what I was thinking," Bart said. "If anyone was in the chapel, we could walk right into their hands, since we don't know where the opening is."

We backed down the steps and continued our explorations of the tunnel. As grateful as I was for the silent hinges on the ancient door, my unease increased when I thought about someone using these tunnels often enough to keep the hinges oiled so the doors could be opened and shut quietly.

We'd only traveled a few feet when we discovered another door, identical to the first, but this time on the left side of the tunnel.

"This should be under St. Gregory, I think," I whispered.

Bart listened at the door, then pulled on the rusting iron ring. The door swung silently and easily open. At first glance, I thought the room was exactly the same as the other two, with benches around the wall and a steep stairway leading up, until Bart shined the light around the remaining walls. This one had a second door nestled against the steps.

"The plot thickens," I whispered.

"Wish I knew the layout of the churches up there," Bart said. "It would sure be nice to know what's coming and where we might end up."

"Guess we'll have to discover as we go. I can't imagine what they could use these tunnels for that they would keep those hinges in such good repair. I hope we don't blunder into the something—or the someone—that's the reason. I don't need any unpleasant surprises."

"Mmm," Bart said, in what I considered agreement. "Let's see where this goes." He pushed on the door near the stairs. Nothing happened. He shined the light around what should have been the casing, except there was none. The door was simply set into the hole made in the stone. Near the top, a simple straight small rod had been inserted into the stone to keep the door from opening. Bart slipped the rod back and pushed on the door. It swung open as the others had, quietly and easily.

This room was a replica of the rest: rough wooden benches around the wall and steep stairs leading up, but with no second door.

"Should we try the door at the top of the stairs or continue in the tunnel?" I asked, hoping for the latter. I'd developed a small sense of security in this dark, cold stone tunnel that I didn't feel when I thought of opening a door and surprising someone in the churches above.

"Let's keep going. We'll assume each set of stairs leads to a chapel. Seems like there were at least three churches and a small chapel, plus those first buildings we passed on the left when we came up the walk. I don't remember what they were."

I didn't remember either. I just remember being surprised at the number of buildings in the complex. As we progressed through the little rooms, the same kind of black garbage bag full of blankets rested under a bench as we'd found in the first room. The mystery increased. Why would they need that many blankets?

If these rooms had been used to hide villagers from invading armies, I could understand the need for all the separate little areas. The priests could have used the different rooms so others wouldn't know who was being given sanctuary. Or in case of mass evacuation of a small village, each extended family could have a room. That would cut down on the noise and problems created by putting a large number of people in a single room and afford a little privacy not usually available during those dangerous times. But these blankets were not left over from medieval times, and were definitely more recent issue than either World War II or Vietnam. Surplus from the Karabagh war?

I didn't have time to discuss it with my husband. He was already out the door and into the tunnel again, taking the light with him. I hurried to catch up, knowing that when Bart kicked into Interpol mode, he could easily forget I was with him and go off without me. When he got caught up in a case, he became single-minded, concentrating on the mystery at hand and forgetting everything else, including his wife.

The tunnel began a shallow descent and slight curve to the right. We'd traveled several feet without encountering further doors, when suddenly we came upon a door in the left side of the wall and a fork in the tunnel. Bart peeked into the room. Same everything: silent door, benches, and steps leading up.

"Eeny, meeny, miny, mo? Which way do you want to go?" I asked, unwittingly creating a little rhyme that had Bart wrinkling his nose at my poetic skills.

"Let's assume we're still under the walkway," he said. "The tunnel to the right would lead to whatever those large buildings were on the left as we came in. If I counted correctly, that last room should be under the first church on the right as we entered the complex. So where does the tunnel go from here?"

"No matter where it leads, I'm with you all the way."

Bart paused and shined the light in my face. "Much as I love having you with me, Princess, I wish you weren't here right now." He leaned down to kiss me.

Anticipating a quick peck before continuation of our explorations, I slipped my arms around his neck and pulled my husband close. "You don't get away as easily as that this time. I've missed you."

Bart's arms went around me and he hugged me close, kissing my neck and my ear and finally finding my lips. "I've missed you, Princess. I couldn't stop thinking of you, especially when I thought you'd be getting the results of your tests and we'd know if your dream was just that or was reality. I nearly got myself killed I was so distracted." He kissed me again, then pulled quickly away. "And I could do the same again. We'd better find out who's here and why, and hope we have some quiet time together before I get you out of danger and on your way back to California."

He didn't give me time to reply, just grabbed my hand and headed down the tunnel that forked left. It inclined rather sharply for about twenty feet, then suddenly dead-ended at a door that resembled the others we'd encountered thus far. But it wasn't exactly like the others. Instead of an iron ring, it had what looked like a stick protruding through the door. When Bart pulled on it, the door opened and we were hit by a blast of cold, snow-filled air.

Bart doused the light and peeked out into the storm. "I think we're on a mountain side. Looks like there's nothing below us but the hill."

"A door into the side of a hill? Are you sure about that, Sherlock?" I asked, wondering how that could be hidden from view.

"Do you doubt my powers of observation, Dr. Watson? See for yourself. Don't lean over too far or you'll fall out. Clever the way they camouflaged the door. Check this out." Bart moved back so I could feel the outside of the door. It was covered with dirt, small rocks and even a couple of bushes appearing to grow from it so it would look totally natural on the hillside.

"Clever, indeed. What do you suppose it is? A 'bail-out-and-run-for-your-life' type exit?"

"Could be," Bart said. "Can't really tell without actually seeing where it leads."

"Now what, fearless leader?"

Bart closed out the storm and turned the penlight back on. "Now you're going back to wait with the others and I'm going exploring down the hillside. I want to know who came up that road and why."

"Mostly a good idea," I agreed. "Except that I'm going with you."

"Princess . . ."

"Bart, there's no use arguing with me. I'm going with you. The only question now is whether we want to stumble blindly down the hill in the dark or go back and find another exit."

My husband didn't even pause to consider the question. He grabbed my hand, flashed the light up the passageway, and we back-tracked to the fork in the tunnel to explore that new section. This turned out to be the longest corridor we'd encountered. It seemed to stretch endlessly into the dark, veering slightly to the right. I would never have felt the variation in direction, except that as Bart flashed the light ahead of us, we could see the left wall ahead and not the right.

"Guess you're right about this leading to the first building in the complex," I whispered. "Unless it's bypassing it altogether and leading to another hillside exit. This is going on forever."

Bart stopped mid-tunnel. "Listen."

The sound of voices echoed through the tunnel ahead. Agitated voices. Or were they simply raised in excitement? I could hear both men's and women's voices and it sounded like they were yelling at each other, but in Armenia that could mean anything from a friendly conversation to the beginning of a war. We immediately reversed direction and hurried back from where we'd just come, slipping into the first room we happened upon.

"Let's see what we're dealing with before we reveal ourselves," Bart said, leaving the door slightly ajar so he could see out.

I collapsed on the bench to catch my breath. I didn't seem to have enough of it lately. Or energy either. Suddenly my stomach growled. When was the last time I'd eaten? I wasn't doing a very good job of taking care of Alexandria. I'd have to remedy that, and the only way I knew how was to change this frenetic lifestyle. Bart was so right. I needed to get back to the estate. My baby deserved better than I was giving her, or could possibly give her while I stayed out in the field. If I'd been a policeman—policewoman, to be politically correct—I'd have turned in my gun and my badge at this point. Unfortunately, that would have to wait until the resolution of the current situation.

As they approached the door, I could hear Norik and another man and woman whose voices I thought I'd heard before. But where? I ran to the door and stood beside my husband to hear more clearly.

"I know those voices," I whispered.

"Who are they?"

"Give me a minute to listen." I dipped under Bart's arm and stood nestled against him at the crack in the door. Since he was a full head taller than me, he had no trouble seeing over my head. I could hear the voices plainly now, but where did I know them from? I ran through my day, trying to remember everywhere I'd been and every soul I'd encountered.

"You don't know what you're doing, Maria," Norik rattled in Russian as they proceeded up the passageway.

The American University of Armenia. Maria and Armen.

"Norik, please don't send us back," Maria pled in the same language. "We've got to get out of Armenia. What kind of life can we have here? It will be years before we can get married. Neither of us can find work, even when we graduate with good degrees. Look at Narine. She can't get paid enough as a doctor to make it worth her time working, and with her contacts and experience, I know she could get a job if she wanted."

"Bart, these are the students I met at the American University this morning. How did they find us?"

"Let's go find out." Bart shifted so I could move away from the door enough to open it. We stepped into the tunnel with the penlight on as they came abreast of the door. Maria gave a little squeal of alarm and Armen's arm slipped protectively around her.

"What are you two doing here in the middle of a blizzard?" I asked in English, though I knew full well as I remembered our conversation of this morning.

They stared at me for a second before the light of recognition shone in their eyes. "You're lady in lounge at university this morning," Maria answered in English, looking puzzled.

"You meet before?" Norik asked.

"As she said, we met at the university." I turned to Maria and Armen and repeated my question in Russian. "What are you doing here?"

They seemed stunned into silence at the two strangers standing before them. Norik answered my question in Russian, the language they all seemed more comfortable speaking with me. "They were at the church tonight. Maria's in our branch and Armen is wherever Maria is. Maggie mentioned we were going to Dilijan to get the bees. Since escape was uppermost in their minds, they thought while I was up here, I could get them across the border."

"But how did they find this place?" I asked. "It's not exactly on the main road to anywhere."

"Armen has come with me before to help with the bees. He knew where to come. They borrowed the truck of his brother-in-law, which he wants us to return to his mother after they leave the country."

"Why do they think you can get them out?" I wondered if it was common knowledge that Norik was the person who knew how to cross borders. That could be very dangerous for him.

"I know the country here. We've had the bees all along the border. After the rumors at the university this morning, they decided they had to leave before Armen was forced back into the army. They figured if we were this close to the border it wouldn't be that hard for me to take them across and still get the bees back to town as I'd planned."

Bart motioned Norik a few steps away. I followed. "What's your plan?" Bart asked quietly in English since his Russian skills were minimal. "Are you going to take them out with us?"

Norik rubbed his chin, taking his time with the answer. "I think maybe yes. I think Armen must go to Army again. This not good for him. I think it better they go to Russia. Maria has aunt there who can help."

"Why can't they go legally, with visas?" I asked, worrying about how they would ever get back if they left illegally.

"They not give Armen visa now. Want him in Army. Dangerous time to be in Army for young man in love." Norik paused and added sadly, "Dangerous time to be in Armenia."

"Do they realize they're not just endangering our lives, but theirs, too?" Bart asked. "Three is a lot of people to hide. Five is a crowd."

"We're in danger if we stay," Armen said, apparently hearing what Bart had intended to be a private conversation. "Better to die trying for freedom than hide like a frightened mouse and be caught in a trap."

Bart and Norik shared a thoughtful minute of silence.

Finally Bart broke the silence. "It's your call, Norik, since you're the one with the experience getting people across the border, and you have a family to consider."

"I think on it," Norik said. He turned and paced a few steps into the darkness, out of the little circle of light created by the flashlights, and back again, pondering, weighing, possibly even praying. I would have been if I'd been in his situation.

"*Ha,*" he said finally. "We all go. But I think we do different plan now."

"What's the plan?" Bart asked. "And when do we leave?"

"In morning we leave. You rest now while I work new plan to make sure no insects remain." He flashed an uncertain smile at us. "That how you say it?"

"You'll work on getting the bugs out of the new plan," Bart said.

"*Ha.* I get rid of bugs before they bite." Norik turned to Armen and Maria. "Okay, we all go. Maybe we all die. Sometimes that is better than living." He turned back to us. "In year 451, Vardan Mamikonyon lead Armenian army against Persians who want to wipe out Christianity. He say, 'Unconscious death is death indeed, apprehended death is immortality.' That become battle cry for generations of Armenian freedom fighters."

He spoke to Armen and Maria. "God give us immortality as gift. We choose eternal life with Him, or we choose something less. I hope you ready to see where your choices take you. Tomorrow you may find out."

Maria drew herself up to her full height, which couldn't have been more than 5 feet, one or two inches, and gripped Armen's hand. "I'm ready."

Armen's comment was interrupted by a small sound echoing through the tunnel from the direction they'd just come. Bart and Norik immediately switched off their lights and we all froze where we stood.

CHAPTER 22

Bart grabbed my hand and pulled me back into the room where we'd hidden when we heard Norik and Armen and Maria approaching. Norik followed at my elbow, and Armen and Maria slipped through the door behind him.

We waited breathlessly as the sound of footsteps progressed towards us. How many were in the tunnel? Possibly only one, but if others wore quiet shoes, an army could be approaching.

"Norik, where are you?" Narine's quiet voice enabled us all to breathe again.

"Here." Norik switched on his light and stepped back into the tunnel.

Even in the dim light, I could see Narine's face lined with worry. "The dog started barking again. Henrik said to tell you another car is coming up the road. You need to come now."

"I come." He turned to us. "You rest. Tomorrow will be hard day. I come back when it's time to leave."

They hurried back down the tunnel, neither of them speaking. The four of us stood silently for a minute until all sound had completely disappeared, then Bart turned on his light and flashed it around the room. "You two might as well spread out some of those blankets and get what rest you can. Morning is only a few hours away. We'll take the deluxe accommodations next door." I'm sure the irony of Bart's comment was lost on the young couple.

We waited with the light until they'd spread the bag full of blankets on the floor, fashioning a bed of sorts. As soon as Marie knelt down on one side, we left the room, pulling the door shut behind us.

I looked up at my husband as he hesitated in the tunnel. I knew exactly what was going through his mind. Should he take me into the next little sanctuary room and make sure I got some rest, or should he follow Narine and Norik down the tunnel and find out who else was on the road in the blizzard?

There was no decision to be made. Neither of us would be able to sleep, or even rest, not knowing who else braved the storm in the middle of the night on a road that led only to a centuries old, locked monastery and a humble shepherd's cottage.

"Let's go, Lochinvar. Onward, in pursuit of the never-ending quest. Or should I say never-ending guests?" I tried to make my voice sound light and filled with energy.

"Princess, you need to get some rest." Bart shined the light in my face. "You must be exhausted. You look terrible."

So much for trying to fake it. "Flattery will get you nowhere, my dear husband. You know as well as I do it would be an exercise in futility to try to sleep. Neither of us would close our eyes, and even if I did, the minute you thought I was asleep you'd be up and gone, leaving me behind. Sorry, Charlie. Won't happen. Let's go see what natives are restless tonight. Then maybe we'll have a couple of hours to catch a quick nap."

Bart stared at me for a minute, shook his head and leaned down to kiss my chin. "When you get that look on your face with your chin set like that, there's no use arguing. That has to be the most stubborn chin in the world."

"You're a quick study, Bart. Let's go." I really didn't want to go anywhere but to bed. I was exhausted. There didn't seem to be any energy, or even a drop of adrenalin left in my body to keep it moving. But I knew neither of us could rest without knowing what was going on above ground.

As my thoughts focused on what might be happening up there, I couldn't imagine a single scenario that brought comfort. Had the Army followed Armen and Maria? Had Bart's terrorist friends managed to catch up to him? Or was my would-be assassin closing in again? Maybe all three. Expect the worst and hope for the best. I shuddered to think of facing any one of them, much less all three. But who else had reason to be out in this weather?

Bart moved quickly through the tunnel, his long legs taking long strides. I had to run to keep up with him. There was no hope of catching up with Norik and Narine. They had too much of a head start because we'd waited for Armen and Maria to make their bed. But there didn't seem to be any more entrances or exits as we hurried through the passageway, so we ultimately had to come out where they were.

And where would that be? The farther we went, the narrower the tunnel became. We could no longer travel side by side. It had become a one-man passage that sloped downward in a shallow descent and curved again to the left. I'd ceased paying any attention to the walls. I couldn't have told whether they were hollowed out of the stone mountain or whether they had been formed with blocks of stone as everything else in Armenia seemed to be.

I hooked my finger through Bart's belt loop and moved on autopilot, following blindly behind him, needing his forward momentum to keep me moving. I could probably go to sleep on my feet as we hurried along the never-ending passage. Fortunately the floor of the tunnel was smoother than the sidewalks on Abovian so I didn't have to watch my footing. I couldn't have seen it anyway since Bart had my penlight. Just when I thought we would never find the end, Bart stopped.

I peered around him. Another unremarkable wooden door blocked our path. Bart stood quietly for a minute. I thought he was listening. Suddenly he handed me the light and peeled off his raincoat. I held it for him while he removed his lavender tie and silver gray suit jacket.

"If I'm supposed to be helping with bees, I'd better look a little more casual and a little less like I just left the office." He folded the discarded items and placed them on the floor of the tunnel, unbuttoned his collar button and rolled up his shirt sleeves.

"Good thought. I hope you don't freeze." I handed him his raincoat. "This doesn't feel very heavy."

"I hope that's the least of my worries. When I dressed, I didn't plan on a trek through a blizzard tonight."

I shuddered. A flight on foot over the mountains through a blizzard was certainly not on any list of things I wanted to do, tonight or anytime. Bart donned the raincoat and transferred his gun from his ankle holster to his pocket. I put my hand in my purse on my own gun, hoping we wouldn't need to use them.

Bart reached for the door. I grabbed his arm. "What if the dog starts barking? Their 'alarm system' has been pretty effective tonight."

He pulled on the door handle. "Pray for the watch dog to be inflicted with a sudden case of laryngitis."

"Roger." And I did.

This door proved a little more stubborn than most of the others we'd passed through tonight. It didn't swing open as the others had. Bart gave another fruitless tug, then stepped back and shined the light on it. No lock or bolt appeared to be holding it.

"Okay, Princess. Work your magic here. Locate the release so we can find out what's going on out there."

I took the light from Bart and examined the door and the wall surrounding it. I felt the bumps and protrusions and ran my fingers into the indentations, all different ways our fathers had concealed the openings in the secret passageways when they built the mansion on the estate. Nothing worked. I hated to run my fingers over the rough wooden door. That would certainly guarantee a hand full of slivers. Then I saw the point of a nail that seemed to have come through from the other side of the door.

I wiggled it. It worked, releasing whatever catch had held the door in place. I felt a slight give, switched off the light and tugged on the door handle. The door opened a crack. Bart grabbed the handle and pulled; the door groaned open a little further. It didn't seem to be held by anything, nor did the hinges seem rusty or unused as they made no sound, but something from the other side prevented the door from opening.

Bart poked his head out of the narrow opening he'd thus far created to see what caused the problem. He stepped back into the tunnel, grabbed the edge of the door, and pulled hard. A pile of stones attached to the door swung into the passage. Very clever. I couldn't tell whether this was an ancient design or more modern, but someone, sometime, had gone to a lot of trouble to carve the passageways and conceal the openings.

I followed Bart out of the tunnel and we pulled the stones back into place slowly, planning to leave the door open a crack so it didn't lock, just in case we had to get back into the tunnel quickly. But it slid smoothly shut before we could stop it. Suddenly we stood in the open with no hiding place into which we could safely and quickly flee.

The wind had quieted and the snowfall abated. A car partially blocked the light from the cottage window. Bart pulled his gun from his pocket and pointed to the front end of the car signaling for me to go around that side. He rounded the back end of the car and edged slowly toward the humble house while I crept toward it from the other direction, my hand on my own gun in my purse. We circled the house to make sure no one was outside, encountering nary a soul. Even the dog was missing. Only the goats in their lean-to near the house stirred at all.

The house contained only two small rooms: a kitchen/living area on one side lit by a single bulb in the small ever-present chandelier, and an even more dimly lit sleeping area on the other. Norik and Narine stood in the center of the small living room with Henrik and a man I'd never seen before. LeVon and a youth about his age, apparently Petros, bent over a game board on the kitchen table, ignoring the adults conversing in the middle of the room in Russian.

"I tell you, Norik, something unpleasant is happening in Armenia, but we're not getting the true story from the government," the stranger said, his voice raised in agitation. "No one has radio, TV, or telephone. I went to the office of the Post to find out what was going on with the telephone. No one knew. I walked to the TV station and they said they are making some repairs and TV would be down for a couple of days. Same bad lie at the radio station. In the old Armenia, it happened all the time. Not today. You don't lose all communication at the same time. What's going on?"

Norik studied the bundle of papers in his hands. "You had no trouble getting these documents made, Feliks?"

"If I hadn't been working with old friends, I couldn't have gotten them at all. People are uneasy, more careful." He nodded his head slowly. "No one wants to admit something is going on, but everyone feels it. You'd think the Soviets were back again."

"Something just as bad." Norik shook his head. "Maybe worse. Osama bin Ladin's al Qaeda, along with the remnant of Taliban, is trying to occupy Armenia. Take over the army and the air force.

Replace Kocharian as President. If they succeed, the next voice you hear on TV will tell you the bad news. If they don't succeed, everything will resume as normal and you'll never hear more than rumors about what nearly happened."

An expression of stunned disbelief crossed Feliks's face. He stood speechless for a minute, then wiped his face with his hands as if to rid himself of the remnant of a bad dream. "Is that why you need all these forged passports and visas?"

Norik nodded. "Border crossings will be almost impossible now. We have people who need to get out, who can't wait for the situation to be settled. They will need these tonight. Thank you, my friend, for finishing the job and bringing them up. Will you stay or go back tonight?"

"I go back, but by different road. Are you coming back?"

"Of course." Norik shrugged his shoulders and spread his hands in what I had learned was a typical Armenian expression. "This is my homeland." He put his arm around Narine's shoulders and pulled her close to his side. "We must make it better for LeVon and Maggie. We must make it good enough that Nona and Ryan will return from America to live with our granddaughter, Jade. Armenia can be great. We just need to teach the people how to do it."

"You won't get the chance with terrorists in charge of the government," Henrik interjected. "You'd better get these people where they need to go and get back to town to keep your eye on things."

"What can I do? I am a simple beekeeper and carpet merchant. But I will come, as soon as we are finished here. Narine and the family will stay until . . ." Norik paused. He suddenly looked very tired. "They will stay for a few days before they return."

Henrik put his hand on Feliks shoulder. "Now, you will have something to eat before you return."

Feliks shook his head. "No, I must go. I don't want to leave my wife alone. It will be morning before I get home if I have to take the other road."

Everyone shook hands but there were no lingering good-byes. Feliks went immediately to his car and drove away, using no headlights and driving in the tracks he had made coming up. The storm had passed allowing a pale moon to peek from behind a cloud. Just a few snowflakes fluttered to the ground, probably falling from the trees overhead, not enough to fill in our tracks in the snow.

"What now, Illustrious Leader?" I asked Bart, hoping he'd say it was past time to get a bit of rest before we headed for the border in a few hours.

"Let's check in with Norik, then you are going to bed, such as it is." Bart steered me to the door and poked his head in. "Any change in our situation?" His voice startled the group. Nerves were strung tight.

Norik stepped quickly to the door. "No change." He looked at his watch. "We leave in four hours. You sleep now. Everything okay with you?"

"Where's the dog?" I asked. "Why didn't he bark at us?"

"Petros feed him. And you are with us so no threat." Norik turned and pointed to the collie still eating in the corner. "He will go out again as soon as he finish."

Henrik crossed to the door and asked in Russian, "How did you get out of the tunnel? We've never had anyone leave without our help."

"You hide people often in the tunnels?" I asked.

Henrik glanced at Norik. I couldn't read the look they exchanged. But before either of them could answer, the collie raised his head from his dish, and looking up at the window above him, growled softly.

"Petros, quiet the dog," Henrik ordered in Russian as his hand swept the light switch next to the door. "Narine, the light in the bedroom."

The boy whirled to the dog and put his hand on its head. The collie immediately stopped, but watched the door where we stood, as if awaiting the order to go find whatever was out there.

CHAPTER 23

"Listen for the signal, Petros. You know what to do." Then Henrik snapped his fingers, the cue the dog had been waiting for. He bounded across the room and slipped out the door with Henrik. Norik followed, closing the door quietly behind him. Bart needed no translation to know what was happening. Trouble had found us.

"Come," Norik whispered. "I open tunnel for you."

"Allison will go back," Bart whispered. "I'll stay out here to help."

"Not on your life. I'm with you, wherever you are," I said.

"Go to tree at end of walkway." Norik whispered. I think Bart would have argued with me, but Norik disappeared around the corner of the house, heading toward Maria and Armen's vehicle. The van was nowhere in sight. Come to think of it, neither was Ruben.

Very vague instructions. "'Tree at end of walkway." The only walkway I knew about was the one up the middle of the buildings, between the churches. Apparently that was Bart's thought also. He grabbed my hand and headed in the direction of the church complex.

We could now hear what the dog had heard—a vehicle straining up the steep winding road. The driver shifted into a lower gear, which increased the noise. Suddenly the engine stopped. The night was silent again. We stopped too, straining to hear sounds in the darkness that would indicate the intent of the driver. A car door slammed, then another, and another. We waited. The fourth door shut. At least four people exited that car, maybe five, the fifth taking more time to get out of the middle of the back seat than those by the doors. Or someone retrieving something from the trunk?

We continued our silent flight down the little curved driveway, walking in the tracks of Feliks's car. Feliks!

"Bart, Feliks would have run right into whomever was coming up that road."

"He'd see them coming, unless they were running without lights too."

As we hurried back along the narrow little driveway, being careful to walk in the tire tracks, I tried to visualize the road up the mountain. Where could Feliks have pulled the car off the road to let someone pass without being seen? It had been snowing heavily when we came up. There may have been many places I missed seeing in the storm.

Too soon we had to leave the road and the anonymity of the fresh tire tracks. The tracks our van made when we drove into the parking lot of the complex were now barely visible under the snow—just slight indentations. We followed those tracks until we could see the ancient stone buildings.

It was amazing how much visibility we had. The dark stone and tree trunks contrasted starkly against the brilliant whiteness of the snow. Other than being unable to see where the snow blanketed uneven spots or holes on the ground, there was no need for a light. Which meant, of course, that whoever was coming up the road had no need for a light either.

As we hurried up the stone path between the ancient churches, I was acutely aware of the footprints we were leaving in the snow. It didn't matter how cleverly we hid, a child could find us simply by following our tracks. As I was about to call that to the attention of my husband, he apparently had the same thought.

"Let's muddle the path," Bart whispered. He veered off to one side toward the entrance of the first small church. I caught the vision of his plan and hurried to the next church, walking forwards and backwards several times, then went to the next sanctuary. Bart went back and scuffed our tracks, obliterating individual footprints.

When I reached the end of the churches, I found the tree Norik meant. At the edge of the hill stood a huge ancient tree with black gnarled branches reaching eerily in all directions. Underneath the twisted branches, stone monuments rested with snow piled deep on each ledge and cleft.

Norik had said "go to tree." He hadn't said what to do when we got here. There wouldn't be time to search for an entry back into the tunnel, and Bart didn't want to be hidden away from the action anyway. I circled the tree several feet from it so my tracks didn't appear to lead to it. One side of the tree, the side facing the drop off down the hill, was different than the rest. A long dark slash ran the length of the trunk from the ground to the first main branch just over my head. I took a giant step across the snow, grabbing the rough bark of the primeval tree to keep my balance.

The tree trunk was hollow. I slipped inside. One of the ancient branches was missing, leaving a face-sized hole that overlooked the valley below. Peering out, I saw three dark figures moving toward the monastery, a vivid contrast against the whiteness of the snow that blanketed everything. Movement on the road above them caught my eye. Two more dark figures approached the monastery from that direction.

Where was Bart? If he waited too long, they'd be close enough to see him. And who were "they?" Definitely not the good guys. Their stealthy approach testified to that. But into which bad-guy category did they fall? That meant all the difference in the level of danger to everyone here. The training, motivation, and bloodlust of the local army and that of the al Qaeda was as vastly disparate as night and day. On the other hand, they could be KGB or the everyday run-of-the-mill terrorist hoping to catch Anastasia off guard.

How had they found us up here? Or had they followed Feliks? Or Armen and Maria? Or discovered the absence of Norik and Narine's family? The list of bad guys matched the list of their possible targets.

Their swift approach worried me. What happened to Bart? I hoped he wasn't planning to confront them, or try to take them on himself. Where had Norik gone? And Henrik? What were they doing? Had Bart joined them? How could I find out without leaving the safety of the tree?

The figures on the road were out of sight but the ones below the monastery were clearly visible halfway up the hill below me. The clouds began to thin and I could see the outline of the moon appearing behind them. The crunch of footsteps in the snow became audible. As I turned to peek out the slash in the tree looking for Bart, I saw a slight movement in the shadow of the ancient stone building nearest the tree.

I held my breath, hoping it was Bart, hoping he'd join me in the tree before they reached the crest of the hill. But he didn't, if it was him. Then it was too late. The three figures topped the hill. I pressed against the inside of the tree, away from the hole left by the missing branch, away from the gashed entry into it—and didn't breathe.

Instructions in Arabic were given for one to stay hidden by the tree, another to stay near the first church; the third would join the other two approaching from the road and go to the house.

The man assigned to stay by the tree moved around to the back—directly next to the opening to my hiding place. If he examined the tree, he'd quickly find the opening, and me. He stood close to the tree, so close I could smell the perspiration and see the camouflage patterns on his uniform. He stood absolutely still for about ten seconds, then reached into his pocket and pulled out a pack of cigarettes, leaning his gun against the tree.

At least, he thought he was leaning his gun against the tree. Anticipating his mistake, I reached out my hand to steady the gun, keeping it upright so he'd think the tree was solid. Then he began the search for a match or light. I took advantage of his rustling movements to silently slip the gun inside the tree. He presented an immediate danger to me and to Bart who I hoped stood in the shadows near him. This man needed to be incapacitated.

Before his compatriots had even reached the end of the walkway between the churches, the soldier found his light, lit the cigarette under cupped hands, and backed up to the tree to smoke it. But before he could lean back and discover the tree was hollow, I reached out to compress the pressure points that would render him unconscious. Bart beat me to it. As the soldier slumped forward, Bart caught him and slung him over his shoulder.

We both stood perfectly still for a second to see if our movements had attracted the attention of the two men down the walkway. The only sound in the night was the soft hooting of an owl.

At that moment, chaos broke out by the house: goats bleated, men shouted, and dogs barked. Someone had turned the goats loose. Ingenious. The soldiers were still near the church complex. The goats would obliterate all footprints and tracks near the house.

Henrik called to Petros to gather the goats quickly before they went down the mountain as they'd freeze during the night. But I was certain the goats weren't being gathered. They'd be driven straight out the driveway toward the monasteries and the men attempting to creep up to the house.

I slipped out of my hiding place, taking the weapon I'd hidden there. Bart dumped the soldier into the hollow tree.

"Cover me," he said, and headed around the back of the little church set slightly askew at the top of the complex with me right on his heels. Hugging the stone walls, we stopped at the edge of St. Stepanos, then darted across the gap between the churches to St. Gregory where the rubies were hidden.

We didn't have to worry about our footsteps in the snow being heard. The goats clamoring up the stone walkway between the churches made enough noise to cover the movements of a regiment. As we reached the *gavit*, Bart suddenly pulled me back against the wall of the chapel. The *gavit*, larger than the small chapel it was connected to, stuck out a few feet toward the edge of the hill, offering a shadowed corner in which to hide.

We pressed into that dark corner just as someone ran along the *gavit* wall toward the end of the church. I saw the end of the gun first, and as Bart reached for the soldier carrying it, I grabbed the gun from his hands. After Bart's quick blow to the side of the head, the soldier no longer had a need for his weapon.

Bart left him on the ground and headed for the front of the complex, relieving me of the extra weapon as we moved along the *gavit*. But when we reached the end of the ancient stone building and peered around the corner, we discovered there was no need for stealth. Norik, Henrik, and Feliks each had an unconscious soldier at his feet. At least, I assumed they were unconscious. None were moving.

Henrik hooted like an owl and Petros, now up near the old tree with the goats shouted an order to the dog who began barking at the goats and turning them back. Bart waved at the men and Henrik joined us at the entrance to the *gavit.*

"There's one along the wall and one in the tree," Bart said, handing me the gun again. Henrik followed Bart around the edge of the *gavit*. I joined Norik and Feliks, giving them the weapons we'd taken from the soldiers.

"I'm glad to see you, Feliks," I said in Russian. "I was afraid you might have run into the soldiers on your way back to town."

Feliks stared at me. "Do I know you?"

Norik quickly introduced us.

"I saw you through the window," I explained as Feliks offered his hand at the introduction, "and watched you drive away just before the dog heard the other car. How did you avoid the soldiers?"

"I saw the lights on the road below, parked behind the funerary chapel at the top of the hill, then hurried back through the woods to see who came this time of night."

"Do you know who they are?" I asked.

Norik shook his head. "They wear the uniform of the Armenian Army, but I think they are not regular Army." He bent, took the belt from the soldier's trousers and secured his hands behind his back, then with the handkerchief from the soldier's pocket, blindfolded the still unconscious man. Feliks copied the process with the soldier at his feet.

As I bent to do the same to the third soldier, Bart and Henrik returned dragging their soldiers, and Petros and LeVon drove the goats clattering down the stone walkway toward the house.

"Good job with the goats, boys," Henrik called. "Pen them up again and go on to bed. I think the excitement is over for the night." Then he turned to the men in the circle. "Let's get them in the tunnel where we can find out who they are and what they were after."

With Bart's smattering of Russian, he grasped the concept without translation, and looping one tall soldier over his shoulder followed Norik and Feliks as they headed the few steps down the hill to the tunnel entrance we'd found in the hillside. Henrik and I finished securing the hands of the other two soldiers and blindfolding them, then I dragged mine and Henrik carried his to the entrance in the side of the hill. Bart came back for the poor soldier I was dragging through the snow and slung him over his shoulder.

Narine appeared at that moment and we followed the men into the tunnel, pulling the door closed behind us. Someone had turned on a string of dim lights that ran the length of the passage, but we didn't have far to go. They took the men, now recovering consciousness, to the nearest room under the churches.

Henrik dumped his man in the middle of the floor. "I will make sure no one else is coming to our once quiet and peaceful abode," he said, returning to stand guard at the house.

Bart and Feliks searched the pockets of the soldiers for identification. As I bent to help, the soldier who had been pretending to be unconscious kicked out at me.

"This one isn't Armenian," I said, jumping back out of the way.

"How do you know?" Bart asked, grabbing the offender and sitting him roughly against the cold stone wall of the little room.

"I think he's the one who gave instructions in Arabic to the other two who came up the hill with him. The moon came out just as they reached the tree where I hid and I saw the bent brim on his cap. He didn't want to be touched by a woman just now, a common cultural thing among Muslims who look down on women."

This was Bart's area of expertise. He had spent much time with the people of the Arab nations, ferreting out the terrorists among them. Surprisingly, it was also Norik's. He and Bart conducted their interrogations in Farsi; Feliks spoke Russian to his soldier.

As the adrenalin abated from the excitement, so did my last remaining bit of energy. I sagged down on a rough bench and leaned against the cold wall. Narine sat beside me.

"How does Norik know Farsi?" I asked, wondering what other surprises Norik held.

"He studied the language for his carpet business. He travels to Iran to buy carpets, goes to the big bazaar in Tehran, and to the little villages where they weave them to find the perfect carpets for his customers. LeVon is studying Farsi also."

"You all amaze me with your linguist abilities." I closed my eyes and leaned my head against the stones behind me. "Do you know what they call someone who speaks three languages?"

Narine sounded puzzled. "No."

"Trilingual," I answered. "Do you know what they call someone who speaks two languages?"

Again she paused, then said, "No."

"Bilingual." I opened my eyes and turned to meet her puzzled gaze. "And do you know what they call someone who speaks only one language?"

Narine smiled. "I give up," she said. "I'm sure it isn't monolingual."

"American."

Narine laughed. "A joke. But you speak many languages."

"That was my major; that's what I chose to study. Most Americans don't learn another language unless they have reason to leave the country. The schools don't require students to study foreign languages. As a country, America probably speaks fewer languages than any other in the world, with the exception, of course, of all immigrants with their mother tongue and the missionaries who learn languages to teach the gospel."

"Musharif!" Bart exclaimed, bending over the fifth soldier who had lain quietly with his back turned while the rest were being interrogated.

"Is American oath or you know this man?" Norik asked.

"I know the man, and his name should only be said as an oath. Musharif is one of the top ten men closest to Osama bin Laden. He's been the brain behind some of the most dastardly attacks on civilians across the globe for the last fifteen years, including fatal embassy bombings." Bart sat back on his heels and stared at the man sprawled on the floor in front of him. "But he's supposed to be in Georgia already. He was seen there just yesterday. What is he doing back here now?"

"Ask him," I suggested.

Bart looked up at me like I'd just advocated turning him loose or something equally ridiculous. "I'm sure he's just dying to tell me," Bart said dryly.

"He might be if he has something to brag about." Certainly he wouldn't answer any questions for me since I was a nonentity in his eyes. In fact, Bart would be better off in his interrogations if Narine and I left, now that we knew the identity of at least one of them.

"We'll go do some mundane woman's task like scrub the floors and lick the boots clean so you can make some headway here." I grabbed Narine's hand and we left the room. I didn't know where I was going—only that we needed to leave—and that I wanted very much to find a bed upon which to lay my weary body.

"Are you feeling okay?" Narine asked as we paused outside the door under the tiny light bulb that dangled overhead.

"Do I look that bad?" I asked with a grimace, imagining how terrible I probably did appear after my very long day. Then I saw the expression on Narine's face. "Are you asking as a woman or as a doctor?"

She smiled. "As a woman doctor." Her smile faded and her tone became serious and professional. "How far along are you in your pregnancy?"

"Very early and I'm just tired. Do you still practice medicine with the economy the way it is?" I said, changing the subject to get the focus off of me.

"No, I haven't worked in medicine since Maggie was born. But it doesn't take a medical degree to see that you are near collapse. Let's get you off your feet while they finish here and decide what to do next."

I let Narine lead me along the passageway toward the entrance without the slightest resistance. "I won't argue with the doctor. I think I could probably lay down right here and sleep."

"We can do better than that for you. Is this your first pregnancy? Have you had any problems?"

"Narine, I'm fine," I assured her, sidestepping her questions. "Just very tired. I understand that you have a new granddaughter."

Though Narine walked in front of me and I couldn't see her face, I could hear the smile in her voice as she said, "Yes, my first grandchild. In fact, I was in the States with Nona when the baby was born."

"And now? Will you be able to go see them again with all of this political unrest in Armenia?"

She stopped at the door. "I don't know. It always takes so long to get a visa and they can be so arbitrary about granting one." Then she turned and twisted the protruding nail in the roughhewn door. I helped her pull open the door with the stones attached to it and we emerged into a night brilliant with silver moonlight. The storm had passed completely.

"You can lay on the sofa. The boys will be on pallets on the floor—if they aren't still playing Nardi."

"Where are you sleeping?" I asked, realizing I'd probably be taking her bed if I took the sofa.

"I will go with my mother and Aida and be near Maggie. You are leaving soon, only a couple more hours, so you need to get some rest. The roads are not good and it will be an exhausting ride for you."

Henrik met us, emerging from the dark shadows near the goat pen. "All is well? What have they found out?"

"One is a leader of al Qaeda, just returned from Georgia." Narine turned to me. "What was his name?"

"Musharif. You've probably heard of him. Al Qaeda has been so much in the news lately because they've regrouped, at least those not already caught in the war on terrorists."

Henrik opened the door for us and stuck his head around the doorframe to check on the boys. If they were supposed to be asleep, they weren't. The click of dice on the Nardi board told the story before I even stepped into the room.

Narine didn't come in. "Mrs. Allan needs to lie down," she explained to Henrik, and then she turned to me. "I'll see you before you leave. Now I will go to Maggie and see if she is sleeping." She disappeared into the darkness, apparently familiar with all the tunnels and hidden entrances and not needing Henrik's help to find her way back in.

Henrik didn't come in either, just poked his head inside and told the boys to put the game away and get some sleep. They would have tomorrow to continue. I was about to say it didn't matter, that I would easily be able to sleep through the noise of the game, but then realized it was an early morning hour and the boys actually should be asleep.

LeVon and Petros spread out on the pallets on the floor fully dressed and I sunk gratefully onto the sofa, which had certainly seen better days. In fact, there didn't seem to be a spring left in it. But I was off my feet, and at the moment, there were no bad guys shooting at me, or shoving me into the path of speeding automobiles, or chasing me with knives. And my husband was near at hand. Life was good.

But I hadn't even closed my tired eyes before Bart and Norik burst into the house, with Armen and Maria close behind.

"Sorry, Princess, don't get comfortable. We're leaving for the border right now."

"Where is Narine?" Norik asked, looking into the empty bedroom.

"With Maggie. What happened? What did you find out?"

"I'll tell you on the way," Bart said, taking me by the hand and literally lifting me off the sofa. "Looks like it's now or never to get you across the border and back home safely. Our window of opportunity is closing fast."

"If not already shut," Norik added softly as he hurried out to find Narine.

CHAPTER 24

Armen followed Norik into the night with Maria in tow. Bart and I were right behind them, not because I was moving that fast, but simply because Bart had his arm around my waist and nearly picked me up and carried me.

Henrik met us at Armen's tiny truck. "I'll get you something to eat to take along."

"Thanks, Henrik," Maria said, "but there isn't time."

"Bart, what about the rubies?" I stopped with one foot in the truck. "Who will get them back to Echmiadzin?"

"Henrik and Norik can worry about the rubies. My worry is you and Alexandria. Get in."

As I joined Maria in the back of the mini-camper, I shined the penlight on the varied contents and we moved toolboxes and shifted rolls of electrical wiring to find a place to sit. Lying down was impossible, not only because of tools all over the floor, but because the camper was so small.

Armen got behind the wheel, slid open the window between the little cab and "camper" and passed through a quilt and a wool Army blanket. "You'll probably want to sit on these. It will save a few bruises when we get to the really bumpy roads."

Encouraging thought. But I was so tired now, I figured I could sleep through anything. Even bumpy roads sitting on a cold, steel truck bed. As I rearranged a couple of bundles of insulated wire behind me, I heard Norik and Bart's last minute instructions to Feliks and Henrik.

"Who's the best man to do it, Norik?" Bart asked.

"Vaghinak, I think," Norik said thoughtfully.

"Feliks, can you send him up here? Today?" Bart quickly added.

"I find him. He will come," Feliks said.

"Blast this communications blackout!" Bart slapped the side of the truck. "We need him here now to finish the interrogation. We need to let them know in Yerevan what's happening—right now—not three or four hours from now. I feel like we're fighting a major war with both hands tied behind our backs."

"Ha," Norik agreed. "But we do best we can. We go now."

"One more thing, Feliks. You know Jack Alexander? He's trying to come through sometime today or tomorrow. Tell him what we've learned, and that I'm taking his daughter out of this war zone."

My heart jumped. Dad was coming? And I was leaving as he arrived?

Bart and Norik squeezed into the tiny cab and Armen tried to engage the starter. Nothing happened but a fruitless grinding. That's all we need. A stalled truck. Eventually Arman's persistence won, and the little truck finally sparked to life. Armen backed up the muddy drive and onto the gravel road.

I twisted around and spoke through the open window as we began the journey out of the canyon. "Now tell me what happened down there. How did you find out about Dad? Is he really on his way? And who is Vaghinak?"

Bart slid his arm across the back of the seat behind Norik so he could turn enough to talk to me. "Because of the communications blackout, Musharif decided he was safe in bragging about what was happening. He figured since the wheels had already started turning, there was no way we could prevent it at this point. Who could we tell and how?"

"And what is happening?" I was almost afraid to ask.

"Tonight," Bart began, glancing at his watch. "Last night," he amended, "they gave the alert to take over all branches of Armenia's government. The moles who've infiltrated and become established in the last few years will all be activated and bring everything to a halt in their respective assignments. They'll control all branches of government, the police, the air force and the army."

"And Dad?"

"Jack expected to arrive in the country at midnight with the rest of Anastasia."

"You knew they were coming and didn't tell me? And we're leaving?" I couldn't believe my ears.

"No, I didn't know, Princess. Musharif told me as he laughed in my face. He said even the legendary Jack Alexander wouldn't be able to stop them. Jack would arrive on the scene to witness the takeover and chaos that resulted, and he wouldn't be able to do a thing about it."

"How did he know Dad was on his way here if communication is out?" I didn't want to believe Musharif.

"One of his men traveled through Armenia from Karabagh to Georgia a few hours ago," Bart said. "Only Armenia is blacked out, not the entire Caucasus region."

"Is Musharif right? Nothing can be done? Can't the Armenians fight back? Can't they prevent it?"

"Question not if they *can* fight back. Question if they *will*," Norik said. "Communism take away initiative of people. They used to having supervisor to tell what to do, how to do, when to do. They good at following directions. Not good at acting on their own."

"But they won't let al Qaeda come in and take over everything without question, will they?" I persisted. "Surely everyone knows the evil of al Qaeda and what they'll bring. They'll regress back where they were under Communism, only far, far worse because of the radical Muslim aspect of al Qaeda."

"Many would go back to Communism in a minute," Maria said quietly. "The older generation that suffer so much now all had money, jobs, free vacations, cars, and apartments when the Soviets were in power, all provided by the State—which took all their money to pay for it. That generation had everything but freedom. But they had been without freedom for so long, they no longer remembered what it was like. They forget how life under Communism stripped them of freedom to talk to anyone they wanted to on the street, to choose the job they wanted, their own place to live, instead of being assigned it by the 'People's Party.' Everything was dictated by the Soviets, but they don't remember that now. They only remember the good part."

Stunned by the new insight, I tried to understand the implication of what Maria said. Of course it was possible for a country to be taken over quietly without war or revolution. If people didn't value freedom and progress, if they weren't working toward a better life with hope for good things to come, this change in leadership might seem nothing more than a different boss moving into the office, without realizing what drastic changes al Qaeda would bring.

Maria sighed. "Now that we, in my generation, know what freedom is, when we can watch CNN and American TV and see what we don't have, we desire that more than money and cars and the false security our parents long for."

"What do you see that's so important to you, Maria, that you would risk your life for it?"

"The freedom to get a job, an apartment, to speak out against injustice, to be able to have the power to change my circumstances by my own effort instead of being trapped by government corruption and Old World tradition that smothers the freedom of the individual. I want my children to have the opportunity to live where they choose, be what they choose to be. I've studied your American history. Individual freedom is treasured, maybe abused by some, but it is allowed and available in America. Here I do not have that freedom. It will come, but I cannot wait until I am an old woman for it to happen."

I considered this for a long moment. How many in my own country were even aware of all we enjoyed that others treasured enough to risk their lives for?

Bart interrupted my thoughts in mock disbelief. "What, no more questions? That's not like you, Princess. You always have more questions than anyone has answers."

I ignored my husband's failed attempt at humor. "Are we going back to Yerevan to help?" I asked, hoping there had been a change of our plans too, in light of the revelation by Musharif.

"Not on your life. You're leaving the country as fast as we can get you out. Norik knows of a little airstrip near the border in Georgia. With a little luck, we can be there by sunup. We're not even trying for Tbilisi now."

"With little more luck airplane will also be there. And working." Norik added quietly.

"Bart, we can't just let this happen. We've got to go back and stop al Qaeda."

"Sorry, Princess. You're leaving. Your dad can handle things in Yerevan without your help. I wouldn't dare show my face there if I hadn't done all I could to get you safely away before the fireworks start." Then he added quickly, "If there are any. Musharif wasn't expecting any resistance at all."

I turned back around to Maria. "Is that true? Could they actually take over without *any* resistance? People wouldn't lift a finger to stop them?"

"If I went to work and the friend I'd been working with for a couple of years told me today things would change and he was now my boss, what would I do? I would wait to see what changes he made. Then I would decide if I could accept them or not. By time I discovered I would not like them, it would be too late."

I suddenly understood how clever this plan really was and how possible it would be for it to happen exactly as bin Laden and his cohorts designed. They wouldn't even have to still be *alive* for it to transpire, as long as there was one man who knew the timetable, one man who still had the key components of the plan. All it required for success was for people to complacently accept, as Maria had just suggested, the change of faces in the positions of authority. Faces they already knew and trusted, if the moles had done their jobs well.

I had one last question. "Who is Vaghinak?" Well, two questions. "What can he do by coming up here that's more important than being in Yerevan to help?"

Turning slightly so I could hear him over the engine noise, Norik answered my question. "Vaghinak other mission driver. He very quiet man; have good instincts, much patience with this kind of person. He best interrogator we have." Then Norik turned to Armen and chattered in Armenian, asking, I supposed, from the tone and Armen's short *"Ha"* reply, if he had said the right word.

Best interrogator. A network of frequently used tunnels, possibly not all as ancient as they seemed. People showing up at this isolated location as if it were a convenient stop on the main road to the capital city. A little airport near the border with a single airplane. This group had an organization in place that apparently was accustomed to smuggling people out of the country—and other clandestine activities to thwart antiquated or unrighteous laws preventing freedom of movement.

I twisted around and knelt at the little window between the cab and the camper. "Okay, I'm ready for the rest of the story. Tell me about this network. Who are they? What have they been doing? Did they know about the moles before or did they just find out? How do they know Dad?"

Bart put his hand over mine and squeezed it. "That's more like my inquisitive wife. Glad to know you're still with us and not in an exhausted fog."

"Well?" I persisted.

"Well what?" he asked, feigning innocence.

"Bart, you're infuriating when you hold out on me! Answer my questions!"

"Just checking your interest level. The group is mostly members of the Church, quiet revolutionaries who have been working in small ways to help each other overcome government graft and corruption and bureaucratic nonsense."

"Smuggling people across borders doesn't seem like a small thing," I interjected.

"Do you want your questions answered, Princess, or do you want to argue with my assessment?"

"Sorry. I repent. I want my questions answered."

"Interpol discovered the mole setup a few months ago when they were interrogating someone about something else. The suspect thought Interpol already knew al Qaeda's plan and talked about it. Your dad and mom came here and trained Norik, Henrik, Feliks, Ruben, and Vaghinak, and probably several others I haven't met yet."

Norik took up the narrative. "We quiet rebels. We doing what good man should do, taking care of neighbor, and while we helping him, we teaching him he can control his life. Not leave it to someone else to make decisions for him. Not let others take away his right to make his life better. We fight against unrighteous dominion." Again Norik turned to Armen for confirmation of his terminology, which I recognized as being straight from the Doctrine and Covenants.

Quiet rebels. I liked the sound of that. "But the quiet revolution didn't have time to finish its work, did it?"

"We see," Norik said so softly I hardly heard him.

"Norik, are you saying there is a possibility this won't happen like Musharif said?"

"Two kinds of Armenian peoples. One with no hope. They not believe God know and love them, watch over them. Other with hope. They believe God keep eye on Hyestan all through history and now He bring gospel to us. You see?"

"Yes, I see where you are going," I said. "Continue."

"This hope, like seed Prophet Alma talk about, grow when God answer prayers. Hope become faith He listen to us. We act because we believe He help our small effort and that effort make difference."

But will it make a big enough difference, I thought, as I rearranged the blanket under my knees. When I looked up, we were approaching an intersection. One arrow pointed to Epebah, Yerevan in Russian, the other to Dilijan. Armen signaled for a left turn.

I reached through the window and grasped Bart's shoulder. "Please can't we go back to Yerevan?"

"No."

"Bart, please. These people need all the help they can get. How can you justify spending the time taking me to an isolated airstrip when you need to be in the city? Or you could continue interrogating Musharif yourself and the others with him? You're losing precious time with this detour to the airport."

"No."

No explanation. No discussion. No compromise. Just an absolute, final "no."

Armen paused at the intersection.

"Go," Bart said, pointing in the direction of Dilijan.

"Bart, think about it. You and Norik are needed in Yerevan—or back with the prisoners. Maybe you'd get information to help stop this before it's too late. Maybe you could find out who the moles are and remove them. You're putting one person above the good of many."

"Four," Bart said quietly.

"Four? Four what?" I asked, puzzled at his terse reply.

"We're getting four people out of the country."

"Oh." I'd temporarily forgotten about my Alexandria, and Armen and Maria's flight from Armenia. But still, four people didn't compare to the three million that were left behind! Armen turned onto the main highway, heading for Dilijan.

"We can't go to Dilijan," I protested, remembering the roadblock we'd encountered. "The police and the army are there."

"Give it up, Princess. You're leaving Armenia tonight. Today." Bart corrected himself, acknowledging that it was well after midnight and a new day already.

I tried a new tactic. "Maybe Armen would really rather be helping the cause in Yerevan than leaving."

"No." This time it was from Maria. "No. We must leave now. Armen will not go back to the Army. This is our only chance for a new life. Especially now, with all these horrible changes coming."

"But if we go back, maybe we can stop those changes," I argued. "Maybe now is the time to make a stand and fight al Qaeda. If Norik thinks . . ."

"Norik is a dreamer," Maria interrupted. "His quiet revolution will take too long. I want to live now, not merely exist in the old way, squeezed into my mother-in-law's tiny apartment. I love Suzanna dearly, but I don't want to live in her house. I don't want to wait until we are through university to get married. I don't want to starve while we search fruitlessly for work. We must leave now while we have a chance to get out."

I had no rebuttal for that. She simply wanted in her life all that I already had: the opportunity for her own home, her own life, her own work, and to make her own lifestyle decisions. How do you argue with that?

I tried one last time "Bart . . .?"

"No," he interrupted. "Absolutely, unequivocally, no."

CHAPTER 25

I turned around and tried to make myself comfortable. I felt like a balloon with a slow leak. The energy generated at the news of Musharif's revelations and Dad and Anastasia's arrival dissipated, leaving me limp and exhausted. Not only was I of no use, like a balloon that wouldn't hold air, I was being an impediment to those who actually could be of great help. That made me feel the worst of all. I was keeping valuable people from their important jobs.

Maria turned a cold shoulder to me. I'm sure she now perceived me as her enemy. Unfortunately, I had a hard time fully understanding her position. Maybe if I had lived without hope of controlling my own destiny, I would feel the same as she did. With hope of freedom this close for her, I couldn't blame her for not wanting to return and lose this opportunity. But if she and others like her didn't stand and fight for a better life now, would anyone here *ever* have it?

Freedom wasn't ever free, and even when you had it, there was a constant battle to keep it. I vaguely remembered a statement Mom used to quote. "All that is required for evil to triumph is for good men to do nothing." Right now, we were doing nothing. I wanted to scream and shout in protest. I wanted to cry out in hopelessness. I wanted to run away from this helpless feeling. Instead, I leaned my head back, shed silent tears of frustration, and prayed for this people and their country. It was all in God's hands now.

I dozed, aware occasionally of a bumpier road than usual, but exhaustion and despair blanketed my foggy mind. Suddenly the bouncing and jostling of the truck stopped. I opened my eyes. It was still dark.

Maria moved beside me. In our limited space, only one of us could stretch at a time. No one moved in the cab. I twisted around, knelt to look out the front window, and saw nothing but a lightening of the sky on the horizon. Maria joined me at the window, apologizing for the elbow in my side as she struggled to kneel in the confining space next to me.

"Where are we?" I asked.

"Airstrip just ahead," Norik said quietly.

"And we are waiting for . . .?

No one spoke for a minute, then Norik finally answered my question. "Signal from Ara. He guide us through land mines."

Just what I needed to hear.

"And once safely through the mine field? Then what?"

"Then you and Alexandria and Armen and Maria are out of here. Out of danger." Bart didn't add, "and out of my hair so I can go back and fight terrorists in Yerevan." He might as well have said it out loud. I knew he was thinking it.

"How does Ara know we're here?" I asked. "Or do we wait for the sun to come up so he can see us?"

"He know. We pass . . ." He turned to Armen and asked for the right word. "Sensor," he repeated after Armen. "We pass sensor when we turn off road. It beep. Wake Ara. He wait for our signal when we arrive this spot. He come and lead us through explosive guarding airplane."

Sophisticated system. "How often do you do this?" I asked, hoping for an answer but not expecting any real enlightenment. I didn't get it.

"When needed," was all Norik would say.

Suddenly a face appeared at Armen's open window, the boyish grin as wide as his face. He thrust his hand through the window to shake hands with everyone in the front seat. This was the handshakingest people I'd ever met!

Ara acted as if he was hungry for human company. He chattered in Armenian and Armen answered him in that language.

"What's he saying, Maria?" I asked.

"He wants to know what news we have. He's had no communication of any kind—no radio, TV, no telephone. He's anxious to know what is going on. Armen is telling him about al Qaeda and that we need to leave Armenia."

Ara said something, and Bart and Armen opened their doors and got out with Norik. Bart checked his gun, and Armen pulled a gun from his pocket, checked it, then replaced it. I wondered where he'd acquired it, but didn't question that he would have one as they tried to escape the country. The dangerous unknown would be much less frightening with a little self-defense at hand.

"We'll walk," Maria said. "The trail's too narrow for the truck."

Bart opened the camper door and helped us out. I felt bruised from the jostling and jolting on the pockmarked roads. Ara led us single file through trees that I could now see in the approaching dawn. We were in a pine forest. Occasionally we passed a hole in the ground with a small clearing of damaged trees around it. Apparently someone tried to get through without Ara. I shuddered, hoping he didn't misstep, or none of us did.

We walked silently for ten or fifteen minutes before we came upon a clearing where Ara broke into an easy jog and led us across the grassy airstrip. The little plane, parked in a shelter draped with camouflaging, didn't seem big enough to hold all four of us.

"Ara can take Armen and Maria," I whispered to Bart. "I don't think I'll fit in that tiny little thing."

"You'll fit just fine," Bart assured me. "It's a four seater."

There was no wasted motion or time. The men quickly wheeled the plane out and positioned it according to Ara's direction. I had the feeling he could have done it all himself, but was glad to have the help. He got in and started the engine.

Armen and Maria quickly climbed on board and settled into the two rear seats.

"One last plea," I begged. "Can't I stay and help, please? I'm leaving too many things undone. The rubies, the symposium . . ."

Bart didn't even answer. He just picked me up and literally dropped me into the front seat of the airplane next to Ara. "I'll be home as soon as I can get there, Princess. Take good care of Alexandria." I got one little kiss on the end of my nose before my husband shut the door and slapped the roof of the plane, the signal to take off.

As Ara revved the engine, I put my hand on the window and Bart covered it with his on the other side. My heart ached at this sudden, wrenching good-bye. I wasn't prepared to leave so quickly, without even one last embrace from my husband. Not that I liked lingering good-byes, but this was too fast, even for me.

We headed down the little grassy strip between the trees to the end of the runway where it was apparent we would turn around and fly out toward the other end. Pink clouds tinged with gold floated above the trees in front of us. Any minute the sun would burst over the horizon, but the forest along the runway was still dark and shadowed.

Reaching the end of the clearing, Ara expertly wheeled the little airplane around, revved the engine, and we headed to the other end of the strip. The wheels lifted off the ground as we passed the two men standing by the hanger.

How I longed to be back there with them. One part of me wanted to get my baby safely out of danger, but the other desperately wanted to be part of the action, wanted to help in any way possible to keep al Qaeda from taking over this little pocket of Christianity. After centuries of withstanding Muslim invaders from every side, it didn't seem fair they would now come and do what their predecessors had failed to do—and do it without firing a single shot or brandishing a single sword.

Ara cleared the trees at the end of the runway and turned toward the rising sun. I looked down for one last glimpse of my husband, who, with Norik, had started across the runway toward the truck. They would follow the path of freshly crushed grasses safely back through the minefield.

Armen said something, pointing out his window.

"Che," Ara said, peering at the ground. Then his tone changed completely. *"Ha! Ha!"*

"Speak Russian, please, so I can understand you." I pled in that language. "What's wrong? What can you see?"

"Lots of movement. Someone is following the path we took through the trees to the airstrip."

I strained to see over Ara's shoulder. We were beyond that point now. Ara kept his course, just skimming the treetops until we would have been out of sight of anyone on the ground.

"Any idea who it was?" I asked. "Tell me exactly what you saw."

Armen closed his eyes and concentrated. "One dozen, or more, soldiers walking single file. Probably following the crushed grass trail we left."

I turned to Ara. "What did you see?"

He nodded. "The same."

"Quick. Turn around and dive the field. Bart and Norik are headed back to the truck. They'll be sitting ducks out in that open space. Get them on the ground, and then get us on the ground to help them."

"No! We can't go back," Maria cried.

"Maybe you can't, but I can. Ara, do as I say." I pulled my gun from my purse and pointed it at him. "I know you're on my side, but just in case you had any ideas about listening to my husband's instructions instead of mine, this should weight your decision in my favor."

Ara instantly turned the plane and zipping close to the treetops, dropped over the field, heading straight for the two men who were now little more than half way across the open space.

It was light enough to see the startled expression on their faces, then disbelief as they hit the ground just before we reached them. I dropped my gun back in my purse and looped the shoulder strap over my shoulder to free my hands.

"Now slow and touch down enough for me to hop out. Then get out of here fast." As I reached for the door handle, I had a sudden thought. "Is the airstrip clear of mines all the way to the trees?"

"Stay on this side of the tree line and you'll be okay," Ara instructed as he throttled down. "Ready?"

I opened the door and stood on the narrow metal step.

"Ready, now!" He touched the wheels to the grass. I jumped and hit the ground running, then did a forward roll when the momentum was too great to stay on my feet. As I sprang back onto my feet, Ara revved the engine to take off and I heard an unexpected thud behind me. Startled, I turned to see Armen, gun in hand, execute the same drop and roll I'd done.

"Where did you learn that maneuver?" Armen asked as he joined me racing for the tree line.

"In a very special school. What are you doing here?"

"I thought you might need a little help to even up the odds. Looks like about three to one as it is."

"Does that worry you?" I asked, glancing down the strip to see where Bart and Norik were. How could I tell them what was happening? Would Bart be so furious to see me on the ground he'd fail to recognize the danger they were in?

Suddenly I was aware of my wristwatch tingling on my arm. I squeezed the receive button on the side.

"Allison Allan, what kind of stunt was that?" The anger in Bart's voice was apparent, not to mention the fact that he called me Allison. He reserved my given name for moments of extreme anger or exasperation.

Frantically I pressed the send button. "Bart, a dozen or more soldiers are on their way through the trees, heading straight for you. Get out of the open, but stay on this side of the trees to avoid the mines."

"Are you sure this isn't just a stunt to get out of leaving?" he asked, racing for the edge of the forest.

"You'd better believe it. I don't jump out of moving airplanes just for the exercise. What's the plan?"

"Let's see what they're up to."

Suddenly an explosion at the entrance to the airstrip interrupted Bart's reply. Someone had stepped off the narrow little trail. A fatal mistake. But how many were left? We needed to get by them, to get back to the truck. To get back to Yerevan.

Another explosion, then another shattered the eerie silence. Anguished shouts filled the early morning air. I crouched in the shadow of a tree with Armen somewhere behind me. I couldn't see Bart or Norik. I hoped they understood the danger of advancing beyond the tree line.

No one moved. A deathly quiet settled over the clearing and the forest that rimmed it. Even the birds stopped singing. We waited silently, too. Had any of the soldiers survived? I tried to visualize the scene, then decided I didn't want to ever see the results of the explosions. War was a horrendous thing, and the blasts removed any doubt about us being in the middle of one right now.

Then I had another thought. What had they done to the pickup? Surely they would disable it in some fashion to render it unusable to us. Another even more dismal thought followed right on the heels of that one. The explosions would have removed all traces of the trail. If, by some small miracle, the truck was still useable, how could we find our way back through the mines now that the crushed grass trail had been obliterated?

Black smoke drifted through the trees, creating a haze over our portion of the landing strip.

My wristwatch pulsed again. "Princess, stay put. I'm going to check out the damage."

I bit my tongue to keep from saying, "Be careful." Of course he would be careful. But I wouldn't stay put. I didn't know whether Norik had a gun or not, but Bart would need back up with firepower. I crept slowly forward, hunched over to be as invisible as possible—and to present as small a target as possible. A twig snapped immediately behind me. Armen followed right on my heels.

The acrid smell of explosives filled my nostrils and smoke burned my eyes. I wiped the tears on my sleeve, trying to clear my vision. My husband moved toward me somewhere ahead in the smoke but so did any enemy soldiers who might have survived the explosions. It would be tragic to mistake him for the enemy and shoot him. Friendly fire had already killed far too many in the recent wars throughout the world.

I pressed the transmission button on my watch and waited a few seconds for Bart to press his receive. "I'm almost abreast of the trail," I whispered. "Armen is right behind me. We'll cover you."

"You follow orders almost as good as a cat, Princess. Please try to remember that precious cargo you're carrying and protect yourself." Then he added quickly, "Thanks. I can use the cover."

I moved forward slowly, warily, another few feet, peering through the dissipating haze. Armen touched my shoulder. I jumped at the unexpected contact.

"What's happening?" he mouthed silently.

I motioned with my hand Bart and Norik's movements toward us. When I turned back around, I could see their silhouettes. At the same time, I heard the first sounds from the trail since the explosions. Someone had survived.

Bart cautiously approached the entrance to the trail. Soon the trampled grass would recover from our footsteps and the path would become invisible again. We had to hurry before that happened. But would we find a way through the destroyed portion? Norik followed Bart to the opening in the trees—empty-handed. I was glad I'd made the decision to disobey Bart's order to stay put. Norik wasn't armed.

When they saw us, Bart gestured to Norik to remain where he was. My husband then pointed at me, flashed a five-finger signal, motioned to Armen to wait, and he entered the trees. Armen grabbed my arm and whispered he would go and I should stay. I shook my head emphatically, counted to five and followed Bart into the haze.

CHAPTER 26

Carefully stepping exactly where my husband placed his feet, I trailed a few paces behind him. Smoke hovered above the ground between the trees, making it hard to see anything very far ahead. Faint groaning came intermittently, but nothing moved anywhere, no breeze to clear the smoke away or bird flitting among the trees.

Bart stopped. I stopped, too, straining to hear what he might have heard or to see what he might have seen. Then he moved cautiously forward again, more slowly this time. He repeated the process a couple of times, progressing very slowly into the trees before it dawned on me what he was doing.

Between the time that had elapsed since we'd walked on it and the smoky haze that still hung heavy in the air, the trail had become almost indiscernible. My husband was feeling his way through the minefield.

I sent a fervent prayer heavenward and increased my watchfulness. We had to be approaching the location of the first explosion. I figured the leader had stepped off the trail, triggering the first blast, and frightened soldiers running for the trees had caused the other two mines to explode.

Through the lingering smoke, I saw timber shattered by the shrapnel and the ground strewn with severed limbs and trunks of downed trees. Then the grass disappeared. A large hole filled with portions of fallen trees blocked the path. A shredded cap lay in the crater with dust still settling on it.

Bart went over the first tree trunk, stopped, then climbed easily over the second. I followed right behind, scrambling to climb over with my shorter legs. He stopped at the edge of the crater, listening, watching, then proceeded cautiously into what looked like a no-man's land. Gone was the beautiful green forest with its thick, lush grassy floor. Carnage had replaced it.

The layers of smoke lifted slightly revealing twisted bodies or parts thereof, lying like discarded mannequin pieces in the next crater. The sensation was horrible and strange, like viewing a surrealistic painting where the separate subjects portrayed are real, yet the whole is not.

Bart bent over one of the twisted bodies, heard the wounded man utter a few final phrases, then he stood again. Too late. The soldier was dead. I could still hear agonized moaning somewhere ahead but couldn't tell where it originated through the haze that dissipated too slowly. Carefully following in my husband's footprints, clearly outlined in the dust, I watched for movement in the trees or signs of life as we passed through the wasteland.

I turned off my mind to everything but the need to be vigilant, the need to be aware of life and movement. I blocked the horror of the scene before me, refusing to think about it, refusing to let my mind dwell on scenes I hoped never to see again in my lifetime.

Sensing more than hearing a presence behind me, I whirled. With my gun pointed directly at him, I frightened Norik who was a scant few steps back. Armen brought up the rear guard. They followed orders like I did. Not.

When I turned back, Bart was bent over another twisted body. This one was moving, the source of the anguished cries, the only sounds we'd heard since the explosions. Bart turned, saw us, and motioned for Norik to attend the wounded man. Then Bart proceeded on through the maze of shattered trees and broken bodies.

I glanced back to see Norik pick up the wounded soldier and gently drape him over his shoulder, then I concentrated on stepping exactly in my husband's footprints in the dust.

We slowly continued our silent parade through the mangled forest, finally reaching the end of the war zone. Bart stopped, bent to examine the ground, and stepped out of the shallow crater onto the dust-covered grass. I closed the short distance between us so I would step precisely where he had walked. Norik and Armen did the same. I could hear their breathing close behind me.

Our short walk earlier of ten or fifteen minutes into the airstrip now became an interminable journey back out. Weariness settled over me like the dust on the grass beneath my feet, blanketing my body with leaden lethargy. It became an enormous effort to put one foot in front of the other, to concentrate on placing my shoe exactly where Bart had placed his. My movements were mechanical, my reflexes numbed. If we came upon an armed guard waiting for us, I knew I would not be able to react swiftly or shoot accurately, but I couldn't revitalize my exhausted body or mind. There were no reserves left to call on, no adrenalin to revive and rejuvenate. Even my small gun became a tremendous burden to carry.

With each step, I felt it would be my last and I would have to collapse and let my leaden legs rest. My total focus became the minute when I could lie down, could sink into the black oblivion of sleep. *One more step*, I thought. *Just one more. Then one more.*

I don't remember coming out of the forest. I don't remember feeling anything at finding the tiny truck sitting unguarded in the sun. No surprise. No relief. No joy that we had transportation back to town and that we had found our way through the minefield and survived it. Not even gratitude for our safety. I was beyond feeling emotion of any kind.

I stopped beside the truck, unable to take one single step more. Bart lifted me in his arms, placed me gently in the front seat and sat beside me. Norik climbed in the back to tend to the soldier and Armen started the pickup. I lay my head on Bart's shoulder, closed my eyes, and fell asleep to the sound of a reluctant starter grinding incessantly.

The truck must have eventually started. I was awakened by excited voices and opened my eyes to see Narine running from the little farmhouse right behind LeVon and Petros.

"What happened?" she asked. "What are you doing back here?"

Norik called to her before anyone could answer and she hurried past us to the back of the pickup. Armen and Norik unloaded the wounded soldier and carried him to the fountain. Petros opened the rock-covered entrance and they all disappeared inside.

"Are you okay, Princess?" Bart ran his fingers across my cheek and down the side of my face.

"Give me a minute to see if all the parts are still here and functioning. I'm sort of numb all over right now." I wiggled my toes and stretched in the confines of the tiny cab. "I don't remember ever being so tired before."

"Maybe it's because you've never been in this condition before." Bart removed his arm from behind me and opened the door. "I don't know whether to thank you or scold you."

I was now awake enough to know what was coming and had no intention of sticking around to receive it. Time for diversionary tactics. I mustered all the energy I could summon and pushed Bart out of the truck. "We'd better go see what's happening in the tunnel."

I tumbled out behind him and went straight to the fountain. "We don't know how to get in this way, do we? Maybe we'd better go through the chapel. I think I remember how to open that entrance."

"Allison," Bart began. I didn't like the serious tone in his voice nor the fact that he used my given name. He had decided which to do and I could tell it wasn't to thank me. As I turned to begin my defense, I saw Henrik emerge from the goat shed.

"Good morning, Henrik," I called in Russian, and hurried toward him. "We've brought back a wounded soldier. Will you open the tunnel so we can go see how he's doing?"

Surprise lit Henrik's eyes, but he strode silently to the fountain and activated the automatic opener to the door in the tunnel. I watched carefully so I could do it myself next time. Who knew when we might need another fast escape? Right now I'd be lucky to escape the reprimand I knew Bart prepared to bestow upon me.

I fully understood the importance of obeying the orders of your file leader. I also realized there were times when those orders became null and void in the face of changed circumstances. If Bart thought I could fly out of there knowing he was walking into the arms of the enemy, he certainly didn't know me very well. His orders for me to leave were contingent on the way things were before the soldiers showed up. I did not deserve to be chastised for disobeying orders, even if he was upset that I had endangered myself and our baby.

On the flip side of the coin, I knew the reason he'd signaled Armen to stay behind and let me follow him into the minefield was because he trusted my reactions. Any agent needs backup he can trust—someone who will do what he expects them to do. He had not worked with Armen before, and though he normally would have preferred to have me stay in the background and out of danger of enemy fire, we had worked together and he knew how I would react.

I also knew my husband's reactions, and now that we were safely out of danger, his first thought would be to chide me for endangering Alexandria's existence by jumping from the airplane. I understood that. We both wanted this baby so much. But he could forget the chastisement. I didn't need it, didn't deserve it, and I wanted to know what was going on in the tunnels.

I ducked quickly into the darkness. Blinded by the sudden change from the bright sun to the total blackness of the passageway, it took a minute for my eyes to adjust. I pulled my penlight from my purse. Henrik might not need light to see where he was going, but I did. He paused just inside the entrance while our eyes became accustomed to the change, then hurried through the tunnel to a room with the door slightly ajar, allowing light and the muffled sound of voices into the dark passage. Henrik opened the door, then stepped back so we could enter first. Narine, kneeling next to the soldier, tending his wounds, glanced up as we came in. Silently she shook her head. He was not doing well.

He saw me, whispered "Mama" in Arabic and feebly lifted one hand toward me. I hurried to where he lay on a blanket on the floor. The dying soldier was so young he had probably never even shaved yet. I knelt beside him and held his hand, murmuring words of consolation to him in his language. If he thought I was his mother, I would gladly play the roll for the few remaining minutes he had in this life. In his state, the only thing that mattered was that someone cared for him and he did not die alone.

He spoke to Allah listing the things he had done that would earn him, Khalid, entrance to Allah's presence. As the surprising revelations labored from his pale lips, I glanced at the astonished faces staring at the dying youth. This boy, Khalid, had been an aide to one of Osama bin Laden's chiefs and had committed to memory the offices where moles were preparing to take command. Khalid begged Allah's forgiveness for not fulfilling his assignment to take the information to Musharif who urgently needed this key piece of information to complete the takeover of Armenia, praying that would not keep him from his eternal reward.

"Tell me who they are and where they are. I will tell Musharif," I whispered, still holding the boy's hand. I motioned for Bart to hand me my pencil and notebook from my purse and wrote as he recited places that sounded like American slang and a name to go with each. I'd listed only about ten when his hand tightened on mine, then went limp.

Narine closed his blank black eyes, felt his pulse to make sure, and rendered the verdict we all knew already. Hot tears streamed down my cheeks. How sad to never have had a childhood, to have become a boy-soldier so early in his young life—and now that life was gone.

Bart helped me to my feet and reached for the notebook. I shook my head. "I told him I would tell Musharif. I will keep my word." I headed for the door, then realized I didn't remember in which of the many rooms in the tunnels Musharif was being held. "Does someone want to take me there? I don't know where I'm going."

Norik and Narine led the way. Henrik said he would bury the soldier. Armen would help. Bart and I followed the silent couple down the dark passageway. No one spoke. Could we possibly have the information we needed to stop bin Laden's men? If we did, it was nothing short of a miracle, and miracles like this just didn't happen in the terrorist business. I'd seen lots of miracles in my life, especially since we'd joined the Church, but to expect to have a key piece of information fall right into our hands was too much to expect, even for me, the eternal optimist!

We passed three doors barely visible in the beam of my penlight before Norik stopped.

"Vaghinak is here," Narine said. "He arrived only an hour ago."

"Why you didn't tell us?" Norik asked.

"I forgot when I saw the soldier. Feliks caught Vaghinak before he left for work this morning and sent him right up. He had no trouble with the police as he left Yerevan, probably because of the little American flag in the front window of his mission van, and Feliks had told him about the roadblock at Dilijan so he avoided that and came straight here."

We entered the room to find Musharif lying with his back to Vaghinak who squatted next to him, speaking softly. Vaghinak stood when we came in and extended his hand to my husband. They acted like old friends. Bart introduced me to the man with the warm, sincere smile. I really felt outside the loop. Bart knew most of these people, and they all knew my parents. I was the stranger here.

I waited until Vaghinak completed the update on the interrogation, anxious not only to fulfill my promise to the boy Khalid, but also to see Musharif's reaction to the news. And I wasn't going to let anyone else read the information I had written down. I wanted to give this to Musharif myself—as a lowly woman who Musharif would detest having speak to him.

I truly hated the attitude of radical Muslims toward women. It certainly wasn't the way God had ordained the plan. They had warped and twisted it until women were not allowed to show their faces to anyone but their husband in their home, were not allowed to eat with the family, be educated, work outside the home nor, in some cases, speak unless they were spoken to. Women could be killed for inadvertently showing a portion of their skin, even an ankle as they walked. They were regarded as nothing more than lowly slaves. When they went to the beach with their families, men could wear western-style swimming suits, but if women wanted to get in the water to cool off, they had to do so fully clothed, draped in their *burka* from head to toe. The inequality was shameful.

I stepped over Musharif so I could face him and squatted as Vaghinak had been doing so I was nearly eyeball to eyeball with him. He closed his eyes so he would not have to look at me.

"Musharif, I have a message from Khalid," I said slowly in Arabic, enunciating carefully so he'd be sure to understand every word. "Before he died, I promised him I would deliver it to you myself. He said you needed it urgently. Are you ready to listen?"

No reaction from the man whose arms were tied behind him.

I persisted. "I would like you to open your eyes and look at me so I'll know that you heard what Khalid wanted to tell you."

Suddenly Musharif kicked out violently. His boot barely missed me. If he'd had his eyes open instead of kicking toward the sound of my voice, he probably would have connected. Bart apparently had been expecting some kind of reaction; I had not. My husband grasped him by the shoulders and hauled him up on his knees, then held him tightly in place while I continued.

"I guess you are listening. Here is the message." As I read each item I'd copied as it came from the lips of the dying boy, I watched Musharif's expression. The tightness of his face muscles relaxed the slightest bit. The scowl softened almost imperceptibly. If his eyes had been open, I think they would have been smiling. Definitely not the reaction I'd been expecting. Definitely not the miracle I thought we'd just received. The information was false.

"Have a nice day, Musharif. Give my sympathy to your wives, if you ever see them again." I got to my feet and left the room, perplexed and deflated. I should have known better than to think this kind of information could fall into our hands so easily. But why had a dying soldier lied?

CHAPTER 27

Everyone followed me into the dark tunnel. Norik opened the door to an empty room nearby where we silently gathered. A single, dim light bulb banished the darkness, casting soft gray shadows across the puzzled faces of those assembled.

"Why? Why would Khalid lie on his deathbed?" I shook my head. "It doesn't make sense."

"Why you think he lie?" Norik asked.

"I watched Musharif's face. He wasn't worried at all that we had the information. Therefore, it must have been false."

"Maybe to give you false leads or head you in the wrong direction," Narine offered.

"Maybe the way it was coded is different from what it seems," Bart said.

I stared at my husband. "Of course! That would be the smart thing to do. Give him the information to deliver, but only the recipient would be able to decipher it correctly."

Bart grabbed my arm. "We can work on it on the way back to Yerevan. Let's get moving. We may not be too late yet. Vaghinak, keep working with him. We'll try to find a way to communicate so you can update us, and we can let you know what is going on in town. In the meantime, make sure he stays isolated and doesn't talk to anyone but you. Keep an armed guard posted on him every minute. He's a wily cuss and if there's any way to slip out of our hands, he'll find it."

We vacated the little room without further comment, each of us, I'm sure, wondering what we could possibly do to avert the seemingly unstoppable from happening.

"Wait." I stopped a few steps down the passageway. "We need to take the rubies with us."

"Why?" Bart asked. "They'll be safer right where they are."

"Bart, we can waste time discussing this or you can trust my intuition and we can be on our way immediately. I'll tell you on the drive to Yerevan why we need to have them with us."

"Go for it," he said, giving me a gentle push down the tunnel to get me on my way. "But hurry."

Norik guided me to the *gavit* of St. Grigor's church and I retrieved the rubies from their cache in the hollow column of the pillar, leaving the ancient hiding place empty once again.

We hurried from the dark tunnel into the dazzling sunshine. As I stopped for my eyes to adjust to the blinding light, Norik took Narine aside and quietly spoke to her. She started to protest at whatever he'd said, but he remained firm. She was not happy at his instructions, but agreed to do whatever he had asked her to do. I hated not being able to understand the language. I was totally unaccustomed to the feeling. Because of the dozen languages I spoke, I could usually understand the gist of what was being said since there was a similarity between many tongues. Body language and circumstance also play a big role. Armenian was not like anything I had ever learned.

Bart propelled me toward the truck and Norik hurried after us. Armen ran from the trees when he saw us preparing to leave. "Where are we going?"

"To Yerevan." Bart opened the door of the truck and helped me inside, making sure I didn't tarry for anything, the time factor being so crucial.

"I can be more help there than I can here," Armen said, jumping in the driver's seat. Norik climbed in the back of the little truck and with the grinding of the reluctant starter, we were off, heading back past the marvelous ancient monastery complex to which no one here apparently gave a second thought and down the road through the canyon. Many of the trees still displayed their leaves in vibrant shades of gold, orange, and red that shimmered in the autumn sun. Signs of last night's storm had almost melted away; only a few patches of snow remained in the shadows and shade where the sun didn't reach.

Bart and I turned to each other at the same time and said in unison, "Okay, now tell me why . . ." I held up my hand. "Me first. I want to know about Dad and Anastasia coming to Yerevan. All of them? Except Mom and Mai Li, of course. Do you have an established meeting place? A safe house or something? And I want to know about this organization that seems to be running very smoothly which no one ever really talks about. How long has it been in place? Everyone's apparently acquainted with you and Dad. You must have been here often. Why haven't I known about it? Is there some big secret that everyone else knows except me?"

Bart stopped the flow of questions with a kiss. While I caught my breath, he snatched the opportunity to speak. "That's better. I'll never get all your questions answered before we reach Yerevan if you keep that up. First, there's no conspiracy of silence regarding Armenia. You've been in other parts of the world doing other things and the subject apparently never came up when you were present. In fact, it's usually discussed on site only because when we are somewhere else, those situations determine the discussion."

I nodded. That was true. The current crisis dominated any discussion when Anastasia got together. "Okay, what about a meeting place. How on earth will you know where to find Dad in a city of nearly two million people?"

"In every city we frequent, we have a designated meeting spot. You were right about it being a safe house."

I glanced up at Bart when he didn't continue. He seemed a million miles away. "And that safe house is . . . ?" I prodded.

"Oh, next to the Cascades. You know, those 650 steps leading from Tamanyan's statue to the Monument to Fifty Years of Soviet Armenia on top of the hill."

"I do just happen to know the place. One of very few I'm acquainted with in the city. Is that where Dad will be?"

Bart was definitely preoccupied with something. Since I had to bring him back from wherever his mind carried him for each answer, it was apparent he'd kicked into Interpol mode and was working on some piece of our current puzzle. "Earth to Bart. Come in, please."

"Mmm. Sorry, Princess. What were you saying?"

"Just asking if that's where we're meeting Dad."

"Yes, we'll go right to the safe house—assuming we can get there without any problem. I hope they won't have disbursed yet and we can get in on the planning and assignments, and not have to scramble to find out where everyone is and what we should be doing. Drat it! I hate not being able to communicate with anyone! This is maddening."

Norik knelt at the window between the cab of the little pickup and the camper. "Now you know how Armenians feel with no electricity and no way to communicate. Most Americans spoiled. Never know how rest of world struggle." He patted Bart on the shoulder. "Except you, my friend. I think your Tibetan prison much worse than Soviet prison."

Norik's comment stunned me. Bart *never* talked to anyone about his six months in the Red Chinese prison in Tibet where they nearly beat him to death. How did Norik find out? Maybe Norik and Bart had compared conversion stories. That was where Bart had learned about the Church—from a Frenchman who shared his cell and who'd taught him the gospel, then was killed before they could escape. However Norik discovered it, knowledge of this episode in Bart's past made him one of a very elite inner circle.

Bart nodded and turned to Norik. "Our generation is, for the most part, totally unaware of hunger and deprivation. We haven't experienced the inconvenience of being without power for more than small amounts of time. But ours is such a young country and we've developed so fast, our grandparents and great-grandparents were the pioneers that struggled to make America what it is today. It's truly the promised land and God has watched over and helped us. Much like He is doing now in Armenia."

"*Ha.* Now Armenia become our promised land." Norik was quiet for a minute. "How we break code on names boy give us?"

"Well, if we were almost anywhere else in the world right now, we could fax Allison's notes to the safe house where everyone's supposed to be meeting. They'd immediately begin deciphering the code and with any luck, by the time we arrived in Yerevan they'd have broken it and made assignments to our people to hit these places and find these people before they can do any damage." Bart rubbed his forehead as if to ward off a headache. "But since we can't get the information to David Chen to start on it, I guess we'll have to work on it ourselves."

"Did you say the entire Anastasia team is coming? Sky is excellent with codes, too. Not that the rest of the team will do us any good while we're on the road." As I pulled my notebook from my purse, I offered up a silent prayer for some heavenly help. At this point it looked like that would be the only avenue from which any assistance would be forthcoming

Bart studied my hastily scribbled notes as I held them up for all to see. "Make another list, Princess, so we can see each one on a separate line. Maybe that'll give us a better picture of what we have."

I tore off that page and started a new list: head honcho house, chaos, decadence tower, Mafia media, pep place, spook house, money bags, degenerate generator, fuzz farm, and hero.

"Why would they use American slang?" I asked as I wrote.

"Young Muslims wouldn't be familiar with American terms. They're not allowed to watch TV or listen to radio broadcasts. Muslims see American society as corrupt and decadent and they don't want their youth contaminated by exposure to our music, TV, or movies. This code would be as much to keep the carrier from really knowing what was going on as to befuddle an enemy," Bart explained. "Probably didn't plan on it falling into American hands, and even if it did, how many Americans would know what the Armenian counterpart of that would be?"

"Okay, there's your list. The first part will probably be pretty easy. It's the names that will give us problems. Here's the first one. Head honcho house. Who has any idea what that could be?"

"Head honcho means top man, right? How about the Presidential Palace on Marshal Baghramian Avenue?" Armen suggested.

"Sounds right to me," Bart said.

I wrote it next to its slang counterpart. "Next is chaos."

"What mean 'chaos?'" Norik asked.

"Confusion, disorder, commotion—everything sort of a mess," I explained.

"House of Parliament big place of confusion and disorder," Norik said. "Across street from Presidential Palace. Usually chaos when they meet. Also place of assassinations."

"I'll buy that. Thanks, Norik. Now decadence tower?"

"Tower. The big TV tower on the hill," Armen said. "It's a communications tower and TV center. You can see it from all over the city."

"Well, if they broadcast American soap operas, decadence tower would be a good name for it." I jotted that down and read the next on the list, "Mafia media?"

"Media: newspapers, TV, radio. Any of those the Mafia uses more than any other?" Bart asked.

"I think no," Norik said slowly. "I think maybe telephone— Armentel. Mafia own. Conduct all their dirty business on cell phones."

"Sounds good. Next on the list is pep place." Silence. "Come on, guys. You were doing so good. Let's see. Pep, energy, vitality . . ."

"Energy," Bart said. "But electrical, gas, or nuclear?"

"All comes under Ministry of Energy," Norik said.

"Great. I assume that is an office that controls the whole shebang. How about spook house?" I asked as I scribbled Norik's answer.

"Spies are called spooks," Bart said. "The KGB handles spies in Armenia."

"*Ha*. Spook house would be KGB headquarters," Norik agreed.

"Money bags is next. Sounds like a bank . . ."

"Ministry of Finance," Armen interrupted. "A powerful arm of the government."

"Got it. Okay, what's your take on degenerate generator?" Silence again. Not even any guesses. "What generates degeneracy? To degenerate is to decline, to grow worse physically, mentally or morally. To generate would be to promote it."

"Radio!" Bart said. "The radio would help degenerate morals with the decadent music it plays from America."

"Ha," Norik agreed. "Armenian music not have bad words. American music filled with bad words and ideas. Not good for morals of our youth, but they listen anyway. Radio and Broadcast Center near my house."

"You're doing great, guys. Only two to go. Next is fuzz farm. At least, I think that's what he said."

Everyone was silent.

"Mmm," Bart mused. "Fuzz is slang for police. They'd definitely have someone moled up in the police department."

I wrinkled my nose at Bart's pun, but had to admit it was funny. Neither Armen nor Norik caught it. So much that each side said got lost in the translation. It delighted me we were able to work together so well and understand so much when language was so evolutionary and ever-changing. Even these simple code words would have been hard to decipher for Norik by himself, or Bart and me without a native's help. With Armen's knowledge of American music and slang from watching TV and his familiarity with his Armenian culture, he was probably best qualified of the four of us to do it alone.

"Police department," I said aloud as I wrote.

"That's probably the Ministry of Internal Affairs," Armen corrected. "That's like your Chief of Police. They oversee all arms of the police department."

I made the correction to the list. "Okay, here's the last one: hero."

Again there was no immediate answer.

"Who is your greatest hero?" I asked.

"Real or folklore?" Armen asked. "Armenian or Soviet? Local or national? There are so many possibilities. Military or civilian? Artist, musician, writer or scientist? We have many heroes in Armenia and everyone has his own."

"What have we covered and we'll see what's left. Maybe that will help. Princess, read the list so far."

"We've got the Presidential Palace; House of Parliament; Communications tower and TV center; Armentel which is phones; Ministry of Energy; KGB headquarters; Ministry of Finance; Radio and Broadcast Center; Ministry of Internal Affairs, which is the police. And hero, whatever that is."

"So they've covered the leaders and those in charge: President and Parliament, Mafia, KGB, and police," Bart listed. "They've covered communication and media: TV, radio, telephone. They have someone with energy and finance. What's left?"

"Transportation?" I asked.

"That's it. The hero would be David Sassoon, legendary savior of early Armenia. His statue is one of the famous landmarks of Armenia, located at the David Sassoon Railway, Metro, and *Marshutka* Station. One of the main transportation hubs on Tigran Mets Avenue," Armen said. "If you stop traffic in and out of there, you can have a major breakdown in transportation in a very short time."

"Bravo, guys. Now if I only had heard the rest of the last word he started. It sounded like he was trying to say cat, but that wouldn't make any sense. Anyway, now we have the rest of this code that goes with each place. But as Norik said, this won't be a cake walk." I smiled over my shoulder at Norik, who was concentrating on the scribbles in my notebook

"This make no sense," he said.

"You're right. It makes no sense at all. It's definitely in some kind of code, and I could easily have written down the wrong thing. I was listening to Arabic and translating to English as I wrote, so I may be way off base with all of this. Probably should have just written it in Arabic but my writing skills aren't as good as my listening and speaking ability. Bart, any ideas on this part of Khalid's message?"

I handed Bart the little notebook and leaned my head back on the seat. All that concentrating gave me a headache. Or was a lack of sleep causing it? Or stress? I closed my eyes and thought about the letters that looked liked strange names. But were they? The sounds I'd copied from the lips of the dying soldier weren't necessarily the sounds those words might have if they came from the lips of someone who spoke English. He was probably saying them phonetically and had memorized them as someone else had spoken them.

We had the places, but who of all the people in those places were the moles? Who were the ones we needed to get to before they could carry out their orders for destruction or to aid in the takeover of Armenia?

CHAPTER 28

"Wake up, Sleeping Beauty. We're here." Bart kissed my cheek and nuzzled my ear. A very pleasant way to be awakened.

"We're where?" I looked around and didn't recognize anything, except that we were in a city instead of the mountains.

"Yerevan. We'll walk a couple of blocks to the safe house and stagger our arrivals. Armen, you can let us out here. After you park the truck, you and Norik come from different directions and a few minutes apart. Come on, Princess. This is where we bail out."

Armen pulled the little pickup next to the sidewalk and we jumped out. I looked around to get my bearings. Yes. There was the boat restaurant where I'd eaten my popcorn the other night when the little gypsy man sent me to Opera Square. "Where from here, O fearless leader?"

"I thought you knew your way around this part of the city," Bart said, steering me into the park.

"I know that if we walk through the park and cross that street, then traipse through another little square, we'll be opposite Opera Square."

"Good girl. But if we continue on this street, we'll end up at Tamanyan's statue at the foot of the Cascades. That's where we're headed." And we weren't losing anytime getting there. No dawdling to people watch. But as we cut through the park to get on our street, the popcorn man was making his magic again.

"Oh, Bart, smell that. Let's get a bag of popcorn to nibble on. I think I'm going to starve to death trying to keep up with you. Don't you ever get hungry when you're on the job?"

"Occasionally. My mind usually doesn't let my stomach overcome my better judgment to stop. Eating on the job can get you killed."

"Well, Alexandria and I are starving and it will only delay us thirty seconds to get a bag of popcorn. Time me."

I pulled a hundred dram note from my purse as I hurried toward the popcorn man and wiggled two fingers at him. He had just finished filling two flimsy little plastic bags with popcorn and I traded him my money for his popcorn before Bart, even with his long stride, caught up to me.

I tossed Bart his bag of fresh, hot popcorn as we hurried through the park. "Now I can face the world. Or the terrorists, or whatever we're on our way to face. Nothing seems quite so bad on a full stomach, whereas the sharp pangs of hunger tend to increase the problem manyfold."

"Agreed. That must be why I keep you around—to take care of me and make sure I eat regularly."

I was double-stepping to keep up with my long-legged husband. "What I don't understand is how you keep your energy level up when I'm not around to make sure you eat occasionally."

"Pure adrenalin," Bart said with a mouth full of popcorn. "When I'm on the job, I never think about eating."

"Guess that's how you keep your boyish figure. Did you get all those coded names figured out while I napped?"

"No. None of it made any sense to me. Norik and Armen didn't have any ideas either. If David or Sky can't figure it out, we'll just have to go in blind and see if we can feel our way through. At least we have a starting place, which is more than we had at this time yesterday."

We crossed busy Mashtots Avenue with the Matanadaran Museum of Ancient Manuscripts at its head and the huge statue of Mother Armenia hovering over the city with her unsheathed sword. I couldn't tell if she was pulling it out or putting it away. It was an interesting statue. With the Muslim cultures surrounding Armenia—and having overrun her several times in the past, did having a symbol of a woman give them confidence that they could overcome the country? Did they see her as a sign of weakness, or as a sign of strength, resilience, and compassion? Funny the things your mind conjures up when it doesn't want to concentrate on something.

In only one very short block we reached the foot of the Cascades. I finished my small bag of popcorn as we paused by the rose garden and gazed up the 650 marble steps on the finished portion of the monument.

"It's a shame these were never finished. The guide book says when the Soviets pulled out, they took their money and their managers and most everything is still standing as it was the day they left. This would rival the Spanish Steppes in Rome if it were finished. At least they are planting flowers and improving it. The picture in the guide book shows overgrown weeds and graffiti all the way up the steps."

"Sure looks better than it did the first time I saw it about four years ago. In fact, the whole city looks better. Things are slowly improving in most quarters and I expect this will become a destination place in the next ten years." Bart took my hand and pulled me toward the buildings lining the little plaza at the foot of the Cascades. "We go up this little alley. The safe house is an apartment on the third floor. Hope everyone is still here."

The entrance to this building was similar to the entrance to my apartment. Or my former apartment. It was pretty apparent I wouldn't be going back there again. I would like my clothes, though. I was getting very tired of wearing this same pantsuit.

We dodged the refuse littering the dirty marble staircase and sent several cats flying off in fright to the floors above us as we ascended the first flight of stairs. But as we rounded the landing onto the second flight of stairs, it became apparent that someone took pride in living there. These steps were swept clean and the wall had been painted. There was also a handrail which had been freshly painted. At the top of these stairs a couple of cheery red geraniums greeted us from their glazed ceramic pots.

"Mmm," Bart said. "New tenant. Or new owner. Probably means she will be watching whoever comes up the stairs. Not good. May have to move from here. Nosy neighbors sound a death knell to a safe house."

"Agreed. Let's hope we can get through this crisis without interference. What's the cover on the house?"

"A young newlywed couple from the church live here. Aram and Mariam Matanyan."

"I suppose they're part of the organization."

"Yup. Most of those in the organization are members of the Church. Members recruit people who have the vision of what Armenia can be, those who have hope of a future. Many Armenians are so disheartened, they only want to leave. Or they've given up on leaving and are just eking out a day-to-day existence with no hope of improvement. The organization started when people like Norik and Narine decided things wouldn't happen on their own and they needed to get things moving in the right direction."

I nodded, watching one of the few cats that didn't seem afraid of us trail along behind. "Make good things happen instead of waiting for someone else to do it, if they ever did."

"Exactly. Here we are." As Bart knocked on the door, the cat caught up with us and rubbed against my ankle. When the door opened, the cat invited himself in before I could stop him.

"Oh, I'm sorry," I apologized to the tall, dark, curly haired young man who stood in the door. "I had no idea he was headed inside."

"It's okay. We belong to him. My wife feeds him and he keeps the rest of the cats off our landing. Mutually beneficial." He stuck out his hand. "I'm Aram."

I shook his hand. "I'm Allison. I take it you already know my husband."

Bart extended his hand to the young man who spoke very good English. "Good to see you, Aram. How ya doin'?"

With his dark eyes looking very serious, Aram replied, "Normal," and waved us into the room.

"Normal? What do you mean?" I asked, stepping into the small but very neat little apartment.

"Normal, as opposed to crazy. Some days it is very crazy around here."

"Glad to hear things are normal, but does that mean Anastasia hasn't arrived yet, or that they've been here and are already gone?" Bart asked.

Aram motioned to a closed door. "Jack's in the office with a couple of your people. We're expecting a few more to filter in."

I hurried to the door and knocked as I opened it. "Anybody here?"

Dad jumped to his feet and smothered me with a bear hug. "Bunny, it's good to see you." Then he held me at arm's length and scolded, "But what are you still doing in Armenia? You were supposed to have gotten out of here two days ago."

"Kind of hard with few airplanes leaving the country. And no communications to find out when the next one is. Besides, I just knew you'd rather have me here than be worrying about me hopping around Eastern Europe trying to get home, with the terrorist alert so high right now. Have you talked to Mom lately?"

He put his arm around my shoulder and walked me to the window that looked out on the Cascades. "I talked to her a couple of days ago. She's managing, but she's still in a lot of pain. She won't get out of the hospital until the weekend. They wanted to keep her long enough to make sure there wasn't any infection. Nedra was driving her crazy already but Mai Li arrived to man the control center. I think Margaret will send Nedra home before she ever gets released, and Jim and Alma should be back soon, so she and Mai Li will be able to handle things until then."

I looked up into my father's weary face. "How are you doing?"

He smiled, a rather forced smile, I thought. "I'm managing, too. I wasn't ready for this situation to erupt right now. Thought I'd be able to get home before this broke, then come back."

I hugged him. "She'll be okay with Mai Li there, and I'll be home as soon as I can get there. It's you I'm worried about, not Mom. When did you sleep last? Or eat?" I put my hand up to his face. "Frankly, my dear, you look ghastly."

He laughed. This time it was genuine.

"Here, I brought you a present." I handed him the notes we'd been working on in the truck and showed him what we thought were the offices where moles could be found.

"Unfortunately, we couldn't decipher the rest of the code. At first glance, these look like names, but when you look closer, they don't make a lot of sense. We hoped Sky or David could break the code."

"If you two are through with the family thing, can I break in for a hug?" The pleasant cultivated voice could only belong to Else Elbert, the fourth female member in Anastasia. I whirled around into the outstretched arms of the ever-elegant Else. A tall, slender Norwegian, Else was related to English and European nobility, an expert in self-defense and personal protection, probably the best marksman in the group, and she treated me like her younger sister.

"How are you doing, my beautiful little Allison?" She pulled away and kissed both my cheeks.

"Never better. I'm with the people I love most. That always improves even a good day. I like the new way you're wearing your hair." Else's normally blonde shoulder length hair was now stylishly short and a lovely hue of magenta, a color I'd discovered very popular with Armenian women. She pirouetted so I could see the back as well as the front.

"Thanks. Thought I could blend in a little better than with my natural color. You're perfect already with your beautiful black tresses." Else was a knockout in her tangerine-colored leather suit and matching boots. The mini-skirt and scoop-necked jacket molded to her model's figure and knee-high boots left a goodly portion of her long slender legs exposed. Made me feel downright dowdy.

I laughed. "Else, you will never 'blend in' anywhere. You stand out like a bright red poppy in a field of dandelions."

"If you two are through with the mutual admiration society, can I get in here?" I turned as Dominic Vicente came out of the woodwork. I hadn't even seen him in the room which was unusual because Dom usually took center stage with his cocky and egotistical but sweetly endearing personality.

"Dom! I can't believe you're in here working instead of out flirting with all those beautiful Armenian women." A native of Spain, Dominic trained as a youth to be a bullfighter and had retained both the attitude and the grace of the profession. He whirled me off my feet as he kissed my cheek in an affectionate greeting.

"Glad to see you," Dad said, striding across the room as Bart came through the door. "I take it my headstrong daughter did her usual number on you since I had word you were getting her out of the country."

"Sorry, sir. I tried," Bart said. "I even had her on an airplane, but she bailed out to save my skin."

I slid next to my husband and put my arm around his waist. "It's a long story which we'll tell you when this is all over. Were you ready to get started when we interrupted?"

Dad nodded and called Aram. "Is anyone else here?"

"Armen just arrived. David and Lionel should be back any minute. They went to get pizza for everyone. I saw Rip Schyler coming up the stairs with Norik. Everyone else is waiting at Margarit and Sarkis's so we wouldn't have too many people here. Normally it wouldn't be a problem, but things are different now." Aram went to open the door for Sky and Norik.

Dad wasted no time getting everyone settled down to business. No time for extended greetings and there didn't need to be introductions. I was the only newcomer to the group. As I listened to Dad's brief preview of operations, I discovered Anastasia had spent a fair amount of time in Armenia since the assassinations in the House of Parliament, and had been instrumental in forming this group that was at the core of the "soft rebellion" working against corruption and graft in the government. This same group would be the key players in finding the moles in each of the agencies or offices we'd deciphered from Khalid's list.

As Dad began assignments, Sky and Lionel came in carrying three boxes of pizza each. "Time out." I held up my hands in the familiar signal and stepped over Bart's outstretched legs. I snagged a box as they passed me and put a couple of pieces on a napkin for my father.

"Everyone grab a couple of slices before our illustrious leader begins so you can concentrate on what he is saying instead of what might be left over by the time the pizza gets to you. Here, Dad, you don't get a choice. You just get to gobble this up while everyone else chooses theirs. Then you'll be ready to start when they're ready to eat."

Since Mom wasn't here to do it, it was up to me to look after my father, who never did a very good job of taking care of his own creature comforts—much like my husband. Of course, it stood to reason, since Dad had trained Bart and taught him everything he knew, including that eating was a luxury only indulged in when things slowed down enough to enjoy it.

The pizza was quickly distributed and Aram handed out cold cans of soft drinks to accompany it. Just as Dad cleared his throat to call the group to attention and begin, someone, some very loud and impatient someone, pounded on the door. Those shouts in Armenian needed no translation.

CHAPTER 29

Aram swooped a box from the shelf by the desk and tossed it at Norik as he headed for the front door. Norik handed out pamphlets about the Church to everyone and opened a set of scriptures that were in the box. Armen pulled five more Bibles from the shelf and handed them to us to share.

"Open scriptures please to St. Matthew 28:19–20 in New Testament." Norik calmly ignored the incessant pounding at the front door. "Bart, you read please."

I watched in amazement as each member of Anastasia got into the scriptures and into the role play immediately. Bart read quietly, "Go ye therefore, and teach all nations, baptizing them in the name of the Father, and of the Son, and of the Holy Ghost; Teaching them to observe all things whatsoever I have commanded you: and lo, I am with you alway, even unto the end of the world. Amen."

Despite the loud voices at the door, Norik continued. "That is why we here, and that is literal promise. He will be with us always. You know that. I know that. Armen, will you give us opening prayer?"

Armen stood with folded arms and bowed head and would have prayed, except that two men burst noisily into the room at that point.

"Who are you? What are you doing here?" the smallest one demanded. No guns were obvious, but I had no doubt they were armed, and probably just itching to wave their weapons around in a show of authority. This had to be KGB and they were not being the slightest bit subtle about it. Things had definitely changed in Armenia. Were we too late to help preserve normalcy? Were we too late to prevent the takeover?

"We study gospel of Jesus Christ," Norik said calmly. "You wish to join us?" He motioned for Armen to move away from his chair and I quickly slid closer to Bart and offered a portion of my seat.

That, of course, didn't produce a calming effect on the two men.

"You don't fool me. Who are you? I want to see passports and visas of everyone in the room." His English was passable, his breath atrocious, and his body odor the worst of anyone I had ever encountered.

"Please to sit and join us," Norik said. "You see what we study. You like, we teach your family."

"Passports," the nasty little man demanded, "Now."

I pulled mine from my purse and offered it to him since I was sitting closest. He examined it, looked at me, then back again at the passport. "What are you doing in Armenia?"

"My husband and I are members of the Church from America and today we're helping the members plan agendas and learn how to improve our surroundings. We study the gospel of Jesus Christ to follow the example He set. Have you heard of the Church of Jesus Christ of Latter-day Saints? Maybe you've heard of the Mormons? We're the same group. Mormon is just a nickname. I'd be glad to talk to you about what we're doing in your country. Jon Huntsman is one of our members, you know. I'm sure you've heard of Mr. Huntsman. You've probably met him several times since you seem to be an important man in the government. Did he tell you about the Church and what it can do for your family and your country?"

"Quiet," the nervous little man shouted. He was rattled. He hadn't expected my discourse, and the mention of Jon Huntsman discombobulated him even more. Since the earthquake in Gyumri and Spitak in 1988 that had killed over 35,000 people, Jon Huntsman was a revered name in Armenia. He had poured millions into helping people help themselves and rebuild their lives. The name of Huntsman opened almost every door in the country.

Bart offered his passport and took up where I left off, beginning a discourse that sounded suspiciously like the first discussion, with a few more references to Jon Huntsman thrown in for good measure.

"Enough!" He pointed at Dad. I held my breath. My father calmly produced his passport and identification, then imitated our approach, talking about how families could be together forever under the Mormon faith. My jaw dropped open and Bart gently closed it for me. He only let Dad get a few sentences out before he commanded him to be silent. Which was a good thing. I had no idea my father even remembered that much of what we had told him.

Norik was next and he unleashed a torrent of Armenian that left me totally in the dark as to content. The man seemed satisfied by Norik's answer and was about to quiz the lovely Else, who could have kept up the pretense just fine, though she was not a member. We'd talked extensively about the Church and I knew she could hold her own in a discussion with someone who knew nothing about it simply by bluffing her way through, not to mention her photographic memory which could probably give an instant replay of all our conversations.

But as he pointed at Else, his large companion who had remained silent in the doorway advanced into the room and whispered something in the smaller man's ear. The little man paused, glancing around the room at the rest of the group that were obviously not Armenians, but all of whom could have been Americans. In a scene right out of a B-movie, he said with a quiet, threatening tone, "You will be watched." Then he turned and followed his larger companion out the door.

Norik started singing, "As I have Loved You" and those of us who knew it joined in—in the language of choice. I thought it was a fun kind of slap in the face of the KGB, until Sky got up from his seat in the corner and silently pointed to something in the crevice between the woodwork on the door and the wall, at the site where a bookcase nestled right up to the door. A listening device. The big creep had planted a bug while our attention focused on the little man.

We acknowledged we knew it was there, and when we'd finished singing the single verse of the song, Norik launched into the first discussion, treating the members of Anastasia as a group of people investigating the Church. Dad slipped out, conferred with Aram for a minute, then came back in with something written on a piece of paper and held it up for everyone to see while Norik continued his lesson.

"Komitas chapel. Thirty minutes."

The pizza was cold but no one seemed to notice. We finished it all before Norik finished his discussion. The members of Anastasia paid rapt attention to every word of the lesson, which delighted me. They were all good people, actually all Christians, but from many different denominations. We'd had conversations about the Church with several of them separately, but they were now a captive audience, learning what we believed and they were enjoying it!

When Norik finished, he called on Aram to give a closing prayer. Just like a real meeting, which, of course, is what we wanted the KGB to hear. Wonder if any of them actually listened to Norik's lesson?

As we made departure noises, a cute young woman with lots of curly black hair opened the front door. Aram hurried to meet her, motioned her to silence, and took her into the study. Standing next to the bug, he said, "Hi, sweetheart. Did you find everything you needed for your cleaning project?"

Before she could answer, he turned to the rest of us. "Mariam wants to paint the apartment, but she says before she can paint, she has to scrub the walls and woodwork. Seems like a waste of time to me when you could just paint over it, but she insists it has to be clean for the paint to be right."

By that time, Mariam had been shown the listening device and she picked up on the role play. "Yes, I've got everything I need. Are you finished here so I can get started? I thought I'd begin in the study when you're through."

"We were just leaving," Dad said. "Good to see you again, Mariam. Have a nice afternoon, if there is such a thing when you tackle a project like that."

Mariam laughed. "I like to clean because it feels so good after it's done."

"When do you want to meet for the next discussion?" Norik asked as we all headed for the front door, trying not to seem like we were hurrying away.

"Same time, same place, next week?" Dad asked. General agreement and we left, flocking down the stairs as a group. As we passed the apartment with the bright red geraniums outside the door, I couldn't help but smile and wave at the peephole, fairly certain this was the point of origin of the KGB visit. If so, I imagined the person responsible for the call would watch us leave as they'd apparently watched us arrive.

When we reached the street, Norik motioned for us to accompany him. Dominic and Lionel went with Armen. Aram joined us in time to volunteer his services as guide to Dad and Sky, which left Else on her own. She turned down my invitation to join us.

"I've been there before. I'm going to do a little reconnaissance on my way. The Diana Shop is on the corner just above the meeting place. I want to check out their new arrivals, as well as the Interpol office on Komitas. I'll be there by the time you are." She smiled at Dad as he opened his mouth to speak. "Don't worry. I won't be late."

"I'd freeze to death if I had that much of my skin exposed," I said as we watched Else flag a cab and maneuver gracefully into the back seat without exposing any more of her incredible legs than were already bared.

"Not to worry, Princess. I'm the only one who gets to see that much of you, and only in front of a nice warm, roaring fire."

"We have an Interpol office here?" It just dawned on me what Else had said.

"We do. A small office just behind a little shuka on Komitas Street. Else coordinates our operations here with that office, as much coordination as there is. We're usually pretty independent, but in case we need backup, it's nice if they know what we're doing."

Norik was watching *marshutkas* as we walked toward Opera Square. Apparently the right one came along. With a downward flick of his wrist, he signaled a passing minivan to stop and we scrambled aboard the crowded little vehicle that looked like it wouldn't make it to the top of the next hill.

A woman hoisted her child onto her lap and freed the seat beside her. Bart sat down and pulled me onto his lap. Norik stood in the doorway with another man who gave up his seat to an older lady who'd boarded behind us. I did a quick count. Eighteen people in a minivan that was designed to hold twelve. But everyone was so gracious and cordial and accommodating it was like a big happy family. The *marshutka* went a block then stopped for a young woman with two small children. I couldn't imagine they'd find room anywhere, but she handed her children in and passengers took them on their laps, someone else held her shopping bag and she stood beside Norik all the way to the top of the hill at Hyestan Trading Post. She passed her money to a passenger who in turn passed it along to the driver. Norik handed her children down to her, then the shopping bag, and she disappeared into the metro station.

"Can you picture that happening anywhere in America but a very small town?" I whispered to Bart.

"Nowhere that I've been recently," he said.

Similar scenes were repeated all the way up Komitas Street until Norik signaled the driver to stop at Vratsakhan. As we disembarked, I could see the Diana Shop across the street on the corner but Else was nowhere in sight. We hurried down a sloping shady sidewalk, dodging vendors with melons and fruit, string beans and potatoes and deep purple eggplant.

Fresh bread was being delivered to a tiny little box of a shop that looked like it had been built from someone's leftover materials. No wrapping, no covering, just stacks of freshly baked loaves in many sizes and shapes which the deliverer unloaded from the trunk of a car, piled onto a box lid and carried to the open plywood door of the kiosk. If I hadn't just had pizza, I wouldn't have been able to resist the tantalizing aroma.

People of Yerevan going about their business as usual in the lazy warmth of the beautiful October afternoon had somehow diluted the urgency I'd felt this morning. As we approached the pink stone chapel, *marshutka* number ninety-six stopped in front of the building and Dad, Sky, and Aram piled out. Down the street from the other direction several people on foot approached the neat looking two-story building.

"Hurry up, people. Let's make every minute count," Dad called as some slowed to chat. "We may be too late, as it is."

With Dad's reminder of the situation, the friendly chatter ceased as Norik held open the door and everyone filed into the wide, white-tiled foyer. A door stood open on the far side of a set of steps leading upstairs and I could hear the sound of running water and a beautiful piano rendition of my favorite hymn.

"Baptismal room," Norik said, pointing at the door. "We have baptism this evening. It take much time to fill font so elders start early." The music stopped as we headed up the stairs and a couple of young missionaries poked their heads around the door.

"Ah, Elder Minasyan. I think he be very helpful to us." Norik spoke rapidly to the very handsome young Armenian, then called to my father. They consulted together and Dad invited the young man to join us.

"Could you hold your meeting in the font room so we can keep an eye on the water?" Elder Minasyan asked.

"Sure, why not," Dad said. He called those back who were climbing the stairs and we filed quickly into the baptismal room. Else flew into the room with David Chen and Oswald Barlow, the last two members of Anastasia who hadn't made it to our meeting at Aram and Mariam's apartment. They'd been to Sissian with local Interpol agents restoring control of the microwave relay stations. One battle won. One step forward.

"Okay, people," Dad said, standing at the front of the room with his back to the baptismal font. "Let's get to work." There was much scraping of wooden chair legs on tile floor as we hurried to find seats. The chairs were not like our seats at home. These were little narrow wooden chairs with upholstered seats, and I noticed the Armenians in the group sat very close together—three on two seats.

"I think you all know, with the possible exception of Elder Minasyan and his companion, what we're up against. Today is the day Osama bin Laden's al Qaeda plans a quiet but complete takeover of Armenia. Moles have been unobtrusively slipping into key positions in the government and other crucial areas so that when they received the signal, they'd be ready to take command. For the most part, we don't know who those people are. You were briefed last night on what to look for and how to identify them. We think we know some of the offices where they're functioning. We need each of you who are familiar with these offices or places to go in with a member of Anastasia, ferret out the moles, and neutralize them, however you can. We want them taken alive if possible so the coalition on terror can interrogate the prisoners."

Dad looked into each of the faces turned to him before he began again. "When Aram reads the places we've listed, take the one you're most familiar with. We're working against two clocks: finding the moles before the signal is given, and before the KGB, who has been alerted, join the party. So sharpen up and let's get this done. Everyone have your radio watch? Keep them on. Even without other means of communication, we should be able to stay in touch over the short distances we'll be involved with using these. Call back here with any questions or problems."

Aram stood with my list of notes and began reading the places we'd deciphered from the American slang. Apprehension and misgivings overwhelmed me. Except for their Anastasia counterpart, they'd be left to their own imagination and devices to "neutralize" the enemy. There was also the language problem; Anastasia and the Armenians would need to find a common language to communicate for those who didn't speak English. And what if we had the wrong targets? What if we ended up in all the wrong places?

"The Presidential Palace," Aram read first. "Who can get inside, find the mole or moles, what the assignment was to be, and stop them?"

No one spoke for a minute except those who were translating for Armenians who didn't speak much English. Then a middle-aged woman on the back row stood a little uncertainly. She had very black, short, straight hair and bright red lipstick. "Meri and I are friends with Mrs. Kocharian," she said through an interpreter. "We've been working with her on a committee trying to improve our schools and teachers. We can get into the Presidential Palace, but I'm not sure what to do once we get in."

"Else, you go with . . . What is your name?" Dad asked.

"Tsovinar." The woman sitting beside Tsovinar rose. I assumed she must be Meri.

"Okay, Tsovinar and Meri. Else will go with you. She'll know what to do. You have your assignment. Go." Dad turned to a young man with pencil and paper in his hand. "Babken, log these assignments as they're made so we'll know where everyone is."

I noticed crutches leaning against the wall near the young man. Nothing said you had to be in perfect physical condition to fight. All you needed was a willing spirit. Everyone could make a contribution in their own way. Good for him.

"The House of Parliament," Aram read as Tsovinar, Meri, and Else left the room.

"The twins work there as security guards on the night shift while they finish their degrees at the university during the day," Elder Minasyan volunteered. "They can get in easily enough but they've only been working there a few months and I don't know if they'll know anyone that well or not."

Dad looked out at those assembled. Our numbers slowly increased as people came in quietly and took their seats. "Are the twins here?"

"Not yet," Aram said. "They're still in class, but they'll be here."

"We won't wait," Dad said. "Write that down, Babken, and we'll talk to them if they get here. Dominic, you're paired with them if they come. Go on with the list, Aram. We don't have time to dawdle."

Aram looked at my hand-scribbled list and read, "The TV center."

An attractive young woman with brown hair twisted atop her head under a knitted tan beret stood slowly and hesitated before she spoke in an almost apologetic tone. "I have a puppet show there. I know the place and the people pretty well."

Dad glanced down at the name Babken wrote next to the assignment and announced, "Loretta gets the TV station with David Chen. On your way, people," then he paced behind Aram. I knew my father could feel the time slipping away but I couldn't think of a better way to do this that would be any faster.

"Armentel," Aram read.

The Mafia media, I thought.

"Naira and Lucine clean their offices every day and know what's going on there," Elder Minasyan offered.

Two tall, slender sisters rose from the back row, one with dark hair, the other with a copper-colored, shoulder length hairdo. They looked very uncomfortable volunteering for anything.

"Can you handle Armentel with Oz? He'll tell you what to look for and help you every step of the way." Dad's voice was gentle and encouraging. Oz stood as they both nodded and the trio hurried out of the room.

"Department of Energy?" Aram said.

A wiry young man stood near the door. "I can do that. I spend a lot of time straightening out our invoices there."

A young woman with a little baby in her arms stood beside him, her mouth set in a determined line as if to say, where he goes, I go. I understood that mind set completely. Dad opened his mouth to say something which I assumed would be "this is no place for babies." I cleared my throat loudly and after glancing at me, he shrugged and assigned Bart to go with them. That caught me by surprise. I thought

I'd be with Bart, then realized there weren't enough agents to go around. We'd have to be separated.

Bart squeezed my hand and jumped to his feet to leave the room with Sarkis and Margarit, according to the names Aram gave Babken to write down.

"Skip the next one," Dad said. "We'll do that last."

Aram skipped the KBG Headquarters and went down the list to Ministry of Finance.

A young woman stood that I'd seen before, the young adult I'd given my beautiful bouquet of peach roses to the night I met Bart. It seemed at least one lifetime ago, but in reality, it had been less than twenty-four hours.

"I'm working on my MBA and have a mentor in those offices. I know the layout of the offices and many of the people pretty well. I can handle that."

"Sky, you go with . . ." Dad paused for her to fill in the blank.

"Milena," she said over her shoulder. She hurried out of the room with an aura of confidence that was refreshing to see. Sky had to hurry to catch up, and he was not one to dawdle, even if he was the oldest in the group. Rip Schyler was our grandfather figure, in his early sixties with doctorates in criminology and abnormal behavior. He was Dutch, fluent in several languages, and I frequently teased him that one of his best was body language.

"Radio Center," Aram said, searching the room until he spotted a delicately beautiful young woman with auburn hair. "Lilit, you've spent a lot of time there with your new music programming. You know a lot of people and can move about freely. Can you handle that?"

Lilit got to her feet and looked around anticipating her Anastasia partner. Dad assigned Lionel to go with her. Lion was French, funny, a flirt with a weird sense of humor, quick as a gazelle, and graceful as a dancer. I had to admit, they made a very attractive couple as they left the room together.

"The Ministry of Internal Affairs." Aram stopped and looked at those who were left.

"Any volunteers for the police?" Dad asked.

A little old man, even shorter than me, stood and came forward. "In another life," he began slowly in Russian, "I used to work there. I still know some of the old guys and if we start remembering the good old days, which really weren't," he said with a wink in my direction, "I can probably find out what you need to know."

I instantly fell in love with this beautiful old man. He had expressive penetrating eyes that sparkled when he smiled and a prickly, almost white mustache. What had he already experienced in his lifetime, enduring decades of Armenia's turbulent and tragic history? At this point, didn't he deserve to sit back and let the younger generation do this kind of work? It was a sad fact that you were never too old to have to defend your freedom and chosen way of life. I admired him for volunteering.

"I will go alone. That will be less suspicious. I know what to look for. I've done this kind of thing before." He offered his gnarled, sunbrowned hand to those of us in the front of the room. When he came to me I couldn't resist the impulse to kiss his cheek. I had no idea who this little old man was, but his spirit spoke to mine and I recognized a friend.

He turned and left the quiet room and no one spoke for several seconds. Then Dad broke the silence. "What was his name?"

"Vanik," Babken said as he wrote down the assignment.

"Transportation's next," Aram said as we heard the front door close behind the memorable old man.

"We can do that." A spritely young woman stood and pulled the young man to his feet who sat beside her. "We're Rita and Roman. My brother works at the Department of Transportation and I worked there before I went to New Mexico for my master's degree so I know a lot of people there, too. We won't have any trouble snooping around."

"Norik, you'll have to go with Rita and Roman. We're out of agents," Dad said. Norik left with the two young people who didn't look any more like brother and sister than Bart and I.

"Wait a minute, Dad. What about me?" Too frequently I was treated not as a full fledged agent, but as my father's daughter, or Bart's wife.

"Sorry, Bunny. I need you somewhere else. We'll get to you and me in a minute." Then he turned to those remaining in the room. "This is only a partial list of places we think will have moles installed. For those of you who don't have trained agents to work with, remember what you were told last night and check that list of things against those employed in that office or department. Allison will remain here with Babken to field your calls. This will be our control center for this operation. You were briefed on how to work the communication watches you were given. If you have any questions, Allison can answer them for you. Aram, you get the dubious honor of checking out KGB headquarters with me. Hopefully they'll not only get off our back, they'll cooperate and work with us. Let's move."

With that, Dad blew a kiss in my direction and hurried out of the room with Aram close on his heels.

CHAPTER 30

I couldn't believe it! Stuck in a makeshift control center—a baptistry of all places. And I was supposed to be a resource for all those people out there and any problems they'd encounter? I don't think so. I was probably the least informed person in the group. Certainly the least experienced agent in Anastasia.

I took a deep breath and looked around at those left in the room. I'd been struck by the number of young people; the majority of those volunteering to help were between the ages of twenty and thirty with only a few older than that. As Maria said on our way to the airplane, this younger generation yearned for freedom and apparently they were willing to put their lives on the line for it.

"Anyone else familiar with someplace that might be vital to a takeover of the country?" I asked.

Babken pointed at a couple sitting by the window. "Avetik and Syuzanna are doing residencies at the hospital. Would that be somewhere they should go?"

"Good thought, Babken." I turned to the young couple and spoke to them in Russian. "Will you two go hang out at the hospital and see what's going on? Listen for gossip, for things out of the ordinary, for people murmuring about their jobs or supervisors, or recent changes in key positions. We don't have anyone to go with you, but you can call in if you find out anything or have any questions."

They left immediately, passing a couple of guys just coming in—obviously the twins. Identical twins. Dominic jumped to his feet. "I'll brief them on our way. Have fun, mi amiga bonita."

"Be sure to write down their names, Babken. You all may know them just as the twins, but it would be nice for the rest of us to know who they are."

"Samvel and Gagik," Elder Minasyan offered as Babken jotted their names on his paper. "How long do you think this will take?" the young elder inquired politely. "We need to prepare for the baptism."

"Of course. Is there somewhere else in the building we can go and be out of the way but still accessible?"

"Yes, I think you could use the empty room we use as an additional dressing room every Saturday when a large group is baptized. Today's a special baptism. Only one family so we won't be using the extra space. It's their wedding anniversary and they wanted to celebrate in this unique way."

"Nice way to celebrate an anniversary! Thanks. We don't want to interfere with the work that needs to go on. Can I help you, Babken?"

The young man, probably about twenty, flashed a grin of gratitude and handed me his pencil and paper, then struggled to his feet with the help of his crutches and hobbled along after me. Elder Minasyan carried a small table from the foyer into the bare room and his companion dragged the chairs along that had been behind it. Half a dozen people brought their chairs from the baptismal room and we were soon set up out of the way. Elder Minasyan and his companion left to finish preparations for the baptism.

Babken and I sat behind the table we'd positioned to look straight out into the foyer. From this vantage point, I could see people coming and going and a lot of activity behind frosted glass doors across the hall.

"What's going on in there?" I asked, pointing at the door that had just opened for the third time in less than a minute.

"That's the mission office."

"Are we in the way here? I hate to interfere with mission business. Will we get anyone in trouble by being here? Should we have asked anyone's permission before we set up?"

Babken smiled. "You ask a lot of questions, don't you? Do you expect answers to them all?"

I laughed. "I guess I do ask a lot of questions, and yes, I usually expect to have them all answered. Otherwise, what's the point of asking them?"

Armen answered. "We're okay. We aren't interfering with anything. President and Sister Beckstrand went to Tblisi to hold a branch conference there and took the Butterfields with them, so the office staff and district presidency is in charge and there isn't as much going on as usual. What can I do? I feel pretty useless sitting around here doing nothing."

"I'll need you, and probably everybody else in this room, to help me as our people call in with questions or problems. I certainly won't have all the answers and you know the area and the customs, so you are my panel of experts. And my first assignment to all of you is to think about other places that al Qaeda might target in their takeover of Armenia. If you wanted to paralyze the government here, if you wanted to have someone in a key slot in any other office or department, where would you put them?"

A pert redhead raised her hand. "I'm Ofelia. I don't know if this is what you mean, but there have been some new guards hired at the American Embassy where I work. I know they go through a thorough security check before being hired, but these guys give me the creeps."

"I'd classify the American Embassy as a pretty important slot, Ofelia. Have you mentioned it before to anyone?"

"No, I'd never really thought about it before last night at our meeting with your Mr. Schyler. Then I remembered that about a year ago this new supervisor was hired. All the old guards that had been working there for quite a while seemed to quit for some reason, and the new guys are really creepy. They've all been hired by this guy who is a real loser."

"Is there someone you trust there that you can talk to?" Bells were going off in my head as we talked. This was exactly the scenario we'd expected.

"Yes. I work for Mr. Infanger. He's head of the USDA."

I stared at her long and hard as I prayed for guidance to make the right decision. "You're sure you can trust him?"

Ofelia nodded. "I know I can."

"Get to him immediately. Tell him what you just told me, and all that we've been discussing here. You can have him talk to me on the Dick Tracy if he has any questions, but all of those guards and their supervisor need to be quietly detained where they can't talk to anyone until this is all over. Don't they have a detachment of Marine guards that can handle all of that quietly and efficiently?" Ofelia nodded, jumped up and hurried out the door.

As she left, a raven-haired girl with big beautiful solemn dark eyes raised her hand. "I'm Anna. I don't know if it's important, but at work the other night I overheard a conversation that gave me goose bumps. These two men that come in all the time were talking about 'when it happens' they needed to have someone at Echmiadzin to make sure they had the support of the Catholicos. Out of context, I had no idea what they were talking about, but after our briefing last night, I've been thinking about that conversation. It really makes sense when I think about al Qaeda and their plan."

I remembered the influence the Armenian Apostolic Church had on everything in Armenia. Yes. It did make sense. "Do we have someone who can get close enough to the Catholicos to talk to him about this?"

Armen leaned forward. "My mother works for LDS Charities. The Lundgreens have met with the Catholicos several times regarding the humanitarian aid they're providing through the Church. Mom translates. We could send the three of them to talk with him. I told Mom what's going on and she was anxious to help however she could."

"Can you get them right on it?"

"I can be at their office in fifteen minutes, and if they're there, it's just thirty minutes to Echmiadzin—if Martun's available with the van." He raced out without even waiting for the go signal. I agreed with Bart. Not having communications made this twice as hard as it had to be. One phone call to the office to tell them what to do would save so much time.

"Thanks, Anna. No one had thought of the church." As I turned from directing Babken to add that to his growing list of people and places, I looked up to see a tall, slender white-haired man enter the room. When he came closer, I was surprised to see he was much younger looking than his beautiful white hair suggested. He said something in Armenian which I didn't understand. I introduced myself in Russian, a language I was sure he could speak since his was the generation used to using it.

He stretched out his hand and I shook it. "I'm happy to meet you, Allison. I'm Valodia. Since the meeting last night, I've been trying to think of the less obvious places al Qaeda would infiltrate, but that might be important after the fact. What about the mayors of all the townships in Yerevan?"

"Good point, Valodia. If they have any influence or power in their little areas, the terrorists would be wise to have someone at the side of the power broker—unless they have taken over the office themselves. How do we handle that?"

"I've known the mayor of Ajapniak for years. I can work with him, and we have members in each of the massivs and villages who know their mayors and can get close to them."

"Thank you, Valodia. You know what to do if you turn up someone suspicious or obviously where they shouldn't be?"

"I do." He turned to leave, then stopped when he spotted someone he knew. A thirty-something woman had been talking nonstop with a striking looking brunette since they came in to the baptistry together, then kept up the conversation after we moved into this room. I wasn't sure they'd heard a thing that had been going on the entire time.

Valodia approached her. "Alla, you know the mayor of Komitas. Do you know if he has anyone on his staff or in his office that's been acting different lately, or that you would deem suspicious, or that the other employees are having problems with?"

"I'll go snoop around and see what I can find out." Alla smiled. "I've been wanting to try out this fancy watch you gave me." She kissed the woman next to her on the cheek and hustled out of the room with Valodia right behind her on his way to contact other members.

I sat back astonished. "Is the whole district involved in this?" I asked no one in particular but just threw it out to anyone who happened to be listening.

Alla's friend answered with a shake of her head that sent her long hair rippling over her shoulders. "There are no secrets in Armenia," she laughed. "If one knows, everyone knows."

"Nunik, what about you?" Babken asked the woman. "You've worked at several places in the last couple of years since you graduated from the American University of Armenia. Anything that might be helpful in your employment?"

"Not that I can think of this minute, but I did remember that President Minasyan teaches at the International School and one of his students is the Mafia don's son. President Minasyan might know something. I think he's in his office right now."

I jumped to my feet in excitement. "Is his office nearby?" I'd discovered many things from the young man who might be an older cousin to this student in the lounge at the American University. This might prove an excellent lead to follow.

She laughed and stood—all six feet something of her towering over my five feet-four-inches. "Very near. In this building, in fact. I will talk to him." She swept out of the room with her long skirt whirling about her legs. If I interpreted her body language correctly, this attractive young woman was accustomed to making grand entrances and exits.

I walked to the window and looked out into the little alley alongside the building, wondering how each of the assignments progressed at this point. Grapevines were changing color along the high fence, and someone reeled in their washing on the highrise building next to us, pulling the line along as they emptied it many stories above the alley. I felt a rush of gratitude for the convenience of my washer and dryer. And for the convenience of telephones and communication systems of every kind. This would have been so much easier if we could have called Yerevan as soon as we'd talked to Khalid and Musharif.

I wondered how Vaghinak was doing with Musharif. Had he discovered any other information we needed to have? But how would we find out with no way of communication? The distance was too great to use the radio wristwatches and there simply wasn't any other method available at the minute.

I felt, more than heard, someone enter the now quiet room. There were only two or three people remaining besides Babken and me, and I turned, expecting to see Nunik returning either with President Minasyan or with some word from him. Instead, Vaghinak stood quietly at the desk. It gave me a little shiver of precognition. I'd simply thought of the man and he appeared out of nowhere.

"Mrs. Allan, I have report."

I hurried around the desk and stood next to him. "Where's Musharif? Did you get something from him?"

"Yes. He said time for takeover is tonight at 6:15, when most offices closed and workers gone home. Moles will make changes in their area so all will be in place when workers return tomorrow."

"How did you get him to tell you this?" I couldn't imagine Musharif offering anything more than he had already given us.

"He say if we know, we panic and make mistakes, but too late to do anything about it, even if no mistakes." Vaghink dropped his head. "Sorry, Mrs. Allan. Then he bite cyanide capsule and die, laughing at us. I not know he have capsule in his mouth."

I quickly tried to console the tenderhearted man who plainly felt personally responsible for the terrorist's death. "Oh, Vaghinak, it's not your fault. Terrorists frequently conceal a capsule under a false tooth. You might never have found it even if you'd known what to look for."

Then the import of what he said hit me. Stunned, I dropped into the chair behind me. This might make a huge difference in how everyone went about what they were doing to ferret out the moles. Then again, Musharif was a master at deceit. What if this last bit of information he'd given was false? What if it was supposed to lead us totally astray? Could they be taking over sooner and he'd given us this tidbit to make us relax a bit? It only took me a few seconds to realize this wasn't a decision I should be making on my own.

As I started to buzz Dad on the Dick Tracy, I remembered we had over a dozen radios out there and I didn't know anyone's number. "Babken, at the meeting last night were numbers assigned to everyone, and if so, do you happen to have a list of those numbers?"

Bless my father for his foresight and Babken for his diligence. Babken produced the neatly hand-printed list of those who had been given a watch radio and their corresponding number. I was even on the list and Bart. How did Dad know we'd have our watches with us? He must have assumed any good agent would come equipped with whatever he needed, and since that was one of our handiest gadgets, we'd be prepared with ours. I was so glad I tucked them into the case, even when I thought I wouldn't use them.

I programmed Dad's number into my little radio, pressed send, and waited for Dad's response. With him at KGB headquarters, I wasn't sure he'd get back to me immediately. I might have to wait until he was able to talk freely.

Suddenly his voice, clearly audible, came over the radio and the content made it apparent he was in the middle of a conversation. "Once we were enemies, Ivan, during the cold war. Now we work together for the good of Armenia." Then he stopped transmitting. At least I knew he got the buzz and that he would call me back as soon as he could. Interesting. Everything changed after the cold war and the fall of the Soviet Union. Former mortal enemies now found themselves on the same side of the table, working against new and possibly even more deadly enemies than before.

Vaghinak excused himself, saying he'd be right back, and went into the mission office across the hall. I glanced at Babken's notes. If Dad, who was the last to leave, was already inside KGB headquarters talking with his guy, I wondered how everyone else fared. How would Else, Tsovinar and Meri approach Mrs. Kocharian? Would she be receptive? And how on earth would they find out if anyone was "inside" the Presidential Palace?

As I looked over each of the assignments and those who had volunteered to go to the various places, I couldn't even imagine how many different approaches would be taken. Every single office, department, or ministry would be so unique from the others. And how would all these young adults handle their assigned tasks? Did they actually have the knowledge and the sophistication to brazenly enter these places and attempt to uncover the bad guys? I was glad most of them had Anastasia's expertise with them, but it would still remain up to the locals to do the bulk of the talking and fancy foot-work that would find the answers. Anastasia would handle it after someone had been identified.

I glanced at my watch. Three o'clock. If what Musharif told Vaghink was true, we had barely three hours to find and neutralize as many moles as possible. The mole had been removed from the Air Force, if what I'd learned earlier today was true. Armenia's little air base was safe. But what about the civilian airport?

"Babken, what about Zvartnots? Was anyone assigned there?"

"Yes, that was one of the first to come to our attention, after the air base. Gegham and Nelli live on the airport and he discovered someone in an office he shouldn't have been in, searching through files he had no clearance for. Those first two were our 'head's up' that we had trouble coming."

"What about the Army? Is anyone in the commander's confidence that can watch there?"

"Davit got himself called back from the Turkish border and assigned to some special task in headquarters with criminal law and forensics. He's working on that now."

Ahh, Davit, the scrupulously honest young man that I didn't want to meet on the border of Georgia when we thought to sneak illegally across that perimeter.

Nunik swept back into our little control center with the aplomb of a prima donna, followed by a tall, distinguished man in his late forties. She introduced him as President Minasyan, the District President of the Church in Armenia.

I extended my hand. "I've already met a handsome young Minasyan. Any relation?"

"My son."

"Artur is the first Armenian missionary to Armenia," Nunik explained.

"You must be proud of him." I said. "He struck me as being extremely capable, and very polite and proper."

"Thank you. How can I help?"

I motioned him into the chair opposite the desk and came around to sit beside him. "I understand you have a son of the Mafia don in your class at the International School."

"That's the rumor. I don't know if it's true."

"I was told two brothers control the Mafia and the KGB. I spoke to the son of the head of the KGB this morning and gleaned some interesting information. I'm wondering if we could also get valuable information from the father of your student."

President Minasyan thought for a minute. "Possibly."

"I assume you've been briefed about what's going on."

"Yes, I was at the meeting last night." He smiled. "With all of my young adults. Are you trying to turn them into a bunch of spies?"

I tried to gauge the seriousness of his remark, but the smile in his eyes was genuine. I returned the smile. "No. We don't want them to become spies. We just want to help them have the freedom they deserve."

"Well said." The smile vanished and he leaned forward. "If his father *is* head of the Mafia, we could use them to help us. They don't want al Qaeda or anyone else taking over. Their status quo is too lucrative. They don't want to share their business profits, illegal as they are, or have someone else change the system so they have no profit at all."

"How would you use them?" I asked, having no idea of my own to offer.

"I will go talk with him about his son. Then I will turn the conversation to this subject. I will see what he has to say and come back to tell you."

"Thank you, President Minasyan. I appreciate your quick response." We shook hands and he left without even returning to his office. Crises produce strange bedfellows. Who'd have thought we'd be calling on the Mafia for help. The same group that apparently wanted me very dead. Or did they? Who had tried to kill me? The two suspects highest on my list were the Mafia and the KGB. And now we were enlisting the help of both of them. Would I ever know who had been trying to end my turn on earth? More important, was I still on their list of "most wanted?"

CHAPTER 31

Since none of our members had private vehicles, public transportation was mainly everyone's mode of travel. How long did it take to cross the city in a *marshutka*? I didn't think they took taxis more than was absolutely necessary. At about 1000 drams per trip, a cab cost ten times as much as a *marshutka* at only 100 drams per ride. The metro was a bargain at 40 drams, but it only formed a shallow S curve through the city and this chapel location wasn't near a station. All of that travel would take time. How many had actually arrived at their destination by now?

Then I had a happy thought. Most were traveling with Anastasia. Our agents would opt for the fastest way of reaching their target and they had money to pay for taxis, where many of the members here couldn't afford the extravagance. So I might expect results any time now from some of the first out, with a lot of heavenly help, a little bit of luck, and much ingenuity and courage on the part of these inexperienced people who were willing to find and confront the enemy.

As I studied Babken's list, a couple in their thirties with a baby wandered in and spoke to Babken and two young girls who had remained quiet throughout the whole process of assignments. The young father introduced himself as Varuzhan and his wife as Silva.

"And who is this?" I peeked around Silva's shoulder at the darling little boy who was hiding his face from me.

"Hovhannes," Silva said with a smile that spoke volumes about her feeling for her son.

"We came to help. I don't know what we can do, but we don't want Hovhannes to be raised under bin Laden's influence. "He's the most . . ."

Varuzhan had to stop and gain control of his emotions before he could continue. "He's the most precious thing in our lives. We waited so long for him. Now we have the Church, our son, and our life is good. How can we help stop these terrorists from taking it from us?"

Wow. He'd certainly put things in their proper perspective in a hurry. I must never forget that this wasn't just the usual "take out the bad guys" scenario. This was a country that had been through things I couldn't even imagine, horrors even the most "on the edge" movie directors would consider too horrible to put on film. And just when things started looking up for them, along comes bad guy bin Laden and his al Qaeda monsters ready to shoot the ark out of the water and sink the whole population back into the dark ages.

"Thank you for coming. If you'll act as my panel of experts when everyone starts calling in, I think that would be the greatest thing you could do. We're expecting things to start happening any minute; I don't know whether we're actually going to get some results, or will just need help solving some problems with assignments. I assume you were at the meeting last night and know everything that's happening." They nodded silently.

As I looked at the four people in front of me, and Babken beside me, I couldn't help but think this was the strangest control center situation I'd ever been in. People wandering in and out, limited means of communication with agents in the field for instructions or feedback, and it seemed everyone in the whole district had become involved. Well, maybe not everybody, but I was amazed at the number of "recruits" helping Anastasia. I'd be very interested to know the exact number of members in the "soft revolt" organization. Were all of these young adults actively involved in the "rebellion" effort? Or had many simply come to do what they could when they got wind of the operation?

In America, when you spoke of teenagers and young adults as rebels, it had a totally different connotation. In Armenia they had something real to rebel against, and it appeared they were not afraid to put everything on the line to do it. I wondered if they realized how dangerous this activity could be. Al Qaeda didn't pussyfoot around. If they thought their cover was blown, they'd have no reason not to blow away the person ready to expose them.

Vaghinak came back into the room and shook hands with Varuzhan and Silva. This truly was the handshakingest people I'd ever seen! He turned to me. "What you need me to do now?"

I handed him Babken's notes on assignments. "Unless you can think of some place or someone else we should check out, I guess we're sort of just stuck waiting to hear from everyone."

Vaghinak studied the list and passed it to Varuzhan and Silva who silently read through the names and places on the sheet of yellow paper. No one spoke. The feeling in the room wasn't really helpless resignation, but bordered on it. Minutes passed. No one else came and my Dick Tracy remained maddeningly, ominously silent. What was happening out there? As the minutes ticked by, tension replaced resignation

But I still had a problem I hadn't addressed. Could I just sit on the information Vaghinak had given me until Dad called back? Or should I try to contact each of the partnerships out doing their thing? Who might be most affected by knowing the deadline?

Suddenly my Dick Tracy vibrated on my arm, startling me. Even though I'd anticipated the communication, it still surprised me. I glanced at the incoming number. Else. Made sense.

"Yes. Else?"

"Mission accomplished."

"Else, even for you that's incredible. How did you do it? Who was it? And what did you do with the mole?"

Else laughed. "You and your myriad questions, Alli! We'll come back there and report on our successful gossipy tea party, unless you need us to go somewhere else first."

"Not right now. Come on in. We're anxious to hear what you found." Yes! One down. How many to go?

I hadn't turned up the volume on my Dick Tracy so I wasn't sure anyone else had heard the good news and I happily announced to the dismal looking group, "We have a success story! Else, Tsovinar and Meri are on their way back to tell it."

There was no applauding, but the sense of relief and excitement in the room worked just as well in expelling the tension. One victory was great, but what had been that particular mole's assignment? Eliminate President Kocharian if he wouldn't cooperate? Or eliminate him anyway and replace him? If someone planned to take out the president, who was prepared to step into his place and where would he be found?

The House of Parliament? I buzzed Dominic on his Dick Tracy. "Si, Alli. What's up?"

"Dom, Else just found the mole in the Presidential Palace. We have word—not verified—that the takeover time is 6:15 tonight as soon as most offices are closed and people leave. Thought you'd like to know in case that helps you identify someone lingering behind to do his dirty work. Also, think about the possibility someone planned to eliminate Kocharian. Who would be the logical replacement and where is he right now? Hope your twins are up on their politics."

"Gracias, bella. We're making some headway here. Amazing the information you can glean when you get a little bull session going with the guys."

"Keep up the good work and let me know if you have a breakthrough." I sat for a minute with Babken's list in my hand, going over the rest of the assignments. Who else would benefit most from the piece of information Vaghinak got from Musharif? Loretta and David Chen were next on the list at the TV Center and there was probably a shift change there about six o'clock.

As I buzzed David, I thought about the multicultural make-up of Anastasia. David was of Chinese descent, a very private person, one of our most diligent and conscientious agents, as well as the pilot for Anastasia's Lear jet and helicopter.

"Yes, Allison?" With David, there were no nicknames. He was David, not Dave, and I was Allison, not Alli, which everyone else called me. He was also one of my very favorite people. I knew I could depend on him no matter what.

"Received an unverified report takeover will occur at 6:15, when most people have left the offices. I didn't know whether that might effect your plans, and can't tell you whether it's even true, though it does sound logical."

"Yes, it seems a plausible time for the conversion of the government."

"How are you coming?"

"Loretta knows many people and we've garnered much information. She's introducing me as a producer interested in doing some long-term shows on Armenia. It's opened a lot of doors. She's quite an actress."

"Keep me posted if you find out anything. You've probably already thought of this, but from the standpoint of al Qaeda, who would have the most to gain in taking over the television center and what would they do after they had control?"

"Thanks, Allison. I'll think about that and we'll be in touch."

Next on the list: Oz with Naira and Lucine at Armentel. When I first thought about them cleaning the place, I wasn't sure they'd be able to discover anything important, but with gossip and "bull sessions" producing valuable information already, the three were in the perfect position to uncover what we needed to know. Often cleaning ladies went about their business almost invisibly, and were able to go in and out of meetings and offices unhindered. I hoped this was the case at Armentel.

I buzzed Oz and while I waited for him to answer, I thought about all we'd been through together. I'd met him when Bart and I, honeymooning in San Francisco, had become involved with a diamond heist. Oz was with the FBI then, but came on board Anastasia immediately after that and had shared in almost every other case we'd worked on since. Oz didn't add to the international flavor of the group—he was one hundred percent American for generations.

"Sorry I couldn't get right back to you, Alli. We about got busted and Lucy came up with the greatest story you've ever heard to get us off the hook. These Armenians are really clever. I'm the official representative of an American janitorial service getting ready to open a business in Armenia. I'm checking out how the work they do differs from our employees in America and Europe."

"And what have you found?"

"You can't believe how much harder they work here. We have so many time- and labor-saving devices at home for cleaning. These people really earn the pennies they make. And that's what it is. Pennies."

"Sounds like you've found a new crusade. Oz, we have a report, totally unverified, the takeover is 6:15. Don't know if that will be helpful but keep it in mind. Have you identified any possible suspects?"

"Yeah, a couple. Both fit all the criteria, plus both are power hungry, hard-driving individuals with 'wanna-be' written all over them."

"Any ideas how to tell which is our bad boy?"

Oz paused a minute, then said, "If we haven't figured it out by 6:10, we'll take them both out to dinner, just in case."

I wasn't sure exactly what he meant by "out to dinner" but figured he could handle whatever he saw coming. Along those lines, I hoped he had the vision to see any left hooks before they connected with his chin.

I signed off and buzzed Bart at the Ministry of Energy with Margarit and Sarkis—and their baby. I wondered if any of the places looked anything at all like I pictured them as I talked with our people there. Probably not. But I knew what this one looked like. It was on the corner of Abovian and Issahakyan—right in front of my apartment—make that *former* apartment.

"Hi, Princess. What's up?"

"Time."

Bart shot back immediately. "What does that mean?"

"Vaghinak's back from Dilijan. Musharif told him the takeover was 6:15 tonight. I don't know whether to believe him or not, but thought you'd like to know, in case it's for real. How's it going at the pep place?"

"Slowly, but not because of my partners. They're a couple of fire-balls. Margarit and the baby are a real hit and she's been talking to every woman in the office while Sarkis worked the male employees. All you have to do is start a conversation on discontent in the work place and everyone comes forth with all sorts of information—which they think are just gripes, but from which we are gleaning great stuff."

"Do you have a major suspect, or suspects?"

"I have my eye on one character who's my personal favorite in the top ten most obnoxious bosses. If he's your normal run-of-the-mill Armenian, I'll eat my hat."

"You don't wear a hat. Get back to work and let me know if you find anything. Time's running out."

"I'm only too well aware of that, Princess. Oh, here comes the mad Russian again. He'd make Stalin look like a saint." Bart disconnected before I had a chance to ask him if he'd like to run up to my apartment and rescue my suitcase. I truly would love something else to wear. However, this wasn't a fashion show and I was presentable so a change of wardrobe appeared way down on the list of things to worry about right now.

Dad still hadn't returned my buzz. *That* was something to worry about. He must be going head-to-head with the KBG—or were they just talking about old times in the cold war? I looked back at Babken's list. Rip Schyler and Milena at the Ministry of Finance were next under Dad. I buzzed Sky.

"Yes, Allison." Sky must have been in a closet. His voice echoed.

"Where are you? You sound like you're in a tunnel or something."

"You wouldn't believe the halls in these government buildings. I swear they're the length of a football field. What's up?"

"The time to stop these creeps. Musharif told Vaghinak the takeover would be at 6:15, but he could have been lying."

"It may not matter, Alli. Milena's been having a heart-to-heart with her mentor for the last thirty minutes and she's pretty sure she knows who the mole is. We're trying to figure out a way to confirm her suspicions. When we do, we'll bring him in."

"Don't bring him here, Sky. I'll find out where you can hold him, but we don't need that kind of vermin here at the Church. Good luck." Where *could* we take al Qaeda? Interpol normally had no authority to arrest, but Anastasia did. Did Interpol have somewhere we could stash these creeps until the coalition on terror could come for them?

One of the young women who had been listening to my conversations on my Dick Tracy came hesitantly over to me. I had to strain to hear her quiet voice.

"I'm sorry to bother you, but I think Davit could lock them up at the army base. He'll know who to talk to so he can have them held safely away from everyone else."

"Great idea." I checked Babken's list but Davit wasn't listed on it. "Does Davit have a communications watch?"

Her big brown eyes looked uncertain. She shook her head slowly. "I don't think so. He wasn't at the meeting last night. My sister and I could go talk to him at the base."

"Thanks." I turned to Babken. "Do we have an extra Dick Tracy she could give Davit?"

Babken shook his head and unstrapped his from his wrist. "She can give him mine."

"Thanks, Babken. You won't need yours as long as you and I are just sitting here." I turned to the shy young woman in front of me. "I don't know your name." We needed name tags to keep track of everyone around here. And would I be able to remember all these names after I finally learned them?

"Anichka. My sister is Laura." Laura stood and came around in front of the desk by her sister.

"Security might be high at the base, Anichka. Do you know how to get hold of Davit if they won't let you on base?"

She nodded. "Some of our young adults are stationed there. I'll find someone to get him for us if we can't get on base to find him."

I looked at the two sisters who didn't look old enough to be out of high school and certainly not old enough to have any experience doing this kind of work. Then my favorite scripture, D&C 84:88, popped into my head. "*For I will go before your face. I will be on your right hand and on your left and my Spirit shall be in your hearts and mine angels round about you to bear you up.*"

"Go for it, girls. Say a prayer first, and be very careful. I'm a great believer in guardian angels, and I expect you'll have some celestial company on this errand."

As they turned to go, Vaghinak stood. "I could drive them. I need to do something."

I nodded, my mind leaping ahead to envision what they might encounter and how they would handle it. At least if Vaghinak drove them, he could watch out for them. As often happened, some of our guardian angels turned out to be very mortal beings.

How many of these innocent people were we putting in harms way? A very heavy feeling began as a lump in my throat and spread downward, growing as it went until it hit the pit of my stomach. Distress and misgivings numbed my mind. How many untrained, naive young adults had we sent into the den of the lions? How many of those lions were very edgy right now, anticipating their big moment just a couple of hours away? How many fingers were on the trigger, watching for someone to come at the last minute, afraid their cover would be blown just as they were finally about to accomplish the job they'd been trained for years to do?

I looked up as someone entered the room, anticipating a familiar face—but certainly not *this* familiar face.

CHAPTER 32

The tall, handsome Armenian walked slowly into the room, glancing only briefly at the three remaining people, a handicapped young man and a young couple with a baby. The slightest hint of a smile flashed in his dark eyes, then as they narrowed, the smile disappeared. I had a sinking feeling this wasn't a cordial social call.

"You missed presentations, Mrs. Allan. I'm terribly disappointed. I expect more from you."

"Dr. Grigoryan." I couldn't think of another single thing to say. My mind and tongue were paralyzed by surprise—and a sudden rush of fear. Why was this man here? How had he found me? And why should I be afraid of him?

"I thought to find you in hospital when you didn't come to seminar. I thought you step in front of another car." He stepped toward me. "Instead I find you healthy—here. Please explain."

Alarm bells went off in my head and my danger antennae tingled big time. "Dr. Grigoryan, I'd like you to meet some very special people." I stood and pointed at the youth sitting next to me behind the desk. "This is Babken. Dr. Garik Grigoryan is in charge of a special symposium at the American University of Armenia at which I was supposed to speak today."

Where was my purse? I'd dropped it on a chair as we moved from the baptistry to this room. It was now on the floor next to Silva. Somehow I needed to get to it without alerting Garik about my intentions.

I stepped to the side of the desk to introduce Varuzhan and his petite wife, Silva. As I did so, Varuzhan stood and took a step forward to shake hands with the stranger. Dr. Grigoryan did an unexpected step back and kept his arms stiffly at his sides. Varuzhan stopped, puzzled at the blatantly unfriendly behavior.

I continued to work my way around the desk. Of all the times for Garik to suddenly appear. The makeshift control center had been full of people for the last hour, or at least people coming and going constantly. Now, when we numbered only four adults and a baby, the biggest threat of the day materialized. But exactly what was the threat? And why did I suddenly fear this man? I definitely felt this wasn't a friendly social call, nor even a simple chastisement for my absence at the symposium. Dr. Grigoryan had something more sinister in mind.

As I attempted to casually retrieve my purse from its place next to Silva, I thought of the four innocent people in the room and various scenarios flashed through my mind. Babken couldn't get to his feet without his crutches and that took him at least half a minute. Varuzhan's first thought would be to protect Silva and their precious Hovhannes. I didn't want any of these people in danger of any kind.

Just what did Garik want? From the intense look in his dark eyes, it was serious business. As he took a long step toward me, I knew I was about to find out and knew just as surely I wouldn't like it one little bit.

I sneezed. Then I sneezed again. I dove for my purse on the floor next to Silva. With one hand I grabbed a tissue from it and covered my nose as I sneezed again, and with the other I located my gun as I balanced my purse on the edge of the chair.

Garik had stopped, momentarily put off by my sneezing, but when I seemed to be under control, he resumed his ominous advance. Please don't let me have to shoot him, especially in front of these good people, I prayed.

Suddenly the front door exploded open and high heels clattered across the tile floor in the foyer. A petite bundle of energy burst through the door, spotted Babken and headed straight for him. She took his face in her hands, kissed both his cheeks, then whirled around and greeted Varuzhan and Silva, bestowing a kiss on the sleeping Hovhannes. Without even a glance at Garik who had stopped in his tracks as the middle-aged whirling dervish flew into the room, she turned to me. "We come to help."

"We" being the three young adults who streamed in at a much slower pace than the take-charge woman who preceded them. These were three very attractive people. Without introducing herself, she pointed to Hripsime, her daughter, Stepan, her son, and Karine, her son's wife. That she was proud of her beautiful family was obvious. That she would be able to handle anything I assigned her was also obvious.

"I'm *very* happy to meet you all." They would never know just how happy I was! "I'm Allison Allan. This is Dr. Garik Grigoryan from AUA. And you are . . ." I shook her hand as I waited for her name.

"Melanya. What we do to help?"

"If you'll all just sit down for a minute, we'll talk about it. I think Dr. Grigoryan was just leaving."

No one sat. Babken struggled to his feet and moved between me and the tall menacing stranger. Varuzhan stepped to Babken's side. As short as I was, I could see over the heads of these two valiant human shields. Everyone turned to look at the man suddenly faced by double the numbers of two minutes ago.

"You will present your paper at symposium tomorrow as agreed?" he said, backing toward the door.

"I'll be in touch, Dr. Grigoryan."

Garik turned on his heel and disappeared. Before I had a chance to catch my breath, the Dick Tracy tingled on my wrist. "Yes?"

"Bunny, you wanted to talk to me?"

"Dad! Yes." I gathered my thoughts and got back on track. "Vaghinak's back from Dilijan. Musharif told him the takeover was at 6:15 tonight when most of the offices had emptied. Then he bit into a cyanide capsule and returned to Allah. I wanted to know if I should pass the information along, or if you thought it might be one final lie to throw us off."

"Have you told the others?"

"When you didn't get back to me, I started to contact them, then got sidetracked with something else." I decided I wouldn't bother him right now with my fright of a minute ago. "Should I let the rest know?"

"Yes. Any news yet?"

"Else said they've taken care of the one in the presidential palace and a couple of others are close. We've had a steady stream of volunteers go out to other places we hadn't thought of so even if we don't stop all of them, we'll definitely put a crimp in al Qaeda's plans. How'd you do with the KGB?"

"Found one of my old counterparts from the Russian side of the cold war and we had to do some reminiscing before I could twist his arm into coming over to my side on this one. He said he'd get his people into the offices we've designated and take over."

"I assume you told him you didn't want to turn the whole thing over to him—just have his help after we'd identified them?" I could see nothing but trouble if they came blundering in just as our teams were finishing their investigations.

"That was what took so long. He wanted to blaze in and arrest everybody. I finally convinced him we'd turn the moles over to him as soon as we caught them. I wasn't sure of his motives."

"Were you satisfied he was genuine and there were no moles at their headquarters?"

"I think he's genuine, Bunny, and I left it up to him to find a mole if there was one. I'm convinced there is but he's better equipped than any of us to decide who and take them into custody."

"Are you coming back here now, Dad?" Though I figured there was safety in numbers, and our numbers had increased significantly, I wasn't confident Dr. Grigoryan would give up so easily. I still didn't know what he'd planned, just that it wouldn't have been pleasant. I'd be more than happy having anyone from Anastasia hang around here to help.

"Yes. We'll be back shortly. Finish notifying the rest of the groups so they'll know about the deadline. We'll assume Musharif actually told the truth, though I can think of a dozen reasons for him to lie with his dying breath."

"Makes me feel really good passing along a possible lie. Not."

"Maybe he wanted us to discount it as a lie. At any rate, get on it, Bunny."

I did, keeping Melanya and her offspring waiting while I gave Lionel and Norik's groups a "heads up" on the takeover time. I also told them to be on the lookout for KGB who would probably try to muscle in on the investigation. I really didn't believe they'd sit back and let someone else do their job, especially foreigners they'd been sworn enemies with only a decade ago.

"We have many offices to visit in Department of Transportation," Norik said as I was ready to hang up. "Is anyone to help us? We not finish investigations before 6:00 with only three of us."

"Yes. I have four people here right in front of me just waiting for an assignment. I'll send them right over. Melanya can call you on her way to find out where to meet you."

I quickly explained the situation to Melanya and her family and they flew out of the control center in a flurry. I'd no sooner finished sending them off, when my Dick Tracy tingled on my wrist. "Yes?"

"Problem at Echmiadzin," Armen reported. "The Catholicos isn't taking visitors. We can't even get in to see him."

I had a hard time hearing Armen. "You're cutting in and out. Why can't you see him? Who won't let you?"

"One of his priests says he's sick today and not able to see anyone."

"Speak louder, Armen. Do you believe that?"

"It's possible."

"What if the priest is the mole and he's keeping everyone from seeing the Catholicos today?"

"I thought of that. I'm not sure what to do."

"Armen, where are you? Your reception is horrible."

"We're on our way back to Yerevan."

"Call me again when you get closer. These little transmitters weren't made for long distances."

"Will do."

My Dick Tracy tingled again. This time it was Dom.

"We've hit a little snag at the House of Parliament. Seems all the guards on the evening shift have been hired in the last six months and it appears all of them had just returned from living abroad. They claim to have come back to help rebuild their country. Those aren't the vibes I'm getting here. We'll need some backup. I think the whole shift, including their supervisor, needs to take an extended break from work tonight."

"Dom, buzz Dad. He's available and he'll put you in contact with the 'containment' people. Else's on her way here. Want me to divert her to help?"

He laughed. "You can always divert the lovely Else my way. On second thought, I'll buzz her myself and let her know where to meet me. Hasta la vista, bella."

Before I had time to give any more thought to Armen's problems at Echmiadzin, my wristwatch communication system buzzed to life. "Yes?"

"Allison, do we have a place identified to incarcerate the moles once we've determined who they are?" David Chen asked.

"Does that mean you've discovered the one at the Television Center, David?"

"Loretta's convinced it's the supervisor, and I agree. The longer we talked, the more nervous and jumpy he got. I invited him out to dinner tonight hoping to quietly get him out of the place, but he has to work late. I'd slip him a mickey or a knock on the chin when no one was looking and get him out of here if I knew where to take him. I assume you don't want him back there."

I thought momentarily of sending the KGB to remove him, but still had reservations about calling them. I wasn't one hundred percent convinced they were on our side yet.

"David, get him into a taxi however you can, conscious or not, and call me back. I'll tell you where to take him as soon as I make a call."

Things had started rolling and it didn't look like they were going to slow down. I needed to contact Anichka to see if she'd talked to Davit at the army base, which was my holding place of choice. I couldn't reach her, but Vaghinak answered when I tried his number.

I breathed a quick prayer of thanks I'd gotten through to him. "Have you found out anything yet, Vaghinak?"

"I call you back. Can't talk now." He cut off abruptly. What on earth was going on? Had Anichka ignored her buzz because she'd been busy or was she in trouble and Vaghinak was trying to bail her out?

Ruben, the other mission driver who had spirited us out of Yerevan and gotten us through the blizzard to Dilijan, poked his head in. "*Barev-dzez.* If you need me, I be in office with Dr. Arram." The pleasant-looking man in his thirties behind Ruben smiled at me, then hurried through the frosted glass door. He'd been in there a couple of times already this afternoon. Must be the mission doctor. I waved to acknowledge Ruben's hello and his offer as my Dick Tracy tingled on my arm. "Yes?"

"Lion here at the Radio Center, Cherie. Lilit had a long tete-a-tete with our suspect and we now have that woman in custody. Sort of out cold, but otherwise okay. She's the prime suspect and when the opportunity to detain her presented itself, we jumped on it. But as soon as we find a place to put her, I think we're going back and spend some more time there, just in case there is someone else on al Qaeda's payroll. This seemed too easy. Where do you want her?"

Before I could answer, my radio buzzed. "Hang on, Lion. Incoming call." I answered to find David Chen on the line.

"We have the supervisor in the cab. Loretta says if you don't have a place yet, we can take him back to Loretta's apartment. She lives alone and we can tie up the suspect and leave him there. We'll get back to him before the drug I slipped in his coffee wears off."

"Great. Wait at Loretta's apartment for Lionel and Lilit. They're bringing one in, too. In fact, you and Loretta better stay there to handle incoming traffic."

"Roger."

I buzzed Lion back. "Does Lilit know where Loretta lives?"

After a quick conference with Lilit, Lion came back on. "Yes. She does."

"Good. Take your prisoner to Loretta's. David Chen and Loretta will be waiting for you there."

Another incoming call before I'd even signed off with Lionel. It was Sky announcing results in a quiet, matter-of-fact fashion. "Allison, the mole in Finance only needs a final disposition, not incarceration. Where's the drop off point?"

"Does Milena know where Loretta's apartment is?"

Sky asked and she did.

"Take the body there. What happened? Was it a public disposition or were you able to do it quietly and unobserved?"

"Frankly, it was a mess. I'm glad Milena's such a strong person. She'd been interviewing her sponsor for at least half an hour, and I was observing, trying to tell how much of his end of their conversation was the truth and how much bull he was feeding her."

"Your favorite thing to do." I smiled to myself. "Read the body language."

"Yes. Well, he'd built up a pretty strong case against one of his subordinates and Milena was just asking a few final questions to make sure we didn't head off on the wrong track. I started to pick up a lot of agitation on his part, then outright hostility, and suddenly he pulled a gun on her. There's no doubt in my mind he would have shot her right there if I hadn't hit him first. She was pretty shaken, but she's bounced back fast. I think the fact that he deceived her had a more devastating effect on her than the fact that he was going to kill her. He'd masqueraded as her friend and advisor for several months and she was quite taken in by his act."

"Maybe it wasn't an act." I suggested. "Maybe the only false thing about him was his mole role."

"Now who's the psychologist?" Sky asked with a chuckle. "I'll pass along that observation. It might make her feel a little better. Got to get him out of here fast. Adieu."

Before I could scribble the results of Sky and Milena's work on the finished side of the paper along with Lilit and Lionel, Ofelia hurried in accompanied by a taller, slender young woman she introduced as her twin sister, Lili. These two were definitely not identical twins. I wouldn't even have pegged them as sisters.

"All taken care of," she beamed. "Mr. Infanger alerted the Marine guards. They called a meeting with the civilian security personnel. All the civilian guards in the meeting were popped in the clinker until they could sort out who was who."

"Popped in the clinker?" I laughed. "Where did you learn those terms, Ofelia? That couldn't have been part of any English class."

"She watches American detective shows," Lili said. "We all learn a lot of English by watching American TV."

"I hope you don't believe Americans are like they're depicted on the soap operas and movies from Hollywood. Most of that is garbage, everybody sleeping with everybody's husband or wife. America really isn't like that."

Ofelia laughed. "Of course. We've known lots of Americans in the last few years. I work with many at the USDA, plus all of the missionaries who've come, but it's a good way to pick up new words and phrases. We've got to run now, but we'll be back to see if there's anything else we can do."

As Lili and Ofelia hurried out the door, I took a deep breath and said a quick prayer of thanks that things seemed to be falling into place. I definitely appreciated the celestial help we must be receiving to have this coming together. Were things going to quiet for a minute so I could figure out what to do about Echmiadzin and the Catholicos before Armen called back?

My watch tingled before I could even exhale. "Yes?"

"Crisis at the House of Parliament." Dominic's usual light-hearted voice came across the airwaves tense and somber.

CHAPTER 33

"Dom, what's the problem?" I turned up the volume on my Dick Tracy to catch his whispered reply, then stepped to the window so those left in the room couldn't hear, just in case this wasn't for public consumption.

"We called Jack, Aram, and Else to come help us. We had the security guards unarmed and were ready to turn them over to the KGB to move to a holding area for interrogation by the Coalition on Terror. But when the KGB arrived, they started shooting the place up before they even knew who were the good guys and who they were supposed to be taking into custody. We need a medic here fast and on the Q.T."

"Dom, who's hurt?"

"Alli, get a medic here who won't ask a lot of questions and who's someone we can trust."

I whirled around to the three people remaining in the room. "Do you have a doctor you can trust?"

Varuzhan stood immediately. "Dr. Arram."

"The man who came in with Ruben? Is he the mission doctor?"

"Yes. He's one of us."

I raced across the foyer and threw open the door to the mission office. Ruben sat behind the desk talking on the phone as Dr. Arram leaned over it working on papers. I pointed to both of them. "Come with me! I need you. Do you have your medical instruments with you, Dr. Arram?"

Dr. Arram tossed his pencil on the desk, grabbed a black medical bag from the corner and followed immediately. By the time we reached the front steps, Ruben flew through the door right behind us.

"Several members of Anastasia are at the House of Parliament and they've just called for a doctor. Go quickly. You can contact my father, Aram Matanyan, Dominic or the twins on your way to tell you where to come. They're all there."

They jumped into the mission van, backed into the alley and hit the street with tires squealing as Ruben accelerated around the corner. With his reputation of being the fastest driver in the mission, I was so glad he was here right now, whatever the emergency

But what was the emergency? If the KGB had shot up the place without regard for who was supposed to be taken into custody, had Dad been hit? Was a mole in the KGB using this as an excuse to take out a few of Anastasia's best? Or had a trigger-happy agent simply misread the situation and jumped the gun? There was always the possibility someone in the KGB took the opportunity to settle an old grudge against Dad, or Anastasia in general. Even if the Russian KGB no longer operated in Armenia, many of the same people were still in place now that Armenia had its independence from Russia. Far too many enemies in the spook business. It was hard to know just who your friends were.

I buzzed Dominic. "Dom, what's happening there?"

"Later, Alli, no time to talk. Do we have a doc on the way?"

"Yes. Is Dad okay?"

No answer. I buzzed Else. A breathless voice answered with a single word. "Else."

"Tell me what's happening," I pleaded.

"Later, love." She disconnected.

I buzzed Dad. No answer. Did that mean he was too busy to answer or he couldn't? I sent a prayer heavenward and called Ruben. "The minute you get there and find out what's going on, please call me immediately."

"I will, Mrs. Allan," he promised.

I hurried back inside to find Varuzhan, Silva and Babken waiting wide-eyed to hear what had happened.

"Forget you heard that last call and don't mention it to anyone. Dom must have had some reason for not wanting anyone to know about the need for a doctor."

They nodded, and a heavy, uncomfortable silence settled over the room. If there were no secrets in Armenia, I hoped this was sufficient to keep Dom's request confidential. But what had happened? And why was there such a cloak of secrecy about calling a doctor? I was too worried about my father—and everyone else at the House of Parliament—to try to get this groups minds on something else. When my Dick Tracy alerted me to an incoming call, I pounced on the receive button without remembering to turn down the volume.

"Yo, Alli. We're returning with a few slightly unconscious possibilities. We couldn't decide which was the real mole so we bought coffee for the entire office and doctored it up. Do we have a holding tank for these poor unfortunate people who will wake up in a few hours with a horrible hangover?"

"Do Lucy and Naira know where Loretta lives?"

In a minute Oz came back on. "Yes, but they said it was on the ninth floor of an apartment building."

"Is there an elevator?" I asked.

Another pause. "Yes."

"So you shouldn't have a problem. How many do you have anyway?"

"Three taxi's full. An even dozen."

"Good grief, Oz. What did you do, drug the whole department?"

"You will remember, Alli, Armentel was the 'Mafia media.' There turned out to be so many suspicious characters here we just decided to have a party and take the entire group. We got them into the taxis under their own staggering power, and now they are out cold. Lucy and Naira will take them to Loretta's apartment. I'll stick around here. Is anyone available to come and help me out?"

I looked up at Varuzhan and Silva. Varuzhan nodded, told Silva to stay behind with Hovhannes, and he literally ran through the front door.

"Varuzhan is on his way, but in case it takes him too long to get there, buzz Sky and see if he's in your area. He can bring along Milena to help with the cover and the language. In the meantime, how's your Russian?"

Oz laughed. "Not as good as yours, but better than Bart's. I'll fake it until I get help. Later, lovely lady." He was pumped with adrenalin. I could hear it in his voice. Wish I felt as good as he did right now.

I glanced at my watch. 4:30. Only five minutes since Dom's call. It seemed hours. What was happening there? To take my mind off the

House of Parliament situation, I glanced down the list Babken had meticulously recopied so I now had my own on which to scribble and scratch and track all our people, checking off their successes.

The Presidential Palace had been wrapped up. Check. I ignored the next, the House of Parliament, and went on to the TV center. Loretta and David Chen had handled that. Check. A single mole. Oz with sisters Lucy and Naira had possibly gone overboard at Armentel, but then again, maybe not. Check mark there. Dad and Aram completed their visit with the KGB, but I wasn't convinced that was a done deal and who would know for sure until the House of Parliament situation was resolved? Still, I checked it off with an asterisk beside the check mark.

I forced myself to continue the list and not dwell on the House of Parliament. Milena and Sky were through with the Ministry of Finance and Lilit and Lionel were delivering their mole from the radio center to Loretta's house. Two more check marks. Ofelia and Lili had taken care of the American Embassy. I added that to the list and checked it off, and wondered if I should have sent anyone to the other embassies in town; I knew for certain there was a French, British, and Russian embassy. Probably too late. And these other places were definitely more important. Any residual fallout that we hadn't handled by 6:15 would have to be unraveled after the fact.

Of course, these were only some obvious people that had been discovered. There was a possibility of several in each office, any one of which may be able to step in and take the place of the mole removed in the last few minutes. Guess we'd find out when the magic hour rolled around.

Babken struggled to his feet and excused himself. I could hear him laboriously climbing the stairs to the second floor as I pondered the rest of the list. We still had no word from Bart, Sarkis, and Margarit at the Ministry of Energy. Vanik had also been strangely silent from the Ministry of Internal Affairs. Had he aroused suspicion and they'd put him behind bars? I couldn't stand the thought of that brave little old man in jail.

Then I remembered Vaghinak at the army base with Anichka and Laura. I tried again to reach Vaghinak.

"I am here," he answered.

"What happened? Is everyone okay?"

"We finally find Davit. While he arrange for place to hold prisoners, he is arrested by vice commander. We figure this is mole on army base. Davit about to be shot when he very calmly call down the wrath of heaven on this man who has gun pointed at him. Commander come in just then and demand to know what is happening. If not for Davit's reputation as honest man with much integrity, commander let him be shot. Instead, commander put them both in cell until truth can be discovered. We slip away and we're on our way back."

"Vaghinak, are you near the Ministry of Internal Affairs? I'm a little concerned about Vanik."

"Not too far. Maybe five minutes. We go there now?"

"Yes, please. Let me know how things are going there. I haven't heard from him since he left here."

"What else happening?"

How I wanted to tell him about the House of Parliament and send him there to find out for me. But I knew I should find out about these other places first. We certainly had enough people at the House of Parliament already.

"I haven't heard from Bart, Sarkis, and Margarit at the Ministry of Energy or Norik with Rita and Roman at the Ministry of Transportation. I'll check in with them now. Thanks, Vaghinak."

I'd sent Melanya and her children to find and help Norik. Had they found him? And what, if anything, had they discovered? We were close to the deadline, and the time was ticking away, each hour speeding by faster and faster it seemed.

As I started to call Bart, Armen buzzed me, this time coming through clearly. "Allison, we're back in Yerevan and on our way to the Komitas chapel. Have you found a solution yet?"

"Not yet. Come on in and we'll talk." Good grief. Found a solution? I hadn't even had time to think about it yet!

Hovhannes was awake and Silva had been feeding and entertaining him to keep him quiet. She reached for my hand and spoke softly, breaking into my frantic thoughts. "I'm not being much help in any other way, but I can pray for you, and I have been doing that."

I squeezed her hand. "Thank you. I think prayer is what's going to help most of all right now."

"As usual, that wrong, Mrs. Allan."

I didn't have to look up to see who the voice belonged to. This time I knew a sneeze wouldn't save me.

CHAPTER 34

"Prayer not help. You please come with me—quietly, but if not, so be it. You come just the same." He dropped his already hushed voice, "Or I hurt woman and child."

I stood slowly, scooped my purse from the chair, looped it over my shoulder, and faced Dr. Garik Grigoryan, whose malevolent expression now distorted his once handsome features. Silva started to cry out but I leaned down and touched her shoulder as I moved by her.

"Dr. Grigoryan wants to talk to me about the symposium at the American University of Armenia. I missed my classes today. Will you handle things here until I get back?" I slid Babken's paper to the edge of the table so she'd see it and hopefully notify Bart or someone on the list what had happened, and as I grabbed my red raincoat from the chair, slipped my own list into the pocket.

I walked slowly, deliberately toward Dr. Grigoryan, my eyes locked on his, hoping he could read the warning in them not to touch this woman or her child. I handed him my coat and turned so he could help me put it on. Strangely, I felt no danger at this minute—while we were in the church. When we left, I was afraid it would be a totally different story. He took my arm, as he had done countless times the first day or two I was here. This time it wasn't just an irritation. This time it made my skin crawl.

Dusk faded into darkness as we left the foyer of the church. A long black Mercedes waited at the curb. I couldn't see the front end, but I was sure it would have three yellow lights on the huge silver grill. All my training told me not to get in the car and the little voice in my head said over and over: "Once in the car, you've lost control.

They have control." But if I didn't go with Garik, how would I find out what this was all about? Who was Dr. Garik Grigoryan and who was he working for? What did they want?

I slid across the back seat and Garik settled in beside me. He reached up and slapped the back of the driver's seat, speaking quietly to the driver in Russian. "Let's go." I glanced at his face as the car maneuvered under the streetlight and onto busy Kochar Street. His expression surprised me. A soft smile curved his lips and his dark eyes glittered with confidence.

"Where are we going?" I asked. I really didn't expect him to tell me, but thought if I wearied him with questions, he might break down and reveal a few secrets before we reached our destination so I'd be prepared for whatever he had in mind. I loved surprises under other circumstances, but not this particular variety.

"You see soon enough, Mrs. Allan." He leaned back against the plush leather seat and stretched his long legs out as far as they would go, straightening the crease in his slacks and brushing an imaginary piece of lint from his jacket.

Neatnik though he may be, I interpreted these actions as a sign we were on our way to see his boss. He wanted to look good. Impress the head man that he had managed to get me there without mussing himself up in the least.

"How did the seminar go today? Were you pleased with the presentations?"

He answered without looking at me. "I very disappointed you not there. You spoil my whole agenda."

"I'm terribly sorry. Something important came up and I just couldn't be in two places at the same time." I almost laughed. This actually sounded like a civilized conversation.

"Did you enjoy the presentations?" If I could provoke him into talking to me, I might discover what was coming.

"They were . . . " He paused. "Boring. Enlightening. Repetitious."

"In other words, you didn't listen to any of them."

Garik turned to me in surprise, stared for a minute, then he smiled. "I did not listen. You not there. You supposed to be there."

"Why did the symposium depend on me being there, Garik? Or was my mother the one that was supposed to be here?"

Garik turned his head again and looked out the side window. He didn't want to look at me. He didn't want to speak to me. And he didn't want to listen to me either. I watched to see where we were going, to see if I could identify any landmarks and give someone a clue where to find me. If everyone wasn't already too busy with their own jobs.

Bart hadn't checked in for a long time and Dad . . . Well, Dad must have problems of his own that I couldn't even imagine. I just hoped he hadn't been the reason for the frantic call for a doctor.

"Garik, this is a beautiful evening for a drive, but I haven't had anything to eat for hours. Is there a possibility we could stop and get a bite somewhere? I'm going to embarrass myself with a very loudly growling stomach in a few minutes if we don't."

He tried to ignore me.

"Please. I'm starving."

"No. No time to eat. Not important." He continued to keep his head turned and stared out the window at the passing lights.

"Maybe it's not important to you, but I'm very hungry and . . ."

"Mrs. Allan, please. Not now."

Not now. Did that mean, "Don't bug me, I'm thinking, preparing my statement for Mr. Big and I need to concentrate"? Who was Mr. Big? What did he want with me? Is he the one who'd been trying to kill me—and since he couldn't do it with his car, he was now prepared to do it face to face? But why? That was the question on which this whole Armenian trip hinged. What was the real reason for my being here?

When I saw a sign to Zvartnots Airport, I fingered the tiny buttons on my Dick Tracy in the dark, pressed Bart's number and held down the send button on my watch. "Are we taking a flight somewhere? This is the road to the airport, isn't it?"

Garik nodded absently without looking at me, but remained silent.

"I'm really not ready to leave Yerevan yet, Dr. Grigoryan. There is so much I haven't had a chance to see." We passed the airport exit. What else was on this road? Where did it lead? Then I remembered—this was the way we'd gone on our bus tour to Hripsime, Echmiadzin and Gayane.

I thought a minute about the Dick Tracy. I hadn't used it for so long I didn't remember all the wonderful little things it was supposed to do, though I vaguely recalled I could open every channel and send continuously without keeping my finger on the send button.

I closed my eyes, settled back on the seat and recalled the day in New Mexico when Jared, our brilliant inventor friend, introduced Bart and me to the special new gadgets he had just put together for us to use. I mentally walked through his instructions, recalling all the little details that had slipped into the recesses of my mind. I activated the "continuous send to all channels" mode, then started talking and prayed it would broadcast clearly long enough to lead Bart to wherever I was being taken. Armen had sent a message from this very area and it was so broken up and unclear I could barely understand him.

Then I started chattering. "I know what we're doing. Since we didn't get to see Zvartnots Temple ruins, you're taking me there now. How thoughtful of you, Dr. Grigoryan, but you really didn't have to bother tonight. We could have done it some other time."

Garik ignored me, continuing to stare out the window at the lights that flew by faster and faster now that we were out of the heavier traffic and heading into the country.

"Oh, we passed the temple. I guess we're heading somewhere else. Let's see, what else is on this road?" I had to keep talking as long as I could, not having any idea how the reception was back in Yerevan, or if we were out of range of the little Dick Tracy's capabilities already.

"St. Hripsime Church must be close, and then Echmiadzin Cathedral just beyond that. Please, tell me where we're going, Garik. I feel silly playing guessing games."

"Don't play games. Don't talk."

"I always talk when I get nervous. And in case you haven't figured it out already, I'm nervous right now because I don't know where we're going. If you'll tell me, then I'll relax and quit talking."

"Relax. We almost there."

Almost where? St. Hripsime church disappeared into the blackness behind us so that couldn't have been our destination. I didn't know what else might be in this direction, except Echmiadzin Cathedral.

"I have one last guess, Garik. Are we going to Echmiadzin? That's the only other thing I remember on this road."

"You talk much. Please to just relax and enjoy ride in nice car." His voice sounded a little more edgy now.

Did that mean we were approaching our destination? Had anyone heard my transmissions or were we so far away the little communication watch wasn't transmitting anything clear enough to hear? And was anyone on the other end free enough to find me if they did know where I'd been taken? Maybe they were all so busy with their own crises . . .

Then I saw the lights of a little town, and the familiar traffic circle adorned with glass cases containing models of the famous ancient monasteries, churches, and cathedrals of Armenia. Echmiadzin. We skirted the walled portion of the huge complex and the car drove around the back, through a gate with a sentry, and behind the immense apartment of the Catholicos. Why did they call it an apartment when it was in fact a huge, long two-storied building with L-shaped wings extending on either end of the tall columned entry? A palace might be a better description than apartment.

"Do I get a private audience with the Catholicos tonight? That was sweet of you to arrange, Garik, but I wish you'd have told me. My husband would have been delighted to come with us and meet him."

Garik turned abruptly to face me. "Husband?"

"Of course. That's why I'm *Mrs.* Allan, not Miss. Or are you just surprised that Bart is here in Armenia? I was. Not only is my husband here, so is my father." I didn't know whether sharing this little bit of information would help my cause, but I didn't think it could hurt. At least he'd know I wasn't here all alone and totally vulnerable. Well, I was totally vulnerable, and even alone right now, but with others of my family in the country, I did have the possibility of aid—I hoped.

Garik sat up. "Where they are?"

"My father's meeting with the KGB, and my husband's conducting other business in Yerevan. I'm sure they'd love to meet you and talk with you about your work. Dad especially would like to thank you for extending the invitation to Mom to participate in the symposium. She was so excited about it." That part was totally true. The part about Bart loving to meet him would only be true if Garik hadn't delivered me to someone with malevolence in mind.

"I'm the only child of my father and mother. Dad is very protective of me, and so is my husband. They would not feel kindly toward anyone who harmed me in any way." I leaned toward Garik. "I just thought you'd like to know that little piece of information before we get wherever you are taking me."

He showed no discernible reaction. The car stopped. We had arrived. I pointed to the Catholicos apartment, positioning my Dick Tracy directly in front of my mouth and said as loud as I dared, "Do they really let Americans go in the residence of the Catholicos here at Echmiadzin?" Then I prayed. *Please let someone hear that who will know what to do and where to find me and don't let Garik figure out what I'm doing.*

He didn't answer. Wasn't even paying any attention to me, in fact, as he peered out the window looking for something or someone in the semi-darkness of the driveway.

"You didn't answer my question, Garik. Am I to have an audience with the Catholicos?"

Again Garik ignored my question, but apparently he saw what he was looking for. He exited the car and held the door for me, extending his hand to help me out. A man approached from the back door of the residence, conversed quietly with him, then signaled we were to follow him into the dimly lit hall. It was a beautiful place, even for a back hall. I had to assume it was dimly lit because I was being smuggled in—not because someone was trying to hide any dinginess, or because of lack of power, or shortage of funds to pay the electrical bill. This didn't look like a residence where anyone scrimped on anything.

Another whispered conversation and Garik nodded, removed a handkerchief from his pocket, and proceeded to blindfold me. Or attempt to.

I grabbed the handkerchief from him. "Sorry, Charlie. I'm not into blindman's bluff. I'll go with you, only because I am insatiably curious about who wants to kill me and why, but I go on my own power and free from blinders."

Garik didn't know what to say. The other man did. He reamed Garik out in Russian and told him in no uncertain terms he'd better control his captive—or he would. I didn't think I'd like that one tiny bit.

Apparently Dr. Grigoryan was not an experienced kidnapper. He'd been properly aggressive at the outset, but now didn't seem to know quite what to do in the face of the guard's insistence that I be blind-folded—and my resistance to the idea. That might be a good thing. Then again, was I better off in the hands of amateurs or professionals?

We compromised. I tied the blindfold, arranging it so that I could still see through the single long flap I left hanging in front of my face, and let Garik tie my wrists. I was able to position my arms so as soon as I relaxed, my bonds loosened and didn't cut off the circulation. I might even be able to wriggle free if I had a chance to work at it.

Now that I was properly secured, as a prisoner should be, the guard relaxed a bit. My condition had the opposite effect on Garik. He wiped the moisture from his forehead on his sleeve, and his sweating palms on his coat jacket. He was clearly out of his element. Would that work to my favor, or against me?

I began to feel nervous myself. It had seemed a good idea to accompany Garik to discover who wanted to kill me and why. But what if this didn't have anything at all to do with the attempts on my life? As we entered a door almost hidden in a pillared alcove behind some statuary and greenery, I decided this had definitely been a very bad idea.

Garik took my arm and helped me down the stairs, a long, steep set of stairs that I thought would go on forever. With a sinking feeling in my stomach, I had the fleeting thought we might be descending into the kingdom of Hades, never to return or be seen again. Why hadn't I obeyed my training and listened to that little voice—and not gotten into that car voluntarily with Garik?

When we finally reached the bottom, it was so dark I couldn't see anything through the linen handkerchief over my eyes—until the guard opened a door. Bright light blazed out into the dark corridor and even through the filter of the handkerchief, what I saw chilled the blood in my veins and made my knees go weak.

CHAPTER 35

Tied to a chair, with his head wrapped in a makeshift bandage, Jack Alexander looked like he had just come through a war. That was bad enough to see Dad barely conscious, his head lolling on his chest, but just behind him sat Mom in a wheelchair, her ghost-white face a portrait of anguish and pain. I thought I must be hallucinating, until I glanced around the room.

The Catholicos, recognizable even through the linen handkerchief from pictures I'd seen, sat in a wingchair near the big mahogany desk. Clearly, he was not happy about the current situation in the room and as I looked closer, he didn't look too healthy, either. At his shoulder stood a priest, or someone dressed in a priest robe. It appeared the Catholicos was also a captive—in his own home.

The focal point in the center of the room was the big mahogany desk. Seated at the desk dressed in a black priest frock with a clearly triumphant expression on his face, the silver-haired man who had broken into the estate—The Fox—motioned the guard to bring us in. Behind him and to his right stood the man in the navy blazer leaning casually against the wall of bookshelves with his arms folded. He was the one person in the room whose presence didn't make sense. Bart said he was my contact. He was supposed to be on my side. Unless he was a double agent. At that thought, I breathed a tiny sigh of relief and checked out the rest of the inhabitants of the richly appointed library.

A few more men whose faces I didn't recognize, some in priestly attire, some in street clothes were scattered throughout the room. And along one wall in straight-backed chairs with their hands tied behind them, Else, Aram, and the twins, Samvel and Gagik, looked miserable. The gang was, indeed, all here.

At least most of the gang who had been at the House of Parliament. Dom was missing. Ruben and Dr. Arram were absent so I assumed they hadn't arrived before the rest of Anastasia and helpers were taken.

But how had they managed to get Mom from the hospital in Santa Barbara to Armenia? And how had they taken Dad and Else? I'd seen them both in action and neither would have been easily captured, unlike my incapacitated mother. As soon I entered the room, the Fox ordered Garik in Russian to put me in a chair facing my parents and remove the blindfold. Garik silently obeyed and with shaking fingers removed his handkerchief from my eyes, then remained standing directly behind my chair.

"Hi, Mom. Looks like you made it to Armenia before the symposium ended after all." I tried to sound cheerful and unafraid, though my heart was beating like there was no tomorrow. Ohhh. Bad analogy.

No response from Mom. Definitely not a good sign.

"Ah, yes, the symposium," The Fox gloated, his beady little eyes gleaming like a fox who just caught a hen. Guess it was an appropriate expression. He had three very desirable hens in his grasp, if I correctly guessed what was coming.

He steepled his fingers and leaned forward on his elbows. "You are so boringly predictable, Mrs. Allan. Valiant daughter races to fill injured mother's empty shoes in Armenian symposium. And you." He swung the chair around and flung a long, slender finger at my barely conscious father. "You speed to the scene of every rumored terrorist plot, along with your squad of over-rated agents. This was too easy," he wailed.

Did I dare say anything or should I follow the lead of my parents and Else and simply let him rant and rave until we knew what was going on? I bit my tongue, wanting to remind him he only had four of the ten members of Anastasia and to not be too hasty. Then I had a terrifying thought. What if he actually had captured the rest of the group and they were all on their way here as prisoners? I caught Mom's eye and saw fear that I'd never seen there before. And something else. Mom's eyes were glazed—she had been drugged and was still under the influence of whatever she'd been given.

He swung the chair again and waved his hand toward Else. "And the elegant Miss Elbert in your high fashion clothes. Too bad there's no place to conceal a weapon in that outfit—too bad for you, that is. Speaking of weapons, Dr. Grigorian, please remove the gun from Mrs. Allan's purse. I assume that is where she carries it."

Garik opened my leather bag and removed the gun, then pocketed it. I glanced at Else while their attention was on the gun. She winked and glanced down. I followed her glance and saw her working her wrist ropes.

"Tsk. Tsk. So predictable," the Fox sneered, leaning back in the leather desk chair. "You all could have made this more challenging. You've taken almost all the fun out of my game by being so true to character. No surprises. No real competition. You deciphered each of the clues on schedule, but then, I made them easy so you would. You appeared where I'd planned for you to be, almost without exception." He turned, leaned forward in his chair and pointed his bony finger at me. "Although *you* did give me a start when you disappeared instead of appearing at the symposium as planned."

At this, I could hold my tongue no longer. "I didn't think I was supposed to get to the symposium," I blurted. "I thought you were trying to have me killed before it ever began."

"Have you killed? My dear, what do you think I am? A murderer?" He plopped back in his chair with a pout and stared at me. "Well?" he prompted when I didn't answer.

"Yes, as a matter of fact, that's exactly what I think. You tried to kill me—to have me run over by a car three different times, then stabbed in Hripsime's tomb, again in the Temple of Fire under Echmiadzin, and finally gunned down at St. Gayane and the Opera."

He shot forward and slapped his hand on the desk, causing even Dad's head to jolt upright. I jumped in my chair. "If I'd wanted you dead, you would be dead. Those were only children's games—a test."

"And what did it prove? Did I pass or did I fail your little tests?" I began working the bonds on my wrists, taking the clue from Else, slowly, carefully, trying not to move discernibly while I looked the Fox in the eye. It looked like it would be up to us to get us all out of here. Neither Mom nor Dad were in any shape to help, and I was fairly certain Aram and the twins, Samvel and Gagik, would not be able to intervene. As for the rest of Anastasia . . . unknown. Still working on the moles? Or captured and on their way here?

The sneer returned to his face. "The results of the test were just as I expected. You reacted fast enough to stay alive, even to avoid injury."

"Did that disappoint you?" I shuddered remembering my close calls with death. This man was definitely a mental case. A very dangerous mental case.

"Not at all." He leaned back in his chair again, rocking back and forth slightly. "I would have been keenly disappointed if you hadn't been quick enough to figure out what was happening and prevent it. But if you'd failed and died, my plan would have worked almost as well."

It was frightening to watch his quick transition from one emotion to another. Would he order us shot on a whim if we didn't please him? And what did please him? What did he want? The obvious answer, of course, was to have Anastasia annihilated. Anastasia had interfered with the terrorist agenda too often, preventing al Queda's radical Muslims from their avowed purpose: eradicating Judeo-Christian governments and introducing a new world order. A radical New Islamic world order. How and when seemed the only remaining questions. I needed to play for time.

"Then I'm so very glad I didn't spoil your fun. I'm a little puzzled though. Forgive me for being dense, but I'm not catching the connection between you and al Qaeda. Or was that just a huge plot you cooked up to get Anastasia here?"

The Fox stared at me without speaking; stared with those glittering, beady little black eyes for the longest time. I couldn't read his mind, couldn't read his body language, couldn't even imagine what he might be thinking.

He picked up a gold pen that lay on the desk and leaned back in his chair. "That is why you are there," he pointed at me with the pen, "and I am here." He tapped the pen slowly against his cheek, looking as if he were deep in thought.

Slowly he swivelled the chair around and looked at Dad with his head still hanging forward, indicating he hadn't regained consciousness yet. I could see him breathing, and could see a small amount of dried blood on the scarf that covered the top of his head in a makeshift bandage. The wound didn't look that serious. Why was

Dad still out? Had they drugged him, too? Maybe he was injured far more seriously than it appeared.

The Fox continued his examination of my parents, turning his attention next to Mom. She kept blinking her eyes, as if to clear her head. Her hands gripped the arms of the wheelchair until her knuckles were white. The heavily casted broken leg stuck out in front, resting on a slender pallet that extended from under her seat. She looked horribly uncomfortable in the chair, in a great deal of physical pain, and I couldn't even imagine the mental anguish she must be experiencing, watching through drug-fogged eyes all that was happening and knowing she wouldn't be able to do a thing to prevent it.

"How did you manage to get Mom out of the hospital? I'm sure there was still a guard on her room."

"Americans are so gullible. It was too easy having a man masquerade as a doctor moving her to a Los Angeles specialty hospital for treatment. The guard is invited to go along in the ambulance, the last thing he ever does." The Fox shook his head as he stared at my parents.

"The fools administered too much drug to them. This is taking much too long." He turned back to me, less animated, almost depressed. "I worked hard on this plan, bringing you together so your deaths would coincide with the takeover of Armenia, a powerful statement to the world of the brilliant organization and daring courage of al Qaeda, masterminded, of course, by me." He paused, tapping the gold pen absently in his palm.

"You said was," I prompted. "Has your plan changed?"

He glanced at his watch, then back at my drugged parents, especially my father. "I have a timetable, a very specific timetable and I must not vary from that. I must be at the Television Center for the broadcast before 6:15. It is time to leave now. I planned for Jack and Margaret Alexander to watch their only daughter die, then each of their friends, then Jack would watch your mother's life ebb from her, leaving him to die alone in the end. But it would be fruitless to kill you if they weren't conscious enough to feel the anguish."

"If we're all going to die, will you clarify a few things for me? Am I to understand this whole symposium was just a ruse to get Mom here?"

He smiled again and leaned forward with a gleeful look in his eyes. "Brilliant, don't you think?"

"Then why did you stage the accident so that she couldn't come? Just to get me here?"

"You follow very well. I knew you would not be able to resist the urge to help, Miss Do-Good. Your dossier is full of that—putting yourself on the line for someone else. So I knew you couldn't possibly turn down the opportunity to help your own mother."

While he was in such a bragging mode, I had several other questions. "What about the rubies?"

"Ah, yes. The rubies. So nice of you to mention the jewels. I'll take them now."

"You think I have them? I think you need to ask your little gypsy where they are. He spirited me out of my apartment so he could search my luggage." I was only venturing a guess here. I didn't really know for whom the gypsy worked.

The Fox focused his sharp eyes on me, searching my face to see if I spoke the truth. "Mmm, I should have known I couldn't trust the little monster. No matter. He will give them up when I demand the rubies—or his life."

"What were you going to do? Ransom them a second time? Ask the Catholicos for an exorbitant amount of money to have them returned?"

"Of course. The world revolves on money. Everyone has a price. You can buy anything or anyone in this world for something, and that something is usually money."

I needed to change the subject before he reconsidered and pressed further for the rubies, and discovered that I actually did have them with me right now. "How about Bart and Dad—they were already in this part of the world working on other problems. Was that arranged by you, too?"

"Of course. They were the easy ones to get in place. Always showing up in the terrorist hot spots, interfering with bin Laden's glorious plans for world domination by his radical Muslims. Then you simply expand the crisis, blow it out of proportion and Jack Alexander calls his people in from all over the world to bring 'justice' and 'equity' to all."

"You've apparently been working on this plan for a long time. At least two years. I'm very impressed, Mr. . . . I don't even know your name."

"To you," he sniffed, dismissing me as totally unimportant, "my name won't matter." He pulled back the black robe from his wrist and glanced at his watch. "I can't wait any longer. I have an appointment at the TV center to broadcast to the world that Armenia is now in the hands of al Qaeda, and is their new center of power."

"How long do you suppose the Coalition on Terror will let you keep your center of power?" My heart plummeted to my stomach. Did that mean David and Loretta had the wrong person in custody from the TV center? And how about the rest of our group? Had all their efforts been in vain?

"We will keep the center of power as long as we hold hostage the million and a half inhabitants of Yerevan, and all the 'brave' Americans who ignored their government's recommendation to leave the country, and other foreign nationals who remained. We have planted explosives in every historic building and every village throughout Armenia, and in every block in Yerevan. The explosives are set to blow simultaneously when the first is activated. Who'd dare try to stop us when the end result would be the deaths of nearly two million people?"

I could hardly believe what I heard. "That would be another act of genocide," I gasped.

The Fox leaned back in his seat, tapping the gold pen against his palm, a smug look on his face. "Then the arrogant Coalition on Terror had better think well before they act as they will be responsible for the extermination of the Armenian people and the devastation of their country." He glanced at his watch again. "Enough. It is time to bring this to fruition."

But something bothered him. He sat tapping the pen in his hand, thinking, pondering, a frown creasing his forehead. Something bothered me, too. I hadn't been able to work my wrists free from the ropes yet. How could I do anything to prevent this from happening with my hands tied behind me? I didn't have a plan for when I did get free, but at least I'd have two hands to do it when the time came.

Slowly a smile spread across his face and he sat up, slapped his hand on the desk, then stood, sending his chair flying backwards across the room. I glanced at the man in the navy jacket still leaning casually against the bookcase, hoping he was on his toes and ready to intervene to save my skin when The Fox started getting out of hand. But he avoided my eyes and seemed to have no interest at all in what was occurring in the room at that minute. I was so glad Bart had said he was on our side. Wish I'd known that when I first arrived in Armenia. It would have saved me a lot of trauma, though now that I thought about it, he hadn't been able to prevent the attempts on my life. He'd better redeem himself now.

Dad might be coming around a little; Mom still appeared to be fighting the effects of the drugs, blinking and shaking her head. Else looked beautiful, calm, and unperturbed, a perfect candidate for a fashion magazine cover with her long, slender legs artfully crossed and her head cocked slightly to one side. It didn't look like she had freed her hands completely yet either. The three boys just beyond her sat with expressions ranging from horrified anticipation to unbelief.

"I will take you all with me to the Television Center where you will be executed on live television so the world can witness for themselves the genius and power of al Qaeda. By the time we reach the center, the drugs will have worn off sufficiently for your parents to be fully, painfully aware of what is happening to their organization—and their daughter. Then I will announce al Qaeda is in control of the Armenian Army, Air Force, all government offices, and even the Armenian Apostolic church. Armenia is no longer Christian, but Muslim."

CHAPTER 36

As The Fox gleefully pronounced our death sentence, I searched the eyes of the man in the navy jacket, the only ally in the room with hands free to stop this maniac. He studiously avoided my gaze. I felt the minute I moved, Garik's hands would immediately be on my shoulders, holding me in place. It seemed apparent he was the puppet of The Fox and would probably do anything he was ordered to do, even if he was squeamish about doing it.

I increased the effort to loosen my bonds not knowing if Garik could see my movements. Was he watching me as I tried to wriggle my wrists free or was he caught up in the drama unfolding before us—the incredible change of expression and mood of the volatile Fox?

What help might the boys be? Were they totally out of their element or could they do something to stop The Fox's plan? Didn't someone say all young men in Armenia had to serve two years in the army unless they were attending the university? Had these boys been in the army? If so, what kind of training had they received? Could they actually take on these professionally trained thugs? And prevail?

The Fox waved his hand at his men. "Get these people in the helicopter. We need to leave this minute so I can make the scheduled broadcast on the triumph of al Qaeda. The whole world will watch the extermination of these bumbling, over-rated enemies of Osama bin Laden and know who was the greatest of them all."

Think fast, Alli. "No, thank you. Sorry, but I'll have to decline your generous invitation."

The Fox whirled on me. "No, thank you? What does *that* mean?"

"I couldn't possibly appear on television. I've worn these same clothes for days and haven't combed my hair or even put on lipstick in that time, either. Thanks, but I'll have to take a rain check on the TV appearance."

The room went totally silent. No one breathed. No one moved. The Fox himself was shocked into immobility for a minute. Then a wicked smile spread over his face. He placed his palms on the desk and leaned toward me, staring into my eyes. "So be it!" He whirled to the man in the navy jacket. "Shoot her now."

I watched in horror and disbelief as the man who was supposed to be my guardian angel, the man Bart said was my contact and had been protecting me, slowly opened his jacket and pulled out his gun. With ice in his eyes, he leveled the gun at my head. I couldn't move. I couldn't react. In my mind, this was not the way this was supposed to play out when I so blithely challenged The Fox about going on TV.

Suddenly there was movement above my head and a shot rang out next to my ear nearly deafening me. Before I had time to compute what had happened, the room swirled with motion. Else leaped from her chair, rolled across the desk and hit The Fox directly in the chest with the full force of her long legs and high-heeled, tangerine-colored, leather boots, sending him tumbling backwards just as the man in the navy jacket slumped to the floor.

Gagik, Samvel, and Aram each bulldozed the man nearest them with a shoulder to the solar plexis of their target, sending all six men crashing to the floor in a sprawl of arms and legs and chaos. The man in the priest frock standing behind the Catholicos struggled to pull the gun from the pocket of his frock. I stood, took one step forward and kicked the gun from his hand as he leveled it at the dazed, drugged Catholicos, then a second kick to his groin totally disabled him. He doubled in pain on the floor.

Dad rolled off his chair and lunged toward Mom's wheelchair, sending it rolling across the carpet and into the corner, out of range of any more gunfire. His glazed stare met my eyes for a split second before he regained his feet and staggered to the corner to shield Mom with his body.

The Fox struggled to rid himself of the corpse draped heavily across him as Else slid off the desk and stuck a spiked heel on his jugular. "You will not move, Marzuk, unless you choose to die immediately, in which case I can accommodate you with a single thrust of my heel. I'd be delighted to rid the world of one more piece of scum."

I turned to Garik standing with the gun hanging limply in his hand, staring at the chaos before him and the sudden reversal of power. "Thank you for saving my life. Now if you'll finish untying these ropes, I'll take my gun back."

Garik slowly shook his head and dropped his hand, pointing the gun at the floor.

"What does that mean? Dr. Grigoryan, whose side are you on?"

He looked around the room and then back at me. "I not know. Until I do, I keep gun."

"I guess that's fair enough, as long as you don't point it at me. I always thought it would be a terrible tragedy to be killed by my own gun. In the meantime, will you untie me?"

It didn't take more than a single tug and the ropes fell away. I ran first to Dad and eased him to the floor with his back against the wall. I cupped his face in my hands and kissed his cheek. He managed a smile. "Thanks, Bunny. I'm fine. Check your Mom."

My plan exactly. From the terrified look in Mom's eyes, it was apparent she was totally aware of what had been going on but knew she was unable to help in any way. I knelt beside her and kissed her forehead, holding her hands in mine.

"You're right. You *are* a tough old bird. I'd never have believed you'd make it home from the hospital by this time, much less all the way across the world."

"Doing it under duress doesn't count," she said, sounding like her tongue was swollen.

"However you got here, it counts." I stroked her hand. "Did they hurt you?"

"I'll tell you later," she managed a weak smile, "when feeling returns to my extremities."

I looked around the room. The twins and Aram had their guys subdued. Garik slumped in the chair I'd occupied only minutes before, the gun cradled in both hands, staring at it, and murmuring over and over, "I kill man. I kill him."

I rose from the floor and gently took the gun from his hand. "Yes, you did, Garik. Sometimes you have no choice. You not only saved my life, but everyone here that had been condemned to death by this madman. And you saved your own skin: they'd have killed you as soon as you outlived your usefulness to them. You weren't aware the games they played were lethal? How did you get involved with them?"

He looked up at me and I could tell he was shaken to the core. He shook his head. "No. I not know Mr. Marzuk bad man. He suggest several months ago we organize symposium. He had names of people who would have important papers to present. Respected experts in their fields. He gave money to University to cover expenses to bring participants here, house them and do conference. He particularly interested in Dr. Alexander. He say she work on something very important."

"And how did you come to bring me here tonight?" I needed to know how involved Garik was in this mess.

"Mr. Marzuk tell me where you are and say I am to bring you any way I can, even if I must hit you over head and carry you. You must be here."

"Didn't you think that was rather strange?"

"He say it very important he meet you here. If you reluctant to come, I get you here by any means."

"But you threatened to hurt Silva and her baby." I truly wanted to believe him, but had to be sure he wasn't just a clever Armenian playing both sides.

"As you see, I have no weapon. I think you come when I say that."

"You think right." I looked at him for a minute, and decided he really was telling the truth. He had been an innocent pawn in the hands of the diabolical Mr. Marzuk. "Thanks again for saving my life, Garik. I appreciate being able to live another day."

The boys had the bad guys face down on the carpet with their hands tied behind their backs. Else still had her stiletto heel pressed deep into the throat of Mr. Marzuk, a.k.a. The Fox, who lay motionless with the blood of the man in the navy coat dripping into his silver white hair and down his forehead. As Dad struggled to his feet, I hurried to help him reach a chair. Then I remembered the House of Parliament.

"Dad, what happened at the House of Parliament? Where's Dom?"

"It was a trap, Bunny. Pure and simple. Dom must have slipped away in the fracas. At least, I hope that's what happened. The KGB came in, led by my old friend, Ivan. He came up beside me to help me take the guards prisoner, then slipped me a double whammy. A gun butt to the side of the head and stabbed me in the arm with a needle full of something. When I woke up I was here. I can't tell you how I felt when I saw your mother here, and then they brought you in. The worst of all possible scenarios."

"And you faked being unconscious to see how this scene would play out."

"Right. I wasn't in any condition to do much of anything anyway but listen."

"Dad, what about Bart, Sky and the rest of them? Were they walking into traps? If this whole thing was simply a setup to wipe out Anastasia, The Fox wouldn't have left his key players exposed—especially when he made the clues so easy to decipher."

"Guess we'd better get back to town and finish mopping up this operation." Dad stood shakily, holding onto the corner of the desk to steady himself.

"So how do we get out of here?" I looked around the room. Garik sat with his head in his hands moaning softly to himself. We had four men tied on the floor, and the captured Fox who now looked more like a red fox than a silver fox with his blood-colored hair. "And how do we get back to Yerevan?"

"We commandeer the helicopter that was going to take us all to the TV station," Dad said. "If we go out of here with guns on us, they'll think we're being transferred to the copter by Marzuk." He removed the magazine clip from his gun. "Give this to Marzuk. Else, he can hold this gun on you and . . ."

"And I'll have my knife to his ribs, just waiting for a single mistake on his part so I can plunge it into his evil heart." Else removed her spiked heel from the neck of The Fox and jerked him to his feet.

"Garik could hold my gun on me and I'll push Mom's wheelchair," I suggested. "Then if Samvel and Gagik carried you, that gets all of us out of here that need to go. We can leave everyone else tied up. But what will we do with the Catholicos? Is he going to be okay?"

"They probably dosed him with the same stuff we got, so he'll come out of it with just a bad headache." Dad rubbed his head. "I'm at that stage now."

I could tell Dad wasn't up to full capacity. In fact, I'd guess he was only operating at about fifty percent but even at fifty percent, he was still head and shoulders above most people in the brains department.

Dad sat down again, his strength gone, but he kept giving instructions on how to exit without detection. "Aram, slip that robe over your clothes. You'll help the Catholicos out and turn him over to the first person we see that looks like he's not in on this. Probably most everyone involved from Echmiadzin is already in this room." Pointing to the men tied on the floor, he said, "Take off their trousers and tie them around their heads so they can't see anything or make enough noise to get attention. We need time to get to the Television Center before anyone can stop us."

Aram pulled on the priest's robe; Garik had my gun and I had Mom's wheelchair at the door, ready to push her through as soon as Dad gave the signal. Else's slender dagger pointed at The Fox's ribs, unsheathed from the waist holster where she concealed it. She allowed him to wipe the blood from his face, then looped her arm through his and he pointed the empty gun at her. I had no doubt that he would go docilely. He knew Else's reputation. She would not hesitate to plunge the dagger between his ribs if he so much as blinked wrong. And he certainly would not want to be killed by a lowly woman, a most dishonorable and ignominious way to die for one of his ilk.

Gagik and Samvel each took one of Dad's arms and held him up between them—a good idea as I wasn't sure how far he could make it on his own steam. Aram brought up the rear steadying the still groggy Catholicos.

Dad gave the signal and Garik opened the door. I pushed the wheelchair through just as the guard who met us on our arrival exited the elevator at the end of the short hall. Garik yelled in Russian for him to hold the elevator. We were going to the Television Center with Mr. Marzuk to make his announcement. The guard punched the hold button and stepped aside while I wheeled Mom into the waiting car, seemingly under the gun of Garik. Else came next arm in arm with The Fox, who appeared to have a gun on her.

Samvel and Gagik dragged my father along the carpeted hall and entered the elevator. Aram brought up the rear with the Catholicos leaning heavily on his arm. The guard stepped into the elevator with us, punched the button and turned to face the door—the opportunity Dad had been waiting for. He slipped the gun from Garik's hand and administered a blow to the head of the unsuspecting guard. Samvel grabbed him to keep him from toppling out the door as it opened, looked out to see who was in the hall, and silently signaled all clear.

We kept our group close together as we hurried to the exit door, the one I'd been brought through less than thirty minutes before. As we left the circle of light on the steps and proceeded into the darkness in the direction Dad pointed, a ghostly form approached, seeming to float along the walk toward us. As the apparition neared, I recognized first the white robes with the purple trim and then the priest I'd met at the cathedral.

"Father Ohanyan!"

The priest came close enough to recognize me. "I remember you. You're the frightened girl with the gun in her purse and an unhealthy curiosity about stolen rubies." Then he recognized the Catholicos on the arm of a tall young man in priest's robes. He quickly searched the faces of the rest of the group, and not seeing any of the familiar people who usually surrounded the Catholicos, demanded, "What's going on?"

"I haven't time to explain in full, Father Ohanyon, but the Catholicos is suffering slightly from drugs that will shortly leave a tremendous headache, and here are your missing rubies." I dug the rubies out of the zippered pocket of my rain coat where they had remained almost throughout this entire ordeal and gave them to him. "I'll leave them both in your capable hands and be back to explain everything later. I'm sure you'll need the details for your report to Washington. I do have one question for you now, though. You knew all along who stole the rubies, didn't you?"

"I strongly suspected it was two of the priests who'd been on probation for unseemly conduct. They had close ties to a wealthy group of the Diaspora in Glendale who would have paid a hefty ransom to have these returned. Where did you get them?"

"I found them in my slippers that evening after our interview. I think we'll find that Mr. Marzuk obtained them from the Diaspora and planned to return them via Mom's briefcase only to ransom them once again to the Catholicos. Father, we left some bad guys tied up in the basement library for the Coalition on Terror. Will you make sure no one disturbs them until someone from the coalition can get here?"

"I think you'd better tell me the story now." It seemed the good priest was also a good agent, not wanting to delay receiving explanations in his case any longer than necessary.

"Sorry, Father Ohanyan. There simply isn't a minute to lose." I signaled Aram to give the Catholicos to the priest and we hurried on down the sidewalk. We met several other priests between there and the little graveled road that led to the helicopter pad, but none gave us more than a glance, since it appeared we had a priestly guide with us. This area was off-limits to most visitors, and definitely off-limits without an escort.

Gagik and Samvel hoisted Mom, wheelchair and all, into the darkened helicopter, already warmed up and waiting for Marzuk. As quiet and cooperative as he was, I had to assume Else had the point of the dagger pricking his skin, just ready to plunge it in at the slightest provocation. Marzuk signaled the pilot to get us in the air. Apparently the man knew his destination, as we immediately headed for Yerevan.

Within minutes we zipped across the city center and landed at the foot of the huge Television Tower on the hill overlooking Yerevan. The pilot shut down the copter, giving me my first opportunity to try to contact Bart. I discovered my Dick Tracy was still on "continuous send to all channels" mode.

"Bart, can you hear me? Can anyone hear me?"

"Loud and clear, Princess. We've been picking up bits and pieces for the last hour, enough to get the drift of what's happening. I can see you from here. Come on in."

I let the twins and Aram help Mom and Dad and raced across the brightly lit parking lot to meet Bart, who burst through the door and caught me in his arms at the foot of the steps. I held on for dear life, never wanting to let him go. Never wanting to leave the safety of his arms.

"You're shaking, Princess. Are you cold? Or is that a residue from your narrow escape?" He pulled away and tilted my chin up to search my eyes. I looked up, but sudden tears blurred my vision. "Are you okay?" he asked. "And Alexandria?"

I nodded, unable to speak for a minute. He hugged me close

again and stroked my hair. Finally able to rein in my emotions, I admitted with a little laugh, "Guess it was just the rush of relief at seeing you again."

"Did you think you wouldn't?" Bart tenderly wiped the tears from my cheeks.

"A couple of times," I acknowledged. "But I made it, and you did, and now we need to get this wrapped up fast." It was amazing how quickly it put my world right when I was with this man I loved so much. I took a deep breath. "The way things have been going, even with The Fox out of commission, I'm not entirely sure things won't start moving at 6:15 with someone else taking the lead. Let's go make sure we've got all the moles. This seems too simple."

"My thought exactly. We broke that code too easily—even with Norik and Armen's help, and then uncovered those moles in every office too darn fast. I think there's still a lot of action just waiting to happen." Bart took my hand and hurried me into the Television Center, while the twins hoisted Mom's wheelchair up the stairs right behind us. Aram took charge of the wheelchair and the twins each took Dad by an arm, steadying him. Dr. Garik Grigoryan brought the helicopter pilot in with his hands tied behind him and Else followed with The Fox.

Employees streamed from the building, anxious to be on their way home. The secretary/receptionist nervously straightened and re-straightened her papers at the front desk in the center of the foyer. I peeked at the papers: a stack of logs for television programming she'd been filling out for tomorrow, and an appointment calendar with several names at the top and lines underneath each. Apparently she scheduled appointments for all department heads, supervisors, and television crews. A worried frown creased her forehead. "You really must leave now. We are closed."

Bart approached her desk and leaning down, spoke quietly to her. "Doesn't someone stay here after hours to answer phones and run the place during the night shift?"

She shook her head, glancing at her watch and then up at Bart. Either she wanted very badly to go home, or she had an appointment. She obviously did not want to remain at her desk and did not want this group of strangers here.

Bart continued to probe, trying to discover who was in charge

and what the procedure was for emergencies. She was totally uncoop-
erative, refusing to give any information or be helpful in any way.
Finally she became exasperated with all Bart's questions and threatened to call the police if we didn't leave immediately. That might not
be a bad thing.

At that moment Dom burst through the door like a bull charging
into the arena for the bullfight.

CHAPTER 37

"Boss man, am I glad to see you!" Dom threw his arms around Dad, gave him a quick hug, and bounced a kiss off Mom's pale cheek.

"Glad to see you in one piece, too," Dad said. "How'd you manage to get out of the House of Parliament when the rest of us got faked out?"

"I was in the back talking to one of the guards. I didn't see any of your 'friends' come in and they didn't see me. I looked around the pillar when I heard the commotion and saw you hit the floor when their head honcho bopped you on the head. I couldn't believe they got the drop on both you and Else." Dom shook his head. "They must be good, boss."

"They're good," Dad admitted, "but I got careless, trusting they were on our team. My fault. Everything changed with the passing of the cold war. These guys used to play by old rules we all observed then. New ball game with terrorists. New rules. What happened when we left?"

"I called Alli to send a doctor when I saw your head wound, hoping they'd stick around long enough for a medic to take care of you. Then I disappeared into the woodwork and tailed you to the helicopter. Decided I'd better do a changing of the guard there. I called on some of your rebels and the Avenisyan's came to the rescue: Garik and his sons, Karen and Roman. We went back and neutralized the whole shift. A whiff of knockout gas and they went down like bowling pins. We replaced them with your rebel band."

I could see the secretary out of the corner of my eye—getting desperate. I glanced at my watch. Ten minutes after six. Only five minutes to the magic hour. I tugged on Bart's sleeve and pointed to my watch. We could always hear Dom's explanation later. I was truly anxious to hear how the four of them had taken care of half a dozen guards—and where they'd put them. Right now I wanted to be in the broadcast room and see what was planned to air at 6:15. Bart glanced at his watch and nodded. We stepped away from the desk.

"Where's the broadcast room?" I whispered.

"This way." Bart led me quickly toward a hallway, staying hidden from the secretary's view by our people crowded around Dad and Dom. "Come on, we'll see what's about to happen there. Maybe David Chen and Loretta got the real mole here and now that Marzuk's in custody, everything at the TV center is contained. Hope that's not just wishful thinking."

"And what about everybody else?" I hurried to keep up with my single-minded, long-legged husband who was bent on getting to the broadcast room. "Did they make sure they had all the moles?"

"They did after we got your garbled message. We reevaluated, decided al Qaeda would have a backup planted, so all the teams returned to their assigned area to ferret out the second mole, or moles, as the case may be."

"What did you find?" I shed my raincoat as we raced through a labyrinth of halls, transferring my gun from pocket to purse as we ran.

"I took Sarkis and Margarit—and Daniel—back to the Ministry of Energy. Sarkis had rooted out the first one, the head of the department, but Margarit found the second one. His assistant. That's basically how it went across the board. We think we have them all, but if we don't, we'll slow them down until our band of rebels can sniff them all out and take care of them."

"Daniel?" I didn't remember any Daniel.

"The baby. Margarit and Sarkis's baby. Little doll. He was a big help in getting people to open up and talk. Everybody loves a baby. Super conversation starter."

"Does that mean I'm growing a little secret agent here?" I looked up at my husband whose expression suddenly mirrored the horror I knew that comment would elicit.

"Not on your life! Don't even think such a thing." Bart stopped at a door with lights on the wall next to it and a sign proclaiming, "No

Entry." He pointed at the door. "This is it. I think it will be a good idea to join them in there. What do you think?"

"Lead on, Lochinvar. We can't stop what we don't know is happening."

Bart opened the door and we silently entered the broadcasting room with banks of microphones, television cameras, and sound controls and equipment on every side. The anchorman sat behind the console facing lights and camera, reading news bulletins into a microphone. The camera man had his back to us. We shut the door quietly and stood against the wall out of the circle of light, not making a sound. My watch showed 6:14.

Suddenly the secretary/receptionist flew into the room at fifteen seconds before 6:15 and grabbed the microphone from the announcer. Before she could utter a word, Bart strode across the room and muffled her mouth with his hand, encircled her waist with his arm and prepared to remove her from the area. I pried the mike from her hand so he could carry her out and twisted it back toward the announcer. "Continue your broadcast," I whispered in Russian, and flashed my gun at the camera man, motioning him to stay where he was.

Bart took her, kicking and trying to scream, from the broadcast room, while the puzzled man at the microphone tried to recover his news broadcast. I followed Bart to the door where I could keep my eye and my gun on the two men, and still help Bart with the furious, fighting woman.

"This makes sense," I said, stripping the belt from my raincoat so Bart could tie her hands. "She'd be the logical next-in-command—or maybe even the first—since she schedules all the appointments and makes out the daily log for commercials and shows. I'll bet she's basically in charge of this whole shebang, making sure everyone is where they are supposed to be, doing what they're supposed to be doing."

"Just to make sure we haven't nabbed the wrong bird, we'd better get a native in there to figure out what the announcer is saying and make sure . . ." Bart stopped and looked at me. "Triples!" we exclaimed simultaneously.

"This would be the place," I said. "Go for it."

I threw my raincoat over the head of the secretary struggling to free her hands and held her against the wall with my gun still trained on the two men while Bart raced back inside, confiscating the mike from the announcer. I heard an announcement in Farsi, a little blurb in Nepali and some elementary Russian.

Suddenly the hall filled with people, Dom leading the pack. Else and The Fox followed, still linked arm in arm with Else's knife at his side. The twins, one on each side, supported Dad, apparently not yet quite steady on his feet, and Aram pushed Mom's wheelchair. Garik Grigoryan and the pilot with hands tied behind him joined the circle while Sky and Lionel approached from the other end of the hall, and David Chen and Oz materialized from behind two of the doors next to us.

I dodged the woman's kicking feet, her upper body still covered with my raincoat to muffle her furious cries, and pointed at the broadcast room. "Aram, run and take the microphone. Keep reading the news on the air like you were a substitute newscaster."

When Aram let go of the wheelchair, The Fox lunged toward Else, purposely taking the full length of the dagger into his rib cage. As he staggered against Else, he pulled a tiny device from a chain around his neck, thrusting it triumphantly in the air.

"For Allah! Infidels die. Al Qaeda triumphs." Then he crumpled to the ground, still holding the deadly device in his hand. I stood frozen in my shoes until Else screamed, "Run. It's a bomb. Get out of here." She grabbed the raincoat-swathed secretary and pushed her down on top of the fallen Marzuk, then dropped atop both of them.

Dad plunged forward, sending Mom's wheelchair flying backward down the hall and the twins dragged Dad on a run to catch the wheelchair. In one amazingly smooth motion, Garik plucked Else off the two bodies on the floor and shoved her toward David and Oz who staggered backward into the room they'd just exited, taking Else with them. Garik slammed the pilot to the floor on top of Marzuk and the screaming secretary, then fell across the three bodies.

Bart came flying through the control room door and tackled me, sending us both tumbling into the room on top of David, Oz, and Else just as the bomb exploded. The noise nearly deafened me as the blast rocked the building, knocking plaster off the concrete walls and shattering glass in the windows.

Bart jumped to his feet and pulled me to mine. "Are you okay, Princess?"

Shards of glass and chunks of plaster fell off my clothes as I stood. "I think so. Mom and Dad. I need to find them." We hurried into the hall that now looked like a war zone. The dust hadn't settled, but it seemed apparent none of the people on the floor could have survived the blast.

"Sound off everybody," Bart called. From various parts of the hall, I could hear Anastasia's familiar voices, including Mom and Dad. Then the twins and Aram answered. Garik had been thrown several feet and lay crumpled in a heap down the hall. I hurried to him and knelt at his side. He opened his eyes as I touched his face.

"You are much trouble, Mrs. Allan." He tried to smile but pain quickly erased his attempt.

"Garik, why did you sacrifice your life? You could have run, too."

"This my fault. I bring you all here." He paused, closed his eyes, and continued, speaking so softly I had to bend down to hear him. "I think maybe you do very good work for Armenia. I not important. Freedom for Armenia is . . . " He stopped, his words failing as his life ebbed from him.

Bart knelt beside me, checked Garik for a pulse that no longer beat, and pulled me to my feet. He brushed plaster from my hair and wiped a smudge from my cheek, along with a tear that probably made streaks down my face. As I leaned against him, he wrapped his arms around me and rested his cheek on my head, enfolding me in my own private comfort zone.

"That was a noble thing for him to do," I was finally able to say.

"A perceived loss of freedom brings out the best in people. Our little band of rebels did themselves proud today. I'm sure none of them envisioned this kind of action when they began their 'soft rebellion' against the graft and corruption in their government, but they certainly rose to the occasion. It would be great if good, decent people everywhere in the world took this kind of action against rotten leadership in their countries."

As everyone assessed their personal damage and that around them, the hall came to life again. Bart shielded me from the carnage the blast had created and led me down the hall to see how my parents had fared.

"It's a major blessing that wasn't the kind of bomb the suicide bombers have been using in Palestine and Israel," I said, noting the walls were still standing, though barren of their plaster.

"That was a personnel device, designed to wipe out people, not knock down buildings. And yes, it was a major blessing or none of us would have survived it."

I stopped in the middle of the hall. "Sure glad I gave those rubies to Father Ohanyan. I'm not sure we could have found anything that remained of them after that blast. Do you suppose we actually stopped al Qaeda?"

Bart draped his arm over my shoulders and moved me along the hall toward Mom's wheelchair. "Well, we sure spoiled their plans for tonight if we didn't. We probably won't know until tomorrow how successful we really were, but at least the first two levels of moles were removed today and some major players are out of action."

"Then the next thing . . ."

Bart immediately interrupted me. "The *next* thing is to get you . . ."

Dad interrupted Bart. "And your mother," and as if they had rehearsed it, they both said together, "Back to California."

I looked at Mom. "Are we going to let them run our lives for us?"

Mom pretended to give it serious consideration. "No, we're not. But I think it might be a very good idea if you took me home so this leg could mend properly—and you could protect that precious bundle you are nurturing. We don't want anything to happen to Alexandria before she even arrives. We'll leave the mop-up operations to the men, go home and prepare to 'fight another day,' as the man said."

I started to object, then bowed to the wisdom of my mother who I could tell was in a great deal of pain. I wasn't feeling too wonderful myself. Nothing that a long leisurely soak in a hot tub and a good night's sleep wouldn't cure, but that probably wouldn't happen tonight in Armenia.

"Okay, I'll go. On one condition."

"And that is?" Bart raised one eyebrow.

"That you promise to bring me back here on vacation."

Bart breathed a sigh of relief. "Of course, Princess. I promise we'll come back."

Dad laughed and winked at Bart. "He'd promise you the world just to get you out of here, you know."

I nodded. "Probably. But a promise is a promise and I'll hold him to it." I linked my arm through Bart's and looked up at him. "We do have a little unfinished business to wrap up before we leave. Father Ohanyan will have plenty of questions and . . ."

"And that can wait until morning," he said, wiping some dust off the tip of my nose, then bending to kiss it. "Right now, little mother, you are going to get some rest. First thing tomorrow, we'll tie up your loose ends, then get the two of you safely home. We have a band of rebels who've tasted their first real victory and are ready for further instruction. When we get that done . . ."

"When you get that done, there will be another crisis, and another, and Alexandria will be a grandmother. But you promised me some rest right now. I could use some food, too. Anyone up for that?"

The twins, Samvel and Gagik, began suggesting places to eat. While they settled on the Hotel Armenia for dinner, suggesting it would also have a good hotel room, I sneaked a peek back down the hall and said a silent thank you and good-bye to the enigmatic Dr. Garik Grigoryan. Would I ever know how many times he had saved my life? Twice in the last hour—at Echmiadzin, and here a few minutes ago, for sure. But had it been him that pushed me out of the way of that car? My tired, muddled mind wasn't up to solving mysteries right now. Later I could sort out all the unanswered questions.

We walked arm in arm from the Television Center and into the cold, clear Armenian night. The city of Yerevan spread across the valley beneath us, lights glittering like jewels on black velvet.

"How about if we sneak off for a quick bite to eat, just you and me, and let everyone else do the group dinner thing?" I suggested. "Then we can check into a hotel room with a nice hot shower . . ."

"And I can be your personal back scrubber. Your favorite thing." Bart pulled me close. "But you deserve it, and I can't think of anything I'd rather do right now."

He waved at the taxi driver standing beside his car at the curb. "Hotel Armenia," he said, as we settled into the cab, then wrapped his arms around me and held me tight.

"Mmm. You always know just what I need," I murmured contentedly, snuggling as close as I could get.

"You're easy to please, Princess. Just promise you a good meal and a hot shower and I become a hero."

"It takes more than just a promise, Charlie. But since you usually follow through, that qualifies you as a hero." I enjoyed a few minutes of peaceful bliss, until my mind starting asking questions again. "Do you think they really planted explosives in every historical building in Armenia and every block in Yerevan?"

Bart stiffened. "Where did you hear that?"

"The Fox gloated that the Coalition on Terror wouldn't dare stop the takeover because al Qaeda would blow everything up and wipe out Armenia and its entire population if the coalition tried to stop it."

Bart released me and sat back in the seat. "Wonder if they notified anyone in the Coalition of that, or if it was just a shot in the wind to throw you off?"

"No idea. That would take an incredible amount of explosives, and a lot of time and effort to set up. And how do we stop it if it's true? He said they were rigged so that if one went off, they all would. The chain of explosives only makes sense on the ones in Yerevan— not the ones all over Armenia in the historical buildings. But what a tragedy if it is true. Bart, how do we find out?"

"Send a bomb squad to check out some of the historical buildings—the most important ones first." Bart slipped back into Interpol mode and I could tell my musings had temporarily cost me my promised dinner and hot shower.

I sighed and pursued the subject, knowing it was beyond my control now. "Since the magic hour is past, do we have communication reestablished? Can you just call someone and have it taken care of?"

Bart surprised me. He immediately called Dad on the Dick Tracy, told him about the possible threat and suggested the Armenian army could handle that task. When Dad asked where we were and what we were doing, Bart replied he had just taken on the most important assignment of the night—feeding his hungry wife and making her comfortable. How did I ever get so lucky as to find a sweetheart of a husband like that?

"How many more moles do you think are in place just waiting to be activated—maybe in another go-around?" I asked, snuggling back in Bart's arms.

"We got two levels tonight—and three in some cases—but only in the areas we thought of. Definitely damaged their organization but you can bet we only scratched the surface. It will be an on-going struggle to ferret out the rest and stop them. But the little group of rebels have tasted success, and learned a lot. They'll be able to handle it. I'm sure Jack will leave a couple of Anastasia operatives in the country to help."

I started to say something, but Bart interrupted. "No, Princess, it won't be you. You're off the assignment calendar for good, except in the Control Center, where you'll be the greatest help. Jack and Margaret are recruiting additions to Anastasia; the workload's getting too heavy for the ten of us to handle with terrorist activity increasing all over the globe. You'll have your hands full keeping track of everyone—and Alexandria." He rested his chin on my head for a minute. "Wonder what she'll be like? Quiet and introspective like her dad, or inquisitive and into everything, going every minute like her mom?"

"Hopefully she'll have the best of our traits instead of the worst."

Bart didn't answer for a minute. "I wonder what kind of world she'll come into? Things seem to be accelerating, getting worse all the time. More war, more evil . . ."

"Just be grateful we have the knowledge the Lord is in charge of everything, and it will all happen according to His timetable. I'm not even going to worry about it for a minute. Right now I'm going to concentrate on creature comforts, of which I've had none in the last twenty-four hours—precious few in the last sixty-four."

"You're right." Bart kissed my forehead. "We've done all we can do for the world tonight. Now I need to pamper and spoil my princess for a few hours before I send you away. So forget about al Qaeda, and bombs and bad guys. I'd even accept a little pampering myself."

"I can certainly handle that," I promised.

We settled back to enjoy the rest of the short ride to the hotel. I couldn't help thinking about the work left to be done. There would be lots of "mopping-up" to do and it would take more than this little band of rebels to clean up after The Fox and his al Qaeda plot to take over Armenia.

Even thinking about it exhausted me. The war on terror would be never-ending until the hearts of greedy, power-hungry men were changed forever. I said a silent prayer for freedom fighters across the world, for all those ordinary people doing their bit daily to preserve their way of life, and for the extraordinary ones like these we'd worked with in Armenia who took a long step forward and put their lives on the line for freedom. Bless them all.

ABOUT THE AUTHOR

Lynn Gardner is an avid storyteller who does careful research to back up the high-adventure romantic thrillers that have made her a popular writer in the LDS market. For her first novel, *Emeralds and Espionage,* she relied on her husband's expertise as a career officer in the Air Force, interviewed a friend in the FBI, and gathered extensive information on the countries in which her adventure took place. Additional extensive research in Hawaii, San Francisco, and New Mexico allowed her to create exciting stories with realistic settings for her other novels.

When Lynn's scheduled trip to Thailand and Sri Lanka was canceled because of raging fires in Southeast Asia, her son and daughter, who both work in the garment industry, were able to visit these countries. With specific instructions from Lynn on sites she'd researched, they gathered the information and took the pictures she needed to make her novel as vivid as all of her others have been.

For *Amethysts and Arson*, Lynn traveled solo 6,000 miles, from coast to coast, through sixteen states, to discover historical sites and other important targets in the major cities of the South for her villain arsonist to destroy.

Jade and Jeopardy takes place on her home ground in California, and also returns to the East coast, to a few favorite locations she fell in love with on previous research trips.

For Opals and Outrage, Lynn went all the way home to her roots in Idaho where she was born and raised, was married and began her travel adventures with her husband of the last forty-five years. She attended high school in Rigby and Blackfoot, and knows and loves the country in southeastern Idaho.

Lynn and her husband, Glenn make their home in Quartz Hill, California where they just returned from eighteen months in the Armenia Yerevan Mission, which Lynn describes as the greatest adventure of all. They are the parents of four living children.

Among her many interests, Lynn enjoys reading, golfing with her husband, traveling, beachcombing, writing, family history, and spoiling her six granddaughters and four grandsons.

Out of Nowhere

Picking up momentum as they ran, Ashlyn and Austin stumbled down the trail toward their parents, laughing and trying to see who would reach the table first. Laura and Joe sat under a shade tree talking and holding hands.

"Aren't you guys a little old to be acting that way?" Ashlyn asked, secretly thinking how cool it was that they were still affectionate with one another. "It's embarrassing the way you two are always holding hands and kissing."

"I'll *never* be too old," Dad said, smiling at his wife.

Austin rolled his eyes at his mother's silly grin and tried to appear disgusted, but his broad smile gave him away. "Okay, okay, enough. Can we eat?"

Laura kissed her husband on the cheek and rose, laughing. "Have a seat. It's all ready."

After Austin blessed the food, the family ate, laughed, and talked to their hearts' content. The river swished and babbled its way down the canyon, and a slight breeze cooled their skin while the sun beamed brightly. The weatherman had predicted a perfect day, and he had been right.

All too soon it was time to pack up and prepare to leave. While Joe and Laura cleared the picnic site, Austin and Ashlyn played a game of Frisbee.

"Come on, Ash!" Austin yelled as he once again missed the Frisbee. "You throw like a girl!" He paused for a moment, catching his breath. "Are you doing this on purpose or do you really stink?"

"All right, buddy, let me show you just how bad I am at this," she taunted. "Your ego is going down!" With a full swing, she threw the disc hard and fast.

Austin ran back as fast as he could. Jumping high in the air, he caught the Frisbee and turned around in a victory dance. Suddenly, a shot rang out. The force of the shot pushed him back, and he fell to the ground.

Ashlyn screamed as Joe and Laura ran from the parking area to find her hovering over his body, crying and screaming. Austin lay on the ground, covered with blood, the Frisbee still in his hand.

Ashlyn held his other hand while Joe called 911 on his cell phone. Laura grabbed the picnic blanket and used it to cover her son, then sat cradling his head in her lap while crying. After finishing the call, Joe laid his hands on Austin's head and gave him a blessing, then stood over his still body with tears rolling down his cheeks.

Ashlyn didn't hear the police and ambulance arrive, but as they pulled her away from him, she knew her best friend, her brother, was dead.

Ashlyn's whole world went black.

* * *

The next few days were a never-ending nightmare. The police questioned her over and over again. Did she see who had done it? *No.* Where had the shot come from? *The trail where they had walked.* Did anyone have it in for Austin? *Absolutely not.*

The police's questions seemed endless while Ashlyn's went unanswered. *Why? Who?* And again, *Why?*

Ashlyn was frustrated that she couldn't give the police the information they were looking for. They asked the same questions so many times that Ashlyn felt they wanted her to change her answers. She knew she should be grateful that they were trying to solve the crime, but she felt angry instead. Her brother had been shot in cold blood, and here they were asking her the same questions.

Joe's best friend, Bob Bradley, worked for the Salt Lake Police Department in the Criminal Investigation Bureau, and he finally persuaded the investigators to stop the questioning and focus elsewhere. The forensics report came back showing that the bullet had come from a .45 and was a clean shot to the heart. Austin had died immediately. Whoever had shot him knew how to handle a gun.

The report also showed that the shot had come from the direction of Austin and Ashlyn's hike. But no clues were found in the secluded area, and since the ground was so rocky, no footprints were found. The authorities concluded that either someone had purposely shot Austin or had mistaken him for someone else. Either way, they told the family, it would be difficult to find the shooter.

On the morning of the funeral, the long-awaited white envelope arrived. Austin was to serve in Denmark. Since Laura was the only member of her family who had joined the Church, she had always hoped missionaries would one day touch her family's hearts as they had hers. She wept as Joe called the Church mission office to let them know the situation.

Ashlyn could hardly contain herself as they closed the coffin. Joe said a family prayer, the last they'd have with Austin. Tearfully, the family slowly made their way into the chapel, where Austin's friends sat together. They, too, were in tears. She glanced at Dave. He sat with his mother and stared straight ahead, a look of pain on his face. His mother cried.

After the family was seated, the congregation sang "How Great Thou Art," one of Austin's favorite hymns. The funeral continued with a eulogy given by Ashlyn—a beautiful talk that touched the congregation with laughter and tears—and with moving talks, songs, and testimonies. Another one of Austin's favorite hymns, "Abide With Me," closed the service, and the funeral was over.

Later that night, after friends and family had left, Ashlyn clung to the thought that her family would be together forever. She knew she would see Austin again. But that comfort always led her back to a whole trail of "whys," "what ifs," and "if onlys."

If only I hadn't thrown the Frisbee so far or *What if it had been me? Why him? Why not me? He had so much to give.*

The trail went on and on, but it always led to the same question: If someone was out to kill, why take one of the sweetest, purest people on earth when they could have taken her, a person with so little to offer anyone?

Late that night when the sorrow was unbearable, Ashlyn quietly made her way out the door and to the car. Hardly able to see through her tears, she drove to the cemetery and walked to her brother's grave. As she sat by the graveside, her body was racked with sobs.

"I'm so sorry, Austin," she cried. "So very, very, sorry. You deserved to live and I should be lying here. It was my fault. I never should have thrown that stupid Frisbee. I was trying to show off, and you paid the price for it. Please forgive me. Austin, you're the best friend I've ever had. Please don't leave me here."

Suddenly, Ashlyn remembered the words Austin had spoken the day he died.

"You have to find out for yourself. I can't do it for you."

Ashlyn lay by her brother's grave, trying to remember every detail of their last talk. It seemed like a lifetime ago. She cried until her body gave in to exhaustion and finally, with a tearstained face, she slept.